The Next
PRESIDENT

JOSEPH FLYNN

BANTAM BOOKS
New York   Toronto   London   Sydney   Auckland

THE NEXT PRESIDENT
A Bantam Book

PUBLISHING HISTORY
Bantam hardcover edition published June 2000
Bantam mass market edition / May 2001

All rights reserved.
Copyright © 2000 by Joseph Flynn.
Cover design by Aenee Sheen.

Library of Congress Catalog Card Number: 99-059476.

ISBN 0-553-57666-6

Published simultaneously in the United States and Canada

Bantam Books are published by Bantam Books, a division of Random House, Inc. Its
trademark, consisting of the words "Bantam Books" and the portrayal of a rooster, is
Registered in U.S. Patent and Trademark Office and in other countries. Marca Reg-
istrada. Bantam Books, 1540 Broadway, New York, New York 10036.

PRINTED IN THE UNITED STATES OF AMERICA

OPM   10 9 8 7 6 5 4 3 2 1

ACKNOWLEDGMENTS

Writing this book would not have been possible without the help of:

Catherine and Caitie, who put a smile on my face every morning, come rain or shine.

Joseph T. Flynn, Martha Flynn, and Mary Coates, my favorite philanthropists.

Mike Daly, state director for Senator Dick Durbin (D-IL); Anne Dougherty and Marlene Carls, senatorial staffers; Vickie Karten, California friend and graphic designer; Laura Hammond, RN, MSN.

David Vigliano, stalwart agent, who was there every time I needed him.

Beth de Guzman and Nita Taublib, my editors, who never called off the search and in the end brought this story safely home.

I thank you all.

AUTHOR'S NOTES

This story makes reference to historical events, well-known institutions, and actual places . . . but it takes literary license with many of them.

For example, the Phoenix Program was a genuine CIA operation, and the U.S. Army's 1st Logistical Command is also real, with the responsibilities mentioned in the story. However, the PANIC unit, all its personnel, and its activities are purely fictional. Likewise, the Treasury Department has no Departmental Internal Management and Oversight unit.

The James C. Petrillo Music Shell was a Chicago landmark for many years, but long before 2004, when I have Del Rawley about to speak there, it will have been replaced by a new and differently sited band shell. This and other liberties have been taken so as not to give the wrong ideas to impressionable minds.

Also, the McLellan M-100 sniper rifle has not yet—thank God—been invented. The current generation of such weapons is fearsome enough.

PROLOGUE
April 1971

J. D. Cade thought he'd never have to kill anyone again. He'd come home to southern Illinois from the war at age twenty having killed five men. Four under orders, one on his own. To his mind, that was more than enough to last him a lifetime, but that was before he heard of Alvy Mc-Cray. Alvy was someone who, as Texans liked to put it, needed killing. Needed it right away.

At six feet two and 175 pounds, J. D. was tall and rangy. His sandy brown hair hadn't been cut during his last six weeks in the army and was already long enough not to mark him as a soldier. His eyes were a clear pale blue and his face was unlined and unblemished, but he'd always had a self-possessed air about him that made people trust in his abilities, and made it unlikely anyone would ever guess he had ten thousand dollars in stolen cash stuffed in the bottom of his duffel bag.

J. D. knew the McCray name, of course. The Cades of Illinois and the McCrays of Kentucky had engaged in a blood feud from the mid-nineteenth century to the outbreak of World War II. That conflict had damped the fires of the feud by killing off dozens of Cades and McCrays, and leaving the survivors with their fill of death.

Now, in the wake of a far less popular war, up popped this ex-marine Alvy McCray, who'd come home and was doing his damnedest to start the hostilities all over again. Alvy had been hitting every bar, tavern, and roadhouse in southern Illinois where a Cade might take a drink and whipping the ass off every last one he found. J. D.'s cousin Ben had nearly been killed, and he lay in the hospital with his recovery still uncertain.

Alvy was described as a big, mean, rawboned sonofabitch, but the outcomes of the attacks were predetermined by the fact that he had begun each one with a sucker punch. With his victim at his feet, he would sneer, "I'm Alvy McCray, and your sorry Cade ass is mine anytime I want it." Then he'd jump in his pickup truck and speed back across the Ohio River to Kentucky before the cops could arrive.

When the authorities in Kentucky received inquiries from their counterparts in Illinois, they replied that as far as they knew, Alvy McCray was a law-abiding young man, and for every time Alvy was alleged to have battered a Cade in Illinois, his father and wife always swore that he was right at home on the family farm outside of Paducah.

The credibility of these alibis was assisted in no small measure by the fact that many of the local cops were also named McCray. So if the McCray family was not actually cheering Alvy on, they were at least tolerating his assaults on the Cades as not particularly troubling.

J. D.'s second night home, he drove down to Kentucky. The sun was disappearing as he found the dirt road where the McCray farm was located. As he drove past, he heard shouts and screams coming from a small weathered farmhouse. It sounded to him like some sonofabitch was beating up a woman. Alvy apparently liked to throw a punch at home, too.

J. D. drove a half mile past the house, backed his car into a stand of trees on the opposite side of the road, and waited for the moon to rise. His plan was to reconnoiter. He wanted to get a look at Alvy before he had to deal with him at close range. But while J. D. was still in the car, he saw a figure carrying a rifle heading his way.

The man was moving in a crouch, and the outline of the weapon in his hands was disturbingly familiar. It was either an M-16 or its civilian cousin, the AR-15. Knowing that Alvy liked to get in the first punch, J. D. was certain he'd like to get in the first shot, too. But fifty meters short of the stand of trees where J. D. waited, the rifleman executed a left turn and moved away from him. He hadn't seen J. D.'s car at all.

Puzzled, J. D. eased out of the car and stole down the road. When he reached the point where Alvy had turned left, he realized that he was at the property line of the Mc-Cray farm. It came to him then: The dumb fuck was patrolling his perimeter. On a Kentucky farm. Scary.

J. D. looked at the farmhouse in the distance. A single light burned in a second-floor window. He could imagine how terrified Alvy's wife must be, having to put up with a violent loon like him. Why the fuck didn't she just wait until he fell asleep one night and shoot him? That'd save . . . save everybody else the trouble. A grim smile formed on J. D.'s lips.

To test his assumption that Alvy was a time bomb with a burning fuse, J. D. crept along unnoticed behind him. He waited until he had a large oak to duck behind and a clear path of retreat and then he chucked a stone at Alvy. It caught him squarely on the back of his whitewalled head. A man with the least bit of intelligence might have taken the pelting as a sign that somebody didn't like him—and could just as easily have killed him.

Alvy's response was to turn and empty his clip.

From that point on, the first part of J. D.'s plan was simplicity: He had to focus all of Alvy's anger on him. Which meant all the other Cades had to lie low. Some of the older men thought this was a burden J. D. shouldn't have to bear by himself—until he described how it had felt to have a volley of Alvy's automatic-weapon fire go blazing past his head.

Just in case the stoning Alvy had suffered provoked him into coming armed on his next foray into Cade country, J. D. stuck his late father's army .45 into the pocket of his field jacket.

Then he set up shop in a roadhouse called the Dew Drop Inn that sat next to state Highway 146 just outside the little town of Golconda. That was where Alvy McCray had begun his rampage by fracturing the jaw of Dashiel Cade. It took J. D. five nights of nursing beers before Alvy finally showed up.

J. D. didn't see Alvy walk through the door, but he knew trouble was on the way when the bartender's mouth fell open. J. D. felt as much as saw people move away from him. He discreetly slipped the .45 out of his pocket—the gun shielded from Alvy by his body—and held it close to his leg. He continued to sip beer from the bottle in his left hand and didn't look around.

He picked up Alvy's reflection in the mirror behind the bar. Alvy leaned against the bar three feet away from J. D. and took a particular interest in the name on J. D.'s field jacket.

"You a real Cade?" Alvy asked him. "Or just some college pussy bought some army pussy's jacket?"

J. D. turned his head to face Alvy.

"Yeah, I'm a Cade. J. D. Cade. And from the way those

beady fucking eyes of yours are set an eighth of an inch apart, my guess is you're a McCray. So what're you doing over here in Illinois when you could be back home fucking your sister?"

Alvy cocked his fist, but before he could throw the first punch, J. D. had rammed the .45 into his nose. Cartilage shattered, blood gushed, and Alvy went reeling. But he took the fact that J. D. hadn't shot him dead immediately as an invitation to regroup and charge. Which he lowered his head and did.

J. D. stepped aside and backhanded him viciously across the side of his face with the .45. On the rebound, Alvy's head slammed into the edge of the bar and he landed flat on his back. When Alvy's eyes regained focus, he was staring straight up the barrel of J. D.'s weapon.

"That was for my cousin Ben," J. D. told him coolly, "and for all the other members of my family you sucker-punched. Think of it as evening up the score. But if you ever come back this way, it's open season on you. You have the brains to understand that?"

J. D. kept his gun on Alvy as he got to his feet and backed out the door. He could tell from the dumb, sullen rage in the cocksucker's eyes he hadn't had enough. He'd be back.

So he told him, "Like I said, settle your affairs before you come this way again."

Alvy returned two weeks later, storming into the Dew Drop Inn with his AR-15 in his hands. Every last drinker in the roadhouse, and the bartender, ran out the back door. But Alvy'd had time to see that J. D. Cade hadn't been among them. He was about to stomp back outside and find *some* Cade to kill when the public phone rang.

The call could have been from anybody for anybody, but standing there alone in the roadhouse, Alvy knew who was calling and knew it was for him. When he picked up the receiver he heard J. D. Cade's voice, and it was full of mocking laughter.

"You up there in Golconda, Alvy? Well, I'm not very far away. Just down on a little farm outside of Paducah. Found a woman here who just loves a man who'll fuck her without beating her up first. What do you think about that, Alvy?"

Alvy ran to his Ford pickup and jammed the key in the ignition. His tires smoked as he took off south on Highway 146. The roar of blood in his ears drowned out the growl of the truck's engine as he hit sixty on a narrow ribbon of asphalt where the posted limit was forty-five.

The blacktop entered the Shawnee National Forest. Even though the trees wore thick new mantles of spring green leaves, the setting sun sent shafts of light poking through the branches that made Alvy squint. But he kept the gas pedal floored even when the pavement rose and dipped and curved. More than once he had to wrestle the pickup back onto the asphalt.

Then he roared around a curve where the road turned west and the sun hit him squarely in the eyes. At that moment he heard a sharp crack that might have been gunfire. He didn't have time to worry about that possibility because just then a deer bolted out of the trees and directly into the path of his truck. He frantically cranked the wheel to the right, hoping the animal would clear his left fender. But it came to him with a shock that at the speed he was traveling, hitting a tree would be a far more certain way to die. Alvy swung the wheel back hard to the left.

His bumper caught the animal in midbound. The impact swung the deer up and around and its hindquarters smashed through the windshield. At that point, Alvy lost his grip on the wheel, but he managed to jam his foot on the brake. The pickup went into a sideways skid for a hundred feet or so and then the wheels tore free from the pavement and the truck flipped over three times, dismembering the deer and coming to a rest cab down.

By that time Alvy was roadkill, too.

Just the kind of death J. D. Cade had wanted for him.

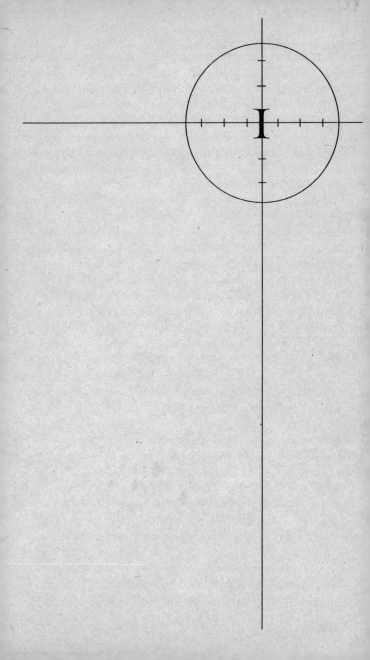

ONE

Labor Day · *Monday, September 6, 2004*

Upward of half a million people filled Chicago's Grant Park chanting for the appearance of the man they believed would be the next president of the United States, blissfully unaware that the lectern at which he would speak was already targeted in the telescopic sight of an assassin.

For most purposes, the day was perfect. The sun shone from a cloudless sky, Lake Michigan glistened sapphire blue, and a breeze off the water moderated a temperature of eighty-two degrees. Streams of people continued to arrive on foot from all directions. Traffic on Michigan Avenue, Lake Shore Drive, and all the east-west streets from Randolph to Jackson was at a standstill. Most motorists simply turned off their engines, stood outside their vehicles, and listened to the coverage of the event on their radios.

But no help was needed to hear the chant of the crowd. It rolled across the lakefront as if the city itself was calling out. Demanding the man who would make history.

"FDR, FDR, FDR . . ."

The throng pleaded for the appearance of Senator Franklin Delano Rawley of Wisconsin, who was already a historic figure by virtue of becoming the first black man to be the presidential nominee of one of the two major political parties.

Presently at the lectern, the city's mayor was doggedly doing his best to finish his speech. A ripple of laughter raced through the crowd as a gust of wind almost carried off the final page of the mayor's oration. Sitting behind the mayor on the stage of the James C. Petrillo Music Shell were the candidate's family and an elite selection of local, national, and party dignitaries. They looked out at the immense, expectant gathering with undisguised joy.

The polls said their man was ahead of the incumbent by only five points, scarcely more than the margin of error, but many of the pundits said this was an election year that would be unlike any other. Two hundred and sixteen years after electing George Washington as its first president, the United States was electrified by the possibility that it might elect Franklin Delano Rawley as its first black president.

"FDR, FD—"

The chant seemed to catch in everyone's throat for a split second and then it changed to a roar as the candidate appeared.

Like rolling thunder, the multitude's shout of approval reached the fifteenth-floor room at the southwest corner of the Hyatt Regency Chicago. It was all the easier to hear because the small floor-level window panel to the left of the room's heating and air-conditioning unit had been carefully removed. The rectangle of thick safety glass and the fat black rubberized seal that had held it in place lay nearby, ready for quick replacement.

J. D. Cade lay in a prone shooting position just back of the empty window frame in the shadows of the darkened room. He'd registered at the hotel the day before under the name of Jack Tenant with his hair colored silver gray by a wash, brown contact lenses over his blue eyes, a well-groomed but newly grown beard, and two-inch lifts in his shoes. He'd checked out via the TV fifteen minutes ago, but a DO NOT DISTURB sign hung on the outside of the safety-latched door to his room. Now he watched through the scope of his McLellan M-100 sniper rifle, the barrel steadied by its tripod, as Senator Rawley arrived on the stage of the music shell some 2,950 yards away.

It had been almost forty-one years since John F. Kennedy was killed by a sniper. The Secret Service hadn't forgotten the lessons it learned from that tragedy, but in the manner of their counterparts at the Pentagon, they had prepared for the last war. The helicopters, the agents on rooftops, the entire security cordon were all positioned on the assumption that no current sniper rifle had an effective range beyond two thousand yards.

The exception to this limit was the .50 caliber McLellan M-100, which was used by the navy SEALs and had an effective range of three thousand yards. The round it fired was powerful enough to shoot down a large aircraft, not to mention kill a man. But the special agents protecting Senator Rawley—Orpheus, by his Secret Service code name—operated under the assumption that this weapon was the exclusive, tightly guarded property of the military.

Nevertheless, J. D. Cade had one, and the hotel room he'd obtained was beyond the security cordon. A picket fence of high-rise buildings on Randolph Street stood between the Hyatt and the park, but he had a clear field of fire, between the Aon Center on the east and the Prudential Plaza Building on the west, to the northeast-facing stage of the music shell.

Senator Rawley, known as Del on all but the most formal occasions, had just stepped onto that stage and was waving to the adoring crowd. He was already in J. D.'s crosshairs, but at the moment the flags on the stage showed that a swirling wind was blowing. Over a distance of almost three thousand yards, a strong wind might move even a .50

caliber round far enough to kill someone walking along Michigan Avenue or sitting on a boat in the Monroe Street Harbor. J. D. had to be patient. When the wind died, so would his target.

Del Rawley was not a classically handsome man, but even seen through the narrow field of vision of his scope, J. D. could recognize the intelligence in the man's eyes and the star power in his smile. Having studied his target, he knew that Rawley was a vet like himself, a former combat medic. He had earned his bachelor's and master's degrees from the University of Wisconsin, had been an educator and an author, had served in the House of Representatives and now the Senate, was a devoted husband, father, and grandfa—

The wind died, the flags went limp, and J. D. Cade squeezed the trigger. The .50 caliber round flew at a speed of 2,500 feet per second, but it had to cover a distance of 8,850 feet. Travel time was 3.54 seconds.

Given the intervention of fate, that was long enough for the course of history to be changed.

What J. D. Cade couldn't see outside the lines of his crosshairs was the man in front of the music shell stage lifting his young daughter, who in turn proffered a rose to the candidate. Del Rawley pricked his finger on a thorn, but bending over saved his life.

The round that should have torn his head off passed over him, streaked between the mayor of Chicago and the governor of Illinois, who were seated behind him, smashed a hole the size of a beach ball through the back of the music shell, and expended its lethal energy by cutting down a six-inch-thick maple tree at its base.

J. D. Cade watched in disbelief through his telescopic sight, stunned that he'd missed. Del Rawley had already disappeared under a swarm of Secret Service agents. First they simply piled on him, but within seconds he was dragged from the stage inside a knot of bodies.

The idea of attempting a second shot never occurred to J. D. Now it was time for him to run. The M-100's features included both a flash suppressor and a sound suppressor, so his shot's point of origin would not be obvious. Nevertheless, his escape would depend on speed. As he swiftly replaced the hotel's window he could see that the scene in the park below had changed from one of a political rally to bedlam.

He'd been careful to wear surgical gloves inside the room, and would continue to wear them for a few more seconds. He had his weapon broken down and stowed inside his suitcase within a minute. The lifts that had been in his shoes were already packed away. Before he'd set up for his shot, he'd shaved his beard but left the mustache. He'd covered the drains in the bathtub and the sink with nylon mesh and retrieved the hair he shed. Those signs of his presence in the room had been packed away, too. He slipped on a pair of sunglasses and exited the room. Now, as a final precaution, he flipped the hangtag on his door asking the maid to clean the room promptly.

Pulling off the surgical gloves and tucking them neatly into the inside pocket of his suit coat, he rang for the elevator with a knuckle. By the time he reached the lobby, news of what had happened in Grant Park was already common currency. Knots of excited people babbled about who might have tried to kill Senator Rawley; others were rushing to the hotel bar to see televised reports; even the staff behind the registration desk was crowded around a radio listening to a frantic reporter tell them what little he knew.

J. D. had to open the hotel door for himself, but he found a cab out front.

At first the driver wanted to stay right where he was and

listen to the news. J. D. said that was certainly his choice, but pointed out that if he remained where he was, he was bound to get stuck in the gridlock that would doubtless engulf the area in the next few minutes, and there would go a day's fares.

The cabbie kept his radio on but asked J. D. where he wanted to go. Hearing the response, he executed a tight U-turn, made a right on Michigan Avenue, and dropped his fare off at the corner of Fullerton Parkway and Lincoln Park West ten minutes later.

J. D. tipped generously but not conspicuously.

Still listening to the news reports, the cabbie bid J. D. goodbye by saying, "Jesus, this is awful!"

"It is a mess," he agreed.

As the taxi disappeared, J. D. walked north through Lincoln Park, attracting no special attention. At Belmont Harbor he boarded a twenty-five-foot cabin cruiser called the *Wastrel*. Below deck he doffed his coat and tie and rolled up the sleeves of his white shirt. He'd chartered the boat in Milwaukee under the name Jonathan Helm, and though he'd paid for it through Wednesday, he'd be returning it in the four and a half hours it would take him to make the ninety-mile cruise north.

He eased the boat out of the harbor. Once out on the lake he ran the craft a mile offshore and then turned north. He proceeded at a steady twenty knots. Just above Kenosha, with no other craft in sight, he stopped long enough to dump the M-100, the surgical gloves, the shorn hair, and the phony credit cards, obtained from a computer hacker, which had financed his travels—all of which went overboard tied inside a black trash bag. According to the chart he'd studied, the water at this point in the lake was over four hundred feet deep. He also rinsed the gray coloring out of his hair and changed into casual clothes for his arrival at the Milwaukee Yacht Club.

He returned the boat to its home berth and, slipping on a blazer, he took a taxi to the private aviation terminal at Mitchell International Airport. Here a Citation executive jet waited for a client named Martin Byrd who was going on a gambling junket to Las Vegas.

Once he was aboard, reclining in a plush leather seat, he told the cabin attendant that he was a low-maintenance passenger. All he'd require would be a soft drink and a pillow for the nap he planned to take during the flight.

The woman smiled and said compassionately, "You do look a little tired."

"It's been one of those days," J. D. agreed.

She brought the drink and the pillow, and promised no one would disturb him.

J. D. fidgeted, unable to get comfortable, as the executive jet climbed smoothly into the sky. He knew sleep wouldn't come easily. He'd left his job unfinished today, and if he did get to sleep, it would still be waiting for him when he awoke.

Five hundred miles to the south of the climbing luxury plane, in Carbondale, Illinois, J. D. Cade's son, Evan, opened the front door of the neat gray frame house on Lark Lane in response to the hammering of Officers Glenn Axton and Hoyt Campbell of the local police department.

Evan Cade, at age twenty-one, lacked his father's height by an inch, but was easily taller than both the cops facing him. He had moderately long black hair, green eyes lit by a mocking intelligence, and a long, lean musculature that camouflaged a sturdy frame.

"There's a doorbell." Evan indicated it to the cops with a nod. "No need to wear out the real estate."

Officer Axton, a stocky blonde with a pugnacious face that looked at home atop his blue uniform, had eighteen months in with the department. Which made him the senior man over the slender, laconic Officer Campbell by six months. Axton asked, "Are you Evan Cade?"

Evan nodded. He saw that these two cops didn't look a whole lot older than him, and they were nervous about something. They didn't have their guns drawn, but each of them had his hand on the butt of his weapon. Evan wasn't sure whether he should be afraid of these goofs or laugh at them. What he did was memorize their names and badge numbers.

"Can we come in?" Axton inquired in a demanding tone.

"No," Evan responded deadpan.

While the cops were busy frowning and formulating a response to this rebuff, an approaching female voice asked, "Who's there, Evan?"

A still-vital woman of eighty appeared next to the young man. She had iron gray hair, piercing blue eyes, and a ramrod posture that would have pleased any drill instructor in the land. She looked surprised to see two policemen on her doorstep. "Are *you* the ones creating such a racket? I thought you were going to break my door down!"

Officer Axton knew enough to backpedal just a little.

"We're here on a serious matter, ma'am. May we come in?"

"I already told them no, Grandma," Evan said.

"Have they said why they're here?" Belle Cade asked.

"Just what you heard: *a serious matter*," Evan said, pitching his voice low for the last three words. Then he continued in a normal tone. "They do seem to have their hands on their weapons, though."

The cops quickly dropped their hands to their sides and had the decency to blush, but this wasn't enough for Belle Cade.

"What is the meaning of all this?" she demanded, and

when the cops weren't quick to answer, she added, "I'm calling my lawyer right now."

She left to make the call.

Evan told the cops, "You guys are in for it now."

Axton looked like he was about to grab Evan, but his partner put a hand on his arm.

Speaking for the first time, Officer Campbell said in an even tone, "We'd just like to take a look in your closet."

"My closet?" Evan asked, bewildered.

"We want to see your shoes," Axton blurted.

That left Evan even more nonplussed. Then, looking at the two young cops, a thought occurred to him. "You guys didn't get a search warrant before you came out here."

Officers Axton and Campbell turned red once more.

"Too bad," he told them, and closed the door in their faces.

Belle Cade's lawyer, Elgar Guerrero, showed up thirty minutes later. He explained that he would have arrived sooner but he'd stopped at the home of the chief of police, interrupted the man's dinner, and demanded to know why two fine people like the Cades were being harassed in their own home by a pair of his cops. The chief, who hadn't known of the incident, made it his business to find out immediately, and then shared the information with Guerrero, but only with great reluctance.

"I had to threaten to sue him, the department, and the city before he opened up," Guerrero told Belle. Then the lawyer turned his attention to Evan. "Those two young fools overheard a tip about you this evening, Mr. Cade."

"Me?"

The lawyer nodded. "You're familiar with a fellow named Ivar McCray, who was electrocuted a few weeks back?"

"I read about it in the paper," Evan replied. Ivar McCray had been described as a biker who'd died while attempting to manufacture a pipe bomb. He'd dropped the soldering iron he'd been using into the puddle of water in which he'd been standing. "What's that got to do with me?"

"Someone called the police department tonight. Someone who knew that muddy footprints had been found near the dead man's body."

"I read that story," Belle said. "It didn't mention any footprints."

"Exactly," the lawyer replied. "Whoever called the police had private knowledge of that little detail. And whoever that snitch was, he said to see Evan Cade if you want to find the shoes that made those prints."

It was just the Cades' good luck that the two young rattlebrains had overheard the tip when it was phoned in and raced off to become big heroes—neglecting to first obtain the small constitutional amenity of a search warrant.

Had they been able to coerce their way into Belle's home and found anything unfortunate, that could have been a problem. A prosecutor could have argued that permission for a search had been given, and you never knew what a court might rule to be admissible evidence in these get-tough-on-crime days.

"I didn't commit any crimes," Evan pointed out.

"The police have been known to arrest the wrong man," Guerrero told him. "Prosecutors have even been known to act . . . overzealously."

"That's why I called you," Belle told the lawyer.

"A wise decision, but I'm not a criminal attorney," Guerrero reminded her. "I will have the name of one for you by tomorrow morning, however."

"I didn't *do* anything," Evan reiterated.

"Sometimes it matters more what's done *to* you, Mr. Cade," the lawyer advised. "And from what we've learned tonight it's all but certain there's someone who doesn't like you."

J. D. Cade's eyes were heavy, but so far he hadn't been able to sleep. He turned his head and looked out the window. The sky, which had been cloudless at the start of the flight, was now filling with a storm front. A massive cumulus formation bruised with storm cells and bloodied by the light of a disappearing sun stretched as far as he could see. J. D. looked up when a hand fell softly on his shoulder.

"There's some rough weather up ahead, Mr. Byrd," the cabin attendant told him, using the alias she'd been given. "Captain Blevins is going to fly around as much of it as he can, but he asked me to have you fasten your seat belt."

J. D. nodded and complied with the request.

"Haven't been able to get to sleep?" the attendant asked.

"Not yet."

She reached into her pocket and then gracefully lowered herself to perch next to J. D.'s seat. She said in a soft voice, "Sometimes I need a little something to help me sleep." She opened her hand to reveal a small gold pill case, which she popped open. Four red capsules lay within. "Chloral hydrate. I'd get in big trouble offering you these as an employee of the charter company, so this is just from me to you . . . take two if you want them."

Sympathy for the killer, J. D. thought. Far better than he deserved. But he smiled and took two of the capsules.

"Take only one at a time," the attendant whispered. "And if you decide to take one now, you should stick with soft drinks."

He thanked her and she went forward to her seat.

J. D. put the capsules in his pocket. He wanted to see how well the pilot was able to avoid the storm before he drugged himself. He remembered seeing a sky that looked just like this one as he was landing in Vietnam. But the pilot of that charter flight—on Flying Tigers, normally a *freight* carrier—had barreled right through the threatening clouds.

The two hundred cherries on board hadn't sweated what Mother Nature might do to them; the stewardess had just announced that the chances of the plane taking sniper fire were 40 percent.

J. D. Cade had enlisted in the army, but he was drafted into the PANIC unit. Ostensibly he was attached to the 1st Logistical Command at Long Binh. This was the outfit responsible for supplying the army in Vietnam with everything from socks to rockets, canteens to claymores. It worked with area commands, supply depots, and support battalions throughout the country.

Which gave its Pilferage and Inventory Control (PANIC) unit, working out of nearby Saigon, reason to pop up anywhere they wanted in South Vietnam—to see just who was stealing how much from Uncle Sam on any given day. Visits from PANIC were greeted with the fear and loathing that civilians reserved for the IRS. Everyone was careful to tread lightly around the unit's auditors. No one ever questioned what they were doing in any area of operations.

There would have been even greater fear in some quarters had it been known that the unit's auditing function was a cover for a small team of assassins commanded by Colonel Garvin Townes. Townes wasn't really an army officer; that was his cover. He was CIA.

But all his snipers were army recruits. That gave PANIC an extra layer of insulation.

PANIC was an adjunct to the Phoenix Program, the CIA plan to beat the Viet Cong by neutralizing its civilian infrastructure: tax collectors, supply officers, political cadres, and the like. The main problem the program faced was that the VCI (Viet Cong infrastructure) it sought were indistinguishable from the general population. Further complicating matters was the establishment of quota systems. In 1969, for example, eighteen hundred VCI were supposed to be rounded up each month; of these, at least 50 percent were supposed to be found guilty and sentenced. Because of the pressure to meet the quotas, the CIA-created-and-armed Provisional Reconnaissance Units of the South Vietnamese government arrested and interrogated civilians seized at random by the hundreds of thousands, and by the end of the war almost forty-one thousand "suspects" had been neutralized to death.

The Phoenix Program grew so big and grotesque that it came to the public's attention in the United States and generated fierce political criticism and opposition. Moreover, even its architects came to admit to themselves that it was sloppy and inefficient. So PANIC was quietly brought into being. It was smaller and far more selective in its targeting, and its use of an army front allowed it to operate beneath the threshold of public awareness. In the end, PANIC became something of a spite operation—spite with a hard-on. Anyone of any importance that PANIC didn't want to live to see the end of the war, much less celebrate a Communist victory, got added to its hit list.

PANIC's snipers were culled from likely graduates of the army's sniper school at Fort Benning, Georgia. Most of the men—none older than twenty-two—who worked in PANIC liked the idea of being part of an elite covert unit. J. D. Cade, who had joined the army to become a combat sniper, had to be coerced into becoming an instrument of assassination.

Sp4 Jefferson Davis Cade's first assignment had been described to him as a "cupcake." His target, he was told, though a nominal ally, was really a vile rodent who should have been exterminated long ago.

Lieutenant Colonel Nguyen Van Le of the Army of the Republic of Vietnam was stationed at Lai Khe, not far from Saigon, with the ARVN 5th Infantry Division. But in 1965 Le was still a major, and his ARVN company had been assigned to provide support to the U.S. 1st Air Cavalry Division in their battle with three North Vietnamese regiments in the Ia Drang Valley in the central highlands. Once the ARVN came under fire, however, Major Le's men "failed to engage the enemy," as an after-action report politely put it. American soldiers whose flank was suddenly left exposed and took several casualties as a result put it more bluntly: The bastards cut and ran. Major Le led the way, though he did suffer a slight wound to his left shoulder. A GI later testified that he'd seen the major shoot himself—very carefully—with his side arm.

The Military Assistance Command in Vietnam (MACV) pushed for Major Le's court-martial. They felt that his actions set a poor example at a time when the United States was just beginning its buildup of forces in South Vietnam. But Major Le was a cousin of the country's vice president, and the State Department intervened on his behalf. A spokesman for the U.S. ambassador told the military brass it would be "damaging to bilateral relations with the host country if Major Le were to be disgraced." To prevent any damage whatsoever to Major Le's reputation, he was promoted to lieutenant colonel and decorated for having been wounded in the defense of his country.

By the time J. D. had entered the conflict, Lieutenant Colonel Le was preparing to retreat again; he was about to emigrate to France. His mistress was already in Paris setting up his apartment. His suitcases were reportedly stuffed with taxpayer dollars to make his new life a comfortable one. He seemed to think everybody had forgotten about him. PANIC hadn't, and Sp4 Cade had been chosen to emphasize that point.

As the ARVN was supplied head to toe by the Pentagon, and the South Vietnamese feared the PANIC unit even more than the Americans did, J. D. Cade, his spotter, Lieutenant Donnel Timmons, and two other soldiers who arrived in a separate jeep and would actually go over the ARVN's books were admitted to the base at Lai Khe without question, and certainly without anyone's asking to search their vehicles.

Timmons pointed out the South Vietnamese flag flying over the base to his companion.

"See that?"

J. D., who wasn't in a talkative mood, just nodded.

"Colors of that flag tell you everything you need to know about the Vietnamese military: Everything that ain't red is yellow."

J. D. dropped Lieutenant Timmons at the entrance to the base officers' club and drove around back. It was after lunch and before happy hour, so there was no one around to give him a second glance. Fifteen minutes later Timmons poked his head out the back door of the club. "Come on, whitey. Tote dat barge." J. D. grabbed a rifle case out of a concealed compartment behind the jeep's seats and joined Timmons inside. Their shooting stand was upstairs in the club manager's office.

When J. D. entered the room he saw that a large safe in one corner stood with its door wide open. The shelves inside the strongbox had been stripped bare, and a bulging duffel leaned against the wall next to it.

"You major in safecracking at Wayne State, Lieutenant?" J. D. asked.

Donnel Timmons was from Detroit. He'd joined the ROTC in college and discovered he was a natural crack shot. He joked that all the skills he was learning in the army would come in handy when he went home and signed up with the Revolution. Timmons always said this with a smile on his face, but nobody in the PANIC unit planned to vacation in Michigan once they got back to the World. For reasons known only to himself, Timmons had taken a liking to J. D. Cade. He volunteered to take the cherry out for his first hit.

"Not a word about this, Cade."

J. D. saw drops of blood on the carpet leading to a closed door. Explanation enough where the club manager had gone.

"A word about what?" J. D. asked.

The window directly behind the club manager's desk looked out on a street that dead-ended at a parade ground one half-mile away. A man dressed in white was reviewing a formation of ARVN soldiers. Timmons trained his spotter's scope on the man.

"That's him," he said. "Fucker's got a tennis racket in his hand. Reviewing troops dressed like that, the sorry sonofabitch deserves to be killed. Go ahead, Cade, do him."

J. D. already had his rifle steadied on the windowsill, his target centered in his scope. There was no reason to wait. No reason at all. He'd signed up to shoot people. He'd never thought it would be like this, didn't want it to be like this, but here he was, and what the hell could he do? He squeezed the trigger and the man in the tennis whites went down like wheat before a scythe.

Timmons was on his feet, hefting the bulging duffel bag to his shoulder.

"That was cold, Cade. Real cold. Let's blow."

Coming from Donnel Timmons, *cold* was a compliment.

J. D. awakened from his dream with a start. The flight attendant was draping a blanket around him. "I'm so sorry I woke you," she said with a pretty frown, "but you seemed to keep saying you were cold."

J. D. pulled the blanket tight around him. The flight attendant gave him a concerned look but thought it best to say nothing. In a moment he was drifting off once more.

He was back with Donnel in the army again. Setting up for his next kill.

Thirty Secret Service agents were guarding Del Rawley's suite at the Chicago Hilton and Towers when campaign manager Jenny Crenshaw was ushered through the front door.

The candidate looked up at her from the sofa where he sat. "Any news? Have they caught the bastard yet?"

Jenny shook her head. She sat on a facing sofa to one side of Rawley's chief political adviser, Baxter Brown. Jenny was as fair and slim as Baxter was dark and massive. The relationship between the two potential rivals was civil because they respected each other's role. Jenny's job was to get Del to the top of the hill; Baxter's job was to keep him there.

Ultimately, though, Del Rawley was the arbiter of his own fate. A man with a good mind, an intuitive grasp of human nature, and four successful political campaigns behind him, he was subject to only one major criticism: He sometimes made up his mind too soon, and when he did, he refused to accept further counsel. In other words, he showed the supreme self-confidence of a natural leader—which rankled the hell out of people at times.

That was one reason why he kept his inner circle small. In addition to Jenny and Baxter, the only other people close to the candidate were Jim Greenberg, his pollster, and Alita Colon, his press secretary.

"Did Devree and the family get off okay?" Jenny asked.

"They should be landing in Madison just about now," Del replied.

In the first hour after the assassination attempt, the

candidate made two critical decisions: One, he would not let some sonofabitch with a rifle drive him out of the race. Two, he would not expose his family to the dangers he was willing to risk himself.

On the first point the Rawley family was unanimously agreed. On the second, a private family conference was required before agreement was reached. Jenny suspected that Del had threatened to reverse his decision to stay in the race unless his family acceded to his wishes.

"If nobody's been arrested, what *does* the FBI know?" Del asked.

"Well," Jenny sighed, "you wait through all the it's-early-yet blather; you try to be understanding that the problem is difficult when half a million people were on hand and *nobody* saw a man with a gun anywhere; you tell them to knock it the hell off when they start pointing fingers back and forth with the Secret Service over failing to see the attempt coming . . . you do all that and what you come up with is they know the general direction from which the shot was fired."

"That's it?" Baxter asked, incredulous.

"Yeah. They said because the wind was swirling today, and because the shot had to be fired from a very long distance, it's just about impossible to pinpoint where the gunman was. They think he most likely shot from one of the high-rise buildings along Randolph Street."

"Makes you feel real confident, doesn't it?" Baxter asked.

"Special Agent DeVito is being replaced as the head of your protection detail," Jenny told Del. "And, as you've seen, the number of agents around here has been doubled."

The candidate put his feet up on the edge of a coffee table, folded his arms across his chest, and let his eyes lose focus for a moment. Then he shook his head and looked at Jenny and Baxter.

"DeVito stays."

"What?" Baxter asked.

"Why?" Jenny wanted to know.

"It's probably good politics," Jim Greenberg said, entering the room. The slim, balding pollster sat on the sofa with the candidate.

"It's more fundamental than that," Del told them all. "If this man who tried to kill me is so damned elusive, I have to think he was able to make his attempt not because DeVito was negligent but because the assassin found some weakness in the overall protection scheme. Correct me if I'm wrong, but DeVito didn't devise today's security plan all by himself, did he?"

"No," Jenny said.

Del tapped his right foot against the coffee table.

"So I don't think he should be scapegoated. He's done a conscientious job, as far as I can tell, and who could be more motivated to see that nobody gets another crack at me? I'll call the secretary of the treasury and even my worthy opponent, the president, if I have to, but he stays."

Jenny nodded. "Okay . . . I'll pass the word."

"You did a nice job talking to the media, Jenny," Del told her.

Baxter and Jim Greenberg agreed.

Shortly after the attempt on Del Rawley's life, a rumor started to circulate that the assassin had been hired by white racists. By evening, talk radio had picked it up and it was the subject of contentious discussion from coast to coast. More than one black caller had talked about getting even.

Jenny had gone before the media and read a statement that Del had quickly written:

"As of now, nobody in authority knows who attempted to take my life today or what that person's motives were. Anyone claiming to have knowledge of today's events has the legal obligation of sharing it with the FBI. Anyone who claims to have knowledge of today's events and uses that claim to provoke violence against innocent persons is a fraud and is no friend of mine or of this campaign. Furthermore, be assured that when I am your president you may trust in me to use all my resources to oppose *anyone* who would foment racial violence under any pretext."

"Reading that statement was the easy part," Jenny said. "I left Alita to field all the reporters' questions."

"Somebody talking about me?"

The press secretary entered the room, sat on the arm of the sofa next to Baxter Brown, and casually draped an arm over his shoulder. Alita was a small, well-turned-out woman, but she had three older brothers who were boxers, and they'd all given her lessons. She was not shy.

"Guy from the *New York Post* had a tidbit for me," she said.

"What's that?" Del asked.

"He heard PeeVee was thinking about approaching the party chairman, wanting to know if you get plugged, does he automatically get the nomination?"

Congressman Peter Van Fossen of New York was Del's running mate, the vice presidential nominee. He'd been chosen strictly to appeal to voters in the Northeast. He wasn't shy, either.

"PeeVee the VP," Del said, shaking his head with a bemused grin. "I'm going to send that guy to a *lot* of funerals overseas." He looked around. "Doesn't anybody have any good news for me?"

Jim Greenberg said in a neutral tone, "Your poll numbers are up ten points since the attempt. Even in the South."

"Probably just a twenty-four-hour sympathy bounce," Jenny suggested.

A deep laugh rumbled from Baxter Brown. "Yeah, but if not, watch for the president to have someone take a shot at him."

While the others laughed, Jenny said in a tone of mock disapproval, "Baxter, the president has issued a statement deploring the attempt on Del's life, and he promises no effort will be spared to apprehend the shooter."

"While privately regretting that I dodged the bullet," Del Rawley said with a sardonic grin. Then he sighed and asked, "So, madam campaign manager, do we stick to our original plan?"

Jenny nodded.

"Despite Jim's new numbers, the president's got the South locked up. You own the Midwest, and we leave PeeVee at home to protect the Northeast. We make some courtesy calls in the Rocky Mountain states. Then we slug it out for fifteen rounds in California. That's where this race is going to be decided."

On a wooded ridge in the Great Smoky Mountains, straddling the state line between North Carolina and Tennessee, Beau "Dixie" Wynne sat next to a small, carefully built campfire. He'd finished his dinner of freeze-dried beef with dehydrated cinnamon-covered apple slices for desert. Now he was enjoying his daily cup of coffee laced with Irish whiskey as he listened to the radio.

Every news show he could pull in was going on about the assassination attempt in Chicago. But they all kept repeating the same three facts: The candidate had just come onstage, he hadn't even started to speak, and bending over to accept a flower from a little girl had saved his life. Beyond that, nobody knew anything that amounted to a hill of beans.

Dixie had been up to Chicago once for a football game at that mausoleum next to the lake where the Bears played. He'd walked through Grant Park that weekend and could picture the scene where the shooting had happened. He remembered all the tall buildings to the north and northeast of that band shell. Had to be ten thousand windows looking down on it; no way the Secret Service could cover them all.

He tried to imagine the one he'd have picked to do the job. Dixie was a career sniper—for the last twenty-four years with the Gainesville PD SWAT team, for five years before that with a secret army unit he'd never told anybody about.

Dixie thought the way he'd have done it would've been to find an office that was closed for the holiday, one that was right on the far edge of possibility so the Secret Service wouldn't consider it too hard, and then make the shot.

Of course, if the goddamn target wasn't going to cooperate, if the fucker was going to *duck* while your round was in the air, there wasn't a damn thing you could do about that. Maybe tell him, "Hold still now," right before you squeezed the trigger.

That was just what Dixie had done two weeks ago. Told convenience store robber and hostage taker D'antron Nickels not to move a muscle when he gave himself up and came out of that Grab 'n' Go store. Dixie had actually just whispered the thought to himself, but D'antron seemed to listen like he'd heard the word of the Lord.

During the seventeen hours D'antron had held his hostages—a twenty-two-year-old male clerk, a nineteen-year-old single mother with her three-year-old twin sons in tow, and a forty-seven-year-old minister—he'd made a point of having each and every one of his captives scream in pain and/or terror over the telephone to the hostage negotiators.

Once the negotiators had coaxed D'antron's name out of him, they'd discovered this was the *third* time he'd taken hostages while robbing convenience stores. The first time he'd been only thirteen and had done a year in a youth camp. The second time he'd been eighteen but had been so high on PCP that his lawyer had persuaded a brain-dead jury that he'd lacked the capacity to form criminal intent. The jury acquitted D'antron, but the judge remanded him to a locked drug therapy facility—for all of six months. Now, at age twenty, here he came again. Terrorizing three adults and two tiny kids into lifetimes of nightmares before he figured out he better give himself up.

The reason D'antron stopped just outside the store wasn't due to Dixie's importuning or divine intervention; he stopped to pose and flash a smile for the TV cameras. Dixie Wynne shot him through his two front teeth.

Now Dixie was in trouble, suspended from his job and being investigated by internal affairs *and* the state attorney, because D'antron had happened to be a *black* sonofabitch. A bunch of troublemakers was accusing Dixie of being a racist. Which was a goddamn lie. By his own count, of the fifty people he'd killed in his various lines of duty, only four had been black, including D'antron. He shot people *regardless* of color.

He'd shot D'antron Nickels because he knew the little prick was going to keep right on robbing stores and taking hostages, and sooner or later he'd kill some innocent person.

Dixie's lawyer had suggested to him that maybe after such a long, intense standoff he'd been tired and thought he saw something nobody else saw. Or maybe a muscle had twitched involuntarily. There were all sorts of reasons his rifle might have gone off accidentally.

Dixie wasn't about to cop to some excuse that would force his retirement. He told his lawyer to start thinking in terms of justifiable homicide. When he saw the shyster had trouble getting behind that line of legal reasoning, he took off.

His plan was to hide out, live off the land, and listen to the radio every night to see if anyone was coming after him.

But the only news tonight was about the assassination attempt in Chicago. He turned off the radio, policed the area, and put out the fire.

As he slipped into his sleeping bag, he thought again about that sonofabitch lawyer wanting him to say he'd shot D'antron by mistake. Hell. If *he* had taken that shot in Chicago, Senator Franklin Delano Rawley would be dead right now.

Jenny Crenshaw looked at herself in the bathroom mirror before going to bed. Her blonde hair was short enough that she could make it look neat simply by running her fingers through it. But her amber eyes were bloodshot and they didn't have bags under them, they had cargo containers. She looked slim and fashionable in her clothes, but after stepping out of the shower tonight she'd seen that her ribs were beginning to show. She slipped on her cotton nightshirt and thought sarcastically, How sexy!

But who had the time or energy to get laid, anyway?

Her head had barely touched the pillow when the phone rang. She allowed herself a groan before answering. "Hello."

"Oh, my . . . I know that tone. You were sleeping."

The voice in Jenny's ear had the thin, rustling quality of autumn leaves crunching underfoot. Hearing it made Jenny ashamed of having indulged in even a second of self-pity. "Don, how are you?"

"Still terminal, I'm afraid. But aren't we all?" The sepulchral laugh that followed answered the question perfectly.

Donald "Hunter" Ward had been one of Jenny's two political mentors, and now he had a malignant tumor inextricably embedded in his brain. Lee Atwater syndrome, he called it. Her other mentor, Thomas "Killer" Laughlin, had callously abandoned his friend and business partner of twenty-two years shortly after he was diagnosed. His legion of enemies said Tom feared that Don's condition was catching.

"Sooner or later," Jenny said, agreeing with Don's assessment of mortality.

"I'm sorry I woke you."

"It's okay, I wasn't actually asleep."

"I knew you'd be busy after what happened today. But I wanted to talk to you. To tell you that I'm going to be looking out for you." Don Ward laughed again. "And I don't mean from the Great Beyond."

"What *do* you mean?" Jenny asked, a note of concern entering her voice.

"I mean, I was asking myself just this morning if there was really any purpose in prolonging my pain. I couldn't think of one. Then I heard the news about Senator Rawley, and suddenly I saw a reason to keep going a little longer. I have complete faith in your abilities, Jenny, but I'm going to help you. There's a man out there who's trying to keep your candidate from reaching his goal. I intend to work very quietly behind the scenes, like the wraith I nearly am, to thwart that man."

Her first impulse was to warn her old friend of the danger involved in hunting an assassin . . . but he'd clearly implied he'd been thinking of suicide only that morning.

In his own way, Don was a brilliant investigator. It had been said Hunter Ward could dig up the dirt on Santa Claus. So if he wanted to use his amazing mind one more time, for her benefit, before the cancer ate it away, who was she to tell him no?

"Thank you, Don."

"Sleep well, dear Jenny."

After deplaning at McCarran International Airport in Las Vegas, J. D. Cade found a pay phone and discreetly looked around. Nobody gave him a second glance. He dropped a handful of coins into the phone and called his mother's number in Carbondale. As the relays clicked and his call was routed across the country, he did his best to clear his mind of what he'd done that day. He didn't want even the tone of his voice to hint to his mother or—

His son answered, "Hello."

J. D. had to clear his throat before he could respond. "Hello, Evan."

"Dad! Is it good to hear from you."

From the day Evan had first burbled "Da," J. D. had never failed to be gladdened by hearing his son greet him, and this time was no different. And for as long as his son had been talking, J. D. had been able to hear when his voice carried a note of distress. He asked, "What's wrong?"

There was a moment's hesitation and then, "Two cops came banging on Grandma's door a few hours ago."

"*What?*" J. D. asked. "What for?"

"It's okay, Dad. I got rid of them, and Grandma called her lawyer."

J. D. was less than comforted. "Evan, what did they want?"

His son's tone said no big deal; his message directly contradicted the feigned nonchalance. "Somebody called the cops and said I killed a guy named Ivar McCray."

White-hot anger engorged J. D. and he was silent for the long moment it took to repress it.

"I didn't do it, Dad," Evan told him firmly.

"I know, Ev," J. D. replied with quiet certainty. "I know who you are and who you're not." Now Evan was silent. J. D. knew that no young person ever wanted to think he could be completely understood.

But Evan let that pass and continued with his explanation. "I never knew this McCray guy at all. Never laid eyes on him. The whole thing is crazy."

J. D. felt his soul wither. "I'll take care of everything," he said. "Anything you—"

"No." A new defensive tone entered his son's response. "Listen, Dad, I know all this sounds pretty scary. Hell, it *is* pretty scary. But I'm taking care of it. It's my problem, not yours."

Evan was wrong about that. J. D. had brought this on his son. He'd placed the person he loved most in mortal jeopardy.

He'd done it by an act now more than thirty years old.

He'd done it by missing his shot today in Chicago.

Right now the only way he could see to save his son was to make sure he didn't miss the next time he had Senator Franklin Delano Rawley in his sights.

But Evan assured him once more, "I'll take care of it, Dad."

TWO

Monday, September 13, 2004

J. D. knew that his only hope was to get ahead of the Rawley campaign and let it come to him. The surest way for the Secret Service to catch him would be for him to follow along behind, searching for another sniper shot. He was certain that there would be no more opportunities for a long-distance kill. This time he'd have to get in close.

He pulled his car into the parking structure behind the office tower on the Avenue of the Stars in Los Angeles where the Rawley campaign headquarters for California was located. He found his way to a uniformed man at the information desk in the building's lobby and asked for the suite number of the Rawley campaign. The man told him with a smile, never inquiring as to the nature of J. D.'s business.

J. D. wore a dark blue suit, tailored more closely than was the current style. He'd shaved off the mustache that had accompanied him to Las Vegas. He'd had his hair cut two days ago, and when the stylist had asked if he wanted the traces of gray at his temples touched up to match his natural color, he'd said no. Instead, he had the gray *silvered* subtly. He wore a wafer-thin gold Omega watch with a black leather band. His shoes were gleaming handmade loafers.

His appearance, like most in L.A., was carefully calculated. Rich white guy, trim enough for the tapered cut of his suit, relaxed enough not to worry about the gray encroaching on his hair. A man to be approached, not feared. Still, he found it interesting that he hadn't been questioned about his interest in the Rawley campaign, and there were no overt security precautions for an organization whose principal had almost been killed only a week ago.

Looking around casually as he waited for the elevator, he noticed two discreetly placed surveillance cameras, but they were standard equipment for any modern office building. What he didn't see was anyone resembling security personnel.

Not until the elevator doors opened on the twenty-ninth floor, where the Rawley campaign was located. Then two strongly built men with cropped hair, earphones, sunglasses, and good suits held the door open for him. They gave J. D. a serious once-over and one of them gestured for him to leave the car, saying, "Please step out, sir."

Betraying none of the tension that had welled up inside of him, J. D. exited the elevator. He saw a wedge of other bodyguards heading his way, obviously shielding somebody of great importance. Rawley here already? That was sooner than J. D. expected. The morning paper still had him in Colorado. He stepped aside to watch, and he noticed that everyone he could see through the open door of the campaign office was looking on with great interest, too.

But as the security people passed by him he saw it wasn't Del Rawley they were protecting but a legendary singing diva known for her interest in politics. The entertainer was accompanied by a pretty auburn-haired woman in a smart business suit. One of the star's escorts spoke into a tiny microphone at his wrist and J. D. overheard him alerting someone at ground level to have the car ready.

The diva shook the hand of the auburn-haired woman and got into the elevator. When the performer turned, she caught sight of J. D. She lowered her sunglasses for a better look and J. D. saw a canary-eating grin appear on her feline face just as the elevator doors closed.

Then the auburn-haired woman was standing next to him and she, too, had a mischievous smile on her face.

"Consider yourself flattered," she told J. D. with a small dollop of the South in her voice. "There aren't many who get a second look from Marva, much less a smile." The woman extended her hand. "I'm Vandy Ellison. Is there anything I can do for you?"

J. D. shook her hand. "J. D. Cade. If you're with the senator's campaign, I just stopped by to make a contribution. Perhaps you might point me in the right direction."

"I *am* the right direction," she said, her smile brightening. She took J. D.'s arm. "I'm Senator Rawley's chief fundraiser for California, and I'd be delighted to show you to my office."

She led him into the suite of offices. The rest of the campaign staff found J. D. far less compelling than the departed diva, and they were getting back to work. The only person paying attention to him and the honey-voiced Ms. Ellison was a broad-shouldered man with short, wiry black hair, brooding dark eyes, and an aggressively hooked nose. He looked like he might have been one of the singer's security people who'd been left behind, except his suit wasn't good enough and his face was too hard.

The man sat at a desk at the back of the bullpen area, isolated from the rest of the staff, and he watched J. D. and Vandy approach without blinking. Or smiling. When they turned down a corridor to the left, J. D. could feel the man's eyes on his back.

Vandy gestured J. D. into a large office with a view that went all the way to the ocean. She got him seated comfortably in front of her desk, and after she made absolutely sure he didn't care for any sort of refreshment, she closed the door.

Just as soon as she seated herself, J. D. asked, keeping his tone light, "Who's the guy outside, the one who looks like a hit man with a toothache?"

The corners of Vandy Ellison's mouth turned down.

"You don't want to know about him. *I* don't want to know about him. Or why he's even still around. He's not important, believe me."

"Okay," J. D. said mildly.

But he could see he'd hit a nerve. Even taking out his checkbook didn't bring back Vandy Ellison's smile. She looked down and drummed her fingers on her desk, trying to regain her composure.

"I'm sorry if I upset you," J. D. told her.

"No, no, it's not you," she said, shaking her head. Then she looked up at J. D. "Do you know what that man wanted to do?"

"No."

"He wanted to look in Marva's handbag." She gave him a minute to plumb the depths of that outrage, and then repeated it in case he couldn't quite believe his ears. "He wanted to look in Marva Weisman's handbag!"

It took J. D. a moment to remember that Marva Weisman was the diva's name.

"Did he get his way?" J. D. asked.

"He did not!" Vandy Ellison said stoutly. "He also wanted to•disarm her security escort before they entered our offices. Can you imagine? He didn't get that, either."

"He's with campaign security, then? Secret Service?"

"That man," she said, dropping her voice to a conspiratorial whisper, "is Special Agent Formerly in Charge Dante DeVito. He's the sonofabitch who almost let Senator Rawley get killed in Chicago."

J. D. frowned. "I have to admit, I can't see why someone like him would be kept on."

"Del is just a sweetheart, sometimes too much of a soft touch for his own good. He—" Vandy caught herself, realizing she was talking out of turn to a complete stranger. "It doesn't matter, really. That man actually still has his title, special agent in charge, but he's effectively been left with nothing to do. Of course, maybe that's why he was trying to mess up the biggest coup I—"

She caught herself again and apologized to J. D.

"I guess I'm really wound up right now, that's all." She paused and forced her smile to return. "Now, did I hear you say something about making a contribution?"

J. D. raised his checkbook. "I thought I'd donate ten thousand dollars to the cause."

Vandy Ellison beamed—and she told him for just fifteen thousand more he could be invited to a very special performance that Marva would be giving at her Bel-Air home for Del. And, of course, Del would be there as the guest of honor.

J. D. looked up from the check he was writing.

"Am I pushing too hard?" Vandy asked with the same impish grin she'd showed him before.

"I'll let you know when I get uncomfortable," J. D. replied. He signed his name to the check. "The thing is, with apologies to you and Ms. Weisman, my taste in music lies elsewhere."

He handed the check to Vandy Ellison and she accepted both his ten thousand dollars and his decision with good grace. She noticed the Santa Barbara address on the check and commented on how beautiful it was up there.

"Would you mind if I put you on our mailing list?" Vandy asked.

"That would be fine, but I should give you my new address. I've just moved to L.A." He gave her the address of the house he was leasing.

Vandy jotted it down, looking like an angler who'd just landed a trophy catch.

"Well, that's nice," she said. "You're so nearby, maybe we'll see each other again."

She had the savvy to let matters rest there. As she opened the door to her office for J. D., she suggested that he might like to leave by the rear exit.

"Why would I . . . oh, our frowning friend? Never let someone like that see you're afraid of him," he counseled Vandy.

The disgraced agent still sat at his desk. He picked up on J. D. and Vandy as soon as they left her office. Vandy pointedly avoided meeting his gaze; J. D. took it in and returned it without concern or challenge. He might have been looking at a potted plant.

"You forgot your nails," DeVito said in a flat voice just as they were about to pass him.

Vandy stopped and impaled the man with a frigid look. "I beg your pardon."

"Not you, him." He nodded to where J. D. stood. "Guy like you, he needs his nails done to complete the look."

Now there was an element of challenge in the stare the two men exchanged.

Then J. D. shrugged and said, "My manicurist died . . . but thanks for caring."

Vandy laughed wickedly, and DeVito turned to glare at her, his face flushed with anger. He pushed back from his desk and stormed past them. Vandy took J. D.'s arm again and he felt her brush a breast against it in a way that was too emphatic to be accidental.

"Oh, my," she said, still chuckling. "You don't know how much good that did me." She walked him to the elevator bank, waited for a car to arrive, and held his hand in both of hers before letting him go.

J. D. left the building keeping a discreet eye out to see if Special Agent Formerly in Charge DeVito was lurking about watching him, but he didn't see the angry fed anywhere. Still, he couldn't help but feel he'd made an unnecessary enemy.

He also wondered if he'd made a mistake by not accepting the invitation to the diva's private party. But he hadn't wanted to appear too eager. The best way to achieve his goal, he felt, was to have the campaign reach out to him. To *embrace* him.

And since every political campaign was a mainline money-junkie—even one so recently threatened by an assassin—he was sure he'd be hearing from the charming Ms. Ellison soon.

J. D. was also sure he had unseen minders, but they remained invisible as his Lexus meandered through the Westside of L.A. and into Santa Monica. When he was positive nobody was actively tailing him, he turned off San Vicente Boulevard at 7th Street and dipped down into Santa Monica Canyon.

The house he had leased sat on a rise at the rear of a cul-de-sac. It commanded a view of any traffic that might approach its front door. Behind the pool and the garden out back, the wall of the canyon rose at a nearly vertical pitch. The owner had named the place El Refugio. The Refuge. J. D. could only hope.

He put the car in the garage and entered the house. As he walked into the kitchen he looked through the sliding glass doors to the figure seated outside at the table near the pool. The slightly built young man with the long blonde hair stared fixedly at the screen of a laptop computer. His name, truly, was John Smith. But J. D. thought of him by his trade name: Pickpocket.

Pickpocket was a hacker who lifted wallets at high-tech gatherings in the hope that he would find computer passwords among their contents. His batting average in this regard hovered around the .500 mark. Once he had the information he wanted he *replaced* the wallets, and the unsuspecting victims went on their way, cash and credit cards in place, never knowing they'd been relieved of their true valuables.

J. D. had caught Pickpocket with his hand on J. D.'s wallet.

It happened at a MacWorld Expo in San Francisco. The little thief had been disguised as a Japanese businessman, complete with black wig and horn-rim glasses. Pickpocket had immediately offered J. D. money to let him go without a fuss. Nobody in the busy hall had yet noticed their little drama. When Pickpocket saw that mere lucre held no appeal for his captor, he offered something much more useful—a *favor*.

"You make that sound like it's three wishes," J. D. had replied, grinning. "You a genie?"

"Next best thing." Pickpocket had quickly whispered who he was and what he did. "Let me go quietly, I'll get you into any computer system in the country."

At the time J. D. had no desire to become a data-bank robber, but, having founded his own fortune with stolen money, he had a personal aversion to dealing with the cops. He let Pickpocket go. Then, in character with his disguise, the little thief pressed his personal business card on J. D.

"I owe you one," he said, and disappeared into the crowd.

J. D. had forgotten about Pickpocket for three years. But he'd kept his card. And when the time came that he thought a brass-balled pocket-picking computer hacker might be just what he needed, the little thief had answered his call.

J. D. slid the kitchen door open and asked, "Any luck?"

Pickpocket held up an index finger, telling J. D. to be patient a moment longer. The hacker's hands flew over the keyboard, and he looked at the screen as if expecting to see the meaning of life revealed thereon. But whatever appeared, it was less than expected.

"Fuck," Pickpocket muttered. Then he looked up at J. D. and said, "Not yet."

The little thief stood up and stretched, various joints popping audibly.

"I've got to get out. Away from the keyboard and the screen. I need to look at the big picture for a while. The real world, not the virtual one. Maybe I'll get some inspiration that way. You know anyplace within walking distance where I can get a bite to eat?"

Pickpocket was a native of northern California and not familiar with the local environs. J. D. told him there were several cafes on the Third Street Mall and gave him directions.

"I'll be back in a couple hours," Pickpocket said. With a mock salute, he was off.

J. D. noticed that the little thief had left his laptop on the table near the pool. It sat there waiting for J. D. to probe its contents. On the face of things, this would be a perfect time to snoop on Pickpocket.

When J. D. had called on the little thief to repay his debt, Pickpocket hadn't asked why J. D. needed him. He didn't pry, overtly, into J. D.'s personal life. But J. D. knew that the little thief *lived* to learn people's secrets. And the machine that lay so conveniently close at hand might well tell him how far Pickpocket had penetrated the life and times of his mysterious employer.

But J. D. was an experienced hunter. He recognized a snare when he saw one.

And having fallen into one trap already was more than enough for him.

A little over two months earlier, on a Tuesday, the first day of July, life as J. D. Cade had known it came to an abrupt end when he picked up his morning mail. Among the postal odds and ends, he found a manila envelope postmarked Lake Charles, Louisiana—but when he opened it he was certain it had been forwarded from the dead-letter office in hell. Inside were three eight-by-ten black-and-white photos, the first of which showed Alvy McCray dead, broken, bloodied, and suspended upside down in the compressed cab of his pickup truck.

J. D. had opened the envelope as he stood in the doorway of his Santa Barbara home. His first impulse upon seeing the image of Alvy's mortal remains was to snap his head up and look for the marksman lining him up in his sights. His second reaction had been to bolt inside his house and slam the door behind him. With his back against the wall, he looked at the other two photos and was not surprised by what he saw. He half expected a hail of gunfire to slam into his house.

Even when it didn't happen, he was under no illusion that the threat was any less real. He knew there had to be somebody—some minders—watching him. Otherwise there was no point in mailing the photos to him. If he'd been off sailing to Tahiti, his mail—and those goddamn pictures—would just be gathering dust at the post office. Somebody had to be around to make sure he was picking up his mail.

J. D. could all but feel the life he'd built for himself slipping through his fingers. More than thirty-three years had passed since Alvy's death. In that time J. D. had settled in California, married, cofounded L-A-B Fashions with his wife, grown rich, become a father, and raised a son he loved more than life. He'd divorced amicably, sold his share of the business to his ex, and watched his boy go off to college in his old hometown.

But this . . . this was an assault on the very foundation of his being. And it was only just beginning.

The second envelope came a week later, postmarked Paris, Texas. It contained a clipping from his hometown paper, the *Southern Illinoisan*, about the accidental electrocution of one Ivar McCray. McCray reportedly had been building a pipe bomb when he died. He was described as a biker who allegedly was attempting to extort money from a local merchant named Barton Laney. With the clipping were two color photos. One showed McCray's gruesomely twisted corpse—and next to it muddy footprints with clearly defined tread patterns. The other photo was a candid shot of his son, Evan, taken at a sidewalk cafe with one foot resting on the opposite knee. The tread pattern of his sneaker was identical to one of the footprints found next to Ivar McCray's body.

J. D. had no trouble remembering that Evan's girlfriend was named Pru Laney, and he had no doubt that the deceased McCray was a member of the clan his family had fought for so long.

The third envelope, postmarked Americus, Georgia, came the following week—and the contents made clear just what was expected of him. There was another photo. This time it was of presidential candidate Senator Franklin Delano Rawley. Along with the photo, J. D. had been sent a PCR—a personal communications resource.

The PCR had first appeared just after the turn of the

century. A lineal descendant of the cell phone, it included functions for paging, e-mail, web browsing, and global positioning/homing. The last feature was what made the PCR all but ubiquitous by 2004. Global positioning/homing allowed parents whose kids carried PCRs to know where their offspring were at all times. Jealous spouses were also among those most insistent that their loved ones carry a PCR.

J. D. realized that his PCR also had been provided for peace of mind: Someone wanted to know where *he* was at all times. That, and keep in touch. When he turned the unit on he found he had e-mail waiting. A message crawled across the PCR's screen:

www.crosshairs.com   8:00–8:10 P.M. *PDT*   7/15/04

When he accessed the Web site on his laptop that night at eight o'clock, he found the schematic drawings for the McLellan M-100 sniper rifle. Put that together with the picture of the man who'd just locked up his party's nomination to be president and it wasn't too hard to figure out what somebody wanted from him. Put both those things together with the earlier mailings he'd received and there was only one choice for J. D. Cade.

He downloaded the plans for the rifle before they would disappear at 8:10.

J. D. Cade had been shooting rifles his entire life. Passing on a marksman's eye and teaching him to shoot had been the only gifts his father had given him. J. D. had shot in the woods of southern Illinois as a boy; he'd shot in the army; and for the past twenty-five years he'd been a member of the Rancho Durango Gun Club, where he took target practice twice a week.

Six years earlier, in 1998, Jack Wesley, the manager of the club, had come up to him and asked if he'd like to enter a shooting contest back East. The entry fee was five hundred dollars, Wesley told J. D., but all the money was going for a very worthy cause.

A little boy named George Thompson had been stricken with leukemia. His only hope was a bone marrow transplant. The boy's daddy was "Lethal" Leonard Thompson, the legendary army sniper. He'd fallen on hard times, so his friends had set up a charity shooting match to pay for his little boy's medical expenses. Jack thought J. D. might like to take part.

J. D. begged off. But he said he'd like to make an anonymous contribution if Jack would forward it for him. J. D.'s cashier's check for twenty-five thousand dollars didn't reveal his identity. Jack Wesley, an old friend of the Thompson family, thanked him profusely. Then he told J. D. it was a shame he didn't feel like competing, because he was one of the finest freehand shooters he'd ever seen.

Three months later J. D. got a phone call from Leonard Thompson. The old sniper told him not to be mad at Jack Wesley; he'd made him reveal J. D.'s identity. Thompson felt he had to share the news personally that the transplant had been a success and Georgie was going to make it.

Thompson also told J. D. that a friend of his named Walter Perry lived up the coast from J. D. in Santa Cruz. Perry was George's godfather. He was also a master gunsmith, and he'd told Thompson to pass the word to J. D. Cade that if there was ever anything he could do for him in the way of gunsmithing, just give him a call. Thompson gave Perry's phone number to J. D.

All of that made J. D. feel very good, but word of Leonard Thompson's gratitude soon filtered out. Thompson was a much-revered figure among long-range shooters, and if he'd seen fit to thank J. D. Cade personally, why, a host of others wanted to extend their appreciation, too. As late as last year, complete strangers had come up to J. D. at the firing range to shake his hand and tell him what a fine thing he'd done.

Oftentimes they would linger to watch him shoot.

After six years J. D. traveled to the Santa Cruz workshop of Walter Perry and called in the debt of gratitude. He laid the drawings for the M-100 on the artisan's worktable and asked Perry if he could build the weapon for him. The gunsmith knew of the M-100; knew that private ownership of it was illegal; knew J. D. was asking him to commit a crime.

He also knew he'd given J. D. his word, and that his godson was alive and well thanks, in part, to this man. Walter Perry told J. D. where and when he'd be able to pick up his weapon. Not that Perry would be there to deliver it. Not that he would *ever* admit building it. J. D. said that was just the way he wanted it—and before he left the gunsmith he purchased another custom-made weapon, a single-shot .22 in the guise of a Mont Blanc pen.

The first thing J. D. had had Pickpocket do for him was simple enough. He had him clone the PCR he'd been sent. With the clone, however, J. D. could disable the homing function, and unlike the original, it was able not only to receive e-mail but to send it as well.

Pickpocket's next task was more complex. J. D. supplied him with his personal Rolodex database and asked him to look for links between any name in it and the populations of Lake Charles, Louisiana; Paris, Texas; and Americus, Georgia.

"Also," J. D. told Pickpocket, "hack into the system for the Rancho Durango Gun Club, retrieve the guest list for the past six years, and look for connections to me and/or our three southern towns. Then look for extremist groups that might be operating in or around the three towns."

"Extremist groups?"

"Klan, Nazis, whatever."

Pickpocket grinned. Whatever J. D. was up to, it was going to be interesting.

J. D.'s pursuit of his blackmailers was rudely interrupted on the first day of August when he received an invitation-sized envelope postmarked Birmingham, Alabama. In it he found a piece of card stock. On the card was a line drawing done in the style of the children's game hangman. A stick figure with a head, torso, and one leg was dangling from a noose. In the space below was printed $E— — —$.

Evan. His son was being threatened again, and J. D. was being told to get to work.

J. D. told Pickpocket to add Birmingham to his search parameters. He then had the little thief set up a series of phony credit card accounts for him, and after studying Senator Rawley's itinerary and picking up the M-100, he set off for Chicago.

After he'd missed that shot and reclaimed his car in Las Vegas, he found he had e-mail.

Now the stick figure had *two* legs, and the message read $EV— —$.

Evan and Belle Cade sat in the office of Richard Shuster, the criminal attorney to whom they'd been referred by Belle's personal lawyer, Elgar Guererro. Shuster was a stocky man with a wrinkled suit, a furrowed brow, and a blunt demeanor.

"Your father called me this morning, Mr. Cade," Shuster said.

"He did?" Evan asked neutrally. "I didn't know he was even aware of you."

"I spoke with J. D. before you woke up," Belle told her grandson. "He wanted to be sure you were in good hands. I gave him Mr. Shuster's phone number."

"I told your father my record in criminal trials was two hundred twelve wins and three losses. He asked me about the losses. Would you like to hear about them, too, Mr. Cade?"

Evan started to reply but decided to hold his tongue. He shook his head.

"All right. I've spoken at length with Mr. Guererro," Shuster told Evan and Belle. "I've called people I know with the police and the state's attorney. The prevailing wisdom among the authorities, Mr. Cade, is that you killed Ivar McCray."

"That's just plain wrong," Belle asserted.

"Is it, Mr. Cade? Many defense attorneys don't like to know that little detail. I do."

"I didn't kill him. And I don't know where any of this stuff about my shoes and muddy footprints is coming from."

Shuster scratched the side of his head with a stubby finger and stared at Evan.

"Okay," he said after a lengthy examination. "Let me lay it out for you the way the cops see it. They've got this dead guy, Ivar McCray. He dies while supposedly making a pipe bomb. Why was he doing that? To send a message to a businessman who refuses to pay protection money to a gang McCray was fronting. Who's the businessman? A gas station owner named—"

"Barton Laney," Evan interrupted.

Shuster looked at Evan closely again.

"I read the newspaper story the *Southern Illinoisan* ran," Evan said. "It's public knowledge that Mr. Laney tipped the cops about what McCray was trying to do."

"Yes, it is. But what the public doesn't know is that Laney told them what was going on only *after* McCray had died."

Belle looked puzzled and asked, "What's the significance of that?"

"Why wouldn't he have gone to the cops before McCray

died?" the lawyer asked. "Isn't that what most people would have done? Somebody threatens you, you call the cops. So why didn't Barton Laney?"

"Because the man obviously doesn't have the sense God gave a goose," Belle offered. "But Evan can hardly be held responsible for someone else's poor judgment."

"Can you think of another reason, Mr. Cade?" Shuster asked.

Evan replied, "I know what you're thinking."

"Not me, Mr. Cade, the police."

"The police, then. They think Mr. Laney didn't go to them first because he knew somebody was going to take care of his problem for him."

The lawyer nodded.

"Do they think I killed this guy because he was bothering my girl's father?"

"In a nutshell, yes. Things got hairy and you stepped in to save the day for the Laneys."

"Then what? Mr. Laney comes forward to reveal the extortion attempt to make it look like McCray got what he deserved? Wouldn't it have been safer just to keep quiet?"

"The cops are still chewing on that one. But besides the footprints, and some little birdie singing your name to the cops, my secretary told me something this morning that, having lived here only ten years, I hadn't known. She told me the saga of the Cades and the McCrays. Your family and the dead man's have a history of bad blood between them that goes back a *long* way."

Belle's brow knitted. "Evan has no part in that."

"But think how it looks, Mrs. Cade," Shuster told Belle. "Who better to paint into a corner for the death of a McCray than a Cade? Another thing I learned today: Chief of police Billy Edwards' wife, Maura, is a McCray."

Neither Evan nor Belle was comforted to hear that piece of news.

The lawyer continued, "The way I see it is this: If the cops find your shoes and get a match on those footprints, they'll arrest you. If they—"

"Wait a minute," Evan interrupted. "About this whole footprint thing. Am I supposed to be the only guy in town who wears the size and type of shoe the cops are looking for?"

Shuster smiled at what he considered a good layman's attempt at defense work.

"Probably not. But unless shoes are virtually brand-new, the wear and tear they exhibit is distinctive. And let me ask you, Mr. Cade, did you ever wear your sneakers without socks? If so, you might have left flakes of skin, bits of hair . . . maybe they can even find a way to coax old perspiration from the insole, for all I know. Anyway, if they find the shoes, find some source of DNA inside them, they'll likely be able to establish whether they're yours."

Evan had no rebuttal.

"So if they get the shoes and make the arrest by the book, the state's attorney will get a grand jury to indict you. If we can't find a way to suppress the shoes as evidence, we'll go to trial. At that point, to establish reasonable doubt, we'll need to place you somewhere else at the time the victim was killed. Impartial and credible witnesses—not family; sorry, Mrs. Cade—are what you'll need."

Shuster scratched his head again. "That, or we'll have to find someone else to hang for Ivar McCray's death."

Evan Cade joined his grandmother in the living room of her house after dinner. When his grandmother looked up from the book she'd been reading, she saw that something was bothering him. More than just his immediate difficulties. "What is it, Evan?"

He said, "Grandma, if it's all right with you, I'd like to

know about the feud." He'd seen how her face clouded when the subject came up that day at the lawyer's office.

"Oh." She closed the book and put it aside. For a moment she was quiet, seeming to seek her own counsel. Then with a small, decisive nod she began, "The feud started in 1865 with incest, rape, and a hanging."

Belle recounted how Wilbert Cade, returning home from the Civil War, chanced to meet and fall in love with the beautiful eighteen-year-old Edina McCray. Determined to marry her, he finally won the permission of her father, Cullum. Family lore had it that in the end Wilbert had to pay old man McCray a hundred dollars for his consent, a princely sum at the time. Not long after the couple was married, Wilbert returned home from a trip to buy a plow horse and found Edina's brother, Birk, raping his new wife in Wilbert and Edina's bed.

Far from being intimidated by being caught at such a heinous act, Birk was defiant. He said his sister had been his first, their daddy had no right to sell her, and he was taking her home. It was said that the only reason Wilbert Cade hadn't shot Birk McCray to death on the spot was that Edina had pleaded for his life; she wanted to see her brother hang. Birk was tried and convicted of crimes against God and nature.

Having their shame aired publicly did not sit well with the McCrays, several of whom attended the trial. Nor was it lost on them that half the members of the jury who convicted their kinsman were Cades. As was the hangman.

The McCrays came for vengeance a month after Birk's execution. A dozen McCray men — "our jury," as they called themselves — raided Wilbert Cade's farm one night. They hanged Wilbert from an apple tree in his front yard, burned his house and barn, and slaughtered his animals. They let Edina live, but they carved WHORE into her belly.

A cycle of reprisals began that continued sporadically

until the last two official deaths in the feud occurred more than seventy years later. In July 1939 Lawler Cade was found hanging from an oak tree. He was rumored to have informed revenue agents as to the whereabouts of an illegal still the McCrays were running. In December 1941 Ransom McCray was found shot between the eyes in the doorway of his home. He was said to have been the McCray who'd slipped the noose around Lawler Cade's neck.

Further bloodshed was prevented only by the outbreak of World War II the day after Ransom McCray was killed. All of the Cades and McCrays who might have directed their lethal energies against one another were sent off to other parts of the world to kill new enemies.

Evan was more than a little taken aback at the savagery in which his forebears had played a principal part, but he picked up on one important detail of his grandmother's narrative.

"What did you mean, Grandma, when you said the last two *official* deaths in the feud occurred in 1939 and 1941? Were there any unofficial deaths after that?"

At first Belle Cade was plainly reluctant to answer.

"Come on, Grandma," Evan chided. "You can't hold back on me now."

Belle moved to the sofa where her grandson sat and took his hand.

"Evan, this feud has been a curse upon our family for far too long. It nearly ensnared your father . . . and now, I fear, it's placed you in danger."

Evan saw that his grandmother was speaking in deadly earnest, and that frightened him.

"If that's the case," he said, "don't you think I should know everything I can?"

Belle looked into her grandson's eyes and decided that she had to tell him as much as she could. "Has your father ever spoken to you about Alvy McCray?"

Evan shook his head.

Belle told him the story.

Evan was agog. "Dad pistol-whipped this guy with Grandpa's .45?"

He considered his father to be the most easygoing man in the world. If he had any complaint at all about his dad, it was that he was overprotective. His father had tried too hard to make sure that *nothing* would ever hurt him. As Evan had grown older, this paternal hovering had chafed. He'd found it necessary to tell his dad to back off a little, to give him some room to lead his own life. Even if he made some mistakes.

Evan could see now that his father must have had similar protective feelings about the other members of the Cade family. So if this Alvy McCray asshole had been pounding on a bunch of them, threatening to get the feud started again all by himself . . . Evan guessed he could see his dad going off on the guy. Sure was an eye-opener, though.

"Your father did only what he had to do," Belle assured him, seeming to read his mind. "No more, no less."

"And this Alvy McCray flipped his truck after Dad had already left for California?"

"Yes," Belle answered emphatically. "Everything worked out for the best."

Then she added, "It was just a pity that deer had to die."

Pickpocket, who had said he'd be back in a couple of hours, hadn't returned to the Refuge by that evening. Which made J. D. very edgy. He had only one ally and couldn't afford to lose him.

Almost as trying as the little thief's unexplained absence were the hours of enforced idleness. J. D. felt certain it would be a mistake, but it was all he could do not to pick up the phone and force the issue—call Vandy Ellison and tell her he'd changed his mind and would like to attend the diva's fund-raiser.

Instead, he did something that almost always calmed him. He took target practice.

J. D. clipped the picture of Del Rawley from that day's *Los Angeles Times*. He'd scanned the paper as soon as it had been delivered that morning to see if the FBI was making any progress in their manhunt for him. He'd wondered endlessly the past week if he'd made some mistake—other than missing his shot—while trying to kill Del Rawley in Chicago. He knew that if he'd overlooked the slightest detail, it could be his undoing, and the thought circled his mind like a bird of prey.

There had been no news indicating the FBI was on to him, but he'd been able to take little comfort from that. The feds could be following a lead that hadn't leaked to the media yet.

The picture of Rawley J. D. cut out of the paper was a good four-color likeness, about two-thirds life size, he estimated. He found a clay planter in the gardening shed, filled it with potting soil, and took it into the garage. There he taped the picture over the mouth of the planter and wedged it on its side on a shelf approximating his target's height. He found two ladders in the garage to stand in for Secret Service agents and set one just to either side of the picture, giving him only a narrow opening for his target.

He stepped off twenty feet from the target. He took out the pen gun he'd purchased from Walter Perry and examined it. It was a masterful piece of craftsmanship. The black plastic shell gleamed in the overhead light, and the gold trim—pocket clip, band around the middle, and ink-filling lever on the side—gave it a look of elegance. The cap had to be removed for firing. The ink lever was the trigger; first it flipped the nib out of the way on a hidden hinge and then it fired the round. The weapon unscrewed at the gold band to reload a .22 caliber cartridge.

Last week, while waiting to make his approach to the Rawley campaign and futilely trying to draw out his unseen minders, J. D. had made use of his time by purchasing an actual Mont Blanc pen identical to the minigun. He thought a decoy might come in handy. While he was out shopping, he also bought a camera disguised as the remote for a car alarm. The idea that he might need to take pictures surreptitiously had also occurred to him.

Now, looking at his target, J. D. shot the pen gun from the hip, a firing position that would be very hard to detect in a crowd. The round went through the picture's right eye. The sound was no louder than a matchstick snapping. Firing the weapon in a large, crowded, noisy room, it would be effectively silent. Then dropping it in the pocket of an innocent bystander and letting him carry off the murder weapon as bedlam ensued would be child's play. When the bystander eventually happened to notice he had something in his pocket, he'd take it out and leave *his* fingerprints on it.

J. D. reloaded to fire another round at the newspaper photo. The typical minigun was a shoddy piece of work that was fired once from a range of not more than ten feet and then thrown away. But Walter Perry's handiwork was reliable at twice that range and reusable. He fired the second round and it tore the photo of Del Rawley in two.

J. D. went into the house and found a blank sheet of writing paper. He drew a rough oval approximately the size of an adult head. He sketched in eyes, brows, and a nose. As art, it was as primitive as the stick figures he'd received. Which was exactly the point.

He took the drawing to the garage, removed the torn picture of Rawley from the planter, and taped up his drawing in its place. He moved the ladders closer together, leaving only a six-inch opening between them for the drawing. He stepped back as far as he could go, maybe twenty-five feet.

J. D. Cade didn't know who was blackmailing him, who was threatening his son, or what the man looked like. At the moment, though, the crude portrait was sufficient to focus his anger.

He fired the pen gun, and the round struck its target squarely between the eyes.

Across the country in Virginia, in the last light of the day, a man with many names, most of them unpleasant and bestowed on him by his multitude of enemies, cut back a jasmine plant that had gotten leggy. A native of the tropics, the plant would have to be brought indoors before the first frost. But placed in a bright window, it would blossom again in January, its white star-shaped flowers and glorious fragrance delights to the senses.

The name by which the man thought of himself was the Gardener.

An altogether different type of character approached him. Of medium height and blocky build, he had a receding hairline, protuberant eyes, and two large warts, one at either end of a wide, lipless mouth. His name was Harold Starchley, but to everyone who'd ever worked with him he was Harold the Toad.

The Gardener, of course, knew that toads could be useful. They devoured slugs and other pests.

"I talked to the technician, sir. He said Cade must have cloned the PCR we sent him and installed a switch to deactivate the homing function. That's the only explanation for why it works perfectly some of the time and not at all other times."

"Mr. Cade doesn't like us intruding on his privacy."

"If he's cloned the PCR, sir, it means he's taking countermeasures. He's probably looking for us right now."

"Of course he is. Which is why we haven't let him see us."

"But time is passing, sir, and Rawley's numbers are still up."

"You have a point, Harold. Perhaps Mr. Cade needs a bit more prompting." He returned his attention to snipping the jasmine. "Well, we do have our options, don't we?"

THREE
Tuesday, September 14, 2004

That morning's *Los Angeles Times* held news of interest for J. D.

> *Denver—The FBI may have prevented a second assassination attempt against presidential candidate Senator Franklin Delano Rawley. An anonymous source has revealed that another sniper shot at Senator Rawley may have been planned for when the candidate speaks in this city later today. The two speeches the senator will be giving here are at indoor venues, leading authorities to conclude that the attempt would be made as Senator Rawley entered or left one of the buildings.*
>
> *Neither the FBI nor the Rawley campaign would comment publicly on the matter, but it has been confirmed that the Rawley entourage has moved from the Four Seasons Hotel, where it had been staying. New lodgings for the campaign have not been revealed.*
>
> *This potential new threat comes scarcely more than a week after . . .*

J. D. pored over the rest of the story and strained to read between the lines. After what had happened in Chicago, the Secret Service and the FBI had to be going balls out to see that nobody got off another long-range shot at the candidate . . . but were they anxious enough to imagine a threat that wasn't real? J. D. had never been to Denver, not for the purpose of killing Del Rawley.

For the moment, all he could think was that the feds were following a false lead, something that would carry them away from him. He was hesitant to accept that notion completely, but earlier that morning he'd used his laptop to read newspapers from around the country. He thought other papers might have stories about the search for him that the *Times* hadn't printed. But he couldn't find any report that pointed toward him. Either the feds were staying extremely tight-lipped about the investigation or they honestly didn't have a clue as to who had pulled the trigger in Chicago.

All things considered, J. D. was beginning to think he'd gotten away clean.

From Chicago, anyway.

That thought had no sooner occurred to him than he heard a door open. By reflex, he grabbed the sugar bowl off the kitchen table and got ready to hurl it at whoever appeared. But reason soon overtook fear and he set the would-be missile down. There was only one person who would likely be entering the Refuge now . . . and it wouldn't do to let him see just how tense he was.

Pickpocket stepped into kitchen.

The little thief's eyes were bloodshot and had dark circles under them. For the first time J. D. noticed a hint of stubble on the young hacker's chin. But he didn't smell of alcohol, tobacco, or sex. And the smile of satisfaction on the little thief's face looked hard-earned. He dropped into a chair opposite J. D.

But Pickpocket didn't say a word, just kept grinning.

"Lose track of the time?" J. D. asked.

"As a matter of fact, yeah. The first time I thought to look at a clock, it turned out to be four A.M. At that point, I figured I might just as well keep going."

"On what?"

Before the little thief could answer he had to stifle a yawn. Then he started to stand. "I've got to get something to drink."

J. D. gestured him firmly back into his seat.

"I'll get you some coffee," he said, getting up. "You keep talking."

"Make it orange juice." Pickpocket rubbed his tired eyes with the back of a hand. "I was walking around yesterday, looking at this and that, trying to decide where to eat. Just letting my mind drift, you know, to see where it took me."

Another bare-the-molars yawn interrupted the narrative as J. D. returned to the table and set a glass of juice down in front of Pickpocket. He took a sip and continued.

"What struck me was how just about every retail operation in the world is franchised these days: restaurants, bookstores, muffler shops, office supply outfits, you name it."

"So?"

"So I thought, just for the hell of it, why don't I look and see what kinds of places our four target towns have? What do Lake Charles, Paris, Americus, and Birmingham have in common other than being in the South?"

"But your computer was here."

The little thief grinned once more. "You mess with it?"

"No."

Pickpocket nodded, deciding J. D. was telling him the truth. He said, "I don't think I'd have had the restraint."

"*John*." J. D.'s use of his given name prompted Pickpocket to get serious.

"Okay. I stopped into a twenty-four-hour cybercafe

called Digital Ditties, got online, and worked all night."
The little thief leaned forward. "Among the endless list of
franchises our four towns have in common, one name
jumped out at me. PostMaster Plus. All four towns have
PostMaster Plus franchises, and among their other uses they
offer a remailing service. You go into your local store, hand
them an envelope, and for a fee you can have it remailed
and postmarked from anywhere else they have a store. And
they have locations nationwide. Remailing is very convenient when you have to communicate with someone but
don't want them to know where the hell you are. Battered
spouses, government witnesses, people ducking subpoenas,
and the like use it.

"Now, it makes more sense to me," Pickpocket continued, "that whoever is sending you this stuff that's jamming
you up—whatever it is—is using a remailer. Otherwise
what you've got is a group of people spread across the South
who don't like you, or one guy who's doing a helluva lot of
driving."

J. D. frowned.

"What?" Pickpocket asked, sitting back indignantly.
"You think I'm wrong?"

J. D. shook his head. "No, I think you're probably right.
But I also think that people in the situations you describe
are likely to pay for their remailing with cash. So why
should the people I'm after be any different?"

Pickpocket shrugged. "Chances are they're not." Then
the little thief grinned impishly. "But remember how dumb
smart people can frequently be. Look at how I make my living: stealing computer passwords that people are stupid
enough to keep in their wallets."

"Yeah," J. D. said, but he didn't sound hopeful.

"Look, you might not see it now, but this is a big break.
Right off the bat, I made contact with three hackers who

claimed to have a password that will get me into any level of the PostMaster Plus system," he said. "It took me a while to check out their references, but I settled on this guy who calls himself Red. I think he's really got the goods, and I think he's someone we can trust . . . as much as you can trust anyone."

"So how soon will we know if Red's the real deal?"

"It'll take a little while."

"Why?"

"Because Red has to check out *my* references."

"Might it speed things up to do the deal in person?" J. D. wanted to know.

Pickpocket looked at J. D. blankly. "In *person*?"

"If Red is anywhere nearby, I'll add twenty K to whatever you're swapping to move things along." J. D. could see that the canny little thief was getting the idea that he was a man in a hurry, but he couldn't worry about that.

"Hackers meeting in the flesh. Huh. Radical idea. I'll pass it right along. But then I've really got to crash."

Evan Cade had covered the sprawling grounds of Southern Illinois University looking for his girlfriend, Pru Laney. Failing to find her, he plopped down on a bench and stared out at the waters of the campus lake. The fall term had just begun, and he knew that missing classes now wasn't the way to maintain the old 4.0 GPA. But after hearing Richard Shuster talk about how he could be looking at a murder trial, his mind was anywhere but on his classwork.

Shuster's implication about finding someone else to take the rap for Ivar McCray's death wasn't hard to follow: Let's shift the blame to Barton Laney.

What complicated matters was that Evan had spent the better part of the night Ivar McCray had died with Pru

Laney. Alone with her at her father's house. Doing what young people inevitably did when they found themselves in sole possession of private and comfortable quarters.

Hardly the impartial alibi Shuster had told him he might well need.

Now Evan wondered what Barton Laney had been doing that night. But he couldn't imagine asking Pru about it. What would he say? "Hey, babe, you remember that night we had such a good time? You know if your dad was out committing murder right about then?"

Making things even more problematic, now that he thought about it, Pru had seemed to start withdrawing from him after that night. It couldn't have been the sex, because that had hardly been their first time. But little by little it seemed to Evan she had started avoiding him, being busy when he wanted to go out, not hanging out at the usual places—and now he couldn't find her at all. It was like she was dumping him without coming right out and saying so.

Which was why he'd wanted to find her, to see where they stood.

Evan heard footsteps approaching. He looked around and there was Pru, walking along with her friend Jeri Perkins, the two of them lost in conversation, heading for the same bench on which he sat without even realizing he was there.

Evan stood up and said, "Hi."

Both women jumped, startled, and Pru looked anything but happy to see him.

"Sorry," Evan apologized. "Didn't mean to scare you."

He said hello to Jeri, but she was so ill at ease seeing him that she quickly excused herself. Standing there alone with Pru, he thought to make a joke that a lack of personal hygiene must be causing people to avoid him. Instead he put his hands on her shoulders and asked, "What's going on? With you and me."

Pru had long hair that was almost as dark as Evan's, and she had green eyes like his. Friends kidded them that they looked too much alike to be dating; they were probably related without knowing it, and any fooling around would surely be incest. They'd disregarded with glee the possibility of breaking that taboo. But now Pru's shoulders trembled under Evan's touch and she stepped back from him.

"Can't you tell me?" he asked quietly.

Pru's chin began to quiver and tears welled up in her eyes.

"Don't you have anything to say at all?"

"My dad's lawyer told me not to talk to you," she blurted.

She looked like she wanted to tell him more, but the words caught in her throat. She turned from him and ran away. He didn't take a single step to follow.

So they *had* broken up. On the advice of goddamn counsel.

Evan decided to blow off his classes and drive home.

He was far too preoccupied to notice that someone was following him.

Jenny Crenshaw arrived in L.A. ahead of Del and the rest of the brain trust. There were some local people she wanted to see that the others didn't need to bother with, not that any of those people would ever be told they were a bother. She pushed through the door of Rawley campaign headquarters and the first thing she heard was a shouting match.

The honest-to-God, curl-your-hair, quick-call-the-cops kind.

Every staffer in the outer-office bullpen had his or her head cocked in the direction of the verbal brawl, all of them looking properly horrified.

"What the hell is going on?" Jenny demanded, hurrying toward the sounds of battle.

"It's Vandy and DeVito," a woman informed her.

"Where's Paul?" Jenny asked, still moving.

Paul Gilmartin was the state campaign manager and the boss of the California office.

"Paul's kid fell off his skateboard. He had to go to the hospital to be with him," came a voice as she hurried down the hallway.

Jenny threw open the door to Vandy's office and the uproar got *really* loud.

"*Stop!*" Jenny bellowed.

DeVito, leaning on his knuckles, had his very red face thrust over Vandy's desk. Vandy was seated behind the desk and held a letter opener in her fist. Both of them turned to look at Jenny, who at that moment was more royally pissed than either of them.

"Sit *down*, Special Agent," Jenny ordered DeVito.

Nobody was going to bully any woman in the campaign while Jenny ran things. DeVito glared at her a good long moment. But he knew who was in charge of the political side of the campaign, and he knew he was really no longer the head of the protection detail. So he drew himself upright and then took one of Vandy's two guest chairs.

"You can put the letter opener down now, Vandy," Jenny said.

She let it drop on her desk. Jenny took a seat in the other guest chair.

"We're going to talk now," Jenny instructed them, "and there will be no resumption of any shouting. Do you both understand that?"

Vandy gave an angry nod; DeVito's was barely perceptible.

Jenny said, "All right, Special Agent, we'll start with you—" She held up a hand to forestall a protest from Vandy. "In twenty-five words or less, what's the problem?"

"She's trying to interfere with my job," DeVito grumbled through clenched teeth.

"Vandy, your turn. Follow the agent's example and get straight to the point."

"I caught him going through my desk," Vandy hissed.

"She slammed the drawer on my hand," DeVito accused, the heat reentering his voice.

"And I'll do it again if you ever—"

"Stop!" Jenny commanded. "Special Agent, *why* were you going through Vandy's desk in the first place?"

"After . . ." DeVito looked like he wanted to spit blood. "After the attempt in Chicago, every contact by an outsider with this campaign should be given at least a cursory examination."

"He wanted to look in Marva Weisman's handbag," Vandy said deadpan. "I get one of the biggest stars ever to give a private performance that will be a feature story from coast to coast and raise at least a million dollars for the campaign, and he wants to make sure she's not packing heat."

Jenny looked at DeVito in disbelief. The stubbornness written across the man's face was almost tangible. He clearly believed he was in the right.

"Did you really think that was necessary?" Jenny asked quietly.

"I want to check *everybody* who comes in contact with this campaign," DeVito asserted.

Jenny remembered that terrible day just over a week ago when she had wanted this man's *hide*, not just his job, because he obviously hadn't checked everyone and everything that could hurt Del, because her candidate had almost died as a result of that failure. In his place now, she might feel the same way he did. But in her place, she knew that sound judgment was called for by everyone involved in the campaign.

"Were you going through Vandy's desk to find something relating to Ms. Weisman?"

DeVito shook his head.

Vandy was only too happy to tell Jenny what DeVito had wanted. To snoop on another person who only wanted to help the campaign. She filled in the details.

"This Mr. Cade simply wrote a check to our national committee for ten thousand dollars and then went on his way?" Jenny asked.

"Yes."

"Did he do anything suspicious?"

"No. In fact, he declined my offer to attend Marva's performance—where I told him Del would be present—for an additional fifteen thousand dollars."

"Maybe he couldn't afford it," DeVito sneered.

Vandy's jaw muscles bulged. She ratted out DeVito's rude remark to J. D. Cade about his lack of a manicure.

Jenny shook her head.

"That was uncalled-for, Special Agent. You will write a note of apology to Mr. Cade that the campaign will deliver to him. You will also apologize right now to Ms. Ellison for attempting to rifle her desk and for trying to intimidate her with your abusive behavior."

DeVito's eyes bulged and he looked like he was about to go off again, but Jenny wasn't finished with him. She continued in a voice of bedrock certainty, "You will do both of these things or after today you will no longer be a part of this campaign."

"I don't work for you, lady," DeVito snarled.

"Last chance, Special Agent," Jenny said, reaching for Vandy's phone. "Do as I say and do it now or you won't be working for *anybody*."

DeVito apologized, probably at the cost of a year off his life, his voice pitched to the sort of subsonic rumble that usually precedes an earthquake of large magnitude. Vandy started to say she couldn't hear him, but Jenny held up her hand.

"Thank you, Special Agent. Ms. Ellison accepts your apology. Don't forget your note to Mr. Cade. You can make it brief. But make sure it includes the words 'I'm sorry.'"

DeVito got up and left without acknowledging Jenny's last command, but he didn't slam the door behind him.

"You think he'll do it? Apologize to Mr. Cade?" Vandy asked.

"He better."

Vandy waited a moment to make sure DeVito wasn't about to come storming back in and then took a manila folder out of her desk and placed it in front of Jenny. She said, "That's why I slammed the drawer on that jerk's hand. I didn't want him to find that."

Jenny flipped open the folder and saw an eight-by-ten black-and-white photo of a handsome man in a dark suit.

"Who's that?" Jenny asked.

By way of response, Vandy slid the first photo aside to reveal a second one: Marva Weisman. Jenny recognized her . . . and now she realized that the background behind both people was the bullpen area of the campaign office.

Jenny looked back to the first photo. "Is he the man who—"

"J. D. Cade." Vandy nodded.

"DeVito set up a hidden camera?" Jenny asked.

"The staffers in the bullpen area complained that it was getting stuffy out there. When the building maintenance guy came, he took off the vent cover and found the camera. By pure luck, I was passing by. I grabbed the camera right out of the guy's hand before anyone else could see what it was. The maintenance guy didn't seem to speak much English, but he nodded when I pressed my finger to my lips. So we can hope he doesn't go to the tabloids and we don't see any 'Rawley Spies on Own Office' stories. A friend made the prints for me privately. Those are the only ones, and here is the disc from the camera."

Vandy dropped it on the photo of the diva. "Maybe we could do a promotion. Make a donation, get a free mug shot. You think it would work?"

Jenny sighed. "Thanks for handling this so discreetly, Vandy."

"You're welcome."

Jenny looked at the first photo again.

"Nice-looking man, Mr. Cade."

Vandy frowned. She didn't want Jenny poaching on her territory. So she changed the subject. "Somebody ought to throw a net over that DeVito."

"I hope that's what I just did," Jenny replied. "But I'll talk to Del about him."

"I think you better."

Fuck them, DeVito thought. Fuck them both.

He walked out of the campaign office, his vision consciously reduced to a narrow tunnel. If he saw anybody looking at him with a smirk or with pity, he'd shoot them. He reached the elevator bank outside the office and jabbed the call button hard enough to crack the plastic. Then he fumed at the wait for the elevator to arrive.

He should have quit. After what happened in Chicago, he should have just quit and accepted the shame he deserved. But when he'd heard the senator insisted he be given a second chance, he'd bitten down on the opportunity like a starving dog on a bone. He'd thought—however long the odds—here was his chance for redemption.

Yeah, right.

They'd sent him ahead to check out the campaign office in L.A. Make sure nobody had planted a bomb and there was no anarchist with pinwheel eyes licking envelopes for the cause. And the thing was, the office staffers had treated him decently, even though they knew he was the fuck-up who almost let Orpheus get killed. They answered every last question he put to them without blinking. They understood he was only doing what was necessary.

But the big shots who brought in the megabucks, around them he was expected to bow and scrape and turn a blind eye. Even that wiseass who'd chipped in a lousy ten grand . . . he was supposed to get a note of apology. Well, DeVito felt a terrible cramp coming on in his writing hand. Not so bad he couldn't pull a trigger, but much too painful to hold a pen.

That slick fucker J. D. Cade would play pinochle with the Pope before he'd hear Dante DeVito tell him he was sorry. What he would do for Cade was check him out, the way he should be checking everybody out. That redheaded bitch had slammed her desk drawer on his hand, but not before DeVito had seen Cade's personal check with his Santa Barbara address and the name of his bank.

That was enough to get him started. And if Jenny Crenshaw cost him his job about it, he didn't care anymore. The elevator finally came, and it was the same car that show biz bitch had used yesterday. He thought he could smell the scent of her perfume lingering in the air.

Fuck her, too.

Evan Cade wanted to learn more about the Cade-McCray feud, so that evening, with the first touch of autumnal coolness in the air, he drove down Route 51 to visit his father's cousin Ben in the little town of Anna. The two men sat on Ben's screened-in front porch.

Cousin Ben had the typical Cade lankiness, but he was several inches shorter than Evan, and with a full head of dark hair and an unlined face, he looked more like he was approaching forty than fifty. He told Evan the decades-old story of the assault he'd suffered. Alvy McCray had long since moldered in his grave, but Ben Cade's emotions still ran high.

"I was planning to kill Alvy even after your daddy bashed that sonofabitch with your grandpa's old army .45. Hating Alvy and thinking about what I was going to do to him got me started on healing, and with my skull fractured in three places from the beating he gave me, there was some question whether I'd heal at all."

"How did you know what my dad did to Alvy?"

"He came to the hospital and told me. He thought it would cheer me up."

"Did it?"

"Yes. But it didn't stop me from planning to kill that bastard."

"Did you tell my dad that?"

Ben Cade nodded. "He said the way Alvy was going, he'd be dead before I got out of the hospital. Sure enough, he was right. Fucker flipped his truck and killed himself. Damn shame about that deer, though."

That was the second reference Evan had heard to the misfortune of the deer. He took it as a measure of how the Cades valued wildlife far more than McCrays.

"Did you feel . . . I don't know, disappointed, maybe, that Dad left for California while Alvy was still around to make trouble?"

Ben looked off through the screen. Insects were flitting about the yellow porch lights that were just starting to take hold against the deepening night. Finally Ben Cade looked back at his young kinsman.

"I was more than just disappointed. I was mad. I was counting on J. D. to help me steady my rifle when the time came to shoot Alvy." His expression softened. "Try as I might, though, I couldn't convince myself that J. D. had left because he was scared. Your daddy was always a real easygoing guy, you might even say gentle, but I never saw him afraid of one thing in his life."

"Neither have I," Evan agreed. Unless it was of someone hurting me, he thought.

Ben laughed at some private thought.

"What?" Evan asked.

"I'm almost ashamed to admit this, but after Alvy died my anger turned to relief. I'd been spared becoming a killer, and that started me thinking that somehow your daddy had done that for me. Spared me and saved our whole family from having the feud start all over again."

"But how could he have done that? He was gone; Alvy died after his truck hit the deer."

Ben looked at Evan closely, as if taking his measure. He was just about to speak when his wife, Marie, called him to take a phone call inside. When he came back, he poked his head out the porch door and looked up the street. Then he returned to his seat.

He told Evan, "It was just a thought, that's all. That your daddy had fixed Alvy."

Evan nodded . . . but he had the distinct feeling that Ben had been about to give him a completely different explanation. He felt cheated. As if he'd missed out on learning a closely guarded family secret. One that concerned his father.

Ben put a hand on Evan's leg. "That was a neighbor who called just now. He said there's a pickup truck with Kentucky plates parked up the block, and the fella inside is looking this way."

Evan considered the possibilities. "A McCray?"

"Maybe the two of us should go find out."

Evan thought a moment, then replied, "I'll go."

"Okay," Ben conceded. "You go . . . and I'll keep an eye on you."

Evan walked up to the pickup truck. It was a dark blue Ford. The license plate holder said it came from a dealership in Paducah. The guy behind the wheel looked to be in his early thirties. He had sandy hair done in a buzz cut and pale gray eyes. He wore a raspberry Izod polo shirt that was filled to the bursting point with muscle.

"Kind of a preppy look for a pickup truck, don't you think?" Evan asked.

The guy looked back at Evan, studying his face. "My wife buys my clothes for me."

"Does a nice job, too. Was there something you wanted to talk to me about?"

"You're Evan Cade?"

Evan nodded.

"I'm Blair McCray." He showed Evan a badge from the Paducah Police Department. "I'm Ivar McCray's cousin. I've been asking a few questions about his death."

"You can do that in Illinois?"

"Just a friendly exchange of information between police professionals."

"Probably helps when one of those professionals is the chief of police and he's married to a McCray," Evan suggested.

Blair McCray didn't so much as blink. "That does have its advantages."

"So you learn anything interesting?"

"Your name."

"And did you tell your fellow cops anything they found important?"

"I let them know Ivar was too simple to spell *bomb*, much less build one."

Evan took in the implication of that tidbit without comment.

"See, Ivar and me, we grew up together. We were more like brothers than cousins. Ivar lost his daddy early and I lost mine before I was born. But I was older, so I was supposed to look after him. Did a pretty good job for quite a while, too. But you go off to college, meet a girl, find a job, get married, and start a family—you do all that, you got your hands full night and day. Some things just slip. With me, Ivar was what slipped. He never was much at school, and he was easily led. He dropped out of high school and took to running with bikers."

Blair put a chiseled arm on the window frame of the pickup and leaned toward Evan.

"What I'm saying, Ivar wasn't a Boy Scout. He was in with the wrong crowd. He got drunk and loud. Started fistfights easier than he should have. Spent any number of weekends in jail. But extortion and bomb building?" Blair McCray shook his head. "That wasn't him. But somebody went to a lot of trouble to make it look that way."

The look Blair gave Evan told him he had a strong suspicion who that somebody was.

"Or maybe, with all your new responsibilities, you just lost touch with him," Evan suggested in a neutral tone. "He changed and you never saw it."

That possibility pricked Blair's conscience, made him frown.

Evan added, "You talked to the Carbondale chief, he had to tell you about the footprints found near your cousin's body. Two of his uniforms wanted to look for shoes in my closet, but they didn't have a warrant and didn't get to come in. But maybe . . . maybe it'd be a good idea to let you take a look."

Evan was sure defense counsel Richard Shuster would vehemently disagree, but he wanted to see how the idea would play with this guy.

Blair McCray laughed, a deep, somewhat threatening

sound that bubbled up from his overdeveloped chest. "I'd be surprised if those shoes aren't long gone. No, I think we'll just have to find another opportunity to talk, you and me. Sometime when your friends with their shotguns aren't around."

Evan looked up and saw Ben behind the truck with a shotgun; in front of the vehicle was his neighbor, similarly armed.

"Not friends, family," Evan told Blair. "I've got lots of family around here."

Blair started his truck and turned on his lights.

"I know what you mean. I've got a lot of kin right close by myself. And as you pointed out, in-laws, too."

He gave Evan a mock salute and drove off.

Jenny Crenshaw had a hard time falling asleep. Besides having to break up the fight between Vandy Ellison and Special Agent DeVito that day, she'd also heard from Baxter Brown about what had happened in Denver: The FBI had been led to a marksman's notebook.

It had been discovered in a hotel room that looked out at the Four Seasons, where the campaign had been scheduled to stay. The head of housekeeping at the second hotel had been checking up on how well her staff had been cleaning rooms when she'd found the notebook, which had fallen behind a desk and been left there by both its owner and the maid who'd cleaned the room.

The head of housekeeping hadn't known exactly what the notebook was, but the crudely scrawled figures in it seemed somehow angry—*sinister*—to her. She'd taken the risk of looking foolish and summoned the hotel's chief of security to examine it. That gentleman, formerly with the Denver PD, had known exactly what he was looking at: notations for windage, elevation, and range.

The head of hotel security had also known who'd be arriving soon at the hostelry across the street, and so he called the FBI.

None of the data listed in the notebook specified a target. Some of the figures *could* have worked for a shot at the Rawley suite in the Four Seasons . . . or the target could have been something else entirely. But what greatly disturbed everyone was that the last occupant of the room where the notebook had been found had registered under a false identity. No man matching the name or possessing the home address of the hotel guest could be found.

With those disturbing thoughts in mind, Jenny had just drifted off, felt herself sinking helplessly into the teeth of a nightmare, when the phone rang. She awoke with a start, and when the phone rang again she felt a chill, as she feared the call could only be bad news. She grabbed the phone and croaked a dry-throated hello.

"Now I know I've woken you. I am sorry, my dear."

If possible, Donald "Hunter" Ward's voice was more brittle and ethereal than the last time she'd heard it. How, she wondered, could anyone sound that way and still be alive? She took a sip of water from the glass on the nightstand and asked, "Do you have any news, Don?"

"Yes, but not the news you're asking for. I haven't redeemed my promise to you yet, but I will. In all my poking about, though, I'm afraid I've uncovered another threat."

"Another *assassin*?" Jenny asked. The mystery man in Denver? The very idea made her go cold.

"Of the more common variety, Jenny. A character assassin. I haven't gleaned the details yet, but there's a big smear heading your man's way. Very big is the impression I got, and quite soon, too."

"A *smear*? But Del is Mr. Clean. I checked him out myself before I signed on."

"Check again, dear. I wasn't led to believe that this was a whole-cloth attack."

"I don't care what it is. When I hear something like this I just want to go off like—"

Jenny stopped herself before she said the name, but far too late for it not to be inferred.

"Like our esteemed former colleague, Thomas 'Killer' Laughlin?"

While it was said that Don Ward could dig up the dirt on Santa, Tom Laughlin's claim to fame was he could shoot Rudolph out of the sky, red nose and all.

"Yes, Tom could run people through the shredder, couldn't he?" Don Ward asked. "Well, I'm sure in the years the three of us were together you picked up some of his fighting spirit."

"In this business, it's a necessity."

"I heard from him, you know. Quite recently."

After a long pause Jenny asked, "He finally had the decency to come see you?"

Don Ward's laugh was a sibilant wheeze that gave Jenny chills.

"No, no, my dear. He called. He wanted me to leave him all the secrets of my craft. Put down in black and white a primer on the investigation of human frailty. You know, which rocks are the most important to look under, which transoms are the most profitable to peek over, which friends are most likely to have betrayal in their hearts. I told him it was all intuitive, a gift, and it would die with me."

Put that way, Jenny wasn't surprised at the affliction Don suffered.

"I imagine he didn't take that well," she said.

"No. Shrugging off rejection was never Tom's long suit. He seemed particularly disturbed, and more than a little surprised, when I told him I was otherwise engaged."

"You told him you're helping me?"

"I didn't specify what was occupying my final days. I

knew keeping him in the dark would drive him crazy. It's a small pleasure, but one he owes me."

Jenny had no trouble remembering that when she had first gone to work for Ward & Laughlin the two men were the best of friends, as close as brothers. Seeing them come to this, she wondered how long she could continue in politics before she became indistinguishable from her mentors.

"Again, my dear, I apologize for the hour of my call. I'll try to do better next time."

"Call anytime you want, Don," Jenny told him. "And thanks."

FOUR
Wednesday, September 15, 2004

"You had to call my lawyer, huh?"

J. D. Cade answered his son's question with one of his own.

"What kind of father would I be if I hadn't?"

J. D. had taken the call from Evan in the kitchen at the Refuge. He'd given the phone number and the house's address to his mother when he'd called her the day before. Outside by the pool, Pickpocket was negotiating a meeting via his laptop with Red, the hacker who claimed to have the PostMaster Plus password.

"Somebody else's father, I guess. Not mine."

"Can't help myself," J. D. replied. "That's just the way I feel."

"I'll yell for help if I need it, okay?"

"I'd rather not let it get to that point."

"All right. How about I'll call you if I even see trouble coming—and believe me, I'm keeping my eyes open."

J. D. knew he had to cut his son some slack. By the time he was Evan's age . . . well, that was how this whole mess got started. So stepping back even a little wasn't easy.

Even so, he said, "All right."

There was a moment of quiet and then, signaling he was taking his father at his word, Evan changed the subject. Dramatically.

"So how come you never told me about Alvy McCray?"

J. D. almost dropped the phone.

Before he could hope to find the words to answer that question, Evan had another one for him: "Is it true you actually dated a McCray—Lilah, Ben said her name was—or were you just *good friends*?"

The note of glee in his son's voice was unmistakable. But this question J. D. could answer and it gave him the time to regain his balance. "You've been talking to people," he said.

"Yeah. Cousin Ben and Grandma. So what about you and Lilah? You have a Montague-and-Capulet thing going on?"

"Lilah was in my senior class at Carbondale High. She was very . . . earthy."

"Stacked, fast, never took a bath?"

"Exactly," J. D. chuckled. "I was on the outs with my girlfriend of the time—"

"Mary Ellen McCarthy."

"Yes. Anyway, while I was angry at Mary Ellen a teacher asked me to tutor Lilah. I knew it would tick off Mary Ellen to see me with her, so I agreed. But all I did was tutor Lilah."

"Because she was earthy or because she was a McCray?"

"A little of both."

"So why did she cause a big uproar and say you knocked her up?"

"Her child's father was black. Lilah thought that it would be easier for her family to accept that after they learned they wouldn't have to share a bloodline with the Cades."

"Wow," Evan exclaimed softly. Then he added, "I met a McCray recently myself."

J. D. listened intently as his son told him of his encounter with Blair McCray. A chill crept up J. D.'s spine. He suggested, carefully, "Maybe it would be a good idea to come home."

"Leaving might make me look guilty, don't you think?" Evan rebutted.

"If the situation there gets iffy, I don't care how it looks."

Which brought them right back to the nub of the only dispute they had as father and son: J. D.'s need to make sure nothing ever hurt his son, and Evan's need to assert his independence—a divide not easily bridged. Evan, in a quiet voice, chose to return to an earlier subject.

"You were gone before Alvy McCray had his accident, right?"

J. D. was taken by surprise again, but not nearly as much as the first time. "For about a month," he replied evenly.

"Well, that ought to take the edge off the pistol-whipping you gave him. I mean, if the cops ever ask me about Cade-McCray confrontations."

"Evan, I know you're a man now, but you're a *young* man. You may not believe it, but there are situations you're really not prepared to handle. If you think you're in trouble with the police or anyone else, you come home. We'll work things out from here."

There was a lengthy pause, then Evan agreed. Somewhat. "If I need an escape hatch, that's what I'll do. But where's home these days? Santa Barbara? Or this new place in L.A.?"

J. D. gave him the cloned PCR number. "Just call me. I'll let you know where to go."

After J. D. said goodbye and clicked off, he heard a tapping at the kitchen door. Pickpocket was there. He waved him in.

"Saw you were talking. Didn't want to interrupt," the little thief said. After a moment's pause he added, "We've got a meeting for the PostMaster Plus password. Pan Pacific Park."

"When?" J. D. asked.

"Tonight," Pickpocket replied with a grin. "That fast enough for you?"

J. D. nodded and said, "I'll go get the twenty thousand from the bank right now."

Jenny's plane landed in Denver that morning. It was the last day of Del's campaign swing through the Rocky Mountain states before heading to California. But she couldn't afford to wait twenty-four hours for him to come to L.A. The smear that Don had alerted her to might be headline news by then. The warning was a tremendous break for the campaign, and they had to do everything they could to hit back as hard and fast as possible. Damage had to be kept to a minimum and, if possible, redirected at their opponent.

When they got all that sorted through, Jenny wanted to hear if the FBI had anything new about the marksman's notebook . . . and talk to Del about Special Agent DeVito running amok.

Except for dozing fitfully on the plane, she hadn't slept since receiving Don's call. She fell asleep in the cab she took from the airport, and the driver woke her up by rapping on his security shield when they reached the campaign's new hotel, the Brown Palace. "We're here, lady."

She paid the cabbie, went into the hotel, and found a ladies' room off the lobby. She splashed her face with cold water, shook herself to bring her circulation up to speed, and raked her hair into place with her fingers. She was still exhausted, but she knew she'd have to be mentally sharp until the campaign's brain trust decided on a plan of action. Or Del decided it for them.

She looked at her watch. Coming up on eight. Jenny

had called Baxter Brown to notify him that she'd be joining them for breakfast and not to let Del make any appearances before she arrived. She deeply hoped her candidate hadn't overruled that decision.

Del was staying in the penthouse suite, and there were two Secret Service agents on guard outside the lobby entrance to the private elevator. Another pair of agents rode up with her. More were waiting when the elevator doors opened. Del's press secretary, Alita Colon, pulled open the door to the suite as she approached it.

"The fellas called up to let us know you were on the way," she said. "Come on in. I've got juice, coffee, and rolls waiting."

"You just earned a place in heaven," Jenny assured her.

"Great—so long as it's not anytime soon," Alita replied. "Anything new about the—"

Alita shook her head before Jenny even finished. "Nothing . . . and that's part of what makes it spooky. What I heard, the FBI didn't find any fingerprints on that notebook except the ones from the housekeeping lady. So how'd its owner handle it, wear gloves all the time?"

There were several more Secret Service agents in the suite, and there would be others on the roof above them and the floor below. But in the windowless room where Baxter Brown and Jim Greenberg already sat at a table helping themselves to breakfast, no guards were present. Nor would they be after Del Rawley entered the room.

As a legacy of the Clinton administration—during which Special Prosecutor Kenneth Starr had compelled agents on the presidential protection detail to testify to a grand jury—calculated risks were taken from time to time by the politicians who were afforded Secret Service protection. What the agents didn't hear, they couldn't be forced to reveal.

"You look beat, girl," Baxter told Jenny.

"How kind of you to notice."

Jim Greenberg poured her a cup of coffee as she joined them at the table. Alita sat down. They allowed Jenny a grace period long enough to take one sip from her cup. Then they cranked up their stares, silently demanding to know what her emergency was.

She spited them by taking a bite of a cinnamon roll first.

Then she said, "I heard from a very good source last night that Del is going to be the target of a big-time smear. One that might happen any minute now."

Alita and Jim sat back in their chairs, the better to absorb the news. Baxter Brown leaned forward and bunched his huge hands into fists. "Who'd you hear that from?" he demanded.

"Don Ward."

"He's still alive?" Baxter asked.

"Real sensitive of you, Baxter," Alita said, knowing the man was Jenny's friend.

Jim Greenberg added, "If this comes from Hunter Ward, I believe it."

"Believe what?" Del Rawley asked, entering the room. He made a point of watching the door close behind him.

"Have a seat, Del," Jenny suggested. When he sat down and poured himself a cup of coffee, Jenny brought him up to speed.

"It's that motherfucking incumbent," Baxter pronounced. "He's seen that your numbers have stayed up since Chicago, and he's petrified. So look out, brother, here comes the mud."

"If Don says it's coming, it's coming," Jenny agreed. "But the thing I don't understand is how it could be coming from Ron Turlock." Ronald Turlock was the incumbent's campaign manager. "His reputation is that he's a straight shooter."

"Straight into his foot," Baxter argued. "That man has

lost four elections in a row. He'll do whatever he has to do, whatever he's *told* to do, just like any—"

Baxter realized too late where his thought would carry him, and Jenny finished it for him.

"Just like any of us mercenary hack campaign managers, Baxter? Not like you devoted staff advisers who take vows of poverty, chastity, and obedience."

"That'll be enough, children," Del said mildly.

Jenny felt a flash of shame. If Del hadn't stepped in, she and Baxter might have gone at it like Vandy and DeVito. But she was too tired to hang on to the feeling for long. Besides, she had other dirty work to do, and she was the only one at the table who would do it.

"Del, I hate to ask, but I've got to," Jenny said. "Is there anything in your past you maybe forgot to tell us?" Jenny had reread the biography she'd compiled on Franklin Delano Rawley while waiting for the flight to Denver. When the time came to hit back, she hoped to use it to refute whatever charges were made and to remind the public of some wonderful thing her man had done in the period of his life that came under attack.

The candidate frowned at her. He got up from the table, turned away and then back, and frowned again. But he was an honest enough man, and a smart enough politician, that everyone else in the room could see—and they were all watching closely—that he was thinking the question through.

"No," he said finally. "There's nothing illegal, unethical, or shameful."

Jenny nodded. "Okay, then even though Don says otherwise, we have to anticipate a lie. A big lie."

"No doubt from an unnamed source," Alita offered.

"We'll have to be damn quick in exposing it as false," Jim added. "And adept at regaining public favor."

"And subtle while we give the president a swift kick in

the ass so his side won't try something like this again," Baxter put in.

"I agree with the kick," Jenny said. "I don't see any need for subtlety, though."

"This is my life that will be under attack," Del reminded them. "I know what I've done and what I haven't. I'll know better than anyone else how much this smear will hurt me and my family. So I'll be the one to decide the type and the severity of the response."

"But it will have to be fast," Jenny said, and the others all nodded.

"Yes, that it will," the candidate agreed.

Del Rawley still had a busy day ahead of him, but Jenny claimed a private moment with him before she returned to California. He assured her that he was not about to let this notebook flap distract him. After surviving Chicago, it would take something a lot more serious to scare him. Somewhat relieved on that account, Jenny told him about their other problem: Agent DeVito. Was Del really sure he wanted a loose cannon like that around the campaign?

"He wanted a peek in Marva Weisman's handbag?" The candidate had to laugh.

"He also insulted a man who Vandy says is perfectly nice and added ten thousand dollars to our coffers."

Del Rawley sighed. "I think your idea of a note of apology is appropriate."

"Not outright dismissal?"

The candidate shook his head.

"Jim has already told me that my loyalty to Special Agent DeVito has played well with the public; it's been worth two to five points in the polls with a cross section of the electorate. How would we all feel if I fired him now and we lost by a whisker?"

Now Jenny sighed. Del patted her shoulder.

"Look, tell DeVito that I said no more hidden cameras.

Give Vandy a nice bonus for setting up the evening with Marva Weisman. That was a real coup. And you . . ."

"Yes?"

"Why don't you deliver DeVito's apology note to that fellow . . . what's his name again?"

"J. D. Cade."

"Yes, you go see Mr. Cade. Tell him we're sorry. Make sure there's nothing ominous about him, to allay any fears DeVito might have."

"Maybe see if I can hit him up for some more money?"

"I'd be disappointed if you didn't," the candidate told his campaign manager.

When J. D. returned to the Refuge with the twenty thousand dollars to pay off the hacker for the PostMaster Plus password, Pickpocket told him, "You had a phone call while you were out. The machine picked up."

The little thief informed J. D. that he was just on his way out. He had to get ready for the meeting that night at Pan Pacific Park.

"You didn't happen to listen to the phone message, did you?" J. D. asked.

Pickpocket grinned. "What, you think I'm nosy?"

J. D. gave him a look.

"Even out here by the pool, I could tell the caller was a woman. I thought it might be personal. I don't snoop on stuff like that. Not without a good reason, anyway."

After the little thief left, J. D. retrieved the message.

The woman said her name was Jenny Crenshaw. She was the campaign manager for Del Rawley. She wanted to take him to lunch tomorrow and present a note of apology to him from Special Agent Dante DeVito. Would he please call the campaign office to confirm or let her know if he was unable to make it? She left the number.

For a brief message, it gave J. D. a lot to think about.

Could this woman prove to be a better avenue to his target than Vandy Ellison?

Would accepting the invitation and getting only lunch out of it queer any subsequent approach to Vandy? That was, if Ms. Crenshaw wasn't as plain as a scoop of vanilla, would Vandy's nose get put out of joint by learning J. D. had gone out with her?

How many blood vessels had Special Agent DeVito burst writing his apology?

Finally, was Pickpocket telling him the truth about not having listened to the message?

Addressing the questions point by point: He had to accept the invitation. It was too good an opportunity to miss. Ms. Crenshaw, as campaign manager, was the CEO of the election effort. There could be no better way to get close to his target.

If that put Vandy Ellison's nose out of joint on a personal level, he still felt confident that she was professional enough to continue to love him for his money. And given proximity on that basis, he was sure he could recapture at least a reasonable facsimile of her affections. Enough to make her pliable when the time came.

In DeVito, he knew he now had a real enemy, and the more he was around the campaign the more DeVito would hate him. But the special agent would become truly dangerous only if he came to suspect J. D. was anything more than he pretended. Then J. D. would have to consider removing the man somehow.

About Pickpocket: He was the problem that was the most perplexing at the moment. That J. D. needed the little thief was beyond question. But it made him extremely uneasy to think that Pickpocket had learned he had contacts with the election campaign of a presidential candidate who'd almost been assassinated eight days ago.

It would not be difficult for the computer hacker to connect the dots.

The thing was, J. D. couldn't see himself killing Pickpocket even if he did.

He pushed that problem aside for the moment and called Rawley campaign headquarters. Jenny Crenshaw wasn't in, so he left a message: J. D. Cade returning Ms. Jenny Crenshaw's call.

He'd be happy to have lunch with her.

The grand jury in Alachua County, Florida, returned a true bill. Sergeant Beauregard "Dixie" Wynne of the Gainesville Police Department was indicted for first-degree murder in the shooting death of D'antron Nickels, holdup man and hostage taker. The next step in the legal process would be to take the defendant into custody. It would also be the most difficult step.

"The sonofabitch hasn't come back yet?" state attorney Colman Crisp asked chief of police Levon Pettigrew.

The two men sat in the state attorney's office. Crisp was as white as the starched collar of his shirt. Pettigrew was as black as a moonless night.

"The only sonofabitch I see in all this has already been buried," the chief said.

"You *condone* what your man did?"

"I condone D'antron Nickels being dead." Pettigrew leaned forward. "What I don't condone is Sergeant Wynne's being charged with first-degree murder."

"Goddamnit, Levon. That's what it was. None of your cops would ever admit it, but two of the paramedics on the scene told the grand jury they saw Wynne shoot Nickels as calmly and deliberately as if he was a clay pigeon."

"Are those people mind readers? They knew what was in Sergeant Wynne's head? What I learned, those two were never at a hostage situation before. Never saw a SWAT team at work."

"Look, we get Wynne in here to tell us his side, we get some of your people to be more forthcoming, I might knock the charge down to involuntary manslaughter and recommend a suspended sentence. The sergeant's lawyer has already advanced the idea that Wynne might have thought he'd seen something nobody else did, or might have suffered a very unfortunate muscle twitch. I could take that into account. But we've got to take him into custody."

The chief offered no response to that notion.

"I'm trying to be reasonable here, Levon, but if I find out anybody knows where Dixie Wynne is hiding and is holding out on me, I'll charge them with obstruction of justice."

"Nobody's holding out on anybody. Nobody knows where Sergeant Wynne has gone. All we know is he told a neighbor he was going where nobody'd mind what he shot."

"Hunting trip, huh? So you think we ought to just keep quiet and wait for the man to come home?"

Chief Pettigrew smiled thinly. "Let's just say I wouldn't want to be the man assigned to go find Sergeant Wynne."

Without saying so, he hoped his SWAT sniper never came back to town, either.

That evening Evan had been out and about in Carbondale. He'd been at the university library for two hours trying to resume his studies before he gave in and admitted that focusing on schoolwork was simply beyond him for now. And most likely for the foreseeable future.

After that, he'd cruised by Pru Laney's house, hoping that she might be sitting on her front porch on such a pretty evening. But she wasn't, and he wasn't able to bring himself to go ring her doorbell. Driving away from the Laney house, he stopped for fast food, which had all the appetite appeal of a mud pie. He threw away more than half of his order.

What bothered Evan most of all was that everywhere he went he saw Blair McCray's blue pickup truck in his rearview mirror. That sonofabitch was beginning to annoy him.

Feeling frustrated, trapped, and increasingly angry, Evan drove back to his grandmother's house. But he parked on the street, not in the driveway. He got out of his Honda, closed the door, and leaned against the vehicle with his arms folded across his chest.

A moment later Blair McCray's pickup truck turned the corner and approached at idle speed. Just then Evan had second thoughts about being confrontational.

If McCray had decided to take matters into his own hands, the only way Evan could be a better drive-by target was if he wore a sign saying SHOOT ME. But Blair McCray didn't open fire, he just met Evan's stare. The ongoing motion of his truck forced him to look away first.

Then, on an impulse that surprised him, Evan let out a sharp whistle.

The Ford pickup stopped immediately and Evan walked over to it. Blair McCray lowered the passenger-side power window. Once again Evan could see what an imposing physical specimen he was.

"You lift weights, don't you?"

"Yeah."

"Probably know some martial art, too."

He shook his head. "Never had a need. Scrappin' comes natural to me."

Evan snorted. "Well, we're not going to settle this with our fists, then. You mind if I get in the truck?"

McCray was suspicious, and plainly thought Evan might be trying to sandbag him.

"Step back from the door a second."

Evan backed up half a dozen steps. Blair McCray shone a flashlight on him and told him to raise his hands above his head and turn around slowly. The first thing Evan had to do was hold his temper, but he complied, hoping he wouldn't be shot in the back. When he was facing the truck again, the passenger-side door was open.

"Come on in," McCray told him.

Evan slid onto the seat and closed the door behind him.

"You want to go somewhere or just sit here?" McCray asked.

"Here is good," Evan answered.

McCray pulled the truck over to the curb.

"Look," Evan said, "I was thinking maybe I could get a restraining order against you. To keep you from following me everywhere. The thing is, I don't see you paying much attention to something like that. Even if your in-law, the chief, was forced to lock you up for violating the order, there are all those other McCrays you mentioned. Some relative of yours could just take your place, and sooner or later somebody's going to lose his patience, and who knows what might happen then?"

Blair McCray waited silently for Evan to make his point.

"I know you won't take it on faith that I didn't kill your cousin; in your place, I'd feel the same way. So what I'm thinking is this: Why don't we look into Ivar's killing together?"

At the corner of the block, a dark sedan with its lights off glided to a stop. The man behind the wheel pointed a small directional microphone at Blair McCray's truck.

He listened to and recorded every word that passed between Evan Cade and Blair McCray.

"You have some police experience I don't know about?" the microphone picked up McCray asking Evan. "Or are you just one of the Hardy boys?"

"I'm smart, I'm motivated, and I'd like to see the last of you," Evan replied. "If that's not good enough for you, I'll just start looking into things on my own."

"You? All by yourself?"

"Me," Evan affirmed.

Blair McCray's eyes narrowed.

"I'll think on it and let you know." McCray cocked his head toward the Cade house. "Meanwhile, you can tell your granny over there she won't need her shotgun tonight."

Evan turned and saw that Belle Cade was standing in her doorway and, sure enough, his sweet old grandmother held a shotgun. Evan doubted she even knew how to take the safety off, but McCray didn't know that.

"See what I mean about people losing patience?" he told McCray.

As J. D. and Pickpocket got into the Lexus to go to Pan Pacific Park that night, J. D. noticed the bulge under Pickpocket's jacket. Before they rolled out of the driveway, J. D. told the little thief, "Give me the gun."

At first Pickpocket thought to crack wise, and then he considered defiance, but in the end he was smart enough to read the look in J. D.'s eyes.

He handed over the weapon, a Glock semiauto, but insisted, "I want that back."

"I'll take good care of it."

"Yeah, but who's going to take care of me?"

"Ye of little faith." J. D. put the weapon under his seat.

J. D. let Pickpocket out at the corner of Third and Crescent Heights, a half mile from the park. Pickpocket would walk the intervening distance. J. D. would drive on ahead and be waiting in concealment when he got there.

Pan Pacific Park lay between the parking lot of the

Farmer's Market on the west and Gardner Avenue on the east. It ran from Third Street on the south to Beverly Boulevard on the north. A running track at street level formed the boundary of the park, encompassing the playing fields and the picnic area that were set in a hollow a dozen feet downslope.

J. D., Glock in hand, slipped into the park from Beverly Boulevard, the opposite end from where Pickpocket would appear. The park was illuminated, but just barely. Light poles were placed far more widely than on the street and their candlepower was considerably lower. They dispensed small islands of light amidst a far larger sea of darkness.

J. D. carefully made his way through the unlighted area to the midpoint of the western boundary. From there he could see to both Third Street and Beverly Boulevard, and he could look across the width of the playing field to the backs of the houses on Gardner Avenue that abutted the park. Not ten minutes after he settled into place, he saw the little thief arrive on the Third Street side of the park.

Pickpocket had told J. D. that he wasn't given a specific point in the park for the rendezvous; he was just supposed to walk the track and he would be contacted. Looking at the setup now, J. D. felt a moment of regret that he'd taken the handgun from Pickpocket. He wouldn't have wanted to step into such a situation unarmed.

Even so, he thought it was better for both of them to have the weapon in his hands.

J. D. watched Pickpocket enter the park carrying the backpack with his twenty thousand dollars. The little thief walked with a jaunty step, hands in his jacket pockets, just as if he was out for a stroll without a care in the world. Or as if—hands in pockets?—the sneaky little bastard had a backup weapon.

Pickpocket had made it to the long straightaway that paralleled Gardner Avenue when a movement on Beverly

Boulevard caught J. D.'s eye. A light gray sedan was pulling in behind his Lexus. From his angle, he could see two figures sitting in the front seat, but they were too far away for him to distinguish their features.

Just then a deep growl reached J. D. from across the width of the playing field. He snapped his head around to see Pickpocket stopped dead in his tracks on the jogging track, directly opposite J. D. He was standing in a halo of light and seemed to be talking to somebody in the darkness just beyond it. J. D. couldn't hear the little thief's words above the continuing growl of the dog.

At least he hoped it was a dog.

He took a quick look back at the sedan. Two male passengers were getting out. He couldn't worry about them now. He'd told Pickpocket he would protect him and that was what he was going to do. He crept forward, staying in the darkness, just as Pickpocket received visitors in his cone of light. One of the new arrivals was a young woman with hair the color of a maraschino cherry. Red was a girl. She was no bigger than the little thief and maybe even an inch shorter. The other new presence was some sort of mastiff that looked as though it could swallow both of the humans at a gulp and have room for several more just like them.

The woman dropped the leash that connected her to the animal. J. D. brought the Glock up to firing position. It would be an extremely long handgun shot even for him. But he thought that even if he didn't actually hit the dog, he might get the animal to charge him. Then he could dispose of it at a more practical distance.

The monster didn't attack Pickpocket, though. It sat right down on its haunches. And the woman extended a hand to Pickpocket, who shook it. With the dog no longer snarling, J. D. was able to hear Pickpocket and the woman laugh. They sat down on a bench next to each other like long-lost friends and fell into animated conversation.

J. D. decided to give it a few minutes to make sure things didn't go sour. After that, he'd depart. When everything continued to go well, J. D. looked back to Beverly Boulevard. He didn't want to lose his car to thieves. But the two men—one dark-haired, one blonde, he could now see—weren't stealing his car. The dark-haired guy was standing at the front of the gray sedan looking into the park. His gaze appeared to be directed at Pickpocket and his new lady friend. The blonde-haired man was in a crouch, barely visible behind his standing companion. He seemed to be fiddling with the front end of their car.

Then, quick as a snake, his arm shot out and he put something under J. D.'s rear bumper. If J. D. had looked away for a second or had a different angle on the men, he'd never have seen it. The two quickly returned to their car, backed up to have room to clear the Lexus, and pulled out to disappear down Beverly Boulevard.

Puzzlement lasted only a second. Revelation struck like a thunderbolt.

J. D.'s minders!

They'd finally crawled out of the woodwork.

Special Agent Dante DeVito was the last person in Rawley campaign headquarters that night. Earlier in the day he'd written the apology note he'd sworn he would never write. He figured that since he didn't have a stroke right then and there, he ought to be good for the next forty years.

What really galled him, goddamn Jenny Crenshaw hadn't even broken a sweat getting him to do it. She'd just called him into her office and told him to sit down.

"I've spoken with Del about you," she said. "For reasons of his own, he'd like to keep you around. But he said you are to use no more hidden cameras in this office or anywhere else." DeVito reddened, unaware that little secret had been exposed. "He also supported the idea that you will write a note of apology to Mr. Cade, which I will deliver to him."

Jenny leaned forward on her desk and looked at DeVito intently.

"Del and I are far too busy to be nagging you about taking care of this obligation, Special Agent. You might think that if you delay doing it, we'll forget about it. So here's the deal: You will write your apology this minute or . . . well, since your career is already in the toilet, I'll have you follow it. From now on, you'll be the special agent in charge of securing men's rooms for the campaign. You will spend each and every on-duty hour in the company of commodes, urinals, and their attendant odors. If you prove adept, maybe we'll let you hand out towels."

Jenny slid a sheet of campaign letterhead and a pen toward DeVito.

"If you prefer," she said, "you may use this stationery for your resignation. I'll make sure Del accepts it."

DeVito was sorely tempted to do just that, but he refused to give that ball buster the satisfaction. He wrote his apology in eleven words.

> Mr. Cade:
>
> *I acted unprofessionally. I'm sorry.*
>
> Special Agent Dante DeVito

"Thank you, Special Agent," Jenny said. "You may carry on with your duties."

That was just what DeVito intended to do. He might have to do it very late, like now, or very early. Times when nobody else was around. He'd just have to be history's first *covert* Secret Service agent.

Well, no, that wasn't entirely true. The service, in fact, often did things that protectees and their entourages knew nothing about. He'd simply be the first to take that idea one step farther and do things his bosses knew nothing about.

He was going to check out anybody and everybody who struck him as being in any way wrong. He'd do it off the books, and he'd take it as far as *he* saw fit. There would be no interference from Charlie Clarke, who was really running the protection detail now, or from Miss High-and-Mighty, Jenny Crenshaw.

As for that smart-mouthed Cade character—whom De-Vito held responsible for the humiliating note of apology—if he dared show his face anywhere around the campaign again, DeVito would get to know him better than his proctologist did.

In fact, the folder in front of him contained the first of the data he'd collected on the man. Now, if Mr. Romeo Cade made Jenny Crenshaw swoon when she delivered the damn apology—the way he had that Ellison bitch falling all over him—DeVito had no doubt the file on J. D. Cade would continue to grow.

It was a calculated risk, but J. D. left the homing device in place. Doing that would allow his minders to find the Refuge. Removing it, though, would let the minders know that he was on to them. Perhaps they'd even guess that he had seen them put the bug in place. He didn't want to give either of those things away.

Once he was home, J. D. lay in bed in the dark, looking up at the ceiling. He was all but alone in a city of millions. His only companion was a young thief who digitally finessed people out of their property, and even Pickpocket didn't know the purpose for which he labored. Everyone

J. D. had talked to in the past ten weeks, he'd deceived in one way or another. Even his son. But how could he reveal himself to Evan?

Hey, Ev, guess what Dad has planned? He's going to kill someone. Who? The man who otherwise might become the next president.

He could imagine his son withdrawing from him in horror, withdrawing from him forever, if he ever told him the truth.

But son, I'm doing it for you. That's more than my father ever did for me.

His father. Landon Cade. He remembered his father holding him in his arms exactly one time. On his fourth birthday. Holding him and hugging him and singing "Happy Birthday." He even remembered kissing his father then. Smearing frosting from the cake all over his dad's face, and him laughing about it. There were photos of that day in the family album.

He'd looked at those pictures alone in his room on countless nights, wondering why he'd never again deserved to have his father open his heart to him. The only other times his father had shown any feelings toward him were when he'd put a rifle in his hands and taught him to shoot, but J. D. had come to feel that the pride his father had taken in him then might have applied equally to a good hunting dog.

Then as a final gesture of disapproval, when J. D. had tried to show that going off to war wouldn't make him bottle up his feelings the way it had his father, Landon had committed suicide.

"I'd never do that to you, Evan," he uttered as if his son could hear. "I'd *give* my life for you, but never take it away from you."

He'd tried to do everything he could for Evan from the moment he was born. Neither his marriage, his work, nor anything else came before his son. He'd always been there for him, the way Landon never had—save once—been there for J. D.

He thought back to his sniper training at Fort Benning. The instructors had driven into him that the only motive that would psychologically sustain him was the knowledge that what he was doing was absolutely necessary. He had to think of the lives he'd *save*, not the ones he would take. J. D. clung to those words now.

Then he remembered one more lesson from long ago: The success and effectiveness of a sniper is limited only by his imagination.

FIVE

Thursday, September 16, 2004

There was e-mail on the PCR for J. D. when he woke up that morning. It came not from the blackmailer but from Pickpocket. J. D. scanned the message as it scrolled past.

> *Good news/bad news. Good: Got into PostMaster Plus system, found franchise where mail to you originated. Bad: Someone is following me. Meet me at Palisades Cafe, Ocean Avenue, Santa Monica, eight a.m.*

At that moment, the bad news carried far more urgency for J. D. than the good. Who could be following Pickpocket? The FBI? The Secret Serv—Then it clicked into place for him. His minders. The two crewcuts who'd put the bug on his car last night. They'd seen the Lexus parked adjacent to Pan Pacific Park, but they couldn't have spotted him hiding in the darkness. Still, they had to assume he was somewhere nearby.

Pickpocket and Red, on the other hand, had been sitting under a light. Had the minders followed them to see if they had any connection to J. D.? The minders wouldn't have had to worry about tailing J. D. The homing device would lead them to him.

The little thief must have e-mailed J. D. so he wouldn't lead the minders back to the Refuge, not knowing that J. D. had already conceded that secret. J. D. quickly showered and dressed. He wished he'd had the means to disguise his appearance, but the best he could do was to put on a pair of sunglasses and an old Los Angeles Dodgers baseball cap he'd had forever.

As he was about to leave the house, he stopped short. He still had the Glock he'd taken off Pickpocket last night. Did he dare take it with him? He very badly wanted to . . . but in the end he decided he couldn't risk it. There'd be no way in the world he could hope to infiltrate the Rawley campaign if he got arrested for carrying a concealed weapon.

Still, as he drove off in the Lexus he couldn't shake the feeling it had been a mistake to go out unarmed.

The Palisades Cafe was set three steps above the sidewalk on a plaza outside a white high-rise office building. Clusters of tables for two filled the seating area. Patrons purchased their pastries, fruits, cereals, and other edibles inside the cafe's glassed-in storefront and then carried their trays outside to sit in the sun, look at the joggers go by in Palisades Park across the street, and watch the Pacific roll up to the broad beach below the cliffs.

J. D. found parking two blocks away and arrived on foot fifteen minutes early for the meeting. Pickpocket was already there, sitting alone at a table on the edge of the plaza reading the *Times* with his back to the park and the ocean. J. D. stopped at a sidewalk vending machine and picked up a copy of the *Daily Breeze*, the Santa Monica newspaper. He tucked it under his arm and went into the cafe. A moment later he came out with a tray bearing coffee, orange juice, and a muffin.

The plaza was filling up with the breakfast crowd, but a table adjacent to Pickpocket's was available. J. D. took it and sat facing the park and the ocean. Looking down at his paper, he began to talk quietly with the little thief.

"Were you followed?"

"I don't think so."

J. D. looked up, ostensibly to watch a lithe brunette run past in the park. He returned his gaze to the paper and told Pickpocket, "I don't see anybody over there watching us."

"Nobody behind you, either. But last night I was sure a car followed me to Red's."

J. D. looked up again, this time idly staring out into the distance. A large piece of sculpture had been placed in the park opposite where he and Pickpocket sat. It looked like a cross section of an onion rendered in pale wood. Layer upon layer curved inward on itself until at the center there was a cat's-eye of open space, a slit through which the ocean could be seen.

"What did you find out from PostMaster Plus?" J. D. asked.

"Those mailings with Southern postmarks you received? They all came from the PostMaster Plus franchise in Arlington, Virginia. You know anybody there?"

"No."

"Huh . . . that's too bad. Still, you know where Arlington is? It's just up I-95 from—"

"Langley," J. D. finished.

"Yeah. Spooksville. I think from now on we ought to contact each other only by computer. I put all the info you'll need to know inside this newspa—"

Before Pickpocket could finish, J. D. saw a gun barrel emerge through the opening of the wooden onion.

"Get down!" he yelled.

Everyone in the cafe froze at the sound of J. D.'s shout except for Pickpocket, who made the mistake of trying to turn and see the source of the danger. The first shot took him just below his ribs on the left side. The second went over Pickpocket's head as J. D. yanked the slumping little thief off his chair. The round that missed the hacker struck a middle-aged man wearing black bike shorts and a yellow jersey, producing a blood-red blossom on his chest.

By now everybody on the plaza was screaming and running for cover. J. D. was among them, carrying Pickpocket toward what he hoped would be the safety of the high-rise's lobby. Just ahead of them, a young woman stood paralyzed by fear. A step before J. D. pulled even with her, a third shot rang out. A streak of blood appeared on her left shoulder, and though the wound seemed superficial, her eyes rolled up in her head and she collapsed.

J. D. hadn't been the only one to think of running into the building. A knot of people cowered in an elevator bank, all eyes watching for the first available car to take them away from the shooting. A security man for the building was already calling the police. J. D. laid Pickpocket's body down gently near those waiting to flee upward.

A grim-faced man stepped forward, telling J. D., "Let me take a look. I'm a doctor."

J. D. nodded and headed for the door.

Down on one knee next to Pickpocket, the doctor asked, "Where are you going?"

"There are other wounded people out there," J. D. replied.

There was also the information Pickpocket had left for him in his newspaper.

He darted outside in a crouch, doing his best to use the cafe tables for cover. The woman who'd been grazed was still unconscious but breathing regularly. The man in the cycling outfit was now drenched with blood. The shooter was no longer behind the sculpture or anywhere else that J. D. could see.

He duckwalked as fast as he could to where Pickpocket had been sitting. He grabbed the newspaper, folded it, and stuck it in the back of his waistband. Then he hurried over to the wounded man. He had a sucking chest wound, but he was still alive. For one awful moment J. D. considered the possibility that if he took this man back inside, the doctor might decide he'd have to treat him first, leaving Pickpocket to wait. That might cost the little thief his life, and it was possible J. D. might still depend upon Pickpocket for his success.

Caught in his dilemma, J. D. heard the howl of approaching police cars. He knew he couldn't afford any publicity, not even as a good Samaritan. To get close to Del Rawley, he'd have to be completely inconspicuous. He had to get out of there fast.

But J. D. just couldn't leave the wounded man to die. He grabbed the man, lifted him in both arms, and ran with him back to the building. The security man had already pulled the injured woman inside and held the door open for J. D. He laid the wounded man down next to Pickpocket . . . and, just as he had feared, the doctor diverted his attention to the cyclist.

But J. D. didn't have time to linger, much less argue with the doctor.

He got out of the building moments before the police arrived.

J. D. forced himself to walk back to his car. His clothes drenched with blood from Pickpocket and the cyclist, wondering if the shooter might come back for another try, listening for a police siren bearing down on him, it was all he could do not to break into a headlong dash. Still, as much of a sight as he was, he knew he would be far more conspicuous if he ran.

Fortunately, it was still relatively early, and aside from one strolling septuagenarian couple he sent scuttling in horror into the nearest open shop, he made it back to the Lexus uneventfully. Once in the car, he stripped off his shirt and kept to side streets. He hadn't gone more than a few blocks when the PCR beeped, letting him know he had e-mail—and he knew this time the message wouldn't be from Pickpocket.

He pulled to the curb at the first opportunity and keyed the message.

Santa can have his little helpers. You can't. This morning was a reminder. Get to work or someone else near and dear might find himself in similar difficulty.

That was when the realization hit J. D. smack between the eyes: He'd fucked up. Big time. Pickpocket had been smart enough to set up an out-of-the-way meeting that morning . . . but J. D. had been stupid enough to drive almost straight to it in a car that had been bugged. It would have been no great trick for his minders to watch him walk the last two blocks.

And the goddamn bug was still on his car. The minders might be following him right now. He checked his mirrors and looked around, but couldn't spot anyone.

Even so, one of those two crew-cut pricks had to be the guy who'd shot Pickpocket. They'd seen the little thief in the park last night and then again at the cafe with J. D. That was enough to establish the connection.

He put the car back in motion and five minutes later he pulled into the garage at the Refuge. He went straight to his bathroom, stripped, and showered. He put on a pair of athletic shorts and started a fire in the bedroom fireplace.

While the flames grew, he pulled the buttons off his blood-drenched shirt. There was blood on the buttons, too, but he was afraid they'd only melt if he put them in the fire. Same with his Nikes; he'd have to get rid of them later.

Thinking of the shoes made him stop and remember Evan. His son also had a problem with shoes that might incriminate him.

Suddenly the anger that J. D. had carried inside him for over two months became overwhelming. He was being blackmailed into killing a man, his son was being framed for murder, and now Pickpocket had been shot . . . and possibly killed. J. D. felt a searing urge to strike back. Immediately.

But right now he had to dispose of the bloody clothes. He had to put Pickpocket's Glock, the little thief's laptop computer, and the instructions he'd given J. D. for making contact with him into the safe in the Refuge's den. Then he had to—

Amidst the maelstrom of his anger and self-rebuke, a thought found J. D. that calmed him like a lover's caress. To the world at large, and to the Rawley campaign in particular, J. D. Cade was required to present the image of a very civilized fellow. But the blackmailer, whoever he was, already knew his dirty little secrets. That meant there was no need for restraint with the blackmailer's little helpers.

J. D.'s minders were fair game.

Regaining his composure, he began selecting the clothes he'd wear for his luncheon date with Ms. Jenny Crenshaw.

Evan Cade came out of the registrar's office at SIU and saw Blair McCray sitting in his Ford pickup in the adjacent parking area. He walked up to the truck. The day was warm and McCray had the window down.

"You make up your mind?" Evan asked about the idea of them working together.

"How do you plan to play detective and keep up with your studies?" McCray wanted to know.

"I don't. I just withdrew from classes for the fall term."

The Kentucky lawman nodded. "So you're serious. Well, your local chief of police wasn't thrilled with the idea, you poking around in a case where you're his number one suspect."

"Fuck him if he can't take a joke," Evan said.

Blair McCray smiled thinly. "Yeah, I can see where you wouldn't worry a lot about hurting his feelings. Okay, Cade. You want to drop your car off at home, we'll get started."

Evan nodded and turned to go, but Blair McCray called out to him. "Hey, Cade."

Evan turned back. "Yeah?"

"The chief went along with the idea only because I promised to keep a close eye on you—and I'm *real* good at keeping my promises."

Evan Cade gave Blair McCray a long look. "I suppose you can talk like that when you pump a lot of iron and you're naturally good at scrappin'."

Evan left his car in the driveway of his grandmother's house and got into Blair McCray's pickup truck.

"So where do we start, Sherlock?" McCray asked Evan derisively.

"Your cousin was a biker. Let's try to find some of his friends. See if any of them might have been helping him to learn new skills. Say, building pipe bombs for fun and profit."

A flush spread across Blair McCray's face. He started to say something, but he caught himself. "You won't provoke me that easy, Cade." It took the Kentucky lawman a minute to calm down, however. Then he asked, "So what's a clean-cut college boy like you know about the local outlaw bikers?"

"There's a bar down in Anna called Stratford Willie's. Always has a line of Harleys parked out front."

"How do you know about that?"

"It's on the way to my cousin Ben's house. You had to pass it when you tailed me there the other night. You didn't notice, that tells me a lot about your powers of observation."

McCray's mouth opened again, then abruptly snapped shut.

"Almost had you that time," Evan said with a grin.

Blair McCray just turned on the pickup's engine and pulled out.

Stratford Willie's had a dozen Harleys parked out front as Evan Cade and Blair McCray pulled up. The hours on the window said 12 P.M.–2 A.M., but the door was open at eleven that morning.

The bar wasn't serving, however. In fact, only one of the seventeen people inside was even conscious. He was a lanky man sitting at the bar wearing grimy jeans and a decrepit leather vest over a bare chest on which was tattooed a life-sized portrait of William Shakespeare. The man had an acne-scarred face, a long gray ponytail, and improbably clear green eyes. When he sipped from the cup he held in one hand, he revealed a glimpse of white, even teeth. In his other hand he had a dog-eared paperback copy of *King Lear*.

"Coffee's the best I can do until noon," he told Evan and Blair.

"That'll do for me," Blair McCray answered.

"Don't have cream or sugar," the man added, getting up.

"Black's fine."

"What about you?" he asked Evan.

"Club soda?"

The guy grinned and shook his head. "Tap water?"

"Okay."

Evan and Blair seated themselves as the man with the tattoo went behind the bar to get their drinks. The two newcomers looked at the comatose bikers. There were ten men, five women, and one slumped figure whose nest of hair obscured gender identification. One of the women, a generously proportioned strawberry blonde, sprawled back against a chair with her head lolling and her mouth open. She wore a T-shirt that said: *You Can Have It If You Can Take It*. On her dangling left hand was a set of brass knuckles.

The bartender put a cup of coffee and a glass of water down on the bar.

"Coffee's fifty cents, water's free."

Blair slipped a dollar onto the bar.

Evan nodded at the sleepers. "That your classics class?"

The man laughed. "Yeah. The postdoc section. A convivial group." He looked over his two customers with a frank eye. "You're a cop," he told McCray. Turning to Evan, he asked, "But what're you?"

"I'm the guy the cop suspects killed his cousin."

The biker-bartender-Shakespearean gave Evan another, more thorough inspection.

"Don't see it myself . . . but even Sweet Will didn't have *all* the angles figured."

"Did you know Ivar McCray?" Blair asked.

"Yeah, I knew Iv . . . Hey, you're family. *Kin*, as Ivar would've put it. I can see it now. You ran Ivar through a car wash a time or two, he'd look a whole lot like you. You're a McCray."

The bartender returned his attention to Evan.

"Don't tell me you're a Cade."

Evan nodded.

"And the two of you are here together? Well, goddamn! I've read all about what went on between your two families. It's fucking legendary around here. Real epic shit."

"That's kind of how we'd like to leave it," Evan said. "History."

"Sure. You want to lay off Ivar's death on somebody else."

"We'd like to find out who really did it," Evan replied.

"You feel the same?" the bartender asked Blair.

"If that's what happened. The way the papers had it, Ivar was involved in some kind of extortion ring; he died making a pipe bomb to teach a lesson to someone who wouldn't play ball."

The man shook his head. "That kind of shit just isn't one of our local folkways. The brethren are into chemistry, if you know what I mean, but not the kind that builds bombs."

"Crank labs explode pretty good sometimes," Blair reminded him.

"Yeah. But not on purpose. Usually. Anyway, Ivar was half straight—he had a job—and if you ask me, he was nowhere near smart enough to build a bomb."

"Was anyone unusual around recently?" Evan asked. "Somebody who might've put ideas into his head, helped him to build the bomb he was found with?"

The bartender looked at his fingernails, which were as well-tended as his teeth. He sighed, then lifted his eyes to Evan and Blair again. "As a matter of fact, yeah. But I don't think you want to tangle with this dude."

"Why not?" Blair wanted to know.

By way of explanation, the bartender asked, "You ever hear of the ROK army? That's R-O-K, as in Republic of Korea."

Neither Blair nor Evan had.

"They were the baddest motherfuckers in the whole Vietnam War. If it moved, they shot it. If we'd just hired enough of those ROK boys to do all the fighting, there'd be a Disneyland in Hanoi today. Of course, there wouldn't be any Vietnamese left to pick up after the tourists."

"What's your point?" Evan asked.

"The point is, this dude who was talking to Ivar, he was the only American motherfucker I ever saw who looked like he could've been a drill instructor for the ROK army."

"He was Asian-American?" Evan inquired.

"No . . . well, maybe, yeah. Just a touch. I didn't really think about it the time I saw him talking with Ivar, but maybe that's what made me think of the Koreans. The thing that came through loud and clear, though, was that here you had a stone killer. Wouldn't matter to him if you were a bug or a bishop. Get in his way, he was going to step on you."

"You know his name?" Evan inquired.

The bartender shook his head.

"How about where we might find him?" Blair asked.

The bartender shook his head sadly, as if they hadn't heard a word he'd said.

"I don't know," he told them. "But there's another suicidal goddamn fool who's looking."

"Who?" Evan asked.

"Deena over there." He inclined his head at the strawberry blonde with the brass knuckles.

"You can probably tell just by looking, she's in mourning. She was Ivar's old lady."

Deena Nokes woke up snorting, sputtering, and throwing a roundhouse left. Her brass knuckles glinted in the overhead light. But the ponytailed bartender had anticipated just such a reaction and stood well clear of the blow. Some of the cobwebs cleared from the woman's brain and she realized who was standing in front of her.

"Oh, it's just you, Punch," she groaned at the bartender.

"Gentlemen callers, Deena." He gestured to Evan and Blair at the bar.

She struggled to bring them into focus. "Who the hell are they?"

"A cop and his sidekick. A *McCray* and a *Cade*. They're interested in finding that evil-looking sonofabitch who talked to Ivar, the dude you've been looking for."

Deena pressed a hand to either side of her head to steady her visual field.

"Sweet Jesus," she said, looking at Blair, "you must be Ivar's brother."

"Cousin."

Manually aiming her face at Evan, she added, "I don't know you at all."

A shaggy head lifted from a table and bellowed to knock off all the fucking yapping or somebody would get killed. Deena yelled back, "Yeah, you, motherfucker." But when other complaints were registered by disturbed sleepers, Punch ushered Evan, Blair, and Deena outside.

The woman recoiled from the sudden blast of daylight as if she was a vampire. Blair steadied her, but she pulled away angrily. Blair held his hands up to placate her.

"We just want to talk," he said.

"Punch said you might be able to help us find the guy who was talking to Ivar," Evan informed her.

"I haven't found that bastard yet, but when I do . . ." Deena reached around to the small of her back and pulled out a Smith & Wesson .38.

"This man's the one you blame for Ivar's death?" Blair asked.

"Who else? Ivar was talking to him, and right after that the big dummy comes home telling me how he's going to start making us all this money. Then the next thing I know, he's electrocuted dead. Who else am I gonna blame?"

Evan held his breath, waiting to hear if Blair would suggest his name to the gun-wielding woman. There was a momentary glimmer in Blair's eye, but he didn't put Evan on the spot.

"You think you can describe this man who talked to Ivar?" Blair asked. "Give us an idea of what he looks like."

Deena snorted. "I can do better than that. I can show you the picture I drew so I'd never forget the sonofabitch." When she saw doubt in the eyes of the two men, she added, "I'm a tattoo artist. Who do you think did old Shakespeare on Punch in there? You could frame my drawings and hang 'em in art galleries. The ones that don't show people fucking."

She put her gun away and stared at the sidewalk. "We had a nice little business, Ivar 'n' me. He'd hand out fliers, talk to people, show them the tattoos I'd done on him. I'd do all the work in my trailer. It was great. We had all the money we needed. We had all the fun two people could ever want. But Ivar didn't think he was doing man's work. Why'd he have to think that? Why the hell did he have to go and leave me?"

When Deena looked up, there was a world of pain in her eyes, but not a single tear.

"I'll let you help me, since you're kin," she told Blair. "But I'm not too steady right now. You and your friend come to my trailer tomorrow. I'll show you that bastard's picture."

Deena gave them directions and then staggered back to Stratford Willie's, but she stopped at the door and pointed at one of the Harleys.

"That hog was Ivar's. It's all I got left of him. I'm keeping it."

Blair McCray nodded his approval.

The Rawley brain trust met before the campaign charged into the first full day of its crucial swing through California. Del Rawley, Baxter Brown, Alita Colon, and Jim Greenberg were gathered in the candidate's suite at the Century Plaza Hotel. Only Jenny Crenshaw was missing.

Her absence led everyone to wonder the same thing, and Alita gave voice to the question: "You think Jenny got word that the smear is about to hit the fan?"

"Let's just wait and see," Del said calmly. There were still Secret Service agents in the room, and he wanted the conversation confined to small talk until they were dismissed. Jenny entered the room two minutes later and the agents took her arrival as their cue to depart.

The look on Jenny's face was serious enough to confirm everyone's fears, but the reason for her grim expression surprised them.

"Sorry I'm late, but I just had a call from the head of the FBI task force investigating the assassination attempt in Chicago. He told me this information is for our ears only, and I have the feeling he wouldn't have given it to me at all if I hadn't been raising hell with him every day."

"What'd he tell you?" Del wanted to know.

"He said they've figured out where the shot had to originate."

"That's the big secret deal?" Baxter asked, incredulous. "Ten days later, and they finally figure that out. So they have to make it seem like a big deal."

Del put up a hand to forestall any further criticism.

Jenny continued. "The wind was blowing hard that day; I was told that can move a bullet around quite a bit. And there were thousands of windows available as shooting stands. That's what the FBI said made pinpointing the location so difficult."

"But that's not what we're supposed to keep secret, is it,

Jenny?" the candidate asked. "It's not the important thing, anyway."

"No," she answered. Then she told them the kind of weapon the FBI determined had to have been used in the shooting, the McLellan M-100. She explained its exceptional range—the reason why the assassin had been able to get off the shot and then elude capture—and the fact that the navy's SEALs were supposed to be the sole possessors of the weapon.

"Some navy commando was the shooter?" Alita asked, wide-eyed.

Jenny shook her head. "The FBI and the navy say absolutely not. The whereabouts of every SEAL on the day in question has already been checked and they've all been ruled out."

"But somebody got ahold of one of their weapons," Baxter said.

"That's where things get really sticky," Jenny replied. "According to the navy, they can account for every weapon in their inventory. On the day of the shooting. Every day before the shooting. And every day since the shooting."

"Forever and ever, amen," Baxter added snidely.

Jenny summed up. "They say it wasn't one of theirs."

"Does anybody else have such a weapon?" Jim Greenberg asked.

"Not that anyone's admitting, no."

"Is there any other weapon with the same range?" Jim followed up.

"No. Nothing that's accurate, according to the FBI and the Pentagon."

"So we all just *imagined* Del almost got killed?" Baxter wanted to know.

Jenny didn't bother to respond.

Del asked, "Would there be any way for someone

working at the plant where these weapons are manufactured to make illicit copies for himself? I imagine they'd fetch quite a price."

"They're checking into that now," Jenny answered.

"Any further word on the notebook that was found in Denver?" Baxter asked hotly.

Jenny shook her head.

The raw emotions of that terrible day in Chicago had resurfaced in everyone at the table. Added to that was a new sense of dread. If the assassin had a restricted military weapon, he was likely far more than a lone madman, and for all they knew, he'd been ready to try again in Denver. The brain trust mulled their respective thoughts in silence. Then Del Rawley reminded them they still had an election to win. "What's the next order of business?"

Alita Colon was the first to speak. "I hate to say it, but anything new on the smear, Jenny?"

Jenny grimly shook her head.

When the meeting wrapped up, she reviewed her schedule for the day and saw the lunch she had scheduled with the offended contributor, J. D. Cade. For a moment she considered passing it off to Vandy Ellison . . . but then she remembered two things.

The picture she'd seen of the man.

And the fact that Del had told *her* to handle the matter.

Jenny Crenshaw was waiting in front of the Ivy Cafe on Robertson Drive when J. D. Cade arrived. He pulled up in a gleaming Lexus and smoothly handed his key to the valet at precisely the appointed hour. In subtle contrast to his expensive car, he wore a comfortable old navy blazer, a white oxford-cloth shirt open at the neck, khaki slacks, and casual loafers. So he was well-off, Jenny thought, and the only dress code he needed to observe was his own.

The man knew how to make a first impression.

"Mr. Cade?" Jenny asked.

"Ms. Crenshaw?" J. D. replied.

"That's me." She extended her hand to him.

J. D. took it. Her hand felt small, firm, and surprisingly hot in his. Not feverish, but more like her normal temperature was set a notch or two above average, her fire burning more brightly than most. J. D. noted that she wore a wheat-colored linen jacket and skirt, a smoke blue blouse, and shoes with modest heels. A button on her lapel read FDR. No scoop of vanilla, this one.

After a moment they came to the mutual conclusion they'd held each other's hand long enough. The maître d' greeted them. He had Jenny's name on his reservations list but, more important, he also recognized her as Del Rawley's campaign manager. He discreetly inquired about the candidate's well-being and assured her that Senator Rawley had his vote.

Almost as an afterthought, he acknowledged J. D.

The maître d' asked if they'd care to dine al fresco, but J. D. said he'd prefer to eat inside. They were shown to a quiet corner table and a waiter brought their menus. Several of the other tables were filled with celebrities. Usually it was the stars who had to ignore unwanted gawking by the public while they were eating, but now a large number of the glitterati were eyeing Jenny and, incidentally, J. D.

He didn't care for the scrutiny. After the events of that morning, he couldn't shake the feeling, irrational or not, that he should be watching for another gunman. Which was one big reason he'd chosen to eat indoors. Having people look his way only increased his edginess. He took a sip from the glass of water that had been set in front of him.

Jenny noticed her guest's discomfiture.

"I'm sorry," she told him. "Does the attention make you

uncomfortable? Maybe I should have thought of another place."

J. D. understood he was letting his feelings show, and that was the last thing he could afford. He had to hide who he really was and most definitely what he really wanted. He put his glass down, smiled graciously, and said, "This is fine."

A moment passed in silence as Jenny regarded him, frankly taking his measure. J. D. raised no objection, doing his best to look the soul of innocence. Hoping no hint remained in his eyes that he'd been covered in blood not long ago.

"Are you very interested in politics, Mr. Cade?"

"Hardly at all."

Not the answer Jenny had expected, but one that rang true to her.

"Senator Rawley just caught your eye, then?"

"You could say that."

J. D. saw a glint of suspicion crease Jenny Crenshaw's face.

"You're not interested in making a statement, are you?" she asked.

"What do you mean?"

"Well, being able to tell your friends that you made a big contribution that helped to elect the first black president. That's not who you are, is it?"

"No, that's not me . . . and I considered my contribution to be relatively modest."

J. D. thought his response covered all the right bases. It rejected her misgiving and let her know he had real money without being boastful about it. She'd figure out for herself there were further contributions to be had if she played her cards right.

But Jenny kept on pushing. "So who *are* you, Mr. Cade?"

He cupped his chin for a minute, as if searching for the right words. Then he spread his hands in a self-deprecating gesture. "I'm a middle-aged guy who's scratched together a nice net worth. Not too long ago, I was married and my son lived at home. Then my wife left me and my son went off to college. I moped around for a while, but one day I decided I really had to stop letting myself go. I needed a haircut. Just to be daring, I went to a new barber. His shop had different magazines. I picked up one with a big story on your candidate. I read it and thought . . ." J. D. knew he'd be taking a chance here but decided to risk it. "I thought this Rawley guy might actually *not* be a sonofabitch."

Jenny drew back perceptibly.

J. D. gave her his brightest smile.

"Nothing personal, Ms. Crenshaw," he continued blithely, "but that was my prevailing view of politicians. Anyway, in the following weeks I read about Senator Rawley some more and at the same time I also came to the decision that after being a small-town boy all my life, maybe it was time I went to live in the big city. So I thought: I'll move to L.A., and maybe I'll actually vote in this election."

When she leaned forward, he saw that she not only had decided he hadn't insulted her candidate, but was beginning to take a personal interest in him.

"You normally *don't* vote?"

"What, for some sonofabitch?" J. D. asked wryly.

For a second Jenny's face remained blank, but then she laughed . . . and J. D. knew that, at least for the moment, he'd won her over.

"Then I heard the senator speak on TV, liked what he had to say, and I decided if I was going to dive into the political process, why not go off the high board? So I resolved to make a contribution to the Rawley campaign. I dropped off a check. And here we are."

"Why did your wife leave you?" she asked, and he couldn't tell if her interest was professional, personal, or both.

"For another man," J. D. said honestly. But he saw that for some reason Jenny was having trouble with that, true or not. It might be flattering, he supposed, that she'd doubt his wife would leave him for someone else, but he didn't want her prying too deeply in any one area of his life. So he turned the tables and asked, "Have you ever been married?"

"My husband was a navy pilot. He died in an accident."

"I'm sorry." But her answer was perfect: Painful partings were not to be discussed. Not at a first meeting, anyway.

Instead Jenny went down another path. "Were you ever in the military, Mr. Cade?"

"Yes."

She assessed his age.

"Vietnam?"

"Yes."

"Is that one of the reasons you like Del?"

"No. There are plenty of guys who served I have no use for."

J. D.'s answer surprised Jenny once more. But as before, it struck her as true. She tried to peer into him again. "You're a hard man to read, Mr. Cade."

"Is all this part of your job, Ms. Crenshaw?"

"It's part of my nature. I was wondering . . ." J. D. prepared himself to do a soft-shoe around yet another personal question, but this time Jenny Crenshaw surprised him. "Are you sure you don't want to go to Marva Weisman's fundraiser for Senator Rawley tonight?"

J. D. was silent while he tried to sort out just what she was asking him.

Jenny saw his confusion and smiled. "Don't worry, Mr. Cade. I'm not hitting you up for another contribution. Not at the moment, anyway. I'm asking if you'd like to be my escort."

"Oh. Well, that's another matter entirely."

"Is that a yes?"

There was no way J. D. could pass up an opportunity that good.

He nodded. "That's a yes."

"Good. And before I forget . . ." She reached into her purse and brought out an envelope. "I have something here for you. A note of apology from Special Agent Dante DeVito."

J. D. asked deadpan, "Did you have to torture him?"

She shook her head.

"Politics, Mr. Cade, is the art of getting people to see where their self-interest lies."

"Don't tell me you didn't have to twist his arm."

Jenny grinned. "That's *how* you get people to see where their self-interest lies."

"So politics is the art of arm-twisting?" J. D. asked.

"Exactly."

SIX

"Come along, Mr. Cade," Jenny Crenshaw said. "It's time you met the next president."

J. D. smiled as he walked to the limo that had just pulled up in front of the Refuge that evening, but he felt an icy uneasiness grow within him—perhaps because he'd never been chauffeured to a meeting with a man he'd tried to kill. After he slid into the rear of the limo next to Jenny, the driver closed the door behind him. With the privacy screen up, the two of them were ensconced in a cocoon of automotive luxury. A moment later the gleaming black Cadillac glided away.

"Nervous?" Jenny asked.

J. D. looked at her and asked in a carefully neutral voice, "About?"

"Sorry. I forgot about your prevailing opinion of politicians. I thought meeting Del—"

"Actually, I am a little nervous about that." Before there could be any elaboration on that subject, J. D. added, "But I thought you were asking if I was nervous about going out with you."

Jenny looked puzzled for a moment and then she blushed like a schoolgirl.

To spare her any further embarrassment, J. D. changed the subject, running his hand along the leather seat between them and asking mildly, "Is this how you spend campaign contributions?"

Jenny's color had paled from scarlet to pink and she responded, "This *is* a campaign contribution. The owner of the limo service will be at our little gathering tonight wearing his FDR button. Would you like one?"

Jenny took a campaign button from her handbag and offered it to J. D.

"Why don't you put it on for me? Unless I make you nervous."

"Not at all," Jenny averred, rising to the implicit challenge.

She deftly pinned the button to his lapel. For a moment their faces were very close and they looked into each other's eyes. Then Jenny sat back.

"I have to warn you," she said, "our hostess does intend to sing this evening. I've been told your taste in music lies elsewhere, but many of the people present tonight will count it as quite a coup that they were at one of Marva's rare private performances."

J. D. replied, "Nudge me if I fall asleep."

Jenny laughed. "Aren't you at all starstruck, Mr. Cade?"

He shrugged. "The people who work behind the scenes are usually more interesting."

"Like me?"

"Absolutely," he responded with a straight face.

"I can't tell if you're joking, Mr. Cade. I can't seem to get a handle on you."

In a matter of minutes, the limo pulled up at the gates of a Bel-Air estate. Two men dressed in dark suits stepped out of a guardhouse to inspect the occupants of the vehicle. Two others stood at oblique angles to the car, Uzis openly displayed.

Jenny lowered her window and a Secret Service agent looked in and recognized her.

"Good evening, Ms. Crenshaw."

"Hello, Jack."

The agent turned his attention to J. D.

"This gentleman is your date?"

Jenny nodded. "Mr. Jefferson Davis Cade."

The agent consulted a guest list and found J. D.'s name.

"Good evening, Mr. Cade."

"Good evening."

The agents stepped back, the gates opened, and the limo moved on. Jenny raised the window. "No glib remarks for the Secret Service?" she asked J. D.

"I suspect your friend Jack is heavily armed."

"And if he is?"

"Makes all the difference in the world," J. D. answered. "You never smart off to a man with a gun."

Jenny and J. D. entered Marva Weisman's mansion. The household help who opened the door for them was backed up by a security man. Unlike the agents on the gate, J. D. took this guy to be a private hire. The difference, as he saw it, was that the feds looked perfectly willing to shoot you; this guy looked like he wanted to. J. D. intercepted a young woman bearing up under a tray of champagne flutes and helped himself to two. He handed one to Jenny.

"The last time I was on a first date," he told her, "it was in a VW squareback and we went to a burger place on Stearns Wharf."

"Your ex-wife?"

"Yes."

"Was that your favorite first date?"

"No, that was with someone else entirely."

J. D. could imagine the caustic laughs he and Mary

Ellen McCarthy might share at a gathering such as this—but given his reason for being in the diva's home, he was glad his old girlfriend was far, far away.

Jenny whistled softly. "Wow. If you could have seen the range of emotions that crossed your face just now . . . That woman must have really meant something to you."

"She did. Still does."

"Any chance for you now?"

"No. She found the right guy for her."

Jenny squeezed J. D.'s hand. "I have to go make sure our hostess hasn't devoured my candidate, but I'll be back before everyone is seated for the festivities." She kissed J. D. lightly on his cheek. "I'll bet there are times when your old sweetheart is alone, or wishes she was, and still thinks about you."

J. D. watched Jenny go. He'd been lucky. He'd let his guard slip, even more so than he had at lunch, but it had turned out to be a good thing. Jenny had seen real vulnerability and it had moved her. But he couldn't count on being that lucky again. He was playing a role tonight as much as any Hollywood phony on the premises and he had to stay in character.

He had to remember that Jenny Crenshaw was one perceptive woman, too.

J. D.'s resolve not to let his public mask slip was immediately put to the test as he walked into the room where the majority of the guests were awaiting their summons to hear the candidate speak and the diva sing. There among a sea of famous faces were two very ordinary ones that held far more meaning for him.

The first he hadn't seen in over thirty years. Donnel Timmons. J. D.'s spotter and fellow assassin from the PANIC unit in Vietnam. Donnel's natural hairstyle had given way to a closely trimmed cut, more salt than pepper. His lean sixties-radical appearance had morphed into a stronger, more substantial build. But there was no question it was him. And by the stunned look in his eyes Donnel obviously remembered him as well.

J. D. carefully limited his expression to a polite smile of recognition, but knowing there was another member of the PANIC unit present tonight, he felt a chill return.

Not far from Donnel, but fortunately standing behind him where he couldn't see the surprised look on Donnel's face, was Special Agent Dante DeVito. Unlike the general watchfulness of the other security people, J. D. saw that DeVito was zeroing in on him personally.

J. D. moved his gaze off DeVito and strolled in the direction of Donnel, who met him halfway. The two men regarded each other for a long moment and then shook hands.

"Sonofabitch," Donnel whispered, "it's really you."

J. D. nodded and responded in the same quiet tone. "Been a long time, bro. But look at us. Come up pretty far in the world for a couple of old army snipers."

"Is that your man?" Del Rawley asked Jenny Crenshaw. He was looking at a security monitor in an upstairs room of the mansion. The candidate slipped into a sport coat; casual chic was the dress code for the evening. "He matches your description."

"That's him. J. D. Cade."

"Looks like he knows Donnel Timmons."

"Yes, it does," Jenny said, and a thoughtful look crossed her face.

"What is it?" Del Rawley asked.

"I don't know. It just strikes me as curious. Donnel was one of your earliest supporters, and Mr. Cade told me his interest in politics was minimal before he became aware of you."

The candidate returned his attention to the security monitor. "They definitely know each other. Maybe I'll say hello to your Mr. Cade."

"I think you'll find him interesting," Jenny replied.

"Any further word on that smear coming my way?" Del asked.

Jenny shook her head.

"Maybe whoever had it in mind thought better of it," the candidate suggested.

Jenny gave Del a skeptical look.

"Yeah, probably not," he agreed. He opened the door for Jenny. "Well, let's go earn our keep."

The Gardener sat in the study of his Virginia home browsing a well-thumbed book on the life and work of Luther Burbank when the Toad entered and brought him a report from California.

"J. D. Cade entered the Weisman estate fifteen minutes ago."

"In Jenny Crenshaw's company, no doubt."

"Yes, sir."

"He'll be in good hands there."

"Do you think he'll—"

The Gardener shook his head.

"No, not tonight, Harold. Our actions this morning should have increased Mr. Cade's sense of urgency, but I doubt we've made him suicidal."

The Gardener smiled when he saw an expression of disapproval appear on the Toad's unlovely face.

"I know *you* would strike at the first opportunity, Harold. But then, it's unlikely you would have charmed Jenny Crenshaw into asking you along for the evening. If only I had someone at my disposal who combined your best qualities with Mr. Cade's."

Then the Gardener returned his attention to the story of Luther Burbank—who had been quite successful at cross-breeding.

J. D. stood among the other guests on an acre of manicured lawn at the side of the Weisman mansion. At one end of the field of green a small stage had been set up. On it were a baby grand piano and a microphone on a stand. Rows of thickly padded folding chairs—with a center aisle dividing them—had been set up in front of the stage. Dusk was gathering, but outside lights were on and dialed up to a brightness level that J. D. had no doubt was ordered by the Secret Service. A pianist dressed in evening wear went up onstage and started to softly play a show tune.

Donnel had rejoined the people with whom he'd arrived. Vandy Ellison stopped by for a moment and attached herself to J. D. She told him she was very put out that he'd accompanied Jenny to the affair. J. D. said that she'd twisted his arm. "Just so long as she doesn't twist anything else," Vandy replied, and gave him a peck on the cheek before leaving.

Jenny returned as people were starting to take their seats. She led J. D. to two chairs on the far right end of the front row. She had J. D. take the outside seat, telling him, "People will be less likely to notice you if you fall asleep there."

"Unless I fall off my chair," he responded.

Del Rawley took the stage to a chorus of heartfelt cheers. As he let the sound of public approval wash over him, he gave a personal wink to Jenny—and for just a moment let his gaze rest on J. D. Cade.

When the applause died, he began his speech.

"It's often been said that any American child can grow

up to be president, but that's really not a natural ambition for children. Ask a young boy or girl what they want to be when they grow up and they'll speak of careers that capture their imaginations and fill their dreams. Their ambitions will run the gamut from astronaut to zoologist, and all points in between.

"But unless it's part of a family tradition, parents are likely to give a long and uneasy look to the child who comes home from school one day and says, 'Mom, Dad, when I grow up, I want to be a politician!' "

The candidate smiled broadly as his audience laughed.

"In fact," Del continued, "I suspect it may well have been just such an occasion that inspired the people who began the term-limits movement."

J. D. found himself laughing along with everyone else. It was only when Jenny Crenshaw lightly put her hand on his leg to share the moment that the surreal nature of his position hit him: He was laughing warmly at the humor of a man he intended to kill. His head started to spin and there was a real danger he might do exactly what he'd joked about earlier: fall off his chair. He put his hand on top of Jenny's and squeezed as hard as he dared to keep his place.

"The reasons why we politicians are held in such low esteem—and make no mistake, the president is nothing more than the politician in chief—are too well known and numerous to go into on this very pleasant evening. Well, I will mention that we tend to talk far too long at any given opportunity, but I will do my best to keep things brief tonight. I will simply say to you:

"If you as Americans do me the singular honor of choosing me as your next president, I make you the following solemn promises: I will take no actions affecting your welfare without first clearly explaining to you what I see as the necessity for taking those actions; I will try as hard to hear your concerns as I do to tell you mine; I will ask you to make no sacrifice that I am not willing to make or have already made myself; I will put no American ahead of any other American; I will strive with all the strength God gives me to see to it that the opportunities the most fortunate among us take for granted are brought within reach of the least fortunate among us.

"I will do my best for you for as long as you will have me. And when you'll have me no longer, or the Constitution requires my departure, I will express my gratitude to you and bow out as graciously as I am able. Thank you one and all."

The candidate bowed humbly as his audience rose to its feet and delivered a resounding and prolonged ovation. His moment of vertigo past, J. D. stood and applauded with everyone else. Trying to regain his detachment, he looked for any sign that Del Rawley was nothing more than a consummate performer who'd chosen Washington over Hollywood as his preferred venue. But try as he might, he could find no hint that the man's words were anything but genuine.

When Del Rawley thought the moment had gone on long enough, he stepped back to the microphone. Gesturing for silence, he said, as if sharing a secret, "If you'll all just sit down and be quiet, I think there's someone here who'd like to sing for you."

The diva joined the candidate onstage. She lifted his hand into the air, and the applause started all over again. But Senator Rawley scooted quickly offstage.

"Now, how am I supposed to follow an act like that?" the diva asked.

But follow it she did, with a performance for the ages, going back to her early days on Broadway and concluding with the title song from her new movie. By the end the audience was on its feet cheering, clapping, and whistling. The diva bowed, smiled, and basked in the adulation.

The price of an encore, she then announced with characteristic chutzpa, would be a further contribution to the cause. She left the stage while checks were written.

Jenny whispered to J. D., "It's okay. You're with me."

J. D. gave her an amused look. "That's very kind of you. But since I just happen to have my checkbook here with me . . ."

Jenny grinned. "Need a pen?"

"If you don't mind."

Jenny handed him a slim silver ballpoint. J. D. made out a check for fifteen thousand dollars and handed it to Jenny. "Will that do?"

"Very nicely, thank you." When J. D. offered the return of her pen, Jenny said wryly, "No, you hang on to it. In case you ever need it again."

"Deal," J. D. agreed.

"My favorite word," said Marva Weisman. She stood there in front of Jenny and J. D.—and she had Del Rawley on her arm.

The diva gave J. D. the same feline smile she had before.

Del Rawley extended his hand to him.

J. D. heard Jenny speak. Her words were clear but they seemed to come from a great distance. "Jefferson Davis Cade, please allow me to introduce our gracious hostess, Marva Weisman, and Senator Franklin Delano Rawley, the next president of the United States."

Can't you see who I am? J. D. wondered, meeting Rawley's eyes. Don't you know why I'm here? It struck him then that the only flaw in his deception would be to delay taking the proffered hand. So he gripped it as if greeting an old and dear friend.

Del Rawley smiled. "A pleasure to meet you, Mr. Cade."

J. D. and Jenny waited for their driver to bring the limo around to the front of the diva's mansion. Jenny had her arm linked with J. D.'s. Clusters of the glitterati hovered nearby, also awaiting the delivery of their vehicles. The mood of the privileged crowd was buoyant. They had the heady feeling that tonight they were part of a presidency in the making. Every single one of them now wore an FDR button, and with the influence they exerted on popular culture, millions more would soon be wearing them. On top of that, they'd seen a show they'd never forget.

As for the cost, well, it was only money—and they had more than enough of that.

"Now, was that so bad?" Jenny asked J. D.

"Certainly a night to remember," he conceded.

He'd pushed the impact of meeting Del Rawley off to a dark recess of his mind and affected the pleasantly drained mood everyone else exhibited.

"You have to admit, Marva can sing."

"Yes, she can."

Jenny tilted her head back to look J. D. in the eye.

"And what did you think of Del?"

J. D. gave an honest reply. "The man has a powerful presence."

Jenny nodded her agreement.

"He writes all his speeches himself, you know. He'll be the first president in memory to do that. Probably be the first since Kennedy to have his speeches quoted after he's gone."

The reference to the martyred president struck a little too close to home for J. D.'s comfort. He looked around, careful not to let Jenny see anything in his eyes. He noticed Donnel Timmons speaking congenially with a man and two women.

Again he wondered if it was anything more than chance that his old comrade was on hand. Before he could pursue that line of thought, Jenny noticed where he was looking.

"Do you know Donnel Timmons?" she asked, not giving away what she'd seen on the security monitor.

J. D. nodded. "From my army days."

"He's been with Del right from the start. Since New Hampshire. He's a good man."

"I was glad to have him by my side, too," J. D. concurred. He couldn't guess if Donnel's long-term status with the campaign meant his reason for being there was legitimate . . . or if it was a deep cover. J. D. looked back at Jenny. "I had a great time tonight."

"You mean that?"

"Absolutely." He saw that she looked pleased, and impulsively decided to take a big risk. It would be disastrous if it went the wrong way, but if he guessed right, it would add to his aura of innocence. "I'd tell you I'll give you a call, but I can imagine how busy you'll be for the next few months. So why don't you call me after the election?"

Their limo pulled up and the driver stepped out to get the door, but J. D. waved him off. He opened the door for Jenny and helped her into the backseat. Then as he followed her into the car he spotted two men in the crowd who made his heart go cold. One dark-haired crewcut, one blonde. His minders. Clearly they had been at the fundraiser not as guests, but as security. The diva's men? No. Those two didn't take orders from a singer. Which meant they had to be . . .

Secret Service.

He pulled the door of the limo closed before they noticed he was looking at them.

Jenny tugged at his sleeve. "What's so interesting?"

"Thought I saw someone else I know, but at second glance the nose was wrong."

"People in this town change their noses," she reminded him.

J. D. smiled politely at the joke.

Jenny put her hand on his leg. "I don't think I'll wait until after the election to call you."

She looked at him, all but asking to be kissed. J. D. leaned in and obliged her.

Even as he felt how soft her lips were against his, he couldn't give himself completely to the moment. He was using this woman . . . and he couldn't get his mind off the two crewcuts being Secret Service.

And how they weren't around only to see that he did the job, but to kill him afterward.

Unless he got them first.

When the limo let J. D. off at the Refuge, after a good-night kiss from Jenny, it was only ten o'clock. During the week, showbiz people in L.A. were an early-rising community. Many of them had to be on their sets at dawn; others would be busy hatching their next deal not much later. These were facts of life for which the diva's fund-raiser had allowed.

The relatively early hour also allowed J. D. the time he needed to make a brief trip home to Santa Barbara without being missed.

He went to his bedroom and quickly changed into a pair of dark jeans and a navy blue sweatshirt. His spare sneakers were far too white for his liking, so he smudged them to a dull gray with ashes from the fireplace. The bloody clothes he'd burned that morning had been all but consumed. The last remnant was the scorched zipper from his pants. He pulled that from the fireplace and added it to the opaque plastic bag in which he'd put his blood-covered Nikes and the buttons from his shirt. He'd dispose of these items on his trip.

After a moment's consideration, he decided to add Pickpocket's Glock to the bag.

J. D. got the gun from the safe, dumped it in the bag, and put the bag in the trunk of the Lexus, under the floor panel with the jack. Then he lay down under the rear bumper of the car and carefully removed the bug that the crewcuts had put there. He'd leave it in the garage. He was hoping that his minders would still be tied up with their cover duties as Secret Service agents, and by the time they got back to him the presence of the bug would tell them that he was still at home.

As he drove away from the Refuge, though, he watched carefully for any sign that he was being followed. But his was the only car on the quiet residential streets of Santa Monica Canyon at that moment. He turned north onto Pacific Coast Highway, confident that he'd left unobserved.

The traffic on PCH was sparse. He settled into the right-hand lane and cruised at the speed limit. A light breeze off the ocean carried with it a pleasant salty odor. To his right the looming bulk of the coastal hills crowded the road. Just beyond Malibu, his headlights picked up a warning sign along the road: ROCK SLIDE AREA, NEXT 3 MILES.

He'd driven the coast highway and seen that sign, and others like it, more times than he could remember. He'd seen TV clips of the giant boulders that earthquakes and rainstorms had brought tumbling down onto the pavement. But he'd never really thought he was in any danger when he drove PCH.

He hoped his minders would be just as oblivious—right up until the moment he dropped a mountainside on their heads.

J. D. entered his darkened home in Santa Barbara. It felt more like he was revisiting a fading memory than a property to which he still held title. Fortunately for him, the house still held all the materials he'd need to make a bomb.

While PANIC had relied almost exclusively on firearms to carry out its work, and J. D. had used nothing but sniper rifles, the men had been required to attend briefings on other covert means to dispatch certain targets: those who declined to present themselves to the unit's crosshairs.

One such government-funded educational opportunity had been called Improvised Explosives. Included in the curriculum was how to build a blasting cap from bits of scrap hardware and three chemical compounds available at any drugstore. Also covered was how to make fuses, electrical and chemical timers, and radio-frequency detonators. Rounding out the course, the instructor taught them how to make very big bangs using such everyday items as aspirin, vinegar, window cleaner, dandruff shampoo, and even urine.

But J. D. didn't need to work with such mundane materials. As a target shooter who hand-loaded his own ammunition, he had a more-than-adequate supply of gunpowder in his weapons vault. He intended to use all that remained of it for the job at hand.

Though he'd sat through the bomb-making course a very long time ago and didn't recall that he'd been particularly interested at the time, he was able to remember everything he needed to know to build a substantial explosive device. As to how he'd detonate it, he decided on a radio-frequency trigger. To get the part he'd need for that, he went to his garage.

After he finished his work, he left the house and tried not to think that he might never return. He drove to Cabrillo Boulevard and parked. He walked out onto Stearns Wharf, past the closed restaurants and shops. He ignored the sign that said HARD HATS REQUIRED BEYOND THIS POINT and strode to the end of the pier. He threw the bag with the Glock and other items into the ocean. He'd done the same thing not that long ago with his wedding ring.

He returned to the Lexus and, twenty minutes later, at a bend in the coast highway where there was a scenic overlook, he pulled off the road. He stopped in the darkest corner of the parking area. He got out of the car and scanned the adjacent beach to make sure no surfers or homeless people were camping out nearby. When he was sure he was alone, he ran across the highway.

He scrambled up the hillside. He had to climb no more than fifty feet to find a cluster of rocks he liked. Using his hands, he dug a hole in the loose dirt at the base of a large boulder and buried the bomb he'd made. The only part he left exposed was a wire that projected from the soil. The wire would serve as the antenna to receive the detonation signal. The transmitter was a device that no one would ever question even if they saw it: his garage-door opener.

Two minutes later he was back in the Lexus, returning to the Refuge.

Now that he'd baited his trap, all he had to do was lure his prey.

SEVEN
Friday, September 17, 2004

The political bombshell exploded early that morning, just in time to be the lead item on all the network morning news shows and to receive wall-to-wall coverage on the cable channels and the Internet.

Del Rawley had sex with a Communist!

Del Rawley was the father of an illegitimate son!

It was revealed that as a young man, Franklin Delano Rawley had traveled to Paris, France, to visit an expatriate uncle, Turner Rawley. While there, he'd met, slept with, and fathered a son by a woman named Sophie Moreau. Mademoiselle Moreau, now a legislator in the National Assembly, was a longtime member of the Communist Party. Her son, Bertrand, was an architect who said he had no interest in politics. Yes, the young man said, his mother had told him who his father was, and though he'd never met him, he liked what he had read about him. He thought it was amusing that a Frenchman uninterested in affairs of state had a father who might become the president of the United States.

As if that wasn't enough, Sophie Moreau, French Communist, endorsed the candidacy of Franklin Delano Rawley.

"He is easily the best man to be president," she declared. Then she added, "And without a doubt he was the best lover I ever had."

The only bit of political cover the story offered was that Mlle. Moreau also told the world that she had made young Del Rawley leave her all those years ago, when he had wanted to marry her, because she was sure they had different destinies, and no, until now he had had no way of knowing about Bertrand.

"It's all about race, goddamnit," Baxter Brown said. "The Communist angle is a smoke screen. The woman could be a Gaullist, but the fact that she's white—"

"And French," Jim Greenberg interjected.

"The fact that she's white," Baxter repeated, "is the big scare tactic: Lock up your women, white folks, because if Del Rawley ever gets into the White House, look out."

"Race is the big hammer," Alita agreed, "but morality might be the monkey wrench. Until now we had a candidate who was squeaky clean, and that was what made a *lot* of people look past their prejudices or deny them altogether. But if all I start hearing are questions about Del's personal life, then we've got—"

The press secretary bit her tongue as she looked up and saw the candidate in the doorway to the conference room of his suite. Jenny was with him. They joined the other three members of the brain trust at the table. Del looked at each one of them in turn.

"When we talked the other day," he said, "and I told you I didn't have anything to hide, I honestly didn't think about Sophie. I was eighteen, and back then, as she said, I would have married her in a minute. But now I can honestly say I haven't thought about her in years . . . and I certainly didn't know I have a son by her."

Jenny had already heard the explanation; the others were nodding their acceptance of it.

"I've spoken with my wife," Del told them, "and she wants to return to the campaign and be seen at my side."

"Might not be a bad idea," Jim Greenberg told him.

"The FBI hasn't caught that sonofabitch who tried to kill me," Del reminded him. "Neither my wife, nor my children, nor my grandchildren will be exposed to any danger for my political advantage. I don't want to hear another word about that."

The candidate got up from the table and asked his campaign manager to come with him. She returned to the room a moment later. The other three were on pins and needles and demanded to know what Del had told her.

She sat, looked at each one of them, and said, "He's considering dropping out of the race. He told me he won't say one word against Sophie Moreau regardless of her politics, and he wants to see his son Bertrand. Right now he's going to spend a day or two with his family in Wisconsin."

Baxter, Jim, and Alita absorbed the news in silence.

Jenny got to her feet and leaned forward with her fists on the table.

"I'm not going to let Del quit. Our country needs him. The media will be breaking down our doors any minute now for a response and we've got to be ready for them."

"What are we going to say?" Alita wanted to know.

"I have no idea. But we're going to come out swinging. And I'm going to think of a way to gut the incumbent if his people ever try anything like this again."

"You still think old Ron Turlock is a straight shooter?" Baxter asked Jenny caustically, referring to the incumbent's campaign manager.

She had no answer for him.

———

As far as J. D. had been able to tell, his minders hadn't seen him return to the Refuge early that morning. So they shouldn't know what he'd been up to. He replaced the bug under the bumper of his car, went into the house, stripped off his clothes, and fell into bed.

His night's work had given him some satisfaction, but he had far too many other problems for sleep to come easily. Or even grudgingly. Still, he had to have some rest soon or he'd be unable to function. Then he remembered the chloral hydrate capsules that the cabin attendant had given him on the flight from Milwaukee to Las Vegas. He took one and it conferred on him the blessing of three hours of dreamless sleep.

Which meant he was awake again before the sun rose.

The first thing J. D. did after showering and getting dressed was to retrieve Pickpocket's laptop computer from the safe in the den. With it, he took the information the little thief had passed to him for establishing contact via cyberspace.

J. D. booted up the machine and, following instructions, went to a Web site called stickyfingers.com. The home page declared it to be a fan club for the Rolling Stones. One of its features was a trivia quiz about the band. Answer a question right, Keith played a guitar riff for you; answer it wrong, Mick stuck out his tongue at you. Answer the question Pickpocket noted in his instructions with the password he provided and you gained entrance to a private chat room in which you could communicate with the little thief.

Assuming he was still alive.

J. D.'s first question addressed just that point.

John, did you make it?

J. D. waited for five minutes without getting a response. He carried the laptop into the kitchen and made coffee. When he sat down at the kitchen table he saw a reply.

He's alive.

J. D. keyed in the question: *Am I talking to Red?*
Yes.
Do you know who I am? J. D. asked.
Yes.
How is he?
Doctors say serious but stable. After surgery.
Does he need any help with medical expenses?
No, but thanks. Thanks for saving him, too. The paper says you're a hero.

J. D. hadn't seen the morning paper yet. A shudder of relief passed through him that he'd gotten away before the cops had arrived, and that the cap and sunglasses he'd worn would keep him from being readily identified.

J. D. had a suggestion to make.

As soon as possible, consider moving John to another hospital. Under new identity.

An emoticon appeared on J. D.'s monitor: :-)

Then: *Just what I had in mind.* After a pause, Red added, *Pickpocket told me to tell you: When he cloned that PCR for you, he made a second clone for himself—so he could backtrack the anonymous e-mail you received.*

That bit of news snapped J. D.'s head back like a solid uppercut. But the surprise lasted only a second. After all, he had been expecting the little thief to snoop on him.

Did he learn anything? J. D. asked.

The last hangman drawing you received was sent through the server of an S&M bulletin board called lovelock.com. Lovelock operates out of Fairfax, Virginia. Right next to the PostMaster Plus in Arlington.

Right down the road from Langley, J. D. thought.

Red, will you be able to help me? I can pay.

You already have. The 20K, remember? Besides, John and I are already fast friends—and you saved him. I feel like I owe you. Anything we find out, we'll send to stickyfingers.

Then, for security purposes, Red gave J. D. a new password to use.

He'd just logged off when his phone rang. Vandy Ellison was on the line.

"We're having a crisis here," she said. "Jenny asked if you can come in."

The Secret Service watched the news like everyone else, and by the time Dante DeVito was summoned to meet with Charlie Clarke—the special agent who was really in charge of Del Rawley's protection detail—he'd already dismissed the French-lover scandal as a political knifing and nothing more. DeVito knew his feelings were influenced by Rawley's loyalty to him but, Jesus Christ, if politics was getting to the point where people could be held accountable for what they'd done as teenagers, then—

The doors of the elevator in which DeVito was riding slid open, and just as he was about to get out, two guys talking to each other, paying no attention to him, tried to get on. DeVito shot the gap and almost knocked both of them ass over teakettle. They both caught their balance, but the looks they gave DeVito were decidedly hostile.

Barely concealing a smirk, DeVito said, "Sorry, gents. Looks like none of us was paying attention to where he was going."

The two guys didn't say a word, but continued to glare. DeVito's take on them was that they were colleagues. He knew that the protection detail had been doubled since Chicago, but he didn't know these guys. Which was strange, since he knew everyone else who'd been added. But these two pricks with their crew cuts—one dark-haired, one blonde—were strangers to him.

He walked down the hall and rapped on the door of the

hotel room from which Charlie Clarke was working. He opened it and walked in a half second before he was given permission.

Clarke looked up from the desk where duty assignments and diagrams of the rooms in which Orpheus—Del Rawley's code name—would be speaking were spread out in front of him. DeVito pulled up a chair and sat opposite Clarke.

"Have a seat, DeVito," Clarke said blandly. "Don't stand on formality."

"If you're going to tell me about the FBI determining an M-100 had to be used in Chicago, I already heard. Jenny Crenshaw had the guts to tell me."

"Yeah, that's why I called you."

"So it wasn't my fault what happened, except *anything* that could go wrong was my fault. Just like anything that goes wrong from here on in is your fault."

"You're a ray of sunshine, DeVito. Always have been. But nothing's going to go wrong on my watch."

"From your lips to His ear," DeVito said sincerely. "So despite being responsible, I'm no longer the goat, right?"

"Right."

"Yeah, I'm worse than that. I'm an embarrassment. Not only because I was judged too soon, but because I remind everybody else something bad *could* happen on their watch."

"Exactly."

"But I can't be fired because Orpheus—God love him— won't let me be. So what're you going to do with me?"

"I thought I'd ask if you had any ideas about that," Clarke told him. "But my notion was you could play center field. Stand back where you can watch the whole game, then run like hell if you see anybody is about to let the ball get past him."

DeVito knew that Clarke didn't have to be anywhere near that nice to him.

"That's mighty damn decent of you, Charlie. I'll take you up on that."

"I never liked you, DeVito, but I've always respected your abilities."

DeVito laughed. "My ex would agree with the first half of that opinion."

He got up to go, but a thought occurred to him.

"Did we get two new guys on the detail?" He described the crewcuts to Clarke.

Clarke nodded. "Arnold Roth's the dark buzzcut; Bill Danby's the blonde. They're both assholes. Don't look at me like that, DeVito. I'm not bad-mouthing my own men. Those two are snoops sent in to look over all of our shoulders after what happened in Chicago."

"What do you mean?" DeVito asked, puzzled. "They're not Secret Service?"

"They work directly for the Treasury Department. So they are colleagues."

"But they're outside our chain of command? They don't answer to the director?"

"I don't know who they answer to; what I do know is, we might have to answer to them. They're part of something called Departmental Internal Management and Oversight."

"D-I-M-O?" DeVito asked.

"Close," Clarke responded. "D-E-I-M-O-S."

Jenny sent Alita out to face the mob of reporters that had descended upon the Century Plaza and then she closeted herself in her own suite to call Don Ward. She clenched the receiver in a death grip, and as Don's phone rang repeatedly, she muttered a litany of prayers.

"Don't be dead, don't be dead, don't be dead. Have something for me, have something for me, have something *great* for me. Answer the phone, Don, answer the phone, ans— Don, thank God you're there."

"I was expecting your call, my dear," he said in a thready whisper. "But today is not a good day. It took me some time to find the phone, and before that a longer time to remember where my hand was located."

"Oh, dear God, Don. I'm sorry. I shouldn't have bothered you."

"You are *never* a bother, Jenny. I'd have been deeply disappointed if you hadn't called. I know what you want, and I have something for you."

He breathed a wonderfully vicious secret into her ear.

"Don, I love you," Jenny told him.

"No more than I love you, my dear."

Jenny asked Don to promise her that he'd call if he sensed . . . the end approaching. She'd break away from the campaign for a day to see him one last time. He told her she'd do no such thing. She was to make the best use possible of the weapon he'd just handed her and raise a glass to his memory when her man won.

Then the connection was broken. Hunter Ward had left his protégée to her work.

Jenny punched in the number for Ronald Turlock, the incumbent's campaign manager. She was promptly put through to him. "Ronnie, so glad you could find the time to talk to me."

"Jenny, it wasn't me, I swear to God," Turlock told her adamantly. "I never heard of that Frenchwoman; I didn't know she was a Communist; I didn't know Senator Rawley had a love child with her."

"*Love child?* Haven't heard that one for a *long* time. Still, it does sound nicer than *bastard.*"

"You don't believe me, do you?"

"I'm looking at a flash poll we just completed, Ronnie,"

Jenny lied. "You know, since the Commie-and-the-love-child story broke. The news seems to have hurt Del in the South. Your man has his Bible Belt base locked up tight now."

"We always did," came the terse reply.

"The interesting thing is, the numbers right here in California actually seem to be swinging our way in the past couple hours. Good old hedonistic, vote-rich California."

"Our polls don't show that."

"Then your people are keeping the bad news from you."

"Is there a point to this call?"

"Oh, there's very definitely a point. Are you on a secure line, Ronnie?"

"Just say what you have to say."

"Okay, but don't blame me if word gets out."

"What word?" Turlock asked icily.

"I've come across some disturbing news about the incumbent. It seems he has a rather curious congenital condition."

"What are you talking about? The president's in perfect health."

"I'll give you that, but did you know that he's only half a man?"

"What the hell is that supposed to mean?" Turlock demanded, but Jenny could hear the sudden note of fear in his voice. He knew just where she was going.

"The incumbent, poor man, was born with an undescended testicle. The right one, I believe. By the time this unfortunate condition was recognized, the poor little pebble had shriveled completely and had to be surgically removed."

"This is despicable!" Turlock sputtered.

"Well, in a perfect world such a thing would never matter. But this is America. How would the country feel? How would your partisans react to the knowledge that their man had no choice but to hang to the left? Could the nation rest easy at night knowing we're only a teeter-totter accident away from having the first *eunuch* president?"

At this point Ronald Turlock's sputtering became incoherent.

"Such a shame," Jenny commiserated.

"You wouldn't dare," Turlock asserted.

"Me? No, never. But just as with you, Ronnie, there are forces that sometimes operate outside of my control." Jenny's voice turned to titanium. "And I can *guarantee* they'll be out of control if *anybody* tries to smear Del Rawley *ever* again."

Jenny underscored the warning by slamming down her phone.

She thought Don Ward would have approved.

When J. D. arrived at the office tower that housed Rawley campaign headquarters, he noticed an immediate difference from his previous visit: There was a Secret Service presence in the lobby of the building now. The presence took the form of Special Agent Dante DeVito. He grinned at J. D. when he saw him coming.

"I heard you'd been called in, Mr. Cade. I thought I'd take just a moment to speak with you personally." DeVito noticed that the elderly gent behind the information desk was looking on unabashedly. "Why don't we step over here?"

J. D. followed the agent to the far corner of the lobby.

"Did you get my note?" DeVito asked, concerning his apology.

"It warmed my heart," J. D. said evenly.

"You have an attitude about you, Mr. Cade. Most people don't talk to federal officers the way you do."

"Maybe it's just the way I talk to you," J. D. suggested.

He knew he should back off, but that seemed too much like backing *down*, and he simply wasn't in the mood. "As you pointed out, I was asked to come in this morning. Ms. Crenshaw is expecting me."

J. D. started to leave but stopped when DeVito whispered ominously, "I've been checking on you. I know *everything* about you."

DeVito watched J. D.'s eyes and waited for him to respond. In vain. Even so, there was unmistakable tension in the air. The special agent continued, "I know where you were born; I know who you married; I know about your son."

The thought that this man might know anything about what was happening to Evan disturbed J. D. greatly. It took all of his self-control to maintain his composure.

"I know about your business interests; I know where you bank; I know where your home in Santa Barbara is."

Now J. D. felt a sense of relief, and he had to keep that off his face, too. This prick was just fishing. He might have come up with a laundry list of information on J. D. available from public documents, but he *didn't* know anything important. Still, J. D. had to play the injured party.

"That's all the time you get, pal. I'm leaving now." Then J. D. had a flash of inspiration. "And you better tell those two creeps you've got following me they better knock it off, too, before I sue the lot of you."

The ultimatum took DeVito completely by surprise. "What two guys? What the hell are you talking about? I don't have anybody following you."

DeVito's reaction was far too honest for J. D. not to believe him. Which told J. D. that DeVito wasn't yet another minder but an independent antagonist. He continued to play his hand.

"You know who I'm talking about. Those two guys with the crew cuts, blonde and dark-haired, stamped from the federal cookie cutter. They've been following me for days—they were even at the Weisman fund-raiser last night—and I'm sick of it."

J. D. left DeVito standing there trying to sort out what he'd heard. He'd taken a risk telling the special agent about his minders; as far as J. D. knew, those two crewcuts weren't aware that he was on to them yet. If DeVito confronted them directly, that would change.

But he didn't plan for his minders to be around much longer, anyway.

Vandy Ellison greeted J. D. at the door of the campaign office. She took him into a conference room where Jenny was talking with four men and a woman. J. D. recognized the woman. Lucy Gray was the sister of a former California governor. Two of the men J. D. recognized, and two he didn't. Of the former, Ted DeLong was an actor who'd left show business to become an extraordinarily successful vintner; the other was Donnel Timmons.

Jenny saw J. D. had arrived and made the introductions. The two men he didn't recognize, he knew by name. Anders Sutherland was a venture capitalist worth billions; Cormac Conlan was an ex-priest who had written a bestseller called *The Gospel of the Streets.*

"The reason I've asked all of you here," Jenny told them, "is that I'm going to need surrogates to speak for Del Rawley for the next couple of days. Del is back in Wisconsin to be with his family right now. I'm sure all of you have seen or heard this morning's news—"

J. D. raised his hand and shook his head. Jenny quickly filled him in.

Then she added, "Del is considering withdrawing from the race."

"Shouldn't you be with him?" J. D. asked.

"My job is to run the Rawley campaign," Jenny told him. "And I don't intend to miss a beat. So when Del does come back, as I'm sure he will, we won't have lost any ground. That's why I called all of you. In case you didn't know, there are always more requests for a candidate to speak than he can possibly meet. Whenever practical, surrogates are asked to fill in. Now, with Del completely unavailable at such a critical time, there are a number of speaking engagements that just can't be missed. That's why I'm asking all of you to fill in for him. I'm sure you know the general outlines of his positions, and I can provide you with material to fill in specific details."

"But you told me the senator writes all his own speeches," J. D. pointed out. "And even with the facts in hand, there's no way I could hope to match his gift for language."

Jenny said she had copies of speeches that Del had already written. She didn't expect any of them to simply read them verbatim, but to paraphrase them as they saw fit while keeping to the substance of what Del had committed to paper.

Everyone agreed, but J. D. was clearly reluctant.

Jenny provided the others with all the details they would need. On his way out, Donnel tapped J. D. on the arm. "Let's get together and talk."

When the others had left, Jenny asked J. D. if something was wrong.

He told her about the exchange with Special Agent De-Vito as he arrived for the meeting, how the man had all but boasted that he'd been prying into every corner of J. D.'s life. J. D. said he'd like to help the senator, he'd like to help Jenny, but he was really not crazy about the idea of a federal agent with a bug up his butt turning his life upside down.

J. D. mentioned that he'd threatened to sue DeVito if the fed kept up his invasion of J. D.'s privacy, but that would be pretty awkward to do if he were speaking publicly on behalf of the candidate. Perhaps he should decline Jenny's offer, just quietly go about his life as a private citizen. Let DeVito get bored and forget all about him.

Just to be safe, he added, "I'd still like to see you after the election, of course."

The surprising thing was, if he didn't have to kill the candidate she was working so hard to elect, if he didn't wind up dead himself, he *would* have liked to see her.

But J. D.'s story made Jenny far too angry to focus on the personal note; she was not about to let some maverick agent screw up her campaign plans. "I'm going to put that bastard DeVito back in his box and lock him inside. You're more valuable to Del than he is, and it's high time he knew it."

J. D. left the campaign office saying a silent prayer Del Rawley would get out of the race. It would make no sense for the blackmailer to want him to kill a noncandidate. He'd be off the hook then, and just as important, Rawley would get to live. He only wished he could do something to help force the senator out of the race.

He got on an elevator to the lobby with two Secret Service agents. This pair held no grudge against him. They simply gave him a discreet once-over and went back to discussing what they were going to eat during their morning break. J. D. picked up on the fact that the agents would be going to a snack shop in the building.

J. D. let the two feds exit the elevator ahead of him, and he watched them cross the lobby and take an escalator to the lower level. He glanced around to see if DeVito was still lurking nearby, and the old gent behind the information desk correctly guessed what he was doing.

"You looking for that fella you were talking to?"

"Yes."

"He's gone."

"Downstairs?"

"No, he left the building."

"Can I get a soft drink at the place downstairs?" J. D. asked.

"Sure. Food's not half bad, either. Lotta these government johnnies like it, anyway."

That's what J. D. had hoped, that the federal agents working the campaign had established a hangout in the building. A place where his minders conceivably might relax. If so, he thought it was time to rattle their cage a little. Give them some extra incentive to stay close for a while.

Follow him right up the coast highway that night.

He was in luck and spotted both crewcuts the moment he entered the snack shop. The blonde was seated at a table against the wall to J. D.'s right. He was intent on the newspaper in front of him. The dark-haired minder had his back to J. D. as he picked up a saucer and a cup to fill from a self-service coffee urn.

J. D. walked over to an adjacent cooler and helped himself to a bottle of fruit juice. He turned to go to the cashier just as the dark-haired minder stepped away from the urn holding a cup of hot coffee. The collision sent the scalding liquid all over the crewcut's hand, causing him to drop the cup and saucer. J. D.'s slacks and shoes were caught in the splash and that was reason enough for him to let go of his bottle of juice.

Amidst the clatter of breaking ceramic and glass, the dark-haired crewcut turned to confront J. D., holding his scalded hand, his face twisted in pain and anger. "Jesus Christ, why the hell don't you watch where—"

When he recognized J. D. his tirade hit a brick wall.

But now it was J. D.'s turn.

"*Me?* I'm not the one who spilled hot coffee on someone. Look at my slacks and shoes."

"You think *I'm* to blame?" The dark-haired minder looked like he wanted to get into it. He clenched his hands into fists, and when he did, J. D. noticed the ring he was wearing.

Before things could escalate, the blonde crewcut materialized to play the peacemaker. He put his hands on his buddy's shoulders.

"Hey, hey, hey. Accidents happen, right? Nobody's to blame. Let's just get all this straightened out, okay?" He turned to J. D. "You all right, mister?"

"Yeah," J. D. allowed. Then he added, "No thanks to your friend."

The blonde had to restrain his partner once more.

J. D. gave the dark-haired crewcut a look that said he was totally unimpressed and unafraid. Then he turned and saw a wary snack shop manager looking on. J. D. took out a twenty-dollar bill and gave it to him, saying, "Damages are on me. *I'm* the one to blame."

Walking out, he muttered in a voice loud enough for the minders to hear, "Asshole."

As J. D. strolled away, he listened for the sounds of pursuit. He didn't hear any. For the moment, the blonde minder must have prevailed. But J. D. was certain he'd lit a fire. He rode the escalator back up to the ground floor and thought how many times during his hitch in the army he'd seen a ring like the one the dark-haired crewcut wore. It was a graduation ring from the United States Military Academy at West Point. With his marksman's eyes, J. D. had even been able to spot the year that the prick had become an officer and a gentleman.

When he got to the lobby he heard a cool voice ask, "Have yourself a little accident?"

Donnel Timmons was standing there, an amused smile playing at the corners of his mouth.

J. D. glanced at his stained slacks and spotted shoes. "Must have."

"I was thinking we could have lunch today. Catch up on old times. But you probably want a change of threads."

The irony of Donnel's presence struck J. D. once again. He could understand now why it was said that cops always hated a coincidence. He didn't care much for Donnel's smirk, either.

"Lunch sounds good," J. D. told him. "Give me thirty minutes. I'll meet you somewhere."

J. D. changed into jeans, a polo shirt, and sneakers at the Refuge, then got into his car to drive to Gladstone's 4 Fish, on the beach just off Sunset, where he'd agreed to meet Donnel for lunch.

As J. D. guided the Lexus up PCH to the restaurant, his mind went back to his army days. He'd always gotten along well with Donnel. They'd been the odd men out in the PANIC unit. The only ones who hadn't been gung-ho covert warriors. Donnel had been the sole black officer in the unit, and J. D. had been the only white enlisted man who hadn't resented Donnel's superior rank.

Despite their past camaraderie, J. D. couldn't accept that mere circumstance had brought the two of them back together in the context of the Rawley campaign. Two trained assassins didn't just happen to show up in a situation like that. He certainly hadn't and . . .

And what if someone had found a way to blackmail Donnel, too?

Pulling into the restaurant's parking lot and handing his car over to the valet, J. D. saw that his former comrade in arms occupied a corner table on the patio overlooking the beach. A moment later J. D. sat down with Donnel, appreciating his choice of tables. Their conversation wouldn't carry above the sound of the waves crashing on the sand.

A waitress promptly brought drinks and took their lunch orders.

Donnel raised his glass to J. D., who tapped his against it to complete the toast.

"So, you kill anybody lately?" Donnel asked.

"No," J. D. answered. "How about you? You still working for the Revolution?"

Donnel laughed. "Naw, man, I'm a capitalist-roader all the way now. Own a company that makes auto parts for Ford and GM. Got six hundred people working for me and they all call me boss. What kind of revolution could improve on that?"

J. D. had an insight as to what Donnel had used as the start-up money for his business.

"So that safe you cleaned out at that ARVN officers' club turned out to be a bigger bonanza than you ever would have believed."

Donnel's eyes narrowed and his smile faded. "Gave you ten K of that money, as I recall."

Yeah, J. D. thought, but I'm being blackmailed for something else. What if someone had found out about Donnel's heist? Had come to him a *long* time after he thought he'd gotten away clean? Had threatened to reveal his criminal past and ruin his respectable present?

How'd that work as blackmail on you, old buddy? J. D. wondered.

Not wanting to give away his thoughts, J. D. only owned up to his part in the crime.

"I made my money blossom, too. Not long ago I owned almost half of L-A-B Fashions. Sold my share and got rich. We're just a couple of grunts who made good."

"You know the first thing I thought when I saw you the other night?"

"What?"

"Thought maybe it was you who took the shot at Del Rawley."

"Me? I was always the reluctant warrior."

"You were reluctant, all right. But you always knocked 'em dead."

"Then it couldn't have been me. The guy you're talking about missed his shot."

Donnel stared at J. D., who met and held his gaze.

"You know," J. D. said, "I thought the same thing. It could have been you."

Donnel blinked. "Me? I'm black!"

"Yeah, I noticed that right off."

"You think I don't want to see a black president?"

"Donnel, you always talk a good game when it comes to race. But your actions always prove that your favorite color is money green. And let's not forget you knocked even more people dead than I did."

Donnel sipped his drink and looked out at the ocean while he gathered his thoughts. Turning back to J. D., he said, "Thing is, we're both fucked if anyone finds out what we did."

"Yes, we are."

"Wouldn't look good for either of us to be around a candidate for president who almost got shot. People'd be suspicious no matter how innocent we are."

"Yes, they would."

"And we are both innocent, aren't we?"

"Of course."

Donnel's smile returned. "That's what I always liked about you, J. D. We always saw eye to eye."

"Pretty much," J. D. admitted. "Only thing that's different now is, we're not in the army anymore."

Donnel laughed. "You mean I don't get to give you orders?"

"You don't give them and I don't take them," J. D. agreed.

After returning to the Refuge, J. D. took Pickpocket's laptop out of the safe in the den and booted it up. He didn't want to use his own machine so no record of what he was about to do would be on his hard disk. J. D. was sure Pickpocket had booby-trapped his computer to guard against outside snoopers who tried to use it without the proper password.

It took him only a few minutes to find out that his two minders were named Arnold Roth—the dark-haired crew-cut—and Bill Danby—the blonde.

Making that discovery hadn't been hard once he'd seen Roth's ring. The U.S. Military Academy had an extensive Web site on the Net, just like every other university in the country. One feature of the site was a link to pictures of graduating classes. Having seen the year Roth had graduated, J. D. didn't need long to find his picture and name and, playing a hunch, those of his classmate Danby. Both cadets were noted as "hard-hitting" safeties on the academy's football team.

Soldiers *and* jocks. Neither would be the kind of guy who'd take kindly to someone spilling hot coffee on him and then calling him an asshole. Especially not Roth, whom J. D. had pegged as the lead dog. He thought the odds were good that Roth and Danby would be crowding him for the near future.

He surfed over to stickyfingers.com and left a message for Red asking her to find out everything she could about the two minders, using West Point as the place to start.

He then closed down the laptop and returned it to his safe.

He called home to see how Evan was doing, but his mother told him that his son was out, that he'd withdrawn from classes . . . that he was with Blair McCray. Then she spent the next fifteen minutes reassuring him that Evan would be all right. The family would see to that.

J. D. pretended to take comfort in his mother's words so that he wouldn't upset her.

But he was far from reassured.

After leaving the office tower where the Rawley campaign headquarters was located, Special Agent Dante DeVito drove to the federal building in Westwood where the Secret Service had its field office in Los Angeles.

DeVito found an empty office with a computer and helped himself to it. He organized his thoughts by reviewing what he'd learned so far about J. D. Cade. Which only forced him to admit he hadn't found anything suspicious in the man's background. Cade had been in the army, but he'd had an innocuous, noncombatant job. He had money, but he'd made it honestly. He had no criminal record, not even a driving violation. He was divorced, but so was De-Vito. He had a son—and that was the one moment when DeVito knew he'd gotten a rise out of Cade, when he'd brought up his kid—but if Cade was everything he seemed to be, he had reason to get pissed at the idea that DeVito might go messing with his family.

If it wasn't for the guy's cool, cocksure attitude, which DeVito took pretty much as a challenge, the special agent might have gone on to other concerns. But now that he'd learned those two new snoops were following Cade, he thought he'd better look into that situation a little further.

He woke up the computer and it asked him for his password. He flipped the keyboard up and saw the password was taped to the bottom of it. Same place he kept his.

He pulled up a current table of organization for the Treasury Department . . . and there it was, meekly tucked away in a corner. Departmental Internal Management and Oversight (DEIMOS). He clicked on its link and found it had been added to the bureaucracy at the beginning of the year. A listing of its personnel included the names Arnold Roth and William Danby.

Next he checked the list of agents on the expanded protection detail for Orpheus. Neither Roth's nor Danby's name appeared there. So the two snoops were with but not officially part of the Rawley campaign. That gave DeVito a very uneasy feeling.

Who the hell were these guys? he wondered.

If they were on hand to be looking over the Secret Service's shoulder, why would they be interested in J. D. Cade? He was just a campaign contributor. Or was he? Maybe, DeVito thought, he should look harder into the life and times of J. D. Cade.

Look into Roth and Danby some more, too.

Evan Cade and Blair McCray agreed that Deena Nokes was no early riser, so it was early afternoon before they set off for her trailer. They followed her directions south on state Highway 51 to an unmarked dirt road that lay halfway between Carbondale and Anna. The lane led directly into the Shawnee National Forest and was barely wide enough for Blair's truck, but a half mile along the path they came to a small clearing containing two dwellings.

One was Deena's customized, mint-condition, '60s-vintage Airstream trailer, which rested on a neat foundation of well-joined mason blocks. The other structure was a small log cabin that looked old enough for a young Abe Lincoln to have built it on his way north to fame, assassination, and immortality. The cabin was as tumbledown as the trailer was well maintained. The roof had holes in it; the only window was broken out; and the door hung precariously in its cockeyed frame.

Deena, looking much more in possession of her faculties than the day before, stepped out of the trailer to greet Evan and Blair as they got out of the pickup and surveyed their surroundings.

Blair asked, "How do you get to live in a national forest like this?"

Deena inclined her head at the cabin. "One of my great-greats built that. I got a claim on this land. My lawyer says the government's either gonna have to cough up a pile of dough or we'll be in court long enough for me to live the rest of my life here."

"What if the feds sneaked in one night and hauled the cabin away?" Evan asked.

"Just let 'em try," Deena said with a mean little grin. She whistled and called out, "Here, Gorby!" In response, a black bear that had to weigh five hundred pounds came bounding out of the cabin. Evan and Blair scrambled back into the truck. Deena threw her head back and laughed at them.

The bear shoved its muzzle into Deena's crotch and almost lifted her off the ground. She gave the creature an affectionate but solid swat on the head and told it to wait right there. Then she went into her trailer and came back out with a large chunk of honeycomb. The bear snapped it up right out of her hand and returned to the cabin.

"You heroes afraid of a little boo-boo bear?" Deena called out. "What the hell good you going to do me?"

She went back into her trailer, and her visitors quickly followed her inside.

The interior of the trailer was a study in compact living: a breakfast bar fronting a tiny fridge and a two-burner stove; a lavatory on the scale of those found in commercial airplanes; a small kitchen table with two chairs under the trailer's only window; and at the back a black-and-white plaid sofa and a small TV on an end table.

On the walls were examples of Deena's art. Her influences appeared to run the gamut from Munch to Picasso to *Hustler*. Her draftsmanship was both expert and richly detailed.

The trailer was as well maintained inside as outside.

Deena told them that Ivar had purchased Gorby from a carnival he'd happened upon down in Tennessee. The bear was of the performing variety and used to the company of humans. But Ivar had made sure the animal still had its teeth and claws. Otherwise it couldn't have protected their belongings when they were away from home.

"Does that bear actually mind you?" Blair asked.

Deena nodded. "We have an understanding, Gorbachev 'n' me."

"That's the bear's name, Gorbachev?" Evan inquired.

"Yeah. Fella who sold him to Ivar was this old Russian. Said he'd named the bear after his country's most famous real estate agent. Told Ivar the real Gorbachev sold about the whole damn country to the Americans. Now that Ivar's gone, I'm real glad I have Gorby's company."

For just a moment, the pain of her loss showed harshly on Deena's face. Then the look of heartache in her eyes abruptly gave way to a hard glint of vengefulness. "Let me show you the picture of the bastard who killed Ivar."

She took out the drawing she'd made of the man Ivar had said was going to make him rich. Evan and Blair studied it while she deftly made a second sketch for them. While she was drawing, she passed the time by telling them how Ivar had spent his last week alive.

Evan and Blair spent an hour listening to Deena and the rest of the day following her leads.

Among their stops on the back trail of Ivar McCray later

that day, Evan and Blair visited A 2 Z Mufflers in Metropolis, Illinois. They showed Deena's sketch to a thin, grimy
mechanic with a prominent Adam's apple named Bulging
Bob. When Bob's boss happened along and objected to
him taking work time to talk to Evan and Blair, Bob told
the guy to fuck off or he'd burn the place to the ground.

The threat was taken as gospel and Bob was left to continue his conversation.

Bob said he did, in fact, recognize the dude in the drawing. Had seen Ivar with him at a place called Dingle's up
near Vy-enna, giving the town of Vienna its local pronunci-
ation.

Evan thought to ask, "You learn your trade by working
on your Harley?"

"My hog, my daddy's pickup, my grandpa's tractor, and
any other damn piece of internal-combustion machinery I
ever come across. Just like most of us."

"Was Ivar at all handy?" Evan wanted to know.

Bulging Bob noticed that Blair's eyes had narrowed
when he heard the question.

"You mean was he up to building that bomb? I wondered that myself. The way I saw Ivar, he was slow but
steady. It might take him a month to read five pages of an
engine manual, but when he was done that boy knew his
stuff cold. In his own way, Ivar was a real craftsman. You
ever see the work he done on his old lady's trailer? Yeah, I
think Ivar coulda built that bomb—if someone showed him
how. But I still don't think he died the way the newspaper
said."

"Why not?"

"Usin' a soldering iron—any electrical tool—while
standing in a puddle? Nobody's that goddamn dumb. That's
somebody tryin' to make it look like you are."

When Del Rawley got home he was greeted by his entire family and many an old friend from his early days in Wisconsin politics. Everyone urged him to fight the smear and stay in the race. It was only after dinner that Del found the time to speak privately with his wife.

"Does it make a difference that she's white?" he asked Devree, referring to Sophie Moreau.

"No," she replied.

"I've never been unfaithful to you," he told her.

"I know."

"But you're still hurt."

The Rawleys sat next to each other, alone in the family room of their home. Pictures of their children hung on the walls along with academic awards. Athletic trophies resided in a glass case. The three volumes on politics in America that Del had published stood between bookends on a small pedestal table.

"I got mad at first," Devree said. "I wanted to hit somebody."

Del smiled. "I bet you would, too."

"You'd win that bet . . . but when I realized there was nobody to hit, that I'd never get the chance, then I realized how much I had been hurt. We've been married thirty-one years, we've raised a beautiful family, we've built an exceptional life. Now you're running for president, and first someone tries to kill you. Then someone else throws mud all over your good name."

Devree realized the implications of what she'd just said.

"Oh, baby, I'm sorry. I didn't mean that woman in France or her son . . ."

Del pressed his fingertips to Devree's mouth.

"I know what you meant," he assured her. "You don't have it in you to hate anyone."

"Except that bastard who tried to kill you, and the people who think they're smearing you. I can hate them, all right."

"You want me to drop out of the race, Devree?"

She shook her head. "I can't make that decision for you, Del."

"What would you do if you were in my place?"

Devree smiled broadly and took her husband's hand. "The first black *woman* who's going to be elected president? Well, I guess the first thing I'd do would be celebrate my hundred and fiftieth birthday. It'll take about that long before this country is ready for the likes of me."

Del Rawley laughed. Then he leaned over and kissed his wife.

"Only if it took that long to get to know you."

Devree said, "Del, if it were me, I'd fight them till my last breath. That's what makes it so hard to have you keep me and the children all tucked away safe while you're risking your life."

"I couldn't do it if I had to risk your safety or the kids'. I wouldn't do it. Nothing is worth that to me."

"That's probably just what the bastards were counting on. Put you in a spot where you'd need to trot your family out to show what a fine, upstanding man you are. They know you'd never do that. So they've got you no matter which way you turn."

"So what do I do?"

Devree squeezed her husband's hand in hers, letting him know he could always draw on her strength. "You make the choice that you can live with for the rest of your life, and then you don't regret it for a single minute."

The problem was, Del hadn't concluded what that choice would be yet.

"But honey?" Devree said, arching an eyebrow.

"What?"

"You decide to stay in the race, you've got to promise me one thing: You'll fight just as mean and dirty as it takes. You don't give those evil bastards one free shot."

Devree kissed Del and left him to make his decision in solitude.

Del built a fire in the fireplace and stared at the flames until they burned down to embers, long after everyone else in the house had gone to bed. He felt a deep sense of peace just sitting there. The kids were back home tonight, and the grandchildren were there, too, sleeping in makeshift arrangements. He was among the people who loved him most.

It would be so easy just to stay right there.

Then the president called.

Jenny was working late in her suite, making notes on a legal pad when the phone rang. She half expected the call to be from Don Ward. Then again, she half expected Don to keep right on calling even after he'd passed away.

"Jenny Crenshaw," she answered.

"Burning the midnight oil for a man who might drop out?" Del Rawley inquired.

"Well, you know how it is with us obsessive professional women. We sublimate the rest of our lives to our work. Either that or I've found someone I believe in."

"You sure you should believe in me?"

"If it turns out otherwise, it's still okay. I bill by the hour."

Del Rawley laughed. Hearing him, Jenny joined in.

"Thank you, Jenny. I hadn't had a good laugh all day."

"Anything I can do to help. I'm a full-service campaign manager."

She'd provided him with the opening to say that there still was a campaign to manage, but Del Rawley veered in another direction.

"I had a phone call from the president tonight."

"Do tell," Jenny replied with interest.

The tone of the campaign had been harsh and partisan from the outset. For the incumbent to call his challenger was quite a turn of events.

"He said he wanted me to know with no uncertainty that he wasn't responsible for breaking the story about Sophie and Bertrand Moreau."

"Funny, his campaign manager, Ronald Turlock, told me the same thing."

"He called you?" Del asked.

"No, I called him. To register my strong disapproval of the politics of the low road."

"That was all you registered?"

"I might have mentioned two can play that game."

There was a pause in the conversation. Jenny could tell that Del wanted to know just how she had threatened the president, what she could have gotten on the man that would have made him call his challenger personally. But Del was too good a politician to let his curiosity outweigh the advantage of not knowing about—and being able to deny—skulduggery done in his name.

Still, he said, "Devree told me that if I stay in, I have to give as good as I get."

"Sound advice. She knows what she's talking about."

"Yeah. Anyway, the president also told me that he'll make a public statement tomorrow repudiating personal attacks on me. He says when it comes to policy or philosophy it's bare knuckles all the way, but he will tell all his partisans to avoid all personal attacks. And on behalf of the people of the United States, he will urge me to stay in the race."

"Very statesmanlike of him." For a man with one ball, Jenny thought.

"Probably good politics, too."

Jenny finally had to ask the question. "So what are you going to do, Del?"

"Get your opinion."

"Of what?"

"Of how my position will play if I stay in the race."

"What is it?"

"If I stay in, I'll explain my relationship with Sophie to the country just the way I did to Devree and my children. I'll say how at one time I loved Sophie; how I'd love to get to know Bertrand. I won't deny anything. I won't disown anyone."

"You're not going to change your party affiliation to the Commies, are you?"

Del laughed again. "No. That's the one thing I'll openly disagree with, Sophie's politics."

"Then I don't think you have a thing to worry about. The people who don't like you already, fuck 'em, they're a lost cause. The people who support you will love you more than ever. And my gut tells me that of the undecideds, you'll get more than half."

"You really think so?"

"Yes. On the other hand, if you drop out, you'll be abandoning all the people who support you in favor of all of those who don't."

After a long moment of silence, Del asked quietly, "We can't have that, can we?"

"I hope not." Jenny paused a heartbeat, then asked, "So, what's it going to be, Senator?"

"Can you keep a secret, Jenny?"

"Sure. As long as it's to your advantage."

Del laughed once more. Then he told her, "I'd decided to drop out. I mean, I'd just made that decision when the president called. I listened to that man blow smoke at me about how he regretted the personal attack on my reputation, and I didn't believe him for a minute. The more he talked, the angrier I got. That man is a weasel. The country deserves better than him. I can't just let him waltz back into the White House for another four years."

"So, I'll see you soon?" she asked.

"Tomorrow."

"You sure I can't tell the president he's responsible for getting you back into the race?" Jenny asked gleefully.

"Okay, you can do it—right when I'm taking the oath of office."

Jenny put the phone down and thrust her fist victoriously into the air. She'd done it. The president never would have called Del—and made him angry enough to change his mind—unless he was afraid Jenny would go public with his . . . masculine shortcoming.

With a smile on her lips and giving no thought to the lateness of the hour, Jenny resumed her work. Then a thought crossed her mind and she quickly noted it in the margin of the page: *Remember. Get DeVito to lay off J. D. Cade.*

J. D. Cade's plan for two other members of the Rawley protection detail was set in motion when he pulled his Lexus out of the garage at the Refuge at 11:30 p.m. As on the preceding night, the streets of Santa Monica Canyon were devoid of traffic, and most of the lights in the houses he passed were out. The neighborhood had retired for the night.

He drove without haste through the quiet streets, but not so slowly as to arouse the suspicions of anyone who might be following him—and he definitely hoped that Roth and Danby were following him. But by the time he turned north on Pacific Coast Highway he'd failed to see any other vehicle behind him.

Either the goddamn minders weren't watching him or the bug they'd stuck on the Lexus had a range that allowed them to remain out of sight. He had to assume the latter. If he just turned around and went back to the Refuge, and the two crewcuts *were* tracking him electronically, they'd know he was playing some kind of game with them. On the other hand, if he kept going and the minders weren't following him, he'd suffer nothing worse than a pointless drive up the coast.

Not that it was a bad night for a drive. Far from it. The air was pleasantly cool and the sky was brilliantly clear. A nearly full moon hung amidst a thick field of diamond-bright stars. He came to a point in the highway where the infinite black void of the ocean seemed so close at hand he could imagine that he'd just become a space traveler, heading for all those bright lights in the heavens and leaving a violent world behind.

Oncoming headlights destroyed the illusion. J. D. put his eyes back on the road and then checked his rearview mirror to look at the traffic behind him. There was only a handful of cars and he knew that number would diminish the farther out of town he went. Checking the mirror at regular intervals, he tried to see if any of the drivers behind him seemed purposeful in their pursuit.

One of them, in a Porsche, eliminated himself quickly as he zoomed past J. D. In a matter of seconds the sports car disappeared from view. Other cars turned off at Cross Creek Road and Webb Way, and as J. D. climbed the long incline approaching Pepperdine University, he could see only two sets of headlights far behind him. Then one car made a right at the Trancas Canyon Road Turnoff.

Now, with no other vehicles left to cover for them, J. D. could *feel* in his bones that he had the minders behind him. Roth and Danby were going to fall into his trap. He made a conscious effort not to let himself get too excited, but he wanted to exult. The moment when he'd have his first opportunity to strike back for what had been done to him and Evan and Pickpocket was almost at hand.

Better still, payback shouldn't compromise him. Roth and Danby were about to perish in a *natural* disaster. Burying his bomb under a layer of dirt meant it shouldn't leave obvious scorch marks on the rocks it dislodged. The plastic bottle he'd used to hold the gunpowder should be obliterated and the few scraps that might remain from the detonator should be flung great distances. With any luck, they'd land in the ocean. But more important, there should be no reason for anyone to suspect a bomb had gone off. Rock slides just happened. The warning signs said so.

His next step was to increase the minders' sense of urgency. Up until then, he'd been carefully observing the speed limit, but now he floored the accelerator. There was some risk he might be stopped for speeding, but the Porsche that had flashed by him should have flushed out any CHiP or county mountie who'd been lying in wait. If J. D. saw flashing lights ahead, he'd be forewarned.

Meanwhile, Roth and Danby would see that J. D. was hauling ass. They wouldn't know if he'd spotted them on his tail or had some other reason to run. But J. D. was willing to bet they'd take up the chase. No doubt about it if Roth was driving.

J. D.'s heart was racing even faster than the Lexus. He was pleased that no oncoming traffic passed him as he streaked along PCH. A road abandoned to all but him and his prey was what he wanted, what he had to have. His adrenaline rush seemed to carry him to his destination at the scenic overlook with magical speed.

He skidded to a stop a foot short of the drop-off into the ocean. He opened his door and plucked Roth and Danby's bug from the console next to him, where he'd put it before leaving the Refuge. He laid it on the pavement. Then he whipped the Lexus off the overlook and around the bend in the highway. Stopping fifty feet away, he snugged the car up against the slope of the mountainside and turned off the lights.

Seconds later a gray sedan appeared, Roth behind the wheel. He and Danby had followed the script J. D. had written for them. They'd raced to catch up with him and their bug had led them right out onto the overlook. Only J. D.'s car wasn't there. Wasn't where the bug said it should be. Roth killed the engine and the two crewcuts jumped out of their car to look for an explanation.

That was when J. D. should have detonated the bomb. But he wanted to wait until they were back inside their vehicle, where they wouldn't have any chance to run or dive into the ocean. In the next instant, events made waiting seem to be a mistake.

Headlights appeared. A car was coming down the highway, heading toward L.A. One cockeyed beam swept across Roth and Danby on the overlook. They shielded their eyes against the glare, Danby looking startled, Roth pissed. The car, a beater carrying what looked to J. D. like a family of migrant workers, passed the point where the Lexus was stopped. A woman in the front seat pointed at Roth and Danby, perceived them as some sort of threat, and urged the driver to get away from there.

J. D. fervently seconded the motion. "Hurry up, goddamnit!"

But the driver refused to take his rattletrap around the bend at anything faster than a crawl.

On the overlook, Roth and Danby were having a debate over the top of their car. Roth summed up his argument by getting back in behind the wheel and slamming his door. Danby must have wanted to stay and look around, but when Roth turned the engine on, Danby knew it was time to get in or be left behind.

J. D. saw the migrants' car disappear inch by inch around the bend in the road. Backup lights flared as Roth shifted the minders' sedan into reverse. J. D. prayed that the driver of the beater would pick up speed now that he had a straightaway in front of him . . . but he waited an extra second—until Roth had turned his wheels to take up the pursuit—before he pulled out onto the road and sent the radio signal to the detonator.

There was a deep, muffled boom. Then, for a second, nothing seemed to happen. J. D. was rolling again, but Roth was frozen in place, stunned that J. D. had been right there all along and he hadn't noticed. The crewcut's stupefaction was broken by a huge groaning rumble that sounded as if the whole mountainside was about to come crashing down.

One last look in his rearview mirror showed J. D. the horror on Roth's and Danby's faces. Their car was moving now, trying to escape the thundering onslaught. For a moment J. D. saw headlights behind him, but then the lights were extinguished by an immense, expanding cloud of choking dust and flying rocks.

J. D. had to take the long way back to the Refuge, but nobody followed him.

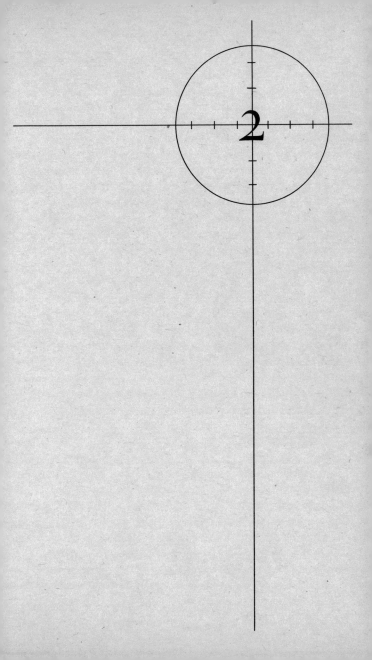

EIGHT

Saturday, September 18, 2004

Dingle's made Stratford Willie's look like the Stork Club, but the joint was jumping when Evan and Blair pulled up just after midnight.

A freestanding wooden structure with an illuminated gravel lot out front, Dingle's faded red paint had chipped off to the extent that the remaining flecks made the building look like it had the measles. The window at the front had been replaced with a sheet of plywood, as had the upper half of the front door. The establishment's name had been spray-painted in neon green.

Evan let Blair lead the way through the entrance. They were noticed immediately by a table of bikers who looked as if their evolutionary climb had stopped well short of *H. sapiens.*

"Sonofabitch, the Girl Scouts sellin' cookies again?" one of the bikers asked.

"Had me a sissy up at Stateville looked like him."

"Which one?"

"The one with the nice ass."

A wave of raucous laughter washed over Evan and Blair

as they made their way to the bar. Blair brought out Deena's sketch. "I'm Ivar McCray's cousin," he told the grinning bartender, whose teeth were as green as the sign outside. "We're looking for the man in this picture. Fella named Bob, down to Metropolis, told us he saw Ivar with him in here. Can you help us out?"

Evan admired how calm Blair's voice was.

"What's your name?" the bartender asked.

"Blair McCray."

"*Blair?*" came a mocking voice from behind them. "Why, that's purtier than Nancy."

The Kentucky cop turned to look at the big-mouthed biker. He was the same bearded, shaved-scalp hulk who'd been reminiscing about his days in the state pen. Blair walked over to him, held out the sketch, and asked, "Have you seen this man? Can you help us find him?"

"I'll help you find my dick is what I'll help you do."

As the biker's audience guffawed at his wit, Evan scanned the pack of outlaws, gauging which one was likely to be the first to join the fight—a fight he was absolutely certain was only seconds away from beginning. After he'd made his selection, and offered a silent prayer for his and Blair's deliverance, he looked for the next two most eager combatants.

Blair continued in a quiet voice. "You keep talking about sissies and asses and dicks and all that. Makes me wonder if my friend and I haven't made a mistake."

"Oh, you made a mistake, all right. A big, bad, *hairy-assed* mistake."

"See, there you go again," Blair told him. "The way you talk, it makes me wonder if this is a *gay* bar."

It took only a heartbeat for Blair's meaning to register in the biker's piggy little eyes. As he heaved his outsized body to its feet, Blair hit the outlaw on the way up, hit him with a left hand that audibly crushed the man's cheek, jawbone, and nose.

Evan had guessed correctly. The biker he'd chosen as the first to jump in reached his hand into a jacket pocket. He never got the chance to bring it out. Evan kicked him in the crotch, and when the man's knees buckled, he kicked him again on the point of his chin.

Spinning to meet the next anticipated line of attack, he saw that the guy he'd thought would be the second to join the fray was actually sneaking away, but number three had pulled a knife that Jim Bowie would have admired, and he appeared to have every intention of burying it in Blair McCray's back, the Kentucky lawman being occupied throwing punches at two other bikers.

Evan plucked a beer bottle off the bar and flung it at the biker with the knife. It caught him smack on the side of the head and shattered. Which served only to get the biker's attention, and redirect the point of his blade at Evan's belly.

Suddenly the light over Evan's head dimmed, as if a black cloud had passed in front of the sun. He instinctively ducked, and the light returned as the bartender, who'd been about to jump on him from atop the bar, went sailing past to impale his leg on the Bowie knife and knock down the biker wielding it. Then somebody tagged Evan with a good shot to the right side of his head. The blow knocked him back into the bar and he held on for a second to keep his feet. He threw punches without ever clearly seeing a target. Left-left-right, the combination he'd been taught at the YMCA. The first punch missed, but the next two landed with satisfying impacts.

Evan was still trying to clear his vision when somebody grabbed him from behind. Somebody who was at least as big as Gorbachev the bear and smelled worse. Before the monster could lift Evan clear of the floor and crush the life out of him, he stamped hard on his assailant's foot. A bellow of pain accompanied his release . . . and then somebody fired a gun.

In the enclosed space, even with the din of the brawl, the gunshot sounded like a howitzer going off. Evan backed up against the bar, wondering if he was about to be shot or if Blair McCray already had been. He blinked furiously, trying to see what was happening, and finally out of his left eye he saw a wrathful Deena Nokes holding a smoking gun in her hand. At that moment he couldn't recall a woman ever looking better to him.

"That was a warning shot," Deena said in a room suddenly gone quiet. "Next one'll go square between somebody's worthless eyes."

A biker started to speak, until Deena pointed her weapon at him.

"The one thing I got to live for," she said, "is finding my Ivar's killer. These two are helping me. Anybody fucks with them fucks with me. Fuck with me, I'll shoot you dead."

Deena looked at Evan and Blair and with a jerk of her head indicated that it was time to go.

They didn't have to be told twice. Hopping nimbly over fallen bodies, they bade Dingle's farewell.

Deena had left her Harley next to Blair's pickup. She was telling the two men she'd give them an escort to the interstate when a biker mama came running out of Dingle's.

The woman was small and pale with stringy peroxide blonde hair. She said her name was LuAnne and pleaded with the threesome to take her with them. She said that when her man, Wendell, came to, he was going to be crazy mean, starting a fight with a citizen and then getting busted up.

Blair McCray started to offer the woman a ride, but Deena told him to shut up.

"How do we know that sonofabitch didn't send you out

here to spy on us? Maybe we take you home and then you call up and tell him and his friends where we are."

The woman looked shocked, but then she had an idea. "I'll tell you what. You take me with you, I'll rat Wendell out." LuAnne revealed that the man in the picture had talked to Wendell earlier that day. He'd paid the biker to start a fight if Blair and Evan came into Dingle's looking for him. Gave him five hundred dollars to beat up—but not kill—the two men.

Evan Cade and Blair McCray looked at each other.

That wasn't all, the biker mama continued. The man in the picture had cut his hair short and shaved, so he looked like a citizen now, and she'd seen him the other day up in Carbondale.

Deena told LuAnne to get on the back of her Harley, and as soon as she complied Deena roared off without telling Evan and Blair where she was going. Forgot all about her promise to escort them to the highway. The two men didn't linger. They drove away from the biker bar as fast as the pickup could go, but they couldn't catch Deena.

Blair McCray glanced back at the bar to see if anyone was taking up the chase.

"Nobody," he said.

"Good," Evan responded, holding a hand to his head.

Blair gently probed his own battered face. Then he said, "That fat jailbird biker fuck is called Wendell and he's making fun of *my* name?"

Evan offered no reply and the rest of the trip back to Carbondale was made in silence.

All the houses on Lark Lane were dark when Blair Mc-Cray pulled up in front of Belle Cade's home. He turned on the pickup's dome light and looked at his reflection in the rearview mirror, delicately massaging his swollen nose. "I might not've been Mel Gibson, but my wife always liked the way I looked. What's she going to think of me now?"

"Maybe you ought to go home to her," Evan suggested in a woozy voice.

"Just as soon as I find out what happened to Ivar," Blair responded flatly.

"Still think I did it?"

"I'm keeping an open mind."

"I saved your ass tonight."

"You also proved you're a lot tougher—and meaner—than you look."

"Only when provoked," Evan informed him.

"So who's to say Ivar didn't provoke you?"

Evan had no answer for that. He gave Blair a bleak look and stepped out of the truck. Misjudging the curb, he promptly lost his balance and almost fell.

"Hey, you okay?" Blair asked.

"What the hell do you care?"

"Maybe I better run you over to the hospital and get you checked out."

"Forget it. You still think I might've killed your cousin. I'll get my grandmother to take me." Evan started toward the house, his steps unsteady, still talking but more to himself than Blair. "Maybe I'll take my dad's advice. Go home to California. Sit in the sun. Surf a little."

Evan bent his knees and held out his arms as if riding a wave. Then he collapsed face first onto his grandmother's lawn. Blair jumped out of his truck and ran over to him. He was about to pick up Evan and take him to the hospital when he saw lights go on in Belle Cade's house.

"Oh, Jesus," he muttered. "Don't let that old lady come out with her shotgun now."

J. D. had been able to fall asleep when he got back to the Refuge, but he woke up early. He'd just finished his shower when he heard the newspaper land outside his front door. He toweled himself off, slipped into a pair of gym shorts, and stepped outside to pick it up.

He went into the kitchen, started a pot of coffee, and turned on the radio to KFWB, an all-news station. He sat at the kitchen table and quickly leafed through the paper. It didn't surprise him that the rock slide on PCH wasn't covered; it wouldn't have been discovered until after deadline. What pleased him was that the paper also failed to report any new developments in the hunt for the man who had shot at Senator Rawley in Chicago.

Nor was there any mention of the suspected shooter in Denver.

He was at the counter pouring a cup of coffee when the radio station broadcast the story of a blockage on the coast highway. He turned up the volume.

"A large rock slide closed PCH last night opposite a scenic overlook between Malibu and Point Mugu. Although no temblors of any significance were reported in the area, authorities say a very large volume of earth was displaced and several massive boulders rolled down onto the roadway. One of the boulders struck a passing vehicle."

The minders or the Mexicans? J. D. leaned in close to the radio.

"Fortunately, it crushed only the back end of the car, and the two men inside, who declined to be identified, were shaken up but unhurt. Crews from CalTrans are busy removing the debris and—"

J. D. snapped off the radio. Sonofabitch. Those crew-cut bastards had escaped.

He was surprised they hadn't come after him already.

Just then his doorbell rang.

———

On the opposite side of the country, the Gardener received word of recent events directly from Harold the Toad. First he heard of Roth and Danby's miraculous survival, and then he was informed that Evan Cade was in the hospital with a concussion.

The Gardener looked grim.

"Do you have any doubt Cade caused the landslide, Harold?"

"No, sir."

"Which means that Cade has identified Roth and Danby."

"He's *spotted* them somehow. He shouldn't know anything beyond that."

The Gardener's baleful look said he wasn't nearly so optimistic.

"This isn't good, Harold," he told the Toad. "Farrel panicking in Illinois and having Evan Cade attacked was a serious mistake. That boy is our primary leverage. We lose him and the entire situation could come undone."

"Cade is already using lethal force," the Toad pointed out.

"Yes, but he's still in the best position to do what we want."

"One of the things we want, sir," the Toad reminded the Gardener, "is for Cade to die after he kills Rawley. Right now it appears Roth and Danby are in greater danger."

The Gardener shook his head in disgust.

"Farrel, Roth, and Danby: They're all critical to the plan, but . . . It's just too bad I don't have more like you, Harold."

"Make a jet available to me, sir, and I should be able to handle both ends of the situation."

"You are a comfort, Harold. Keep a bag packed." The Gardener paused for a moment's reflection. Then he said, "If Mr. Cade thinks he's making us jump, let's remind him who holds the whip hand."

As J. D. approached his front door, he had a moment of real regret that he'd thrown Pickpocket's Glock into the ocean. He just hoped he didn't get shot through his front door. But when he took a quick look out the peephole he saw Jenny Crenshaw on the other side.

Holding nothing more lethal than a black leather notebook and a large white paper bag.

He opened the door. From the look on her face, she had expected to find him wearing more than gym shorts. But he noticed that didn't stop her from quickly checking him out.

"I was worried that I might wake you," she said. "I haven't, have I?"

J. D. shook his head. "I'm awake but unshaved. Would you like to come in?"

She nodded and stepped inside. J. D. closed the door behind them.

Holding up the white bag, she said, "Breakfast."

J. D. offered his thanks. "Would you like to eat by the pool?"

"When in California . . . ," she responded.

He led her through the house and out to the table next to the pool.

"This is very nice," she said.

"Thank you. I take it you dropped by so early because you have news."

Jenny nodded and smiled. "Great news. I've been up all night, dying to tell somebody for hours."

"Can it wait just a bit longer? Let me slip into a T-shirt?"

Jenny acquiesced graciously. J. D. went inside and when he came back out he was wearing not only a shirt but also pair of walking shorts. Jenny had laid out an assortment of rolls and had brought silverware and two glasses for orange juice from the kitchen.

J. D. sat down, helped himself to a pastry, and asked casually, "Good news?"

"Del's back in the race."

J. D. was cutting a cinnamon roll in half to share with Jenny when she told him. He kept his face down, the better to hide his expression.

"I'm just so glad Del didn't decide to drop out," Jenny continued. "It would have been such a letdown for so many people."

J. D. *hated* the news, had to force himself to refrain from grinding his teeth, but when he looked up he had his public mask back in place. He handed Jenny half of the roll.

"I just had to share the news with someone," she added, "and I picked you."

Which J. D. could see only as Fate mocking him. Telling him he'd find no easy way out of his trap. "I'm flattered," he said.

Jenny smiled and then yawned so widely she needed two hands to cover it.

"Excuse me."

J. D. said, "I have that effect on women: 'Not tonight, dear, I'm exhausted.' "

"Uh-huh. Tell me another one. No, don't. I've got to tell you my idea and then get back to my hotel for a few hours of sleep. Del's holding a press conference this afternoon announcing his intention to stay in the race."

"He's coming back to town?"

Of course he was, J. D. thought. No need to have asked, really. Couldn't have a tragedy without all the dramatis personae following their charted courses.

"He's on his way," Jenny said. "Now please, before I pass out, just listen."

She explained how Del had refused to make an issue out of the incumbent's lack of military service, and even after the smear attempt on him, she didn't expect him to change that, not directly. But she thought she had a little more wiggle room these days to make the point indirectly.

"I want you and Donnel Timmons to travel with Del. Sometimes you'll speak to the same audiences he does. Other times you'll speak to different groups but in the same town where Del will be speaking. This will elevate your standing in the public eye, and one salient point the media is bound to pick up on will be—"

"That, black or white, American vets support Del Rawley," J. D. finished.

"You don't sound too enthusiastic."

J. D. knew he had to be careful here. His real feelings were beginning to seep out.

"I guess it's sound strategy . . . but there's still the matter of Special Agent DeVito."

Jenny's energy had all but dissipated until she heard DeVito's name. Then an indignant anger reinvigorated her. "Don't worry about *him*. I'll take care of Special Agent DeVito."

J. D. asked mildly, "Is it really worth the aggravation?"

"I'm going to get Del Rawley elected," she told him. "And I could use your help."

He bit his lip, thinking with black humor that it would be the supreme irony if Senator Franklin Delano Rawley actually needed the help of J. D. Cade to get elected. That his campaign would fail without it. But in the end J. D. shrugged and announced his only real choice.

"Okay, I'll do it."

"You'll be at the news conference this afternoon?"

"Sure," he said, and produced what he hoped was a team-spirit grin.

Jenny reached out and affectionately put a hand over one of his.

"Thanks. This means a lot to me." She pushed back from the table and stood up. "Now I've got to get back to my hotel and get a few hours' sleep."

"You drove here?"

"Yes."

"Then let me call a cab or offer you a guest room. Wouldn't do to have the candidate get back in the race, then have his campaign manager fall asleep at the wheel."

Jenny considered her options. "Does the guest room have an alarm clock?"

J. D. said it did.

"I'll stay here."

J. D. turned off the phones so Jenny's sleep wouldn't be disturbed.

As a token of gratitude, Jenny took J. D. to lunch at the Chaya Brasserie on Alden Drive. Unlike their visit to the nearby Ivy Cafe, they were seated and served without fanfare. Their waitress gave them a bright smile, but no brighter than she gave anyone else.

"You don't mind not being recognized and fawned upon?" J. D. asked.

"I like my privacy when I can get it," Jenny told him. "I'm willing to sacrifice it, though, in order to get what I want. Take a quick look around and tell me what you see."

J. D. didn't know what to expect but followed orders. He didn't see anyone famous. He didn't see the FBI or Secret Service swooping down on him. He simply saw a room filled with smartly dressed people . . . who were wearing FDR buttons. Not all of them, but a lot.

He turned back to Jenny. She was smiling, knowing he'd caught her drift.

"That's why I work through the night. That's why I'm willing to sacrifice my privacy when need be. How many people did you see wearing buttons for the incumbent? No, don't look, I'll tell you. Eight."

"Your man wins, hands down," J. D. told her.

"Oh, the race is a lot closer than that. This part of L.A. is one of Del's strongholds, but it's nice to see the faithful making a public statement. It means they're likely to spread the word to family and friends, and word of mouth is still the most powerful selling tool there is."

"It doesn't bother you, the idea that candidates have to be *sold* to the voters?"

Jenny shook her head. "I hope it doesn't bother you, either. Because that's what I'm asking you to do. Sell Franklin Delano Rawley to the electorate. Sell the hell out of him."

Jenny's aims conflicted so directly with his own that J. D. couldn't keep a frown off his face. Fortunately for him, she misinterpreted his feelings.

"Look," Jenny said, "I know the nitty-gritty of politics bothers most people, but try to think of it like this: Del is selling his vision of what the country should be and how hard he'll be willing to work to achieve that vision, and the people will pay for what he's selling with the currency of their faith, their trust, and their votes. That's the deal, and I don't see anything wrong with it."

J. D. knew he'd been lucky just now, but he reminded himself that he had a smart woman sitting not three feet from him, watching him closely. If he kept letting his real feelings show, she'd start to see through him. He had to focus on what *she* was thinking.

So he addressed himself to her point. "There's a difference between selling your vision and selling yourself."

"Not if you come along with your vision, to make sure it works."

J. D. grinned reflectively. "A telling point. You're a pretty persuasive person."

"God, I hope so."

"And you don't mind the media poking into your private life?"

"Not so far. The truth is, your privacy gets invaded only as long as you're news. For me, that will be until election day. After that, nobody will give a rat's patoot about Jenny Crenshaw."

"But from now until then?"

Jenny stared at J. D. for a moment. Then she said quietly, "My darkest secret?"

"Is entirely your business," J. D. replied with utmost sincerity.

"I had a nervous breakdown," she told him anyway. "It happened seven years ago, when my husband died. I was in a locked room at a private treatment facility for six weeks."

J. D. didn't say a word. Didn't dare.

Jenny shrugged. "You're right. That's nobody's business but mine. And nobody has yet to dig it out and expose it to public review. But if they did, I'd live with it. I'd pay the price for what I hope to gain."

J. D. remained silent but thought that was, indeed, the heart of the matter: paying the price for what you hoped to gain.

Jenny grinned at him.

"Don't look so serious," she told him. "Don't worry. You're still new to all this. I won't ask to know your darkest secret for at least another week or two."

J. D. knew it was time to hold up his end of the conversation, and he evaded neatly. "I was just wondering what some reporter would make of the fact that you spent four hours in a bed at my house this morning."

Jenny laughed mischievously. "He'd undoubtedly make far more of it than there was. But so what? We're both single, we're both well over twenty-one . . . and we both know your manners are far better than they need to be."

"I'll make a note of that."

"Please do. But since this is a business lunch, we'll stick to business. So let me assure you that dealing with the media is a two-way street. We use the newsies as much as they do us."

And Jenny proceeded to tell him how.

DeVito was at the DGA Building on Sunset Boulevard doing a double-check of the auditorium where Orpheus' news conference would be held. Everybody was aware that he'd been looking over their shoulders but nobody complained—even though more than a few of his colleagues now considered DeVito to be bad luck.

Shortly before the audience was due to start filing in, a veteran special agent named Landers sidled up to him where he was standing in one wing of the stage and whispered, "You hear about the two assholes and their accident?"

For a moment DeVito was irritated, thinking Landers had stopped by to tell him a joke when he ought to be working. Then he listened with serious interest to the story of how Roth and Danby had almost bought the farm last night.

"What the hell were they doing out there?"

"Who knows?" Landers said. "Only reason I heard about it was they had to report the loss of their car, and word got out."

Landers left. Left DeVito thinking that, sure, accidents happened. But more often than not they happened to people you hated to see get hurt or die. Not pricks like . . . J. D. Cade.

DeVito looked up and saw him standing there in the wings on the other side of the stage.

J. D. had spotted the Secret Service agent, too, saw DeVito giving him the evil eye. He'd been watching for Roth and Danby, concerned they'd give him more than dirty looks. But then he realized he was safe from them as long as the blackmailer still hoped he'd kill Del Rawley. The crewcuts, if they were well-trained mutts, could kill him only after he smoked the candidate.

Which had to make them more than a little unhappy, knowing he had no such constraints.

On the other hand, unless Jenny Crenshaw was able to fit DeVito with a muzzle, the special agent seemed to have no limitations on giving J. D. grief.

The doors to the auditorium opened and a procession of Hollywood royalty made their entrance. Everyone had been obliged to pass through metal detectors, but once past that egalitarian security procedure, a pecking order as rigid as any in nature took over. The A-list took their places first and then the lower orders filled in around them. Del Rawley's news conference was the hottest ticket in town that day.

Secret Service agents were positioned throughout the auditorium, and one was standing not five feet behind J. D. That wasn't good enough for DeVito. He kept staring daggers at J. D.

Jenny had left J. D. in his present spot while she went to talk with the candidate, so he had no choice but to remain there. DeVito's unblinking stare was beginning to annoy him, however. He considered making a gesture. A mocking salute. An extended middle finger. In the end, he went with something practical: a small test. He darted his right hand under his suit coat.

For all DeVito knew, he was reaching for his handkerchief, but the agent reflexively pulled back his suit coat and reached for his Uzi. No doubt about it, J. D. had DeVito very tightly wound. Before things went too far, J. D. casually removed a notepad and pen from his pocket.

J. D. heard the Secret Service agent standing behind him mutter, "What the fuck?"

The man had seen DeVito go for his weapon, but he hadn't seen any reason for such a move. There was only J. D. between the two of them, and he was harmlessly writing a note. The second agent quickly brushed past J. D. and peered out at the audience. Nothing was amiss there.

The agent asked J. D., "Did you see anything threatening?"

"Only him," J. D. responded, nodding at DeVito.

DeVito's face was twisted in rage. He'd stepped on his dick and been caught at it. He disappeared into the backstage shadows.

A moment later, J. D. heard a quiet voice. "I believe that man was tempted to shoot you."

Donnel Timmons had eased up to J. D.'s side. J. D. took a quick look around. The Secret Service agent who'd just questioned him had departed. Probably wanted a word with DeVito.

"Which man is that?" J. D. asked Donnel in the same soft tone.

"The one that was about to point his automatic weapon your way."

"My way? You sure it was me? Weren't you behind me?"

Donnel chuckled quietly. "Yes, I was. Wondering where the hell I could duck. All the while I was thinking I may be middle-aged, but I'm still too damn young to die."

"What are you two whispering about? We're not going to have any secrets in my administration." Del Rawley arrived with Jenny and another pair of agents.

The candidate greeted Donnel and then extended his hand to J. D.

"Jenny tells me she gave you the short course in campaign politics at lunch, Mr. Cade."

J. D. shook Rawley's hand. "She did, and it makes me glad I'm just a bit player, Senator."

"Oh, we'll get the most we can out of you, don't you worry about that. So how is it you know my friend Donnel Timmons here?"

"From our army days, Senator."

"You were in the same outfit?"

J. D. nodded. "1st Logistical Command. Pilferage and inventory control."

Del Rawley cocked his head. "Didn't they used to call you guys the PANIC unit? I remember trying to get syringes and pressure bandages from a supply depot one time and they couldn't be bothered with me. They were in a big sweat doing an emergency inventory—all because they thought the PANIC boys were about to swoop down on them."

"Must've been afraid of the likes of Lieutenant Timmons. I was just a clerk."

Donnel cut J. D. a look, then he smiled and said, "Don't you believe it, Del. We'd have been lost without J. D. Cade."

Del tossed a glance at Jenny. "There's something going on between these two, all right. Old army buddies, you just never know what they got up to. But we'll find out soon enough. Gentlemen, I'm taking Ms. Crenshaw's suggestion. You two have joined the circus."

Then the candidate stepped onstage to give the most important speech of the campaign to date. He waited for the applause to die and came straight to the point.

"For me," Del told his audience and the TV cameras, "there is no escape from taking responsibility for my actions. I don't deny my affair with Sophie Moreau; I make no excuses for it. Sophie was the first love of my life. While

I don't share her politics, I've learned that I do share a son with her, and I'd very much like to get to know Bertrand.

"There's no escaping the fact that the *great* love of my life is my wife, Devree Harper Rawley, and since the attempt on my life in Chicago, Devree and our children, Eleanor, Bobby, and Colin, have never been more precious to me.

"There's no escaping the fact that my political opponents exposed my affair with Sophie Moreau not because she is a Communist but because she is *white*. My political enemies were counting on the idea that a black man—a black man running for president—having had sex and a child with a white woman would stir revulsion in a multitude of voters, both black and white.

"All I can say to that," Del told them, "is the heart follows its own path. Seeking only a love that fulfills, it cares nothing for race, religion, age, or even gender. If I'm found to be unworthy of the office I seek because of who I fell in love with thirty-seven years ago, so be it. I'll accept that judgment without regret. I am at peace with myself. I wouldn't change a thing.

"But if I get only the votes of those people who still recall their first loves with undimmed joy, there's one more fact that's inescapable: I *will* be your next president."

J. D. watched from the wings with Jenny and Donnel. Del Rawley seemed to be speaking directly to him. Or at least to his experience. He thought of his own first love, Mary Ellen McCarthy, and found himself nodding in agreement.

Then, as at the diva's fund-raiser, the realization that this man could affect him so deeply brought him up short. Made his body jerk. But no one noticed because they were fixated on the candidate, who was receiving a standing ovation from the audience.

Jenny and Donnel were applauding also, Jenny with a

tear on her cheek, Donnel wearing a broad smile. Jenny turned to look at J. D., and it was only then he realized that he, too, was clapping.

Glancing at Jenny and Donnel, J. D. remembered how he'd wished he could find a way to help force Del Rawley out of the race. So he wouldn't have to kill him.

Just then the idea hit him as to how he could do that.

A moment later, his PCR beeped. When he saw who was paging him he excused himself.

"Where's Mr. Cade?" Del asked as he stepped offstage.

"He had to make a phone call," Jenny explained.

The candidate raised an eyebrow. "Hope he got to hear the whole speech."

"He was applauding as loudly as anyone," Jenny told him. "He told me at Marva's the other night about his first love, the girl he should have married. But she got away."

"A lost love? Seems like Mr. Cade and I have one or two things in common." Then Del Rawley turned to Donnel Timmons. "You know, Donnel, the way I recall it, you told me about being in the 1st Logistical Command, all right. But you never told me the PANIC part."

Donnel shrugged, but he didn't avoid Del's eyes. "What can I say? That's like 'fessing up to being with the IRS on April fifteenth."

"Is this going to be a problem?" Jenny asked with a note of concern.

"No . . . no," the candidate replied. "I guess I'm just a little sensitive right now about anything that might jump up and bite me on the ass. I think one no-regrets speech is pretty much the limit for any campaign. So, Donnel, I hope you and Mr. Cade don't have any other secrets that might prove embarrassing."

"Not me," Donnel said evenly.

"Then we'll have to ask Mr. Cade if he has any skeletons in his closet."

The candidate and his retinue departed. Del instructed Jenny to ask J. D. Cade to join him for dinner that night.

"Dad," Evan said, "where've you been? Grandma's been trying to call you—and I just remembered that PCR number you gave me."

J. D. had placed the call from the lobby of the DGA building. His mother must have tried to reach him that morning after he'd turned his phones off so Jenny could sleep undisturbed.

"What's wrong?" J. D. asked. "Is everyone all right?"

"Well, actually, I have a mild concussion and I'm in University Hospital."

J. D. looked around and strained to keep cool. "How'd you get the concussion?"

"There was this fight," Evan said reluctantly.

"With who?"

"I never actually saw the guy who hit me. It was at this biker bar called Dingle's."

"Why were you there?" J. D. kept his voice at a conversational pitch, but he could feel a vein in his head start to throb.

"Blair and I were sort of—"

"Blair McCray?"

"Yeah. We went to this bar looking for this guy and a fight broke out."

"That's been known to happen in biker bars. You might have thought of that."

"The thing is, we found out that the guy we're looking for paid these bikers to beat us up."

"And they succeeded."

"Not as much as they wanted. Deena saved us."

"And she is . . . ?"

"Ivar McCray's common-law wife. Widow now. She's looking for this guy, too."

"And the reason everyone's looking for this guy?"

"We . . . I think he's the one responsible for Ivar McCray's death. Maybe for setting me up, too."

"Does he have a name, this guy?"

"Not that we know. We're not even sure what he looks like. One description says he's a long-haired biker who might have some Asian blood. Another says he's short-haired and clean shaven. Hey, Dad, have you ever heard of the ROK Army?"

The question made J. D. struggle to stay in control. "Yes."

"This bartender named Punch says the guy we're looking for could've been a drill sergeant for them. Were they as bad as he makes out? You know, if it moved, they shot it?"

"Evan," J. D. said firmly, "it's time you came home. As soon as you're fit to travel."

"I guess that means yes. I'll have to let Blair know. But yeah, coming home is my thought, too. I didn't like how it felt as if the world was slipping away from me when I passed out. As soon as they let me out of here, I'm going to let my lawyer know."

"Good."

"Hey, Dad, where are you going to be? Los Angeles or Santa Barbara?"

"I don't know." J. D. hesitated, then added, "I'm going to be traveling with a man who says he's going to be the next president of the United States."

"What?"

"I'll explain later. You can use either house. If you want to stay in L.A., go to the Fred Sands office in Santa Monica. They'll have a key for you. Wherever you go, stay in touch."

DeVito spotted J. D. among the crowd in the lobby. Celebrities of all stripes were lingering to discuss the speech. The fed closed in on J. D. like a fast-moving storm front.

"You're a real wiseass, mister, you know that?" DeVito told J. D.

"If you think I'm a pain, Special Agent DeVito, take a good look in the mirror," J. D. replied. Then he added, "By the way, did you check out your two friends who are also making nuisances of themselves?"

Having Cade ask him about Roth and Danby—after the two had almost been killed—made DeVito take a step back. He looked to see if Cade somehow knew what had happened. But Cade just looked the way he always did. Cool, plausible, unflappable . . . probably wouldn't bat an eye if he was slitting your throat.

"Information concerning the protection detail is classified, Mr. Cade," DeVito told him.

"Has Ms. Crenshaw spoken with you lately, Special Agent?"

"No," DeVito said, not liking the implication.

"Well, I have the feeling she's about to; here she comes now."

Jenny made her way through the crowd to the two men.

"There you are!" she said to J. D., taking his arm. "I've been looking all over for you. Del would like to know if you can join him for dinner tonight." Reacting to DeVito's grimace, she told him, "As for you, Special Agent Clarke wants to see you."

DeVito knew when he was being told to beat it. Knew when there was nothing he could do about it. He stormed into the auditorium and went backstage, where he expected to find Clarke, but the agent in charge had already left. He was told Clarke was accompanying Orpheus back to his hotel suite. But DeVito did see Roth and Danby . . . and the more Cade wanted to know about them, the more DeVito wanted to know about them.

"My name's Dante DeVito," he told the crewcuts.

"We know who you are," Roth responded.

That was just the kind of crack DeVito didn't need right then.

"Is that right, Arnold? That's what you and your friend do? Snoop on fellow agents?"

"Only the ones who fuck up," Danby told him.

"Where do you guys come from, huh? What makes you qualified to second-guess anybody else?"

"You don't question us, we question you," Roth told him.

"You question me, don't hold your fucking breath waiting for an answer."

DeVito gave each of them his class-A sneer and stomped off. More than ever, he felt there was something wrong about those two. More wrong than Cade, even, who had, after all, checked out clean.

So far.

Twenty minutes later, DeVito knocked on the door of Charlie Clarke's command post at the Century Plaza, and this time he waited for a reply before entering. Clarke glanced up from his work. "Take a load off, DeVito."

DeVito pulled up a chair, sat, and waited stoically while Clarke made a note on a blueprint.

When the agent in charge finished, he looked up. "I was told you went for your weapon today with the seeming intention of bringing it to bear on one of Orpheus' surrogate speakers. I wanted to hear from you if I got that right."

Clarke's tone was neutral but he was watching DeVito very closely.

"That's right," DeVito admitted without elaborating.

"You gonna make me pull teeth?" Clarke asked. "Look, DeVito, unlike some people, I don't have a hard-on for you. I thought I gave you a pretty decent second chance." Clarke leaned forward. "What concerns me now is knowing that you haven't gone off the deep end. That you can make it to the end of this campaign in a professional manner and re- tire in peace and quiet. If you don't think you can manage that, I'd appreciate it if you'd tell me."

DeVito answered in a measured voice. "That guy, Cade, he provoked me."

"He provoked *you*? I had Ms. Crenshaw breathing fire at me that you've done nothing but provoke him from the first time you set eyes on the man. She is *pissed* at you, DeVito. She told me about her plan to make you a bathroom moni- tor and I'm beginning to see the wisdom of it."

"I think she's fucking Cade."

Clarke rubbed weary eyes. "So what're you saying here, DeVito? He's Mata Hari, only he's got a dick?"

DeVito clenched his teeth.

Clarke told his subordinate, "My money says you've al- ready done a background check on Mr. Cade. Am I right?"

"Yes."

"And do you have any proof he is anything but a whole- hearted supporter of and generous contributor to Orpheus' campaign?"

"No," DeVito snapped.

"You checked him out down to the brand of toenail clip- pers he uses, didn't you?"

"Everything I could find."

"Even so, the man almost *provoked* you into going for your weapon."

DeVito said nothing. What could he say? That Cade *had* pissed him off right from the start? That the more the SOB got involved in the campaign, the madder it made him? He couldn't say that. So there was only one way he could go.

"Cade told me that our two snoops Roth and Danby have been watching him, too. You know what that's all about, Charlie?"

NINE

"Evan Cade says he's leaving? Leaving town?"

"Leaving the state," Blair McCray told Carbondale chief of police Billy Edwards. "Going back to California." The two men were talking in Edwards' office in the municipal building.

"Well," the chief said philosophically, "there's not a god-damn thing we can do about it."

Blair asked, "Still no luck on connecting Evan Cade to the footprints left at the scene of Ivar's death?"

The chief shook his head. "We both know that we're never going to find the shoes that made those prints. Those suckers are long gone by now."

That had been Blair's original opinion, too. But now he reconsidered whether the shoes had, in fact, been destroyed. "Unless somebody *is* framing the kid . . . Then I bet those shoes are sitting in a plastic bag somewhere."

The chief gave his in-law a cool look. "What? You're literally waiting for the other shoe, or shoes, to drop? Have you really come around to taking Evan Cade's side?"

"He said he saved my life last night."

"Said?"

"Told me there was a biker with a Bowie knife about to cut my gizzard out."

"But you didn't notice?"

"I didn't actually see the guy. Or the knife. I was pretty busy right then. But Evan said he bounced a beer bottle off the sucker's noggin. I do know from looking at Evan's injuries that he caught one helluva punch to the face, and he must have dealt out a couple of good licks himself, the way his knuckles were cut up."

"He was in the middle of a brawl. He didn't have any choice but fight. Doesn't mean he saved your life."

Blair shook his head.

"You know how it is when somebody says something like that. You can tell right off if he's lying. I think Evan Cade is telling the truth."

"Peace comes to the Cades and McCrays," the chief snorted. "Will wonders never cease?"

"Come on, Billy," Blair told the chief. "You're not blood. You're an in-law."

"With *my* wife that's close enough."

"Maybe we've been looking at the wrong end of things here. The story was that Ivar intended to pay back some merchant who wouldn't go along with a protection scheme, right?"

"That's right. Local man who owns four gas stations— whose daughter just happens to be Evan Cade's girlfriend."

"Was his girlfriend."

"Well, sure, if he's leaving town and not taking her with."

"No, I mean right now. While we were riding around yesterday, he told me that Pru Laney dumped him. On the advice of her daddy's lawyer."

Chief Edwards saw the two possibilities to be found in that nugget of information. He went with the one that he liked better.

"Maybe the lawyer didn't want the stink of Evan Cade's situation to rub off on her."

"Or maybe her daddy's got his own problems and his lawyer's going to blame Evan Cade for them. What's that gas station owner's name again?"

"Barton. Barton Laney."

"Sorry," the kid behind the counter at the gas station said, "Mr. Laney's not here."

Blair McCray had just gone 0 for 4. Hadn't been able to find Barton Laney at any of the gas stations he owned.

"You know if he's sick or out of town?"

"Didn't hear anything like that."

"So he's working. But he isn't at any of his places of business."

"If you say so."

Blair thought for a minute. "Who deposits the day's receipts, you or him?"

The kid's eyes flattened with suspicion. He reached under the counter.

Blair told him, "If there's a panic button under there, that's one thing. If it's a gun, don't even think about it." He showed the kid his badge.

The kid left his hand where it was. "That says Paducah, mister. You're not even in the right state."

"Don't I know it. But I am working with your local cops, and all I'm looking for is a way to find your boss. I thought if he comes by at the end of the day to get his money to put in the bank, I could meet up with him."

"Wouldn't that make you a little nervous, somebody you don't know wants to meet up with you and a bagful of your money?"

Blair laughed. "You put it that way, yeah. Look, call the cops if you want. I'll wait right here. But don't call nine-one-one because this isn't an emergency. Just use the business number."

"I don't know it."

"You got a phone book, don't you? Look it up. And don't worry . . . I won't make any sudden moves."

A phone call to the Carbondale PD was enough to reassure the clerk that Blair wasn't a stickup man, but it didn't get the Kentucky cop any closer to finding Barton Laney. So he called Evan Cade in his hospital room.

"Hi. You feeling any better?" Blair asked.

"Sure. The flowers you sent picked me right up."

"I didn't send you any—" Blair realized Evan was jerking his chain again, but this time it made him laugh. "That was pretty good, Cade. You had me there for a second."

"I am feeling better," Evan admitted. "Less woozy."

"Listen, I'm still working this thing. Trying to look at it from another angle. And I'm wondering if maybe there isn't something you know about Barton Laney you haven't told me."

Evan wasn't quick to respond.

"So there is something. Well, if you're gonna take off, Cade, wouldn't it be a good idea to have someone back here doing something that might help you?"

"Barton Laney has four gas stations," Evan told Blair, "but he used to have eight."

Then Mr. Laney's wife got sick, Evan added, and the Laneys were uninsured. He had to sell off half his business and borrow against the rest in a losing fight to keep his wife alive. When Evan first met Pru there was a question whether she'd even be able to continue at the university. But just a few months ago Pru had told him that things were getting a lot better. She'd be able to stay in school and her dad was paying off his debts.

"Then up popped Ivar," Evan said.

Blair realized that Evan wasn't insulting him; he was seeing if Blair understood what had happened.

"How would Ivar have known things were looking up for Barton Laney?" Blair asked. "If Ivar had been extorting money from the man, and he'd tried the scheme, say, a year earlier, all Laney would have had to offer would be a stack of unpaid bills. So how would Ivar have known when to strike?"

"And where did Barton Laney get the money to eliminate his debts?" Evan added.

A moment of silence ensued, during which Blair came to a hurtful conclusion.

"Sonofabitch. Ivar was mixed up in something."

"And when he died under suspicious circumstances, who better to blame than a Cade?"

"Yeah," Blair agreed quietly.

"That guy we were looking for, the one Deena wants to find . . ."

"Yeah, he's the one to talk to, all right," Blair agreed.

When J. D. returned to the Refuge, he took Pickpocket's laptop out of the safe in the den. He booted it up and accessed stickyfingers.com. He hoped that there would be a response to his request for information about Roth and Danby, but there wasn't. There was no sign that the request had even been read.

You out there, Red? J. D. keyed into the computer. *Is John still with us?*

He waited several minutes without getting a reply. Pickpocket's private chat room had the air of an abandoned property.

You're probably just busy, both of you. But if you have the opportunity, I could really use your help. In addition to my prior request, there's someone else I'd like you to check out for me. His name is Donnel Timmons. . . .

He described Donnel as the owner of an auto-parts business, having contracts with Ford and GM, probably living and working in the greater Detroit area. He asked for all the information they could find on the man—but he didn't mention Donnel's service in the PANIC unit or his connection to the Rawley campaign.

J. D. didn't want the cyberinvestigation to come too close to him.

Assuming Red and Pickpocket were even still available to help him.

J. D. had just returned the little thief's laptop to the safe when the PCR beeped. He had e-mail. He briefly hoped that his computer wizards had chosen that means to get in touch with him. But when he read the message he saw it was from the blackmailer—upping the ante.

Our patience is wearing thin. Your performance is laggard. We've hired a second contractor. First one to complete the job wins. Runner-up suffers the consequences.

A second assassin, and J. D. had to beat him in the race to kill Del Rawley or Evan would be framed for murder.

He paused to consider if this was merely a ploy to turn up the pressure on him, force him to act regardless of whether he'd have to sacrifice himself to get his target. It could be a trick. Might even be a sign that the blackmailer was getting desperate.

He would have been inclined to think so . . . if Donnel hadn't been around.

If he hadn't read that story about a possible sniper in Denver.

For the first time, J. D. had to weigh a new possibility. Running. Hiding. Disappearing. Not just him, but Evan, too. He hadn't thought of it before because it meant Evan would have to live his life as a fugitive. But if a second assassin killed Del Rawley, and the only alternative was having Evan convicted for a murder he didn't commit, then it had to be considered.

Considered strongly.

In the meantime, he had a dinner appointment with Del Rawley to keep.

J. D. Cade stepped off the elevator outside of Del Rawley's suite. The Secret Service agent who rode up with him nodded to the two agents who met him as he exited the car. Another pair stood ready in front of the door to the suite. He was certain that more agents were stationed in the stairwells and on the roof.

One of the agents at the door spoke into a microphone at his wrist as J. D. approached, and another man opened the door from the inside. Nobody said a word to J. D. for good or ill.

Then Jenny appeared with a smile on her face.

"J. D., how nice to see you again." She took his arm and led him into a lavish suite.

"Nice digs," J. D. observed.

"It's the royal suite," Jenny said.

"*Royal?*"

"The hotel offered us the presidential suite—"

"But I thought that would be a mite presumptuous," Del Rawley concluded, entering the room. He shook J. D.'s hand and looked him in the eye. "You know, never give the opposition a chance to say you're getting ahead of yourself."

J. D. broke contact with the senator's eyes and looked around. "But this is okay?"

Jenny told him, "This is the only other suite the Secret Service approved for security reasons. After the attempt on Del's life, no one would dare begrudge him his security."

Del gestured J. D. to a conversational grouping of easy

chairs. Jenny asked what she could get them to drink. Del asked for a scotch, neat. J. D. requested mineral water.

As the two men sat down, Del inquired, "You're not a drinking man, Mr. Cade?"

"Gave it up almost twenty years ago." J. D. shrugged.

Rawley nodded and looked J. D. over. "Clean living certainly seems to agree with you, Mr. Cade. You look very fit for a man . . . well, you must be just about my age."

Del and J. D. accepted their drinks from Jenny. She sat down with one of her own.

"I'm fifty-three," J. D. said.

"Two years younger than me, then. You're not actually a California native, are you?"

"No. I was born and raised in southern Illinois. Carbondale."

"Carbondale. That's Senator Paul Simon's hometown, isn't it?"

"Makanda. Just a few miles up the road."

"That's right, Makanda." The candidate leaned forward. "I know I'm being nosy, but I like to be familiar with the people who speak on my behalf. You don't mind, do you?"

J. D. shrugged once more. "I'll let you know if I do."

J. D.'s candor made Del Rawley grin. He looked at Jenny. "We have a man who speaks his mind here. It's clear he's not sucking up for a job in Washington."

"No, that's not what I had in mind," J. D. replied.

"Good. Then you just tell me when I'm getting too personal. I'm curious about your army service, Mr. Cade. How is it that you were drafted? Didn't you have a student deferment?"

"I enlisted, Senator."

Del Rawley searched J. D.'s face. "You *believed* in the war?"

J. D. shook his head.

"Then why join up?"

"The war was an opportunity for me."

"In what way?"

"I wanted to show my father I was a better man than he was." J. D. momentarily lapsed into a memory that was plainly still potent for him. "My father was an infantry captain in World War Two. Saw a lot of fighting. Won a Silver Star in the Battle of the Bulge."

"You thought you had to live up to his record?" Jenny asked.

J. D. shook his head once more. "There was always an emotional barrier between my father and me. He never treated me badly; he just never let me get close. I was told that my father had been a very happy young man but the war had changed him. By the time the fighting in Vietnam started to get everyone's attention, my dad was already opposed to the war. He was a professor at SIU then, and he said anybody who ever opened a history book about twentieth-century war in Asia knew Vietnam was a lost cause."

"But you didn't believe him?" Del asked.

"I'd never read any of those books, and it wouldn't have mattered if I had. The war was my chance to rebel against my father. It was my opportunity to show him I could face the same kinds of trials he had . . . and not let any of them keep me from loving the people in my life."

"But the army, in its wisdom, gave you a clerical job," Del said.

J. D. nodded.

"Were you ever able to reconcile with your father?" Jenny wanted to know.

"No. He committed suicide while I was in Hawaii on R and R."

The door to the suite opened and, under Secret Service escort, a staff of waiters brought in dinner. Del Rawley stood up. "Why don't we eat now? I've done enough prying."

Jenny and J. D. also stood. Jenny put a gentle hand on his shoulder.

J. D. remained silent, wondering if he should feel any shame at using the story of his father's death to bring the inquisition to an end. He decided no shame was called for. It was about time his father was there when he needed him.

After dinner, Del suggested that Jenny find some quiet place to brief J. D. about the stops on the upcoming campaign swing and what he would be asked to say and do. Once they departed, the candidate poured himself another drink and returned to his preferred easy chair.

A moment later Special Agents Clarke and DeVito entered the room. At their request, the candidate hadn't told a soul that they were surreptitiously monitoring his dinner with J. D. Cade. Even Jenny Crenshaw hadn't known. Del gestured the men into the chairs opposite him.

"Well?" he asked.

Clarke glanced at DeVito and then responded to the candidate. "I didn't hear a single word I thought was a lie."

"Special Agent DeVito?"

"I didn't either," he admitted grudgingly. "In fact, everything he said agrees with what I've found out about him. His father taught history at Southern Illinois University. Jefferson Davis Cade enlisted in the army straight out of high school. His father committed suicide while he was in Hawaii on leave. He didn't tell you, but he was there with his girlfriend of the time, one Mary Ellen McCarthy."

Del Rawley smiled pensively.

"That mean something to you, Senator?" DeVito asked.

"Jenny told me that Mr. Cade said he'd let the girl he should have married get away. Probably this McCarthy girl he was with when he got the news about his father."

DeVito nodded, agreeing with Orpheus' speculation.

The candidate told him, "I assume you've been meticulous in your investigation of Mr. Cade—all without result."

"Yes, sir. But with all due respect, there are things you just can't know by looking at the documentary evidence. For instance, I had no idea that Mr. Cade's relationship with his father had been so strained. And, frankly, that was the one thing I heard that bothered me."

"What do you mean?"

"Well, if his father was a combat hero—and that will be easy enough to find out—why would Mr. Cade enlist in the army and then not demand to be in the infantry?"

Del Rawley chuckled. "You never served in the military, did you, Special Agent?"

DeVito stiffened. "No, sir. The war was over by the time I was eighteen. The draft had been abolished. I went to college and then into the Secret Service."

"I'm not questioning your courage, DeVito, only your knowledge of military life. Privates don't make demands of anyone. They are the lowest form of life in the world. If the army put you in a job back then, you did it and kept your mouth shut."

DeVito remained polite but refused to yield on his point.

"Yes, but couldn't he have *volunteered* for combat if that's what he really wanted? He was over there when the war was just about at its peak. If he wanted to prove something to his father, wouldn't he have been able to find some outfit that needed another soldier with a rifle?"

Del considered the question.

"Yes, undoubtedly he could have. But as you implied, there . . ." Rawley sighed as a host of memories returned to him. "There were a lot of grunts dying back then. The way things were, most 11-Bravos—infantrymen—would have thought they'd gone to heaven if they got a job in the rear; guys who were already in the rear weren't looking to head in the other direction. It's not hard for me to imagine that, despite his relationship with his father, young J. D. Cade landed in-country, took one look around, and decided he liked being a clerk just fine. Not many would have blamed him for making that choice, either. I certainly wouldn't."

"So where does all this leave us, Senator?" Clarke asked.

"I think we'll just accept Mr. Cade for who he is."

"But—" DeVito began.

Del Rawley held up his hand, cutting him off.

"There is one thing I've been meaning to ask you gentlemen, though I know it's highly unusual. Most likely unprecedented. But I was wondering—and I'd like to keep this strictly between us—could you provide a discreet but effective handgun that I might carry?"

"You want to be armed, Senator?" Clarke asked, surprised.

"No reflection on you gentlemen. Just think of it as a last line of defense."

The two agents looked at each other. Clarke was transparently dubious, but DeVito responded, "If I still get a vote around here, I say yes."

Jenny had invited J. D. to her suite for their planning discussion.

"You're sure this will look okay?" J. D. asked.

"Remember what I said at lunch? We're both single, we're both over twenty-one, we're—"

"How much over twenty-one are you?" J. D. asked.

The question just popped out. It surprised him that he'd made such a personal inquiry. He warned himself to be careful—something he seemed to have to do repeatedly around Jenny Crenshaw. He resented the fact that he couldn't be himself around her.

But then, if she knew who he really was, she'd run screaming for the Secret Service.

"I'm forty-four," she said. Her tone was neutral but she was watching carefully for his reaction.

"Don't look it," J. D. responded.

"Yeah, not a day over forty-three, right?" But she smiled when she said it. "Now, before you turn my girlish head, let's get to work, shall we?"

"Sure."

Jenny's digs were far more modest than Del's. There was a work area with a six-person conference table. Beyond that was a living room and a balcony. The door to the adjacent bedroom was ajar.

J. D. headed for the conference table, but Jenny said, "Let's be comfortable, okay? These long days are starting to do me in."

She plopped down on a sofa and kicked off her shoes. She opened a three-ring binder on her lap and patted the cushion next to her. J. D. took his place but was careful to leave room between her leg and his. Jenny bridged the gap with the open binder.

She outlined the itinerary for the next week: Fresno, Stockton, Eureka, San Jose, San Francisco, Palo Alto, Carmel, Newport Beach, San Diego, Palm Springs, and back to L.A.

J. D. said, "I'm new to all this, but that schedule looks pretty damn ambitious to me."

"It has to be," Jenny told him. "If we can hold our momentum in California, that'll take us to the first debate, in two weeks—and Del is just going to destroy the president once they're on the same stage together. So the coming days could well be what determines who wins in November."

J. D. nodded, lost in a moment's reverie.

"What are you thinking?" Jenny asked.

"I was just wondering about the cost of ambition. Doesn't the senator miss his family?"

"Of course he does. But after Chicago, he just won't risk their safety."

"Still, he must get lonely."

"Yeah, I imagine."

"Well, at least he still has you."

"Twenty-four hours a day," Jenny agreed.

"Would you happen to have layouts of the places where I'll be speaking?" J. D. asked. "I like to know my environment before I go to work."

"Absolutely."

Jenny flipped to the back of the binder; she had floor plans and photos of the rooms.

J. D. moved in closer for a better look. His leg now touched hers and his arm rested on the back of the sofa just above her shoulders.

It wasn't long before the campaign's business was out of the way and J. D. Cade and Jenny Crenshaw had their hands full of each other. J. D. kissed Jenny. She unbuttoned J. D.'s shirt, her blouse already off. J. D. moved his head back as Jenny slid his shirt off his shoulders. She gave him a frank and admiring stare.

J. D. told her, "Now I know why people get into politics."

"Only in this party," she told him. "The other party cares about nothing but money."

"Some people find that pretty sexy, too."

Jenny removed her bra.

"But what do they know?" J. D. asked.

He took Jenny in his arms and carried her to the bed. "Is this all right?" he asked, putting her down. "I mean, I haven't been with anyone new in a long, long time. Should I have let you carry me off to bed?"

Jenny pulled J. D.'s face down to meet hers. She kissed him and said, "Don't worry. I'll let you know just what I like and what I don't."

As she proceeded to show him what she meant, a small wedge of J. D.'s consciousness detached itself and looked on self-contemptuously, a voyeur from within. It was not concerned with passion, only calculation, and when their physical energies were spent and Jenny lay asleep amidst the rumpled sheets, it drove J. D. to slip out of bed without a sound. He picked up the tiny camera fitted into the remote for his car alarm. Then he silently photographed a nude Jenny Crenshaw.

The bitter irony of what he was doing was not lost on him.

He was falling in love with the woman whose life he intended to ruin.

Roth and Danby were in a room at the hotel two floors below the one where J. D. was taking his pictures. They were getting ready to go out and take care of a problem that had cropped up. Then Roth stopped what he was doing and looked at his friend.

"I can't tell you how much I want to kill that bastard," he said to Danby.

Danby snapped shut the case they would carry with them.

"You have been telling me ever since he almost killed us."

The horrifying experience of nearly being crushed to death had left Roth in a rage; it had made Danby reflective and wary. If Cade could pull off that rock slide stunt so neatly, who knew what other gruesome yet blameless fate he might plan for them?

Despite their predicament, Danby had to laugh.

"What's so funny?" Roth demanded.

"I was just thinking: That Cade is one *dangerous* fucker. We better watch out."

"*He's* the one who better watch out," Roth snarled. He grabbed the case from Danby. "Come on, let's go."

Danby followed. He'd been following his friend Roth for a long time now. But he thought, one way or another, this was going to be the last time.

J. D. Cade pushed through the revolving door of the Century Plaza Hotel.

Dante DeVito watched him from across the street. He sat in a lights-out sedan parked at the head of a ramp leading to an underground garage. He brought his wrist mike to his mouth.

"Does he look like a man who just got laid to you?" DeVito asked.

The figure of another agent appeared in the glassed-in entrance to the hotel lobby. "Me, I've always got a shit-eating grin when I get laid. This guy looks like his dog just died."

"Huh," DeVito grunted. He was sure that Jenny Crenshaw was backing Cade because she was sleeping with him. If he was wrong about that . . . shit, maybe Cade's gripe against Roth and Danby was legitimate.

"Valet's bringing Cade's car up," the agent told DeVito. "What do you want us to do?"

"Follow him home," DeVito responded. "Make sure he's tucked in for the night."

DeVito could have used some sleep himself. He was groggy. But he decided to go back to the campaign offices and look at his file on J. D. Cade one more time. Now that he knew there had been a serious rift between Cade and his old man, maybe something would jump out at him. If nothing did, though, he'd better just close the file and find something else to worry about.

He watched as first Cade's Lexus and then the tail car passed by. When they were out of sight, he switched on his engine and his lights. He told himself he was just following through on this Cade thing now. Even when things looked pointless, DeVito always followed through.

As he pulled out, he didn't notice that he was being followed.

J. D. didn't notice DeVito's men on his tail, either.

Dinner with Del Rawley, sex and betrayal with Jenny Crenshaw, and the second-assassin message had left him badly distracted, his thoughts maddeningly jumbled. He'd taken the first step of his plan to force Del Rawley out of the race without killing him . . . but what if that wasn't enough? What if there was an element of spite in the blackmailer's plan that required the candidate's *death*? Required that his blood be spilled by J. D.'s hand?

If so, what the blackmailer had also done was ratchet up the pressure on him to kill Roth and Danby, too. Because his only hope of getting away clean was if those two were out of the way.

He even asked himself whether he should take out Donnel. Who else could the second assassin be? But that thought made him recoil. Donnel had been his friend. His comrade. They shared the same sins.

With a growing sense of shame, he knew that he couldn't kill Donnel before he learned the truth, whether he was the second assassin. *If* there was a goddamn second assassin.

He was also sure that the more he came to know Del Rawley the harder it would be to take his life. He had to look for a way out until he had absolutely no choice.

But what about *Evan*? a voice in his head shrieked. You're taking too big a risk. Kill Rawley and be done with it. Sacrifice yourself if you have to, but save *Evan*!

As he pulled into the garage at the Refuge, he wondered if he was cracking up.

Yeah, he thought grimly, that could be the way to go.

Get to a place in his head where he wouldn't be responsible for his own actions.

Wouldn't matter then who he killed.

Evan Cade was drifting off to sleep, spending one more night in the hospital for observation, when there was a soft knock at his door. He looked up and saw Cousin Ben step into the room. It was well after visiting hours.

"Were you asleep?" Ben asked quietly, closing the door behind him.

"Just about."

"You feeling better?"

"I still get a little dizzy. It comes and goes."

Ben sat down in the visitor's chair next to the bed.

"Evan, there's something important I think you have a right to know."

Evan rubbed his eyes, coming alert now. He raised the bed to a sitting position.

"What is it, Ben?"

"Well, I heard from your grandma you're planning to go home to California."

"Yeah, but I intend to say goodbye to everyone first."

Ben nodded. "I figured as much . . . but I didn't know if we'd have the chance to speak privately."

"What is it?" Evan asked again.

Ben drew a deep breath and slowly let it out.

"You remember how we were talking at my house? When that McCray showed up?"

"Yeah." Evan remembered thinking Ben had been about to confide in him.

"Well, I think what I have to say has something to do with your current troubles."

Evan recalled the point at which their previous conversation had been interrupted.

"This is about Dad and Alvy McCray, isn't it?"

Ben nodded. "I figured out how J. D. took care of Alvy. I think I even know who helped him do it. And my gut tells me that somehow your daddy's past just won't stay buried."

Then Ben told Evan his story.

Deena Nokes and her sister biker mama, LuAnne, were seated on the late Ivar McCray's Harley at a red light on the outskirts of Carbondale when a car passed by on the cross street.

"Hey, that's him!" Deena yelped.

"Who?" LuAnne asked.

"The bastard we've been looking for. The guy who said he'd make Ivar rich."

"You sure?" LuAnne asked nervously. "All I saw was an old man driving and a girl."

"There was a guy in the backseat. The bastard who conned Ivar. So hold on."

Deena turned off her headlight, gunned the engine, and made a sharp left, running the red light. She followed the car to the entrance of Giant City State Park. Giant City was named for its huge formations of sandstone, which were piled up higgledy-piggledy as if a race of gargantuan toddlers had left their building blocks scattered across the landscape. It was filled with cliffs, ravines, streams, and caves. Hiking on many of its paths could be risky even in daylight, and after 11 P.M. the park was closed to all visitors except those staying at its lodge or cabins.

The car pulled into an empty parking lot. Deena cut the hog's engine and coasted to a stop in the shadow of a huge gum tree. By the light of a full moon, the two women watched. The car's driver and the young woman emerged. Then a man with a gun got out of the backseat.

The man Deena had been trying to find. He marched the other two off along a trail.

Deena snapped the Harley's kickstand down and dismounted. She reached around to the small of her back and grabbed her revolver.

She instructed LuAnne, "You count to a hundred. Not too fast, not too slow. Then ride on down to the lodge and call the cops. Tell them come quick, somebody's getting killed. Don't give your name, just get the hell out of there. Go to my place. If I get killed, you can have the Harley, the trailer, anything you want. Just don't rip me off if I'm only laid up in the hospital, okay?"

Terrified, LuAnne could only nod.

"Start countin'," Deena told her.

When she heard LuAnne begin, she ran off toward the path the others took.

Deena had been a country girl, raised rural. Had to use an outdoor privy until she was ten. She'd learned how to hike and climb and stalk at the same time she'd learned how to stand upright. But that had been a long time ago, and back then she'd had the advantage of being able to steal up on her prey barefoot, the soles of her feet toughened to the consistency of rawhide.

Now, at twenty-eight, she hadn't done any serious physical exercise since the eighth grade, and after all those years in shoes her feet had gone as soft as her conditioning. She was hard put not to wheeze as she followed her quarry, and no way was she going to take off her motorcycle boots.

But Deena had three things going for her: surprise, moonlight, and the whimpering of both the man and the girl. It wasn't loud, wasn't hysterical, but it carried a banshee note of death foretold. And it covered the grunts of her own exertions. Half a mile along the path, on a ledge overlooking a fast-running stream, the man with the gun called a halt to the forced march. He compelled his captives to get down on their knees. They leaned against each other, their bodies shaking, their sobs growing louder and more disconsolate.

As the man raised his gun, Deena lifted hers. She was at least a hundred feet away. Well outside of accurate range for a short-barreled revolver. But the moonlight was bright and her target was stationary. And she could imagine this same murderous sonofabitch holding his gun on Ivar, and then at the last second throwing the soldering iron in the puddle to electrocute him.

Deena fired her first shot.

She was too late to save the man because she missed. The man who'd been on his knees fell to his side, the blood pouring from his skull gleaming oily black in the moonglow.

Deena fired again and hit the bastard this time. Winged him on his left shoulder. She thought her shot might also have struck the girl because she started to crumple just before her executioner fired at her. Only after he saw that his two victims had been disposed of did the bastard even turn to see who was shooting at him.

Just as he did, Deena fired her third shot. Another hit. It looked to Deena like she took off the top half of the fucker's left ear.

The man flinched in pain, but that didn't stop him from locating Deena's position in a nest of rocks and returning fire. She ducked behind the cover of her sandstone barrier as bullets struck nearby. She scuttled to her left. She had only three shots left and knew she must use them to at least drive that sonofabitch off. She didn't want him coming after her.

She poked her head up and took a quick sighting. Sure enough, he'd just started her way. Deena fired again. She missed this time but the shot came close enough to make her adversary retreat. He was back on the ledge. Nowhere to hide there. Deena had to risk her last two shots. She wouldn't have a better chance than this.

Her next shot also missed, but the way the bastard's head snapped around, she could tell he'd felt it pass by, and this shot, too, drove him back. The bodies of his victims lay sprawled just behind him. He popped off two quick shots in Deena's direction, but they were aimed at the place she'd been before; he hadn't found her new spot.

Holding her breath, squinting her eyes, praying she didn't miss, Deena fired her last round. Again it was close, but again she missed her target. But she had the bastard back on his heels. He took yet another step in retreat.

As he did, the girl lying on the ground stuck her foot out.

Taken by surprise, the killer pitched backward, arms windmilling, and he went over the ledge, falling into the coursing water fifty feet below.

TEN
Sunday, September 19, 2004

DeVito had decided to make himself comfortable. He was using Jenny Crenshaw's office at campaign headquarters. It beat the hell out of sitting behind the cramped desk he'd been given at the back of the bullpen. He pored over his file on Crenshaw's squeeze, J. D. Cade.

He'd been at it for hours and was so tired that the words on the page in front of him started to swim. He shook his head. He dipped his fingers into the glass of drinking water that sat on the desk and rubbed his eyes. His vision cleared, but not very much and not for very long.

With damn near blind determination, DeVito pushed on. Try as he might, though, he couldn't come up with anything incriminating on J. D. Cade. On paper, as far as he'd been able to determine, the man was just who he said he was: an honest, successful businessman . . .

Honorably discharged veteran . . .

Father of a son in college . . .

Ex-husband who was decent enough to get along with his ex-wife. The prick.

Fucker had no known vices whatsoever.

Which made him just too good to be true. What did the

bastard do for fun? Sit at home, count his money, and diddle himself? There had to be something.

He got involved in presidential politics, that's what he did for fun. He appeared out of the blue—right after the man DeVito had sworn to protect with his life was almost assassinated—and before you knew it, he was having dinner with the man who might well be the next president of the United States. Which was just plain wrong.

Political junkies developed their habits early. Goddamn Cade hadn't even been registered to vote until a few weeks ago. And all of a sudden he bought his way in at the top? Uh-uh, didn't pass the smell test.

Except the fucker came right out and said that this was the first time in his life he ever felt an interest in politics. And what could DeVito say about that? Go up to Rawley and tell him, "Sorry, Senator, even you're not that magnetic and wonderful and awe-inspiring. Nobody is."

Sure, that'd go over big.

A thought crept up on DeVito's exhausted mind. Caught him when he wasn't looking and disappeared. It was the answer, or a possible answer, anyway, and he had to get it back. But he was so tired now that his *head* was swimming. He reached for the water glass again.

Fine motor control, however, had gone the way of sharp vision for DeVito. He overreached. Pulling back, he knocked the glass over. It went rolling and rattling off the desk.

"Fuck," DeVito muttered.

He bent over to pick up the glass, wondering if he'd fall out of his chair.

Just then a round from a high-powered rifle shattered the window behind him and tore through the file on J. D. Cade that he'd been attempting to read one second earlier. Energized by a flood tide of adrenaline, DeVito rolled away from the desk, chased by a second shot. He huddled in a corner.

Safe.

But DeVito knew at that moment he was just as lucky as Del Rawley to be alive.

Evan Cade was deeply asleep at 2:45 a.m.—it had been an hour and forty-five minutes since he'd last been checked to make sure he hadn't slipped into a coma—when the knot of yelling cops, nurses, and others burst into his room, throwing on the overhead light.

Evan tried to blink away what seemed like a very bad dream. Which promptly got worse when Chief Edwards blurted, "Evan Cade, you're under arrest!"

"What?" he managed to croak in disbelief.

A cop holding an open handcuff reached for Evan's arm, but a doctor intervened. The physician was very young and so puffed up and red-faced with anger that he looked as if he might start venting lava. Instead he let fly with a dire medical warning to the police chief.

"This patient presented with a head injury, the extent of which is still not known. He's being closely monitored to see that his condition does not worsen. If you forcibly remove him from this hospital and submit him to the rigors of arrest and incarceration, you may well jeopardize his health and even his life. If you proceed with this outrage, disregarding my advice to the contrary, my colleagues and I will be only too happy to testify at whatever criminal proceedings and civil actions are brought against you and your department."

Evan was completely awake now, cheered by the doctor's ferocious defense, and ready to offer a thought of his own.

"Besides all that," Evan told the chief, "anything bad happens to me, a great many people named Cade will be extremely unhappy with *you*."

The chief understood: Risk Evan Cade's life and his own jeopardy could well be mortal. Let *that* vengeance happen, there'd be no stopping a resumption of the feud. While Billy Edwards tried to decide what to do, Blair McCray stepped forward and whispered urgently into his ear.

The chief wasn't happy with what he heard but in the end he assented.

"Evan Cade," the chief told him, "you are under arrest and you will remain in this room under police guard until such time as you are fit to be taken into custody." Then he informed Evan of his Miranda rights.

Evan thought it was time to ask, "What's the charge, anyway?"

"The murder of Ivar McCray."

Evan looked at a grim-faced Blair for support but the Kentucky lawman held up a hand, pleading for Evan to be patient. When everyone else had left the room he talked to Evan.

"I don't think you did it. The chief does."

"Why?" Evan demanded. "Why now?"

Blair sat in the visitor's chair, clasped his hands, and hung his head.

"What happened?" Evan asked anxiously.

Blair looked up at him and said softly, "Barton Laney was killed. Shot in the head."

"Oh, Jesus!" Evan gasped. Then he turned pale and shook his head. "Oh, no! Don't tell me . . . please don't tell me . . ."

But Blair did. "Prudence Laney was also shot in the head. She's alive and has been in surgery almost the past three hours. But . . . what I heard, the damage is terrible."

Tears streamed down Evan's cheeks. He couldn't speak. Blair put his hand on Evan's shoulder and then delivered more bad news.

"It happened at Giant City. The responding officers found your shoes in the trunk of the Laneys' car. The shoes that made the footprints next to Ivar's body. They were in a plastic bag."

"Evan Cade has been arrested, sir," the Toad told the Gardener after he'd woken him. "He's being held under guard in a hospital room."

The Gardener pulled himself upright in bed. "Why was he arrested?"

The Toad relayed the report he'd received from Farrel in Illinois.

"That bastard Farrel panicked," the Gardener said, his anger building. "He saw a single hick lawman poking around and he panicked."

"Yes, sir."

"The Laneys had to be killed, but not this soon. They were to disappear *after* Evan Cade had been arrested for Ivar McCray's murder, to make it look like his family had disposed of them to keep them from testifying against him."

"Farrel was not your hire, sir," the Toad reminded him.

"Neither were Roth and Danby." The Gardener swung his legs out of bed and planted his feet in his slippers. He stood and pulled on his robe. "Do you think Blair McCray will be content to stop his snooping now, Harold?"

"No, sir."

"Neither do I. And now we also have to contend with this person who saw Farrel kill the Laneys and then tried to kill him."

"What do you propose to do, sir?"

"I propose we take the situation in hand," the Gardener said, heading for his bathroom. "You're going to Illinois. I'm going to California."

The Gardener stopped abruptly, bringing the Toad up short. "This is going to hit J. D. Cade hard. We'd better contact him again, Harold, and suggest all this is another turn of the screw. Wouldn't do to let Cade think that control of the situation is slipping away from us."

Dixie Wynne was driving east on the Blue Ridge Parkway that Sunday morning. The rising sun made him squint as he pointed his GMC 4 x 4 toward Asheville, North Carolina. He hadn't come down off his mountain to keep holy the Lord's Day. Neither had he left his redoubt to stock up on food, water, or ammunition. He was fixed just fine for those necessities, and he figured he could hold out in the mountains indefinitely.

What was bringing Dixie back to civilization was the fact that today his favorite football team, the Jacksonville Jaguars, was playing the Green Bay Fucking Packers, who'd beaten his Jags in the Super Bowl back in January. Dixie would be dipped in shit before he let a little thing like smoking D'antron Nickels keep him from seeing this rematch.

In fact, the tremendous gravity of the NFL season was tugging him back in the direction of home. Sure, he could make do with some sports bar today, but he longed to spend the remaining weeks of the season watching from his own easy chair, as was the God-given right of any American male. Not having heard a single news report on his radio that a search was under way for him in connection with the Nickels shooting, he was inclined to believe he'd be allowed to exercise that fundamental right.

But just to be on the safe side, before he got to Asheville

he pulled into a service station and put in a call to his next-door neighbor, Tag Olney. Tag's daughter, Nikki, had married a psycho who refused to recognize their divorce decree—until as a favor to the family Dixie had counseled him on what a .50 caliber round from his Barrett M82A1 would do to the psycho's head. At that point the gift of reason returned to the young man and he departed, never to be seen again.

Dixie's call was answered on the first ring.

"Hey, T. O., how's it going, buddy?" he asked.

"Dixie, is that you?"

"None other. My house hasn't burned down while I've been away, has it?"

"No, no. It's right there where you left it."

"Anybody been by asking questions about me?"

There was a hesitation that Dixie didn't like, and then his friend said no, not lately.

"Not lately?" Dixie echoed.

"Well, there was this one fella, you know. You musta forgot to stop your mail or somethin', and one day I saw this fella go up to your box and start pullin' things out. I went over and asked him what the hell he thought he was doin'. He showed me a badge and said he was a postal inspector. Your carrier told him about all the mail buildin' up and he come out to see for himself. Said he was puttin' a thirty-day hold on all your mail. Nobody's been around since him."

"That was nice of you to check, T. O. Fact is, though, I did forget to stop my mail."

"Don't you worry about your place, Dixie. Don't worry about *nothin'*. I'm keeping a good eye on things for you."

"Thanks, buddy. I appreciate it. So long."

Tag Olney hung up his phone to break the connection. Then he lifted the receiver and, without punching in a phone number, shouted into it, "You hear that, you miserable sonofabitch?"

But the fact was, Alachua County state attorney Colman Crisp had only hinted that he would be tapping the phones of Dixie Wynne's neighbors. What he'd *promised* was that he would charge any of them who had contact with Dixie and didn't report it to his office with hindering prosecution and see that they did hard time.

Feeling he was a worse traitor than goddamn Benedict Arnold, Tag Olney called the state attorney's office. Nobody was there on Sunday, of course, so he had to leave his message on Crisp's voice mail. He hoped the damn machine went down and the message never got through. Wouldn't be his fault if that happened; he'd have played his Judas part.

He also hoped Dixie took his message not to worry about a thing as the warning to stay away he'd meant it to be. But Tag Olney felt so shitty about what he'd done he got drunk and didn't even watch the Jacksonville–Green Bay game.

J. D. lay in bed awake under the still-dark California sky. From the nightstand next to the bed came the screen glow of Pickpocket's laptop computer. J. D. had left it there, up and running with the AC adapter on, locked onto the secret chat room. He'd checked a thousand times during the night to see if Red or the little thief would get back to him, and each time he'd been disappointed. Then, just as the first streak of predawn gray appeared in the sky, Pickpocket came online.

I'm back.

You're recovering? J. D. asked.

Yeah. Red says my scars look sexy.

I need your help.

I know. I have a clone of your cloned PCR. I've read all your e-mail.

J. D. remembered Red telling him that.

Sonofabitch who shot me thinks I'm one of Santa's little helpers, huh? He'll learn.

Despite everything, J. D. had to smile.

Got the information you wanted on Roth and Danby. Timmons next. Plus I have a few other thoughts to pursue.

Thanks for your help.

Thanks for saving my ass. I'll get back to you. Download R&D file now.

J. D. did and read the file immediately.

According to the data Pickpocket had collected, Roth and Danby were the Bobbsey twins in olive drab. Classmates and teammates at West Point, they had spent their entire military careers together. From postings with the 82nd Airborne at the beginning of their service to a two-year stint with the Defense Intelligence Agency at the end, they'd marched in lockstep.

Then, having topped out in rank, Roth a colonel and Danby a lieutenant colonel, the two men abruptly switched to the civilian side of government, the Treasury Department. They signed on with a newly formed unit called Departmental Internal Management and Oversight (DEIMOS).

Pickpocket informed J. D. that so far he'd been unable to find a description of this unit's responsibilities or the name of the person who headed it. The little thief said he'd keep on looking for that information.

Whatever nominal job description Pickpocket might find, J. D. knew in his bones that Roth and Danby were waiting to take him out. They had a perfect cover. Working among the Secret Service, it would be their *job* to shoot him as soon as he killed Del Rawley. Those two fucks, they'd probably get medals for smoking him.

Not to mention the personal satisfaction.

J. D. returned Pickpocket's computer to the safe in the den, showered, and was getting dressed when the PCR beeped: e-mail. Had to be from the blackmailer, he thought. He called up the message.

Your son is now in custody. Worst yet to come.

J. D. felt a killing rage surge through him . . . then he remembered Pickpocket had set up the clone to send e-mail as well as receive it. He clicked the reply icon and spoke clearly for the voice-recognition software.

"You've just made a very bad mistake," he told his blackmailer. "I was close to achieving our goal. Now you've left me no choice but to break away from my effort. If there is a second contractor, if you make it impossible for me to succeed, then my life's work will become finding you—only you won't know it when I do."

J. D. hit the send button and clicked off the PCR.

"Because you never hear the shot that kills you," he said aloud.

Before he could take his next step, the phone rang. It was his mother.

"J. D., something terrible's happened. Evan's been arrested and . . ."

He listened closely to his mother's recitation of events. He became so angry he began to shake. "I'm coming home, Mom. Tell Evan I'll be there as soon as I can."

J. D. managed to charter an executive jet for the flight and threw two changes of clothes into a garment bag. Just as he was ready to leave for Santa Monica's small airfield, where the plane stood waiting, his doorbell rang. When he opened the door, he saw Jenny. She'd brought another breakfast, but she immediately saw that something was wrong.

"What is it?" she asked.

J. D. replied, "A family emergency. Can you give me a ride to the airport?"

She could and did. The Sunday morning traffic was

light and when J. D. told her what had happened, Jenny took her eyes off the road to look at him. "Your son was arrested for *murder*?"

"Yes," he confirmed.

"What happened?"

"I have very few details. My mother just called and I know only two things for sure: my son is in a hospital room under police guard, and he wouldn't kill anyone."

"Who died?"

"A man named Ivar McCray."

"Why would the police think your son killed him?"

J. D. sketched a quick outline of the hostilities between the Cades and the McCrays.

"Your family is party to a blood feud?"

"I thought it was history but it seems someone is trying to stir the kettle again."

Five minutes later they arrived at the airport.

"I hope everything works out for your son," Jenny told J. D., sympathizing with the tension she saw in his face.

He nodded. Then he said, "I'm really sorry about leaving you in the lurch. About speaking for the senator, I mean. Please give him my regrets."

"He'll understand. He left the campaign for a family emergency himself, remember?"

J. D. took Jenny's hand. "I like to finish the things I start."

"Me too."

"I understand someone in my position wouldn't reflect well on the campaign. But if you ever need me to write another check, just let me know." J. D. kissed Jenny. "And when I get back, after the campaign if not sooner, I still want to see you."

"I'd like that, too." She repaid J. D.'s kiss with one of her own.

He stepped out of the car, grabbed his suitcase and Pick-pocket's laptop from the backseat, and was gone with a wave.

Jenny watched him go. A son arrested for murder? A blood feud? J. D. Cade had been a hard man to pin down from the start and now she was even less certain of who he was. But after last night she definitely wanted to see him again. And sooner rather than later.

The FBI let DeVito sleep for all of three hours before they woke him for a second round of questioning. His answers were the same as the first time through. He'd been working late, using Ms. Crenshaw's office so he could stretch out. He'd knocked over a glass of water and just as he bent over to pick it up, bang-boom. Somebody was shooting at him. He'd scuttled into a corner, and as soon as he thought it was safe, he called for help.

Was the file on J. D. Cade of any significance? the FBI wanted to know.

"No, it's just a background check on someone who's joined the campaign. I was closing out the file, in fact. You're welcome to look; it all seems pretty harmless to me."

The FBI, which bore the burden of investigating the attempt on Del Rawley's life, now had the added responsibility of investigating the attempt on DeVito's life. DeVito understood that they had their job to do and he told them what he knew. But there was no love lost between the FBI and the Secret Service just then. Each felt the other had fucked up royally at its primary function. The Secret Service had failed to stop the assassination attempt on Orpheus, and the FBI had been unable to find the assassin ever since.

Now the Secret Service faced the added embarrassment

of almost having one of its own agents assassinated. The situation didn't reflect well on anybody or make for a close working relationship. So while DeVito told his counterparts at the bureau everything he knew, he didn't tell them everything he suspected.

What he'd come to suspect—to the point where he'd bet the pension he still hoped to get—was that Cade was linked to Roth and Danby by something more than an unfounded suspicion of the former by the latter. If nothing else, DeVito had ticked off all three men recently, and whoever had tried to shoot him had to be somebody he'd pissed off very badly.

Then there was the fact that he'd felt something was wrong with Cade, Roth, and Danby right from the start. All of them, each of them. That was another thing they had in common.

He'd been tempted to sic the FBI on Roth and Danby. He couldn't do it, though. There were tribal loyalties to be observed. The FBI was Justice Department; the Secret Service was Treasury. If you fouled your own nest, DeVito thought, then it was your job to clean it up.

Looking at it that way, DeVito decided his best bet was to keep going after Cade. Cade might have Jenny Crenshaw in his corner but he had no official standing. He'd be the one who could make the least trouble for DeVito; he'd be the one who was the most vulnerable.

That strategy fit perfectly with the only good thing that had happened to DeVito all morning. He'd captured the thought that had eluded him in the moment before he'd almost died: Check Cade's *recent* past—the last few weeks, months, maybe a year—to see if something unusual prompted his sudden interest in presidential politics. The man's overall history might look squeaky clean but maybe something kinky had cropped up lately.

Something that had landed him smack in the middle of the Rawley campaign.

Special Agent Charlie Clarke walked into the interview room at the federal building where the FBI had been talking to DeVito. Clarke had escorted him there for the beginning of the session and then gone to inform Orpheus of what had happened.

"Come on, DeVito, you're free," the agent in charge said. "I went bail for you."

"You're a card, Charlie."

Despite the lame humor, DeVito was glad to see one of his own. On the drive back to the Century Plaza, Clarke asked DeVito how he was feeling.

"Fine, I'm fine."

"You see a doctor yet?"

"What for? I didn't even get nicked."

"How about your general state of mind, if nothing else?"

"My mind's clear as a bell."

"Yeah?" Clarke looked him over closely, then he said, "Well, you won't have to worry about Cade anymore."

Surprise painted a clown mask on DeVito's face. "Why not?"

"He's left the campaign."

"Why?"

"Family emergency. Jenny Crenshaw just told me his son was arrested and charged with a murder in southern Illinois. Cade flew there this morning to be with him."

Bingo, DeVito thought. Something big—and bad—had just happened to Cade.

Clarke looked at him strangely. "You're smiling, DeVito. A kid getting charged with murder strike you as funny?"

"You know, Charlie, maybe I could use a day or two off."

"Take whatever time you need. Just don't do anything either of us will regret."

DeVito swore he wouldn't but Clarke saw the gleam in those dark Sicilian eyes. DeVito had some kind of plan. For the moment, Clarke was just as glad he didn't know what it was.

He had a million things to do, and when he got back to his command post he was given an urgent message to call Ted Reineke, the special agent in charge of the FBI's local office. Reineke told him he'd just had a call from the LAPD. The two agencies were going to stage a raid off an anonymous tip the cops had received moments ago about the sighting of a man with what had been described as a "sniper kind of rifle." If Charlie was interested, he could get in on it.

The raid took place at an apartment complex for white-collar transients in Marina Del Rey. The apartments were month-to-month furnished rentals for businesspeople arriving in L.A. with new jobs but no permanent place to live. The reputation of the place said it was filled with exciting young professionals who carried on like libertines because they were all away from home and everybody understood that no commitment lasted longer than a weekend. In other words, faces were soon forgotten, and intentionally so.

The combined forces of the LAPD, the FBI, and the Secret Service took three hours to prepare for their strike. During that time, they ascertained that the tenant in their target apartment had obtained his digs under a false identity. They also evacuated the rest of the complex and had to call for more cops to keep the titillated residents from creeping back for a better look at the action.

When the media inevitably arrived, a lie was blandly passed out that the object of official attention was the head of a huge counterfeiting operation. Which explained the federal presence.

The actual assault on the apartment was loud but in no

way life-threatening. Nobody was home. None of the law-enforcement types thought it was wasted effort, however.

Inside the premises they found a McLellan M-100 rifle.

J. D. Cade returned home for the first time in thirty-three years.

He took a taxi directly to University Hospital, asked a blue-haired lady behind the information desk for his son's room number, and was striding toward the elevators when someone called his name.

"Mr. Cade?"

J. D. stopped and saw he'd been addressed by a muscular young man whom J. D. was sure he'd never met before . . . but somehow looked familiar. The man extended his hand and J. D. cautiously took it.

"You are J. D. Cade, aren't you, sir?"

"Yes."

"I recognized you the moment I saw you walking toward me. You couldn't be anybody but Evan's daddy. I'm a friend of your son."

"What's your name?" J. D. asked.

"Blair McCray."

J. D. released Blair's hand and made sure he kept his expression neutral, but there was something about this young man that made J. D. peer at him closely.

"I tried to visit with Evan just now, Mr. Cade, but there was a lot of your kin up there and I thought I'd better come back later. I already told Evan I think he's being set up, but if you'd let him know that I mean to prove it, I'd appreciate it."

J. D. nodded and expressed his thanks. He still couldn't figure out who Blair McCray reminded him of.

Blair recognized J. D.'s scrutiny and answered his unspoken question. "If I look familiar, maybe it's because I heard

that one time you had a run-in with my daddy. Alvy Mc-
Cray."

"Yes, I did," J. D. admitted impassively.

He wondered if the violence would ever really end.
Then Blair McCray gave him a small measure of hope.

"Mr. Cade, I just want to say I'm sorry for everything
that's happened."

"So am I, Mr. McCray. So am I."

Then J. D. Cade said he had to see his son and left.

J. D. was mobbed by aunts, uncles, and cousins until his
mother raised her voice above the din and demanded, "Let
me see my son!"

The crowd parted and Belle Cade stepped forward and
hugged J. D. Then they moved off from the others and sat
side by side in a small lounge at the end of the corridor.
Belle held her son's hand.

"I'm so glad you're here, J. D.," she told him. "When I
heard Evan had been arrested . . . well, I can't recall ever
being so angry."

"Neither can I, Mom. Where do we stand with the murder charge?"

Belle pointed out a man standing among all the Cades
down the hall. "That's Richard Shuster, Evan's defense attorney. He took a sworn statement from a clerk who works
at the Salvation Army store. The clerk remembers Evan's
shoes—the ones the police found—being part of a package
I'd donated two weeks before Ivar McCray died. Mr. Shuster is going to file a motion in court tomorrow to have the
charges against Evan dismissed. What we don't know yet
was who bought the shoes from the resale shop or if they
were stolen. Mr. Shuster told me that's what the police
could claim: Evan had someone buy—or steal—the shoes
back for him. But Mr. Shuster said the chances are very

good that he'd be able to create a sense of reasonable doubt if the case ever comes before a jury."

"I don't want it to get that far," J. D. told his mother. He asked her if anyone was in the room with Evan now.

"No. The guard lets only one of us in at a time, and Evan is sleeping. But you go right in." Then Belle Cade kissed her son's cheek. "It's so good to finally have you home again."

J. D. entered Evan's room without disturbing him. He removed his son's laptop computer and that morning's newspaper from the seat of the visitor's chair and placed them on the bedside tray. He sat down and simply watched Evan sleep.

It was something that had fascinated him since his son was an infant, and it took him back to a far more peaceful time. He realized that Evan was an adult now, but, sleeping peacefully, he looked so impossibly young and innocent that it made J. D.'s heart ache.

When Evan opened his eyes a half hour later and saw his father sitting next to him he exclaimed, "Dad!"

J. D. reached out and took his son's hand. "How are you?"

Evan looked toward the room's door, which was tightly closed. Still, he answered quietly. "It depends on who's asking."

"I am."

"Physically, I'm doing better."

"And otherwise?"

"Dad, this situation has gotten very bad."

He told J. D. what had happened to the Laneys.

"I'm so sorry, Evan." J. D. let go of his son's hand. He knew he was responsible, at least in part, for the violence that had befallen the Laneys. He wanted to look away but forced himself to meet Evan's eyes. "We have to talk."

"I know."

Evan saw that his father was looking for a way to begin and gave him a running start.

"Cousin Ben told me about Dr. Skipaniak."

J. D.'s eyes widened in surprise. "How did he find out about Skip?"

"He read a story in the St. Louis paper."

Evan told his father how Ben Cade had never gotten over his suspicion that his cousin J. D. had somehow managed to contrive the death of Alvy McCray to spare him the need to commit murder and save the rest of the Cade family from a resumption of the feud. Each spring for several years Ben had gone to the spot where Alvy's pickup had struck the deer, hoping to figure out how J. D. had done it.

He'd never managed to arrive at a solution, until one day he read a story in the newspaper of how the chief veterinarian at the St. Louis Zoo, Dr. Steven Skipaniak, had brought down a tiger that had escaped from a derailed circus train. Rather than kill the animal, Dr. Skipaniak had fired a dart filled with muscle relaxant to immobilize the animal.

Ben had thought if a tiger could be darted, why not a deer?

"He called Dr. Skipaniak at the zoo, Dad, to talk to him about it. When the doctor's secretary asked who was calling, Ben gave his name as Mr. Cade."

"Skip thought Ben was me."

Evan nodded. "Ben hung up. But he knew he had the first part of the scheme figured out. You darted a deer. Then he guessed you tied it to a tree. Finally, he worked it out that you severed the deer's restraint at just the right moment—probably with a rifle shot—and defined the path of where you wanted the deer to run by marking it with the urine of predators. With a friend like Dr. Skipaniak, you shouldn't have had any trouble getting what you needed."

"Ben has always been a smart, determined man," J. D. said. He supposed he should be grateful the police—or the McCrays—hadn't been as dogged in their investigation of Alvy's "accident."

"How'd you know Dr. Skipaniak?" Evan asked.

"He's a fellow army veteran. I met him when I was buying a stethoscope as a gift for Mary Ellen McCarthy. She'd just been accepted to med school."

After a moment's silence, Evan said to his father, "Ben told me his story only after he heard I was going home . . . and because he thinks what happened then is somehow tied in to what's happening now."

J. D. nodded. Then he asked his son, "So how do you feel now that you know?"

"Damn shame about that deer," Evan told his father.

"How do you really feel?" J. D. persisted.

Evan took a moment to arrive at his answer.

"I think you took one life to save many others. I think that's what you must have had in mind."

Evan had neatly paraphrased the sniper's code, J. D. thought. *Think of the lives you're saving, not the one you're taking.* In effect, his son had absolved him . . . of the killing he knew about. But J. D. felt that now was the time he must bare his soul—as far as he dared—to Evan. Now was the time Evan might be ready to forgive him.

"Alvy McCray wasn't the only man I killed."

Evan went pale. "Who else?"

J. D. revealed to his son what he had really done in the army—including how he'd shot a U.S. Army major whom a friend of J. D.'s had described to him as "a gung-ho lifer prick who's going to get me and a lot of other grunts killed just so he can make colonel."

J. D. had taken a captured NVA sniper rifle from the

PANIC armory to do the job, but in an act of reckless bravado had returned the weapon uncleaned. To show *his* asshole commanding officer that one of his men had gone off hunting on his own.

Evan offered no words of judgment. He just asked quietly, "What happened to your friend?"

J. D. sighed. "He died. He was fatally bitten by one of the vipers they have over there. If he had to go anyway, I just wish it had been before I . . ."

Father and son lapsed into a long interlude of quiet. During which J. D. thought bleakly that maybe his son wouldn't forgive him. Maybe he'd just lost Evan.

Finally J. D. broke the silence. "Did you know that Blair McCray is Alvy's son?"

The way Evan's mouth fell open, he clearly didn't.

"Yeah," J. D. affirmed. "I ran into him in the hospital lobby. He introduced himself and asked me to tell you he intends to prove you're being framed. He said he was your friend."

J. D. watched his son grapple with that idea.

"Yeah, I guess he is now."

"You think his feelings might change if he knew what I did?"

Evan had no answer for that.

"I've tried to protect you all your life," J. D. told his son, "but I'm the one who put you in the middle of this mess. All I want now is for you to come through it unharmed. I'm going to do everything I can to see that happens. So I have to ask you, Evan—I have to *beg* you—to let me be the one to put an end to it."

Evan looked away from his father and stared out the window for a long time.

When he looked back, there were tears rolling down his cheeks.

He said, "Dad, the bastard who's trying to frame me shot

Pru. Killed Mr. Laney, then shot Pru in the head . . . after I let her walk away without trying to stop her."

"I know, Evan, but—"

Evan stubbornly shook his head.

"How would you have felt, Dad, if someone had shot Mary Ellen McCarthy?"

Del Rawley stepped in front of a mob of reporters in a large conference room at his hotel. His face was grim. His gaze swept all of those present, giving them a chance to look into his eyes. Then he directed his attention at the pool TV camera that would carry his image to the nation.

"This campaign," he said, "will not be stopped."

He paused to let the message sink in.

"By now all of you know that early this morning a member of my security detail, a special agent of the Secret Service, was almost killed by a sniper. He was sitting at a desk in the office of my campaign manager when two rifle shots were fired through the window. These shots came within inches of killing a man of the utmost courage and loyalty. Someone who, like all his colleagues, would step into the line of fire to save the person he is assigned to protect.

"I was nowhere near this particular agent at the time of the shooting. I was never in any physical danger. After conferring with the Secret Service and my campaign staff, we've decided that this cowardly act was intended to serve as a warning that no matter how much protection I have, I will never be safe. It was a bald-faced attempt at intimidation, a symbolic threat to drive me from the race."

Del set his jaw and there was fire in his eyes.

"To the assassins who would substitute the tyranny of the gun for the will of the people, I tell you now that you will *not* win. The American people will not be denied, either by me or by you, their democratic birthright to choose their next president. I have spoken with my family and we are in agreement. We will not run from you. You will *never* drive me from this race. Nor will you succeed in your deadly and hateful ambitions. You will fail. You will be caught. You will be punished.

"Just as soon as we are done here today, I will leave to keep my full schedule of appearances. If you attempt to interfere, you will do so at *your* peril.

"This campaign will not be stopped."

There was a brief moment of silence and then the room erupted in applause, with even the members of the media joining in.

Jenny watched from the wings with tears of pride in her eyes. With her were the other members of the brain trust and Donnel Timmons. Secret Service agents were everywhere. Among them were Roth and Danby.

Del accepted the embraces and handshakes of Jenny and the others as he left the room.

Looking around, he noticed that someone was missing.

"Where's Mr. Cade?" he asked Jenny.

She took the candidate's arm and, excusing the two of them from the others, led him off several paces—a ring of agents moving with them—to a place of relative privacy. There she explained in a quiet voice what had happened to J. D. Cade.

Del Rawley cut to the heart of the matter. "Did the boy do it?"

"J. D. says no, he couldn't have."

"Normal reaction for a father. What do you think?"

"I don't know. I hope not. We'll have to wait and see."

"So we won't be using Mr. Cade."

"He said he understood how things would look. But he offered to make further contributions if we need them."

Del Rawley considered the situation, made private deliberations.

"I enjoyed talking with Mr. Cade last night. We seem to have a lot in common."

"I enjoyed last night, too," Jenny said.

"Let me know how all this turns out. We may not be done with that gentleman yet."

Jenny nodded. "Okay."

Del Rawley walked off, a man on a mission.

DeVito intended to look for the real J. D. Cade in the places he'd called home. He headed for Santa Barbara first. It was closer. But he intended to visit southern Illinois as well.

He had Cade's Santa Barbara address and every intention of breaking into his house. It would be a black-bag job, but he didn't care. He wasn't looking for evidence to convict Cade of anything; he was looking for justification to shoot the sonofabitch when the time came.

He was sure that come it would. He felt it in his bones that Cade would be back.

But when DeVito arrived in Santa Barbara he was immediately frustrated. A huge birthday party was going on at the house next door to Cade's place. It spilled out all around the house and looked as if it was just cranking up. HAPPY 65TH, GEORGE! a banner read. Drop dead, George, DeVito thought, and take everybody to the hospital with you. But he knew he'd have to come back later. Probably much later, and he didn't feel like he had a hell of a lot of time.

Since he was in town, though, DeVito knew there was someone else he could see. He'd pay a visit to the former Mrs. Cade. Maybe Cade's ex wasn't quite as chummy with him as she seemed on paper. Maybe she'd have a few poisonous and revealing things to say about her former husband. DeVito found his way to a large house near the mission.

What Bonnie Evans Cade told Special Agent Dante De-Vito was: "Get the hell out of my house and off my property, and don't come back without a warrant, you prick!"

DeVito left but not fast enough to keep the door from, in fact, hitting him in the ass.

He was about to bull his way back into Bonnie Cade's home when a weasely-looking little guy hissed and beckoned to him from the corner of the house. Then the little guy disappeared without even waiting to see if DeVito followed.

The weasel was standing in the driveway, screened from the view of anyone in the house by a tall clump of hydrangeas. He introduced himself as Raymond Washburn, Bonnie Cade's current husband—but only until he could find a lawyer who could break his prenuptial agreement.

Washburn began to spew exactly the kind of bile about the former Mrs. Cade that DeVito had hoped she would spill about her ex. DeVito asked the bitter little man if he knew J. D. Cade.

"Only slightly," Washburn conceded.

"To your knowledge, did he ever commit an act of violence against anyone?"

"No."

"Did he ever engage in any illegal practice in the business he co-owned with his ex-wife?"

"Bonnie won't let me see the books."

DeVito started to lose patience. This little turd just wanted someone to listen to him bitch.

"Did Mr. Cade ever spit on the sidewalk in your presence?"

Raymond Washburn knew when he was being insulted. "He's never done anything criminal that I've seen—but I'm *afraid* of him."

"Why would that be, Raymond?"

"Because I fucked his wife."

"Yes, but she's *your* wife now, even if you aren't too happy with her."

"I mean I fucked Bonnie when she was still married to him, and he knows about it."

DeVito found this somewhat more interesting, but there was an obvious question to ask. "How *long* has he known about it?"

"Almost two years," Washburn admitted.

DeVito turned to walk away, but the little man grabbed his arm—until DeVito gave him a hard stare.

"He's very cool and calculating, that man. Patient. He could wait a long time."

"Maybe forever, huh, Raymond?" DeVito smirked.

"You'd be afraid, too," Washburn accused, and then he spoke the words that rang in DeVito's ears like thunder, "if someone was after you who shoots the way J. D. Cade does."

"Yeah, J. D. Cade shoots here, has for years," said Jack Wesley, the manager of the Rancho Durango Gun Club.

DeVito couldn't understand it. He'd checked out J. D. Cade down to the dirt under his fingernails—on paper, anyway. And he hadn't found any dirt. Nor had he found any record of J. D. Cade belonging to a gun club. He didn't understand how—

"Is he listed as a member under his own name?" DeVito demanded.

"In a manner of speaking."

"What the fuck is that supposed to mean?"

Jack Wesley didn't like DeVito's attitude one bit. He answered through clenched teeth. "What it means, Mr. Federal Agent, sir, is that Mr. Cade joined the club when my predecessor ran things here. Bert was just about retired, but his hearing had checked out a couple years prior to that. At that time Mr. Cade sometimes used his first name. Jeff. Short for Jefferson. He gave Bert his name as Jeff D. Cade. Which Bert wrote down as Jeff *Decade*. Bert caught the mistake eventually, but Mr. Cade just laughed when it was brought to his attention. Said might as well leave it that way. He seemed to shoot okay under that name."

"And how well does Mr. Cade shoot?"

"Just like I said. He shoots okay."

"You feel comfortable repeating that characterization in court someday?"

"I'll feel comfortable when you get your ass off this property. You got any more threats to make, I'll feel comfortable talking to my lawyer."

The sonofabitch wasn't going to give an inch, DeVito could see. Push him harder, he'd just dig in deeper. No point in that now. He could come back for this asshole later if need be.

He'd already found out the important thing.

J. D. Cade was a shooter.

After Blair McCray left the hospital, he thought it might be a good idea to pay Deena Nokes a visit. See if his cousin Ivar's widow might have found out something helpful.

He drove out to her place in the woods and knocked on the door of the trailer. He looked around for Gorbachev the bear or any other potential threat. He wasn't authorized to carry a weapon in Illinois but, with the Laneys getting shot, he was doing so anyway. He wasn't about to go down without a fight.

There was no response to Blair's rapping on Deena's door . . . but he thought he heard a muffled whimpering coming from inside. He tried the door but it was locked. The rattle of the doorknob seemed to momentarily increase the volume and the pitch of the weeping, and then the sound was bitten off. Whoever was inside had realized her voice could be heard.

"I don't mean you any harm," Blair called out to the woman in the trailer.

"You don't have to shout," came a voice from behind him. "LuAnne 'n' I can hear you."

Blair turned quickly to see Deena Nokes. Gorbachev was with her. The bear started to growl and showed some truly fearsome teeth and claws. But Deena realized the bear was scaring her visitor for no good reason.

"He's family, Gorby," she told the animal. With a whack on the bear's rear, she added, "Go on, git. Back to the woods until we've got a real sonofabitch for you to eat."

Blair was both impressed and relieved when the animal heeded its mistress.

Deena informed Blair, "Whoever that bastard was that killed Ivar, I shot him twice. And that poor girl he shot sent him off a high ledge into the water. But the way my luck runs, I doubt either of us killed him. That's what you're here to talk about, isn't it?"

"Yeah, that's why I'm here."

"Here's your shooter," Blair McCray told Chief Billy Edwards. "This is the man who killed Barton Laney and shot his daughter, Prudence."

Blair slapped a well-rendered drawing down on the chief's desk. He'd persuaded Deena to do an updated sketch of the man she'd seen shoot the Laneys—the same man she'd seen talking to Ivar. Blair had told her it would be a good idea to have the police in on the hunt because that would lessen the chances that the killer would escape if he decided to make a run for it.

He'd also promised that he wouldn't reveal her identity or that she was still seeking personal vengeance.

The chief looked from the drawing to Blair.

"How do you know this is who we want?"

"The person who made the drawing saw the shooting."

Now Billy Edwards was interested.

"You found an eyewitness? Who is it?"

Blair shook his head. "Can't say."

"Bullshit!" the chief bellowed. "Family or not, you can say and you will say."

Blair took a seat. "No, I won't. Not until we get this sonofabitch."

"I'll lock you up."

"Go ahead. But here's how I see things. We get the shooter, I'll produce the witness. You crap around with me and let a killer get away—maybe even shoot somebody else—how's that going to make you look?"

The chief ground his teeth. "I don't understand you at all."

"You still think Evan Cade killed Ivar?" Blair asked.

"We've got his damn shoes!"

"And you found them in . . . ?"

"The trunk of Barton Laney's car. Not far from where he'd been shot in the head."

"You found them in a plastic bag, just like I said you would if someone was framing Evan Cade," Blair reminded him. "Only thing missing was an evidence tag: *Exhibit* A."

"So you don't think Cade killed Ivar?" the chief demanded.

"My witness implicates that man." Blair nodded at the drawing.

"Damnit, you're not telling me half of what you know."

"Let's just catch this sonofabitch, Billy, and I'll tell you everything. What I can say now is that the man has been shot—nicked, anyway—on his left shoulder and left ear. Let's get his picture out on the Net in case he's running."

"Your witness shot this man, didn't he?"

Blair didn't answer.

"How the hell would you feel in my place?" the chief wanted to know.

"Grateful that I know a lot more than I did five minutes ago," Blair responded.

J. D. Cade spent a quiet evening with his mother at her house. They ate dinner and encouraged each other that all would work out well for Evan. As they washed and dried the dishes, they reassured each other that they were in good health. And with each passing moment, neither one was the least bit fooled that they were leaving important matters unspoken.

After they'd sat down in the living room, Belle came out and asked, "You won't be staying long, will you, dear?"

"I have to leave in the morning."

Belle asked intuitively, "You feel trapped by something, don't you, J. D.?"

"Yes."

"But you can't talk about why."

"No."

She kissed her son's cheek. "I think I'll go on up to bed. I pray now before I end my day, did you know that? It seems the closer I come to meeting my Maker the more I want to tell him my side of things. I'll mention tonight what a good son you are and how much I love you."

"Tell him I'll take all the help I can get," J. D. said. "I love you, too, Mom."

Belle Cade stopped at the foot of the stairs and gazed back at her son, looking as though she wanted to tell him something but was uncertain if she should.

"What is it, Mom?"

The old woman's jaw firmed, and she nodded slightly as if to herself. "It was a shame about that deer, J. D."

Belle Cade climbed the stairs, leaving her son to wonder if he could possibly have heard his mother right. Just before he gave in to the impulse to rush after her and ask her to repeat what she'd said, the phone rang.

"Hello," he answered.

"Hi, J. D.? It's Jenny Crenshaw. I called to say hello and find out how things are going with your son."

J. D. was still distracted by his mother's comment and he struggled to regain his focus.

"Um . . . the lawyer said he should be able to have the charge dismissed tomorrow."

"That's great! You really work fast."

Jenny told him that the campaign had a wonderful day. Del's "This campaign will not be stopped" speech had received standing ovations in L.A., Fresno, and Eureka. It had been picked up by all the networks and shown on the prime-time newscasts. She asked if he'd seen it.

"Sorry. I've been pretty busy here."

"Of course. I'm the one who should be sorry. I should have realized. I'm just so excited. Our numbers in California are taking off, and polls coming in from around the country are showing we're making gains everywhere, even in the incumbent's strongholds."

"All because of a speech?"

There was a moment's silence on the line, then Jenny asked, "You didn't hear about the shooting, either?"

J. D.'s stomach knotted and he said, "No."

"Someone tried to shoot Special Agent DeVito very early this morning. Shot at him from a long distance, just like Del. He was working in *my* office. He was just as lucky as Del to have escaped with his life. It's been interpreted as a warning to Del to get out of the race. That's why people are reacting so strongly to his refusal to be intimidated."

A disturbing question occurred to J. D. "Did anybody think that the attempt might have been made not to intimidate the campaign but to cripple it? Even if the shooter found DeVito in your office, who was it he went looking for? It would hurt Senator Rawley's chances a lot more to lose you than DeVito."

Jenny's whisper of fear came across the line, "Oh, my God!"

J. D.'s mind went straight to Donnel Timmons. If there was a second assassin, it had to be Donnel. But J. D. just couldn't see his old friend doing the job for money. Which led J. D. back to the thought that maybe Donnel was being blackmailed, too—and, like J. D., he was looking for any way out short of killing Del Rawley.

But would that include shooting Jenny Crenshaw?

Perhaps Donnel hadn't come up with a plan, the way J. D. had, that would only destroy her professional and personal reputations.

Feeling completely hypocritical, J. D. said, "Please, Jenny, be very careful."

"I will . . . I will."

But he could tell she was badly shaken, not at all sure that she'd have been as lucky as DeVito had she been the one in her office—had she been the one in the crosshairs.

"I think I'll be able to return to California tomorrow," J. D. told her.

She said that was wonderful and updated him on the campaign schedule.

But he could still sense her fear when she said goodbye.

J. D. woke up that morning and understood that Ben must have shared his secret with Belle as well as Evan. His mother knew what he'd done to Alvy, too, but didn't condemn him for it. On the contrary, she was willing to plead his case to the Almighty. Aside from the comfort of having his mother be his advocate, he was glad she knew the real reason he'd never returned home before now, why she'd always had to be the one to visit him in California.

Belle was in the kitchen cooking when he entered the room. She told him to sit down, she'd have breakfast on the table in five minutes. But he looked out the window first. The sky was overcast with clouds so black and massive they looked too heavy to stay aloft.

Up till now, the weather had been the last thing on his mind. "What's the forecast, Mom?"

"Bad," she told him. "That Hurricane Eddie that's been churning around the Gulf of Mexico hit New Orleans last night. The storm front is heading right up the Mississippi River."

J. D. turned from the window, fervently hoping his return to California wouldn't be delayed. He sat down at the table. A copy of the *Southern Illinoisan* rested on it. Next to the newspaper was an open crossword dictionary. That told him his mother still started her day the same old way: scan the headlines, then go straight to the crossword puzzle.

"There's nothing in the paper about Evan," Belle said. "That's a good thing, isn't it?"

"Yes." J. D. picked up the paper and looked at it. "It means the cops haven't talked to the press. They don't want the story to turn around and bite them when they have to release Evan."

"Saves Evan the embarrassment, too."

Putting the paper down, J. D. noticed the guide words at the top of the right-hand page of the crossword dictionary: *de Gaulle* and *Deiphobus*. The latter word drew J. D.'s eye to the entry listed just above it.

Deimos (dee-mos) *n.* [Gr. fear or panic] One of the two moons of . . .

Panic? Roth and Danby worked for an office of the Treasury Department called Panic?

In that moment J. D. knew who his blackmailer was.

Belle put a plate of bacon and eggs in front of him and sat down wearing a look of concern.

"Are you all right, J. D.? You have a very strange expression on your face."

Not trusting his voice, J. D. only nodded.

"You're sure?"

J. D. cleared his throat.

"I'm fine, Mom. In fact, I'm feeling better than I was a moment ago."

Thirty minutes later the two Cades were at the county courthouse in nearby Murphysboro, where they watched Richard Shuster get the homicide charge against Evan summarily dismissed for lack of evidence. The judge instructed the state's attorney that a clear connection had to be made that Evan had repossessed his shoes from the Salvation Army store, or other evidence must be found tying him to the death of Ivar McCray before he would consider reinstating the charge.

That taken care of, J. D. and Belle proceeded to University Hospital. There was no longer a cop guarding Evan's room, and J. D. and Belle entered it.

Evan saw them but didn't smile. If anything, his expression was grim.

"What happened?" J. D. asked.

"Pru died," his son responded. "A doctor told me about ten minutes ago."

"Oh, honey," Belle consoled. She moved to Evan's bed and stroked his cheek.

But J. D. could see no comfort in his son's eyes, only pain and anger.

After hearing that the charge against him had been dropped, Evan talked with his father and grandmother for a minute. Then Belle sensed that they needed to be alone and went out of the room.

"I have to leave," J. D. said. "There's something I have to take care of."

"Me too," Evan replied.

J. D. realized that Evan would try to find Pru Laney's killer and there was nothing he could do or say to change his son's mind. "Let me know if there's any way I can help."

"Yeah. I only wish I'd let you teach me how to shoot better."

"Be careful what you wish for, Evan. Be very careful."

J. D. went to his son and put his arms around him. He looked for some way to dissuade his son from seeking vengeance. But he could find no moral standing from which he could even begin an argument. Evan knew how he'd handled such matters.

"I'll see you as soon as I can," J. D. told him.

Evan nodded. "I love you, Dad."

J. D. felt tears well up in his eyes. "I love you, too."

After saying goodbye to his mother, J. D. took a taxi to the airport. On the way there, he booted up his laptop and checked the stickyfingers.com chat room. There was a message from Pickpocket and it confirmed what he already knew. The name of his blackmailer.

Head of Departmental Internal Management and Oversight (DEIMOS) is Garvin Townes.

J. D.'s old commanding officer, Colonel Townes of the PANIC unit.

He keyed in a message: *See if you can find out what Townes has been doing the past thirty years.*

He thought he'd have to check back later for a reply but it came immediately.

Thirty years? You don't want much, do you?

If you're not feeling up to it . . .

I'm up to it. I just came online because I have some news on your other request.

Preoccupied with Townes now, J. D. couldn't recall what else he'd asked of Pickpocket.

Go ahead, he said.

Re: Donnel Timmons. He was in the auto parts business but sold his company ten years ago. Checking on current activities.

Wondering what Donnel's "current activities" might be, J. D. boarded the waiting jet. It was fueled and ready to go. The flight plan was filed for San Francisco, the day's last stop for the Rawley campaign. Two minutes later the aircraft rose into the threatening sky just as rain began to fall.

Ten minutes after that, a commuter flight from St. Louis touched down amidst a downpour. Special Agent Dante

DeVito stepped out of the plane and sprinted for the terminal.

When DeVito arrived at the Carbondale Municipal Building fifteen minutes later, he was escorted to the office of the chief of police, Billy Edwards. DeVito knew Cade didn't have a criminal record, but his son had been arrested for murder here and he wanted to hear about that. He also thought the local cops should be able to point him in the direction of old acquaintances and former friends who might be able to shed a bit more light on Cade for him.

As a visiting federal officer, he expected prompt, courteous cooperation from the locals, and the chief did extend his hand in greeting when DeVito was ushered into his office, but the man looked decidedly edgy about receiving him.

"Something wrong, Chief?" DeVito asked, taking the chair he'd been offered.

"More than usual."

"And you're wondering if I'm more bad news."

Billy Edwards nodded. "You told my sergeant you're here to talk about J. D. Cade?"

"That's right. You know Mr. Cade?"

"Not personally, no."

"But you're holding his son for murder?"

"Not any longer. The charge was dismissed this morning."

DeVito frowned. "Why was that?"

"Judge said insufficient evidence."

DeVito—the outsider—knew he was about to tread on dangerous ground, but he asked anyway. "The judge an honest man? Not somebody who might be swayed by an unexpected contribution to his retirement plan?"

A sour look spread across the chief's face. "Who can say

what's in a man's heart? You want, I'll take you over to Murphysboro and you can repeat your questions to the judge himself."

DeVito snorted. He'd pass on that one.

"If you don't know about Mr. Cade personally, what about professionally?"

"He left town a very long time ago. Back when I was in grade school."

"Chief, you liked J. D. Cade's son as a killer. You liked him enough to go out and arrest him, whatever some judge said after the fact. You mean to tell me you didn't even check your files to see if maybe his father didn't pass along some bad blood to him?"

"Yeah," the chief admitted, "I did."

"And?"

"J. D. Cade has no criminal record."

Which DeVito already knew. "All that means is he was never charged with anything. What about any run-ins your department had with Mr. Cade that stopped short of arrest? Was there ever anything like that?"

Chief Edwards didn't like this fed at all. But he knew the easiest way to get rid of him was to cooperate—an attitude he wished his damn in-law Blair McCray would take up.

"Well, I found one old report that didn't involve any charges but had to be filed for property insurance purposes. Mr. Cade was involved in a bar fight shortly after returning home from the army."

"What, two drunks slugging it out? Who got the better of it?"

"It's more complicated than that. You have to know some local history to really understand. But the gist of it is, this fellow name of Alvy McCray started up with J. D. Cade and Cade purely beat the hell out of him."

"With his hands?"

"That's what the report says, but I talked to the old-timer who took the report and he told me he heard stories at the time that Cade pistol-whipped McCray."

"And there were no charges for that?"

"It could never be confirmed."

"Why not?"

The chief sighed and launched into a brief account of the Cade-McCray feud, how Alvy McCray had initiated assaults on various Cades, and how most people on the Illinois side of the dispute were not about to say anything that would help one of their Kentucky enemies.

"Huh," DeVito grunted. "So this bad-ass hillbilly goes up against J. D. Cade and it's like he ran into a buzzsaw. Is that the end of the story? Nobody tried to get revenge?"

The chief didn't care to hear his in-laws characterized as hillbillies but kept his temper in check. "Mr. Cade thought it best to leave the state just after the fight."

DeVito rubbed his chin, thinking. "And this McCray character, he didn't try to even the score on someone else in the Cade family?"

"He might have wanted to, but he died."

"Died? Violently?"

"You could say that. He rolled his pickup truck three times after it struck a deer."

The story slithered through DeVito's labyrinthine thought process. "So it was an accident—after J. D. Cade had left the area—but it was awfully fucking convenient."

"For the Cades, the McCrays, and the general welfare, yes, it was. Nobody except Alvy McCray wanted to see the feud start up again."

DeVito had an insight. "This person J. D. Cade's son is supposed to have killed, another McCray?"

The chief nodded. "Ivar McCray."

"That stirring up all the old hostilities?"

"Not so far. But it might. Alvy McCray's son, Blair—he's a police officer down in Paducah—he's come up to look into the matter on an unofficial basis."

"No shit?" A thought struck DeVito. "Better tell him to watch out for stray deer."

The chief wasn't amused "I'll be sure to do that. Couldn't blame it on Mr. Cade even if it happened again, though."

"Why not?"

"He left town this morning."

"What?"

"Word I received was he was in court this morning to make sure his boy got off, visited him at the hospital, and took off in his plane probably about the same time yours was landing."

"Sonofabitch," DeVito muttered. It didn't take a rocket scientist to figure out Cade was going straight back to the campaign. DeVito also sensed he'd learned as much as he needed to know, or was going to find out from this grumpy cop, about J. D. Cade's early years: a pistol-whipping, a blood feud, and an accidental . . .

Death. Alvy McCray messed with Cade, his pickup truck hit a deer. Roth and Danby annoyed Cade, they were almost killed in a rock slide. Nobody got that lucky with his enemies.

"How soon can I get a flight out of here?" DeVito asked Billy Edwards.

The chief looked out his window, where the rain was coming down in such volume he seemed to have a view of Niagara Falls. "Not soon would be my guess."

Blair McCray called Evan from the lobby of the hospital and asked if it was safe for him to come up and visit.

"Yeah. I'm alone right now." Then Evan told him, "Pru Laney died."

"I'm truly sorry to hear to that."

When the Kentucky lawman reached his room, Evan told him, "I feel like such a shit."

Blair sat in the visitor's chair. "I can't see where you did anything wrong."

"It's what I didn't do right that bothers me. I never even tried to talk to Pru. It wasn't like her to just turn and walk away because some lawyer said don't talk to me. We were . . . close. I should have demanded the truth from her."

"Truth can be in short supply a lot of the time."

Evan made sure he met Blair's eyes. "Yeah, it can."

"Your daddy tell you who my daddy was?"

Evan said yes, but nothing more.

"That was part of the reason I came up this way. I mean, mostly it was for Ivar, but when I heard it was J. D. Cade's son who looked like the guilty party, I just had to get involved."

Blair hung his head in reminiscence. "I never knew my daddy. He died before I was born. Before he even knew Mama was pregnant with me, I was told. The only image I had of him was this photograph where he was wearing his Marine Corps dress uniform. The man sure cut an imposing figure for a young boy to look at."

Blair looked up at Evan.

"My mama said, though, it was just as well he died. For both of us. She'd been taken with Daddy's looks, too. But she soon learned he was really an ignorant, violent man. He'd taken to beating her the second week they were married. She said she doubted he'd have allowed her to divorce him. She thought they'd have wound up killing each other, and if I'd been alive when the dam broke, I could have been killed, too.

"I've never had reason to doubt a single word my mother has told me. But I wanted to believe that maybe she just wasn't remembering things right. How could a man who looked like my daddy be anything less than an American hero? And who the hell was this J. D. Cade to lay him low so soon before he died?

"So when I heard about Ivar and you, I wanted to come up here and set everything right. Only you turned out to be anything but what I expected. And for some reason, or maybe no reason at all, the more things looked like you weren't the one who killed Ivar, the more I had to accept that maybe I was lucky my daddy had died before he could lay a hand on me."

"Sometimes life's harder when you do learn the truth," Evan suggested.

"Like realizing Ivar and Barton Laney were connected in some kind of scheme," Blair said. "Or else why would the same sonofabitch kill them both? And Pru—the way she broke up with you and the fact that she was also killed implies she knew what her father was doing."

"She was used. They were all used," Evan said bitterly.

"Yes, they were. And now, I believe, it's time to get back some of our own." Blair told Evan what Deena Nokes had seen and done. He told him how he'd given the killer's likeness to the police for dissemination just in case the man was on the run.

Evan shook his head. "I don't think he is. This thing isn't finished yet."

"No, it's not."

J. D. sat in the bar of the Royale Hotel on Union Square in San Francisco sipping a glass of mineral water, still debating with himself whether Donnel Timmons was a second assassin. He thought it must have been relatively easy for Donnel to get close to Del Rawley at the beginning of the primary campaign. Back then, the candidate had been only one of many, without Secret Service protection, running for his party's nomination and not the presidency. Doing a background check on a seemingly prosperous black businessman who was willing to donate both time and money to the cause would never have occurred to anyone. By the time Senator Rawley won the nomination, Donnel had already established himself as a loyalist. His cover was perfect.

But then why bring in J. D. if Donnel was already in place?

So that if one assassin failed, all would not be lost.

J. D. could see Colonel Townes thinking that way. He could also see Roth and Danby having the task of disposing of both him and Donnel. Whichever of them got Rawley would go first; the other would follow soon thereafter. No loose strings would be left dangling.

That was one possible scenario.

What J. D. was certain of, though, was that Townes was his blackmailer, and if he could devise a way to find him, he could kill him. That would free J. D. and Evan from his clutches.

Del Rawley wouldn't have to die, either.

No sooner had he thought of the candidate than the Secret Service arrived.

A pair of agents entered the bar from the hotel lobby. A second pair moved in from the street entrance. A third pair appeared through the doors to the bar's service area. One of the agents from the lobby whispered into his wrist mike.

Seconds later Del Rawley made his entrance with Jenny Crenshaw, the two of them ringed by more agents. Patrons in the bar spontaneously stood and gave the candidate a round of applause. Del waved and offered his thanks. Jenny smiled. J. D. thought it best to get to his feet also and Jenny spotted him.

Arriving at his table, Jenny said, "The concierge told us you were here. May we join you?"

"By all means."

The three of them sat as the ring of bodyguards took up their positions. Several people openly watched the gathering, craning their necks to get a peek, but none was close enough to overhear the conversation.

"How is your son, Mr. Cade?" Del Rawley asked.

"He's fine, Senator. A bit shaken up but fine."

"How was it that the police came to suspect him?"

J. D. thought how best to put it. "It's somewhat complicated, but it boils down to being too close to people who got caught up in an unfortunate situation."

"Please, I'd like to know the details." The implication was clear: Del would let J. D. back into the fold if he could find political cover; otherwise, so sorry.

"A man was believed to be trying to extort money from the father of my son's girlfriend. When the alleged extortionist turned up dead, suspicion was cast on my son. I'm certain this was done to protect the real killer, but the police like to go the obvious route first."

The candidate's head bobbed in agreement, but for a moment his eyes lost focus as he was carried off by a memory. Stirring himself, he said, "I know what you mean about the police. In 1939 my grandfather was shot and killed by a state trooper in Indiana who couldn't believe that a black man could be driving a new car unless he'd stolen it."

Jenny put a hand over one of Del's and gave it a brief squeeze.

Then the candidate continued. "Well . . . we're glad everything worked out for your son. Were you able to get a room here?"

J. D. shook his head. "No room at the inn."

"I'll take care of it," Jenny replied.

"It's okay," J. D. assured her. "I'll find a room someplace

else for the night. I just wanted to catch up with you and give you the news. I'm going back to L.A. in the morning."

Jenny exchanged a look with Del Rawley. A silent message passed between them. Del said, "Why don't you stay for the speech I'm giving in the morning, Mr. Cade? Be my guest, tell me how you think it's received. Then I think I'll have a moment and we can talk."

Jenny told J. D., "We're not done with our day yet. Del has a formal dinner to attend at city hall that Mayor Wu is giving in his honor."

J. D. said, "They certainly make you earn your money, Senator."

"That they do, Mr. Cade, that they do." He stood and extended his hand to J. D., who rose to take it. "I'm happy about your son's vindication. You must be very relieved."

"I am. My son means everything to me."

Del smiled and clapped J. D. on the shoulder. Then he was off. Jenny lingered with J. D. for a moment.

"I'll get you a room here."

J. D. nodded and looked closely at her. "How are you doing? I didn't mean to scare you."

"I'm doing okay. It took a little while, I guess, but . . . I just hadn't thought anyone would want to shoot *me*. But I told myself that if Del has to carry on, then so do I."

"If you feel like company after your dinner . . ."

"I'd like that." She took his hand for a moment, then left.

J. D. sat down, alone with his thoughts until the concierge arrived and presented him with the key to his room. Alone again until Donnel Timmons joined him two minutes later.

"How's your boy?" he asked.

J. D. looked at Donnel, not really surprised he'd heard about Evan.

"He's having a helluva time, to be honest."

"Somebody out to get him?"

"Certainly looks that way."

"You teach him any tricks of the trade?"

J. D. shook his head. A waitress stopped by and Donnel ordered a drink.

"Bet you'd like to find the sucker who's messing with your boy," Donnel opined casually. "Make *real* short work of that dude."

"You want to be my spotter?" J. D. asked.

"For something like that . . . you ask me nice, I just might."

J. D. thought it was time to change the subject. He asked Donnel if he'd noticed the two crewcuts—the dark-haired one and the blonde—among the Rawley protection detail.

"Yeah, I know who you mean," Donnel said, giving J. D. the impression he'd had them pegged from the start.

"They've been crowding me. Making me think I better forget about my involvement in politics before certain unfortunate truths become known."

"Yeah? Well, that *might* be a good idea."

That was when J. D. realized that Donnel, too, might have been put on notice about a second assassin. Which would explain why Donnel had been so wary about him.

"Thing is," J. D. continued, "even if I leave, they might keep checking on me just to be thorough. They find out about me, they might cast a wider net, and who else might get exposed?"

Even in the low light of the bar, J. D. could see Donnel's eyes narrow.

"Now, *that* would be unfortunate."

J. D. gave him something else to think about.

"I've done some checking on those guys. Their names are Arnold Roth and William Danby. They work for a special section of the Treasury Department. It's called Departmental Internal Management and Oversight. DEIMOS. That ring any bells with you?"

J. D. watched closely for any sign of recognition but didn't see any.

Donnel shrugged. "No. Never heard of it."

"*Deimos* is also a Greek word. It means 'panic.' "

"*Sonofabitch!*"

"Yeah," J. D. said. "Colonel Townes is up to his old tricks."

The waitress brought Donnel's drink. J. D. raised his glass to his old comrade in arms.

"We who are about to die . . . ," he said.

After his toast with Donnel, J. D. retired to the room Jenny had arranged for him.

He wanted to call Evan but felt it was too soon. He didn't want to pressure his son. That might only provoke him into acting more recklessly than he would otherwise. Besides, he didn't have anything new to say.

He considered calling his mother, too. He wanted to explain to her how he'd thought he'd had no choice but to kill Alvy. He wanted her to hear him explain it, not just leave it to Ben to defend him. But she already had forgiven him, so why put her through all that again? Especially when there was someone new he might *have* to kill.

Jenny came to his room shortly after 11 P.M. She was exhausted. Her new sense of mortality had added to the already staggering burdens of her job. She told J. D. that she wanted to go straight to bed. Not for sex, just to be held and comforted.

Ignorance was bliss, J. D. thought. If she knew who he really was, she wouldn't turn to him for comfort, she'd flee instantly. Or maybe she'd find the strength to strike him down . . . and after the way he'd completely abused her trust, maybe he'd have to let her succeed.

But the masquerade continued and they snuggled and talked briefly. She told him of her day, talked about the ups and downs of the campaign, and even confided a humorous secret: the president had only one testicle. She swore him to secrecy about that just before she drifted off.

She was a warm, pleasant weight against him. Her breath on his neck made his skin tingle. He thought of the pictures he'd taken of her in the nude. He'd planned to make a composite of Jenny naked with Del Rawley. Maybe drug Donnel, use his nude body as Rawley's. Post the images on the Internet. No way the candidate could plead a youthful indiscretion in that context. Let the firestorm drive Rawley from the race before the hoax was revealed.

Now, with Colonel Townes in the picture, J. D. didn't think that was going to be enough.

TWELVE
Tuesday, September 21, 2004

Del Rawley's speech that morning was being given in the hotel's Silk Trade Room. The huge, opulent meeting room was already filled with a well-heeled crowd busily chattering and nibbling on their breakfasts of fresh fruit, croissants, and Kona coffee. Jenny, feeling much restored, escorted J. D. to the entrance of the room and vouched for him to the Secret Service agents working the door. One of them still waved a handheld metal detector up one side of J. D. and down the other. Then they let Jenny take him inside.

"I'll be sitting at the head table," she told him. "But I'm way over on the right. You'll be sitting at a table front and center. Del reserved your seat himself."

"How come?"

"He said he wants to get an honest opinion of what he has to say today, and he told me you're the one person he could think of who doesn't have a hidden agenda."

"He's too kind."

Like the other tables in the audience, the one at which J. D. would sit was round. His seat was the nearest to the head table, which meant he'd have to turn his chair around to see Del Rawley speak. Jenny introduced J. D. to a group of local swells who all seemed to know each other and had paid big money for their prime seating. They smiled pleasantly and greeted J. D., and no doubt they were impressed when the candidate, sitting not fifteen feet away, gave J. D. a wave and he casually returned it. As soon as Jenny left, however, envy and resentment reared their ugly heads and the local swells excluded the interloper from their attention and conversation.

That suited J. D. just fine. He looked around casually to get a feel for the room. People were finishing their food. Plates and silverware were being bused away by squadrons of hotel staff. Secret Service agents guarded every door that J. D. could see. More agents hovered around the head table and one stood directly behind the candidate.

Roth and Danby stood at the left end of the head table. Roth made eye contact with J. D. It was the first time they'd laid eyes on each other since the rock slide. Roth looked less than happy to renew their acquaintance. He whispered something to Danby.

J. D. looked away.

A voice asked him, "Coffee, sir?"

J. D. looked up to see a busboy standing in front of him holding a coffeepot.

"Yes, please."

The busboy was a handsome young black man. Handsome but with nervous eyes. And a hand that trembled as he tipped the stainless-steel coffeepot to fill J. D.'s cup. Tiny beads of sweat dotted the young man's brow and upper lip, and he stiffened visibly when a woman at the head table stepped to the lectern and announced that Senator Rawley would speak just as soon as everyone's coffee cup had been refilled.

J. D. looked at the busboy's face. The kid's eyes were unfocused. His head was cocked as if to listen to a voice that spoke only to him. An epiphany rippled across J. D.'s mind;

he knew just what was going to happen next. This kid, for God only knew what reason, was going to try to kill Del Rawley.

J. D.'s eyes quickly darted back and forth and he saw that no one else had a clue. He was the exclusive audience for the drama about to unfold. A soft chiming sound began as the tremor in the busboy's hand tapped the spout of the coffeepot against J. D.'s cup.

J. D. looked for any telltale sign that the kid was carrying a gun. He didn't see any giveaway bulge. Which made sense, because how could he possibly sneak a weapon past all the Secret Service agents? He couldn't. Still, J. D. —having thought about killing Rawley so often himself—was sure the kid was about to make an attempt on the candidate's life.

But using what for a weapon? The silverware? It was ludicrous, but . . . if the busboy succeeded, J. D. Cade would be off the hook.

J. D. would no longer have to kill Rawley. Wouldn't even have to kill Townes. Evan would be saved, and there would be no more blood on J. D.'s hands. Not directly. All he'd be guilty of would be failing to stop a madman. While that might be reprehensible, it was no crime.

He sat and watched without comment as the busboy overfilled the cup and slopped coffee into the saucer. J. D. pushed his chair away as the coffee spilled onto the tablecloth.

"I'm sorry, sir," the busboy told J. D., finally noticing his gaffe. "I'll clean that right up."

But in his haste to put the coffeepot down on the table the busboy accidentally knocked a spoon to the floor. He quickly bent down to retrieve it . . . and his hand reached under the tablecloth. Now J. D. knew where the gun was: taped to the underside of the table.

Through the babble of conversation that filled the room,

J. D. heard Del Rawley laugh. He looked and saw the candidate sharing a joke with the man sitting next to him. There was a glow to Rawley—an aura of intelligence, decency, and humor—that was nearly visible. This was a very special man he was about to let die.

J. D. looked back and saw that the busboy was standing now and had a pistol in his hand. He held it very close to his chest. No one else had noticed. Then the busboy's eyes met J. D.'s. He saw that he'd been discovered, but he was far from deterred. He spun to face the head table and take his shot at the candidate.

But J. D. was already out of his seat and flying through the air at the busboy. As he collided with the kid, J. D. heard a nearby male voice shout, "Gun!"

The gun went off, but J. D. had deflected the busboy's arm upward and the shot went into the ceiling. Then the room erupted in a cacophony of screams and shouts. The busboy still had the gun, but J. D. had his arm and they wrestled for the weapon atop the table. With the would-be assassin lying on top of him and his neck over the edge of the table, J. D. looked back and saw a half-dozen Secret Service agents charging toward them—Roth and Danby at the forefront.

J. D. twisted the busboy's gun hand in their direction. He kneed the kid in the groin to get him to stop struggling for a moment, and forced the busboy's finger to pull the trigger. A shot was fired and Danby went down. J. D. was about to line up Roth for the next shot when agents arriving from another direction piled on top of him and the busboy, carrying them both to the floor.

Within seconds J. D. and the busboy were hauled to their feet. The kid's hands were already cuffed behind his back. J. D.'s arms were yanked backward, and he was about to be manacled, too. But the people who'd sat at his table yelled protests at the feds.

"What are you doing?"

"That man saved Senator Rawley's life!"

"Let him go, he's a hero!"

Popular acclaim was not enough to dissuade the agents, but then their boss, Special Agent Clarke, arrived. "Let him go. He deflected the shot meant for Orpheus."

As J. D. was released, the busboy was taken away, and two men from the audience—doctors, J. D. assumed—knelt over the fallen Danby.

"Are you all right, Mr. Cade?" Clarke asked.

J. D. had a gash on his forehead but was otherwise unhurt. "I'm all right. What about everyone else?"

"You saved Senator Rawley. But the second shot struck one of our men."

"I'm sorry. I did my best."

"I know you did." Clarke shuddered as his adrenaline drained. "I need you to come with me now so we can talk to you about what happened. We'll get that cut looked at, too."

Then Jenny was there. She'd overheard Clarke.

"Senator Rawley would like to see Mr. Cade for just a minute to offer his thanks."

Clarke nodded. He told four of his men to escort J. D. to Orpheus and then bring him to the hotel security room. As J. D. was led away, he received a spontaneous ovation for his bravery.

Not far away, one of the doctors draped a linen napkin over Danby's face.

And Roth stared daggers at J. D.

DeVito appeared in the entrance to the room. He'd been delayed by the storm, and the first flight out of St. Louis had allowed him to arrive only at that very moment. He took in the scene. From the disarray, he drew the only conclusion possible: another assassination attempt. His heart turned to ice at the thought that he was too late.

"Orpheus?" he asked the agent at the door.

The man knew DeVito, knew he'd been away. "Alive and well."

"Cade?" DeVito asked.

"Yeah, I think that's the guy's name. How'd you know?"

"I had a feeling."

"You had a feeling Mr. Cade was going to save Orpheus' life?"

"*Save* his life?" DeVito was thunderstruck.

"Yeah, didn't you see? But one of our guys got it from a stray shot."

"Who?"

"That guy from the special unit."

"Roth?"

"No, the other one. Danby."

First the rock slide, now a stray shot, DeVito thought.

"Where is Clarke going to question Cade?"

The agent spoke into his wrist mike and got a reply. "Hotel security office."

DeVito took off to find the security office.

Cade a hero and Danby dead: a very mixed message for DeVito to chew on. One thing was for certain, though. DeVito was going to sit in on Cade's interrogation. He had to.

He just couldn't get his mind around the idea of Cade *saving* Orpheus' life.

"I don't know why I did it," J. D. told Del Rawley truthfully. "I just saw the gun and reacted. I suppose I would have been safer ducking for cover."

He was with Del in the candidate's suite. Jenny was there, along with the rest of the brain trust, Donnel Timmons, a raft of Secret Service agents, and a plainclothes cop from the SFPD. A doctor applied a bandage to J. D.'s forehead.

"Ducking occurred to me," Del admitted. "Out of the corner of my eye, I saw that man turn. There was something about the set of his shoulders I didn't like. Then I saw the gun in his hand and I couldn't decide whether to duck left or right. But then you came flying through the air and knocked his arm away." The candidate paused as a thought struck him. "Never saw a rear-echelon motherfucker move like that before."

J. D. only shrugged.

The doctor finished his work and stepped away. J. D. and Del Rawley looked at each other. "I'm very grateful, Mr. Cade. Maybe I should have you managing my protection detail."

J. D. shook his head. "Not me, Senator. I'm ready to go back to the rear with the rest of the REMFs."

"I doubt that." Del extended his hand and J. D. shook it. "Now if you don't mind, I have to call my wife and tell her that I'm all right. That I've used up only two of my nine lives."

Before the candidate left to make his phone call, he instructed Jenny, "We keep as close to our schedule as possible." Then Del looked at Clarke. "I know you'd prefer otherwise, but I'm sorry. Short of some sonofabitch actually succeeding in killing me, I'm going to live up to my word. This campaign will not be stopped."

Rawley turned to J. D. "Right, Mr. Cade?"

"You're a brave man, Senator," J. D. replied.

"Stupid, stupid man," Garvin Townes muttered to Arnold Roth.

Roth had called Townes at his suite in the Mark Hopkins Hotel. Townes was watching his television. A video camera had caught most of the important action in the Silk Trade Room that morning: J. D. Cade foiling the gunman; wrestling with him on the table; the second shot going off. The sequence was being repeated endlessly. What wasn't shown was Danby dying, but that piece of information had already been passed along by the anchorwoman.

"He did that on purpose," Roth said venomously.

"Of course he did," Townes agreed.

"I mean he shot Bill on purpose. He *looked* right at us while we were running toward him. Replay the tape in slow motion and watch Cade's eyes."

Townes switched the TV from live feed to replay. He rolled the sequence in slow motion from the television's memory. He saw Cade dive at the busboy, knock his arm up, and grab on to the wrist of the gun hand. Then somehow Cade managed to get his feet back under himself but couldn't keep his balance. He wound up pulling the busboy down on top of him and they landed on the table. Cade's head was bent back over the edge of the table and . . . he was looking at someone or something approaching him.

"Sonofabitch," Townes muttered softly.

Cade forced the busboy's gun hand directly in line with where he was looking. He wrapped his hand around the busboy's gun hand. The busboy stopped struggling—went slack—for some reason Townes couldn't see, and then the gun went off. The busboy's finger was on the trigger, but the pressure on his hand from Cade was what squeezed off the round.

Cade hadn't stopped there, either. He was lining up his next target—Roth. Just before Cade could fire again he and the busboy were buried under a pile of Secret Service bodies.

"He knows," Townes said in a quiet tone. "He knows you and Danby were the ones watching him."

"I told you that rock slide was no accident," Roth said, hatred filling his voice. "He's had too much time. He's hunting *us*."

"Yes, he is." Townes wondered if Cade could possibly have discovered his participation.

"I want to kill him," Roth told Townes. "As soon as possible."

"Soon enough," Townes said.

There was still one move to make before then. It was time to bring a far more direct threat against Evan Cade. Time to do what really should have been done in the first place.

The busboy who had tried to kill Franklin Delano Rawley was named Prentice Colter. He had no connection to any terrorist group. He had no political, racial, or social ax to grind. What he had was an IQ of 175 and an occasional aversion to taking the medication that kept his paranoid schizophrenia under control.

Prentice Colter thought *he* was supposed to become the country's first black president, and Del Rawley had to be stopped from taking Colter's rightful place in history.

Colter's mother had called the SFPD from her home in Oakland as soon as she had seen on TV what had happened. All of the details she'd told the authorities about her son had been verified by independent sources.

Prentice had admitted that he'd carried the weapon into the room when he'd been sent out to fill water glasses, shortly before the guests had arrived. He'd stuck the weapon to the underside of the table while kneeling down and pretending to tie his shoe. Then he went on filling water glasses and waited for his moment to arrive. The crazy fucker had planned and executed his assassination attempt to a fare-thee-well.

The only thing he hadn't counted on was J. D. Cade.

Who had come and gone after telling his story three times to Clarke, DeVito, and an SFPD cop, Inspector Osterman.

"Impressions, gentlemen?" Clarke asked.

"That man saved everyone's ass," Osterman said, "the senator's, yours, and mine. That's my impression."

DeVito nodded, grimly silent. By now he'd seen the tape of the assassination attempt.

"Any part of his statement of events seem off-key?" Clarke wanted to know.

Osterman shook his head. "Not to me. Cade's the odd man out at the table. He's looking around. He sees what's happening while everybody else is yakking. Then at the risk of his own life he does the right thing."

"DeVito? That how you see it?"

"As far as the tape showed, yeah."

The San Francisco cop got to his feet. "Sorry about the man you lost. But for the rest of it, it's just like I said. We all fucked up and got bailed out by Mr. Cade. Now, if you'll excuse me, I've got an appointment with the mayor to get my ass reamed. I imagine you gentlemen will be having your high colonics shortly."

Osterman left and Clarke looked at DeVito.

"You think Rawley will stick up for me the way he did for you?"

"What does it matter?" DeVito asked. "We're both finished."

"The director's en route to San Francisco as we speak. I have to meet him at the airport."

"He say anything about me?"

"No."

"So who's in charge of the detail?"

"Arnold Roth."

"Goddamn."

"Yeah." Charlie Clarke left the hotel security room looking exactly like what he was: a man who had to chauffeur himself to his own execution.

DeVito had thought there was no point telling Clarke that he'd found out Cade was a shooter—and he sure as hell wasn't going to say a word about *anything* to that cocksucker Roth.

What troubled him now was how the hell he was going to talk to Orpheus. What could he say to the man? "Senator, I strongly feel the man who saved your life in San Francisco is the same one who tried to take it in Chicago."

How would he ever be able to explain that? He didn't understand it himself.

Even as bewildered as he was by the idea of Cade as hero, even at the risk of alienating Orpheus, DeVito decided he had to see the man. Right now.

He ignored the chain of command completely—fuck Roth—and entered Orpheus' suite and begged five minutes of his time. Alone.

Del heard the urgency that underlay DeVito's request and granted it. He dismissed the other agents and the brain trust, Jenny leaving very reluctantly.

"Is this going to be about Mr. Cade again?" Del asked.

His tone told DeVito he'd be fighting an uphill battle if it was. So the special agent decided to leave Cade for later—if he brought him up at all.

"I do have a couple of other concerns, Senator."

"And they are?"

"Did you ever get that gun? The one you asked Clarke and me for?"

"No, I didn't."

DeVito handed him a flat, compact semiautomatic. It was his personal weapon. He showed Del how to load a clip, chamber a round, and work the safety.

"It's small enough, light enough to carry in your hip pocket. Nobody should notice."

Del stared at the weapon he held in the palm of his hand, regarding it pensively.

"You think you would have used that this morning if you'd had it?" DeVito asked.

The man who would be president looked DeVito in the eyes. "I don't know. Probably not. My first impulse was to find a hole and dive in."

"That's a sound impulse," DeVito said in a neutral tone.

Del drew the obvious inference. "But it wasn't the kind of reaction that saved my life, Special Agent DeVito, was it?"

"No, sir. Mr. Cade acted heroically today."

"What was your other concern?"

"You've heard that the director has replaced Charlie Clarke?"

"No, I didn't know that," Rawley said with an edge to his voice. "I wasn't consulted."

"You'll have to take that up with the director, Senator. I wasn't consulted, either. My point here is that the new special agent in charge of your protection detail is Arnold Roth. He doesn't know about the little present I just gave you." DeVito nodded at the gun. "Probably just as well we keep it that way."

"Just as well for you or for me?"

DeVito laughed harshly and shook his head. "Pardon me, Senator, but my career is over. The only other thing they could do to me now is shoot me. And I don't think I'd mind that too much. My point is, Roth is a real hard-ass. He can't tell you what to do, of course, but if he learns that you have a weapon, I wouldn't be surprised if you find you've misplaced it real soon."

"You don't trust this man, Special Agent DeVito?"

"Not one damn bit, sir."

"And there is something else you want to tell me, isn't there? Something about Mr. Cade."

DeVito nodded.

"Very well. What is it?"

DeVito had decided that his best course of action was to leave his suspicions aside and just tell Orpheus the most salient fact he'd learned.

"I found out how Mr. Cade likes to relax." The special agent saw a wary expression appear on Orpheus' face. "No, sir, nothing like that. No drugs or hookers or barnyard animals."

"What is it, then?"

"Senator, Mr. Cade likes to fire rifles. At targets over long distances. And he does it pretty well, from what I'm told."

On that note, Del Rawley set off for another full-tilt day of campaigning.

Del's speeches in Palo Alto and Monterey were electrifying. Coming so closely on the heels of the assassination attempt in San Francisco, the emotions of both audiences were raw. People laughed and cried and cheered. More than anything else, they gave off a sense of overwhelming joy that their favorite was still alive.

Every line Del spoke was punctuated by a standing ovation. Handmade signs appeared: WE WILL NOT BE STOPPED! Crowds lined the motor route for miles. People stood shoulder to shoulder along the roadways as if to safeguard with their own bodies the man they wanted to lead the country. The experience was overwhelming.

As soon as the candidate was settled into his suite in San Diego that evening, he sent for Donnel Timmons. As with DeVito, he met with Donnel alone. He even poured their drinks himself.

"The last time I got shot at so often, I just wanted to go home," Del Rawley told Donnel Timmons. "This time I can't even do that."

Del sat in an easy chair, Donnel on a sofa. Each man had his straight scotch resting on the coffee table between them. Neither drink had been touched.

Donnel put his left foot up over his right knee. He gave the impression he was relaxed, not at all uneasy that Del had summoned him for a private meeting.

"You think I did the right thing staying in the race?" Del asked.

"I thought so before . . . before that crazy busboy tried to kill you."

"Devree felt pretty much the same way. She's scared now, but she's mad, too. She doesn't want me to give in. Not just so I can be president, but so whoever wants to stop me will know they won't be able to scare off good people in the future."

"Devree's a smart woman." Donnel uncrossed his legs and picked up his drink.

"Your friend J. D. Cade did quite some number saving my skin, didn't he?"

The shadow of a smile settled on Donnel's lips. "Didn't think twice before he was on that sonofabitch."

Del smiled, too.

"You know, I told Mr. Cade almost exactly that. Told him I never saw a REMF move like him before." Del paused, then asked, "You PANIC boys ever see any combat?"

Donnel took a sip of his drink. "Well, you know, sometimes our jobs took us into AOs that were pretty much Indian country, and you always had to watch out for Charlie wherever you were. But we didn't do any actual fighting, no."

"Who was your CO in that outfit?" Del wanted to know.

"Our commanding officer?" Donnel looked into his glass, as if for an answer.

"Yeah. You remember his name?"

"Was . . ." Donnel looked up. "Was Colonel Garvin Townes."

Del made no overt response to the name, just nodded. Like he'd committed Townes' name to memory. The candidate put his feet up on the coffee table. "If I had my way, Donnel, you know what my motto for the rest of the campaign would really be?"

"What?"

"It'd be 'Let's just get the fucking job done.' "

"Amen to that, brother," Donnel replied.

Jenny had just left J. D. to do an interview with PBS—he'd declined to join her and she'd promised to see him later—and he was on his way to his suite when he passed the hotel gift shop and saw a newspaper headline that stopped him dead in his tracks.

He stopped in and, for camouflage, picked up a couple of magazines as well as the newspaper. Alone in his room, J. D. sat down to read. The newspaper was the *Los Angeles Times*. The reporter's name was Tom Hayashi. The headline read, "Authorities Find Restricted Sniper Rifle in Marina Del Rey Apartment."

The first paragraph told him everything he needed to know.

"A McLelland M-100 .50 caliber sniper rifle, a weapon supposed to be the exclusive property of the U.S. Navy SEALs, and the type of weapon suspected of being used in the assassination attempt against presidential candidate Senator Franklin Delano Rawley in Chicago, was found yesterday in a Marina Del Rey apartment by a strike force combining personnel from the LAPD, the FBI, and the Secret Service. The name of the apartment's tenant is being kept confidential, but a source revealed that he used a false identity when signing the lease agreement. Descriptions of the tenant by neighbors are sketchy, but he is said to be an African-American."

J. D. reread the paragraph several times, and each time he did his heart beat faster.

The M-100 he'd used was at the bottom of Lake Michigan. He had no doubt of that. But what if . . . what if someone else—a second assassin—had also been alerted that the plans for the M-100 had been briefly posted on the Internet? That would explain the weapon the cops and the feds had found at the Marina.

So there was no longer a question that a second assassin existed. No question in J. D.'s mind that Donnel Timmons was that assassin. No question that . . .

He'd placed his son in grave danger by saving Del Rawley's life that morning.

Two thousand miles to the east in Carbondale, Brady Farrel, the killer of Ivar McCray and Pru and Barton Laney, sat at the bar in Jack Duggan's, an ersatz Australian steakhouse. Along with all the other patrons, he raptly watched the TV screen on which J. D. Cade made the lunge seen round the world. The assassin's arm was deflected, the shot went astray, and a voice on the videotape yelled, "Gun!"

"Gun!" echoed the bartender at Jack Duggan's.

Serving a drink instead of watching the tube—he'd seen the tape a dozen times already—the bartender observed a scruffily dressed woman press the barrel of a revolver into the base of a patron's skull. The bartender was twenty-two years old, the holder of a freshly minted bachelor's degree in physical education, and a high-school assistant football coach. He saw his chance to be a hero like the guy on TV and he went for it.

Out of the corner of her eye, Deena Nokes saw him leap over the bar at her.

"No!" she yelled.

Farrel saw help on the way, too. Knowing it was now or never, he jumped from his bar stool to flee.

From that point on, things didn't work out quite as happily as they had in San Francisco. While the bartender deflected Deena's gun hand, he knocked it directly into line with the escaping Farrel. Trying to keep her grip on the gun, Deena squeezed the trigger and shot Ivar's killer squarely through the head. The lethal round continued on and claimed the restaurant's mascot as a second victim. Bruce the parrot, who'd sat in his gilded cage and warbled "Wild Colonial Boy," expired in a burst of multihued feathers.

People ran and ducked for cover, their screams, shrieks, and curses trailing behind them. Deena had held on to her gun, and now the bartender lay at her feet, having serious second thoughts about the doing of heroic deeds.

Deena looked at him and pointed her gun in his direction.

"You *stupid* shit," she said. "I was only holding him till the cops got here."

As if to verify her statement, a police siren wailed in the distance.

"Goddamnit, now what am I going to do?" Deena asked.

"Give yourself up?" the bartender suggested meekly.

Deena booted him in the belly. "I wasn't asking you, asshole."

Looking around at all the terrified people, knowing they

were peeing in their pants waiting for her to shoot someone else, certain she'd never be able to explain her way out of this shit storm, Deena decided the thing to do was run. People cowered and wailed as she raced for the door. All except for one warty, frog-faced sonofabitch standing near the exit. He looked at Deena so calmly she almost wanted to stop and smack him one, ask him if he hadn't been paying attention or what. But she didn't have the time. She bolted outside and ran for her hog.

Harold the Toad followed her out to the parking lot. He'd been on his way to the restaurant to meet with Farrel and tell him that he'd been relieved. The Toad could easily have disarmed the woman who'd killed Farrel and held her for the cops. But that would have ended her usefulness and exposed him to unwanted attention and questioning.

He decided to tail her instead. See if he might work her into his plans somehow.

She got a good lead on him, but following people surreptitiously was one of the Toad's many talents, and riding a poorly muffled motorcycle, trailing long blondish hair behind her, the woman wasn't exactly inconspicuous.

He followed her for quite some time. At first he'd thought she was simply going to make a run for it, head south and get as far away from the shooting as she could. But she soon changed directions and jinked from one back road to another. It became clear to the Toad she had no idea of where she wanted to go, that her anxiety was simply forcing her to keep moving.

He thought she was going to be of no use to him after all and he might as well kill her. He couldn't let her live because she obviously knew something about what Farrel had been doing. Otherwise, why would she have said she was holding him for the police? But before he could act on that decision, the woman turned off onto a path leading into the forest.

Harold the Toad parked his car on the shoulder of the road and followed on foot. He looked on from concealment in the woods at the clearing where Deena Nokes lived. He could see the tidy Airstream trailer and the collapsing log cabin. There was no light on in the trailer but the woman's motorcycle was parked beside it.

She was obviously at home.

The Toad liked this setup. He liked it very much indeed. So quiet and isolated. No one would ever hear any screams.

But first he had a bit of tidying up to do.

Evan Cade was spending his last night in the hospital before being discharged. The day had been one of staggering emotions. Like the rest of the country, he had seen the tape of his father saving Del Rawley's life. He'd watched replays until his eyes blurred.

Every Cade in southern Illinois had come by to exult with him; most of the hospital staff had dropped in to offer praise to his father. His grandmother and Ben had been delegated to speak for the family to the local media.

Best of all, when he'd booted up his laptop to send his father an e-mail, he'd found a message waiting for him:

I was in the right place at the right time, that's all. I'm unhurt. Please tell Grandma. Will call ASAP. I love you. Dad.

Evan couldn't recall ever feeling such a fierce joy before. It carried him through the day but left him depleted that night when he was finally alone. He'd already turned the light out and was drifting off when he heard a soft tapping at his door.

A young woman entered, but she wasn't his nurse. "Evan. Evan Cade, is that you?"

Now, as she stepped forward, Evan recognized her from school. "Jeri Perkins?"

She nodded. Jeri had been Pru Laney's best girlfriend.

"It's kind of late for visiting, Jeri."

"I know. I had to sneak in. I didn't want anyone to see me."

"Why?"

"I have something for you. Pru gave it to me."

"Pru?"

Jeri nodded, handed Evan an envelope, and started to sob softly.

"Pru said to give it to you if . . . if something happened to her. When I heard she'd died, I spent the whole day in bed crying. Then I got scared. I thought about throwing that envelope away. Pretending like I never saw it. But then I thought maybe if you didn't know what she wanted to tell you, you might end up like . . . like her."

The young woman's tears flowed freely and she gasped as if she couldn't get enough air.

"Jeri, are you all right? You want me to call the nurse for you?"

"No, no! I've got to go. Please, don't ever tell anyone I had that. Or even that I was here. Please, Evan, promise me."

"Okay, Jeri. I won't say a word."

She bobbed her head in gratitude and started to go. But she stopped in the shadows near the door. "I saw what your father did today, Evan. He's a very brave man."

"Thanks, Jeri."

"I just wish . . . I just wish someone could have done the same for Pru and her daddy."

"Me too."

Several of the patrons and some of the cops at Jack Duggan's were more upset about Bruce the Parrot getting whacked than the big guy with the hard face and the bandaged ear. In fact, they blamed the big guy—and Archie, the dim-witted bartender—as much as the woman with the gun for the beloved bird's demise.

Now, with the stiffs, both human and avian, removed, the crime scene people from the state police come and gone, and every last witness interviewed, Chief Billy Edwards sat with Blair McCray at the bar.

"So maybe now you think you should've told me your cousin's girlfriend was the witness to the Laney murders?" the chief asked Blair. "You think you should've told me she was the one who wounded that sonofabitch before she came back and killed him?"

"I think she found him before either of us did. I think she did the right thing calling me to come get him. I think she would have testified against him."

"Well, that won't be necessary anymore, will it?"

"No."

"No, indeed. Not after she drilled that sucker from one end of his brainpan to the other. And for all we know, he could be some innocent slob who'd just stopped in for a beer and a steak."

Blair McCray rolled his eyes.

"You really think that guy's name was Jack Armstrong?" he asked, referring to the ID found on the shooting victim's body. "Did he look like an all-American boy to you?"

"He looked shot dead to me, which never improves anybody's looks. And we'll find out who he is soon enough. But what interests me more is finding his killer." The chief gave his in-law a bleak look. "Anybody else held out on me like you did, I'd lock his ass up right now. Being family and a fellow cop, you get one last break. Tell me where I can find Deena Nokes."

Blair regarded the chief innocently. "I haven't heard from her the last couple of hours."

The chief sighed. "You think this woman got it right? That the guy she shot was the one who killed the Laneys. The one who killed Ivar. That Evan Cade wasn't involved."

Blair nodded. "That's pretty much what I think."

"Okay. If that's the case, then from your point of view, justice has been done."

The Kentucky lawman knew what was coming next.

"I think it's time you went home, Blair," Chief Billy Edwards said.

Garvin Townes had arrived in San Diego ahead of the Rawley campaign. He sat in his own hotel suite, not far from where Del Rawley was staying. He'd just sent Arnold Roth, the head of the senator's personal protection detail, out the door with his marching orders.

He'd yet to hear from Illinois, but he had confidence that his new, aggressive strategy for Evan Cade was the correct one—and he'd made it plain that it had better be implemented quickly.

Townes had been lured out of retirement by the prospect of becoming the incumbent's next national security adviser. As the president was a total incompetent beyond the grubby limits of domestic pork barrel politics, the way Townes really saw it was that he would be the president for foreign affairs—which was the only area of government he considered meaningful.

His foreign policy would be simplicity itself: Fuck with us, and we will kill you.

The big picture was, as always, perfectly clear. It was bringing all the endless pixels into resolution that was the hard part. And the most difficult detail, once again, was J. D. Cade.

Townes had to admit to himself he never should have

coerced J. D. Cade into joining the PANIC unit. Cade had intended to be a combat soldier, an army sniper. Had graduated first in his class from the sniper school at Fort Benning. He had been not only a deadly shot but also wonderfully bright. Townes had decided he just had to have this young man. He had been sure that Cade would come to see that he'd been honored by being chosen for an elite covert operation.

What Townes hadn't discovered until later was that Cade had been working out some sort of grudge against his father, and being assigned to a combat unit had been his means of doing so. By denying Cade that opportunity, Townes had thwarted him. Turned the boy sour. Made him rebel to the point where he thought he could choose his own targets, even kill an American officer.

Which, of course, was intolerable.

Townes had no choice but to cast aside his ambitions for J. D. Cade. But he hadn't forgotten him, oh, no. He had kept watch on a regular, if not constant, basis right from the start. And when his men had brought him pictures of how young Cade had eliminated his enemy, Alvy McCray, with a deer—a deer!—it had made him both gleeful and filled with regret. Such a talent as this could have come to full fruition under his tutelage.

He wondered how Cade had felt—what sort of, well, panic had raced through his mind—when he first saw the picture of himself kneeling on the highway, cutting the loop of rope from around the deer's neck.

He'd continued to receive reports on J. D. Cade down through the years. He'd learned with growing disappointment that Cade had settled into the domestic stupor of work and family like any other member of the common herd. Cade's only point of distinction was that he had refused to let his wonderful skills as a marksman wither away.

He'd continued to shoot regularly, brilliantly, and without fanfare. Just as Townes would have wanted.

In an amusing turn of events, Cade had even wound up doing his shooting under an assumed name, a thin disguise at best, but it showed that Cade's instincts were still sound.

He'd always known that the day would come when he'd call on Cade once more. That he'd make him live out his destiny. Even though it would cost Cade his life, Townes would see to it that his last act was one worthy of him—and of Townes.

But J. D. Cade was still insubordinate. Rebellious. Treacherous.

Delaying the hit on Rawley. Killing Danby. Always fighting him so hard.

It should have been different. They should have been such a great team.

DeVito sat in his hotel room with a cold can of soda pressed to his forehead, watching a video of J. D. Cade saving Del Rawley's life. Watching it for the millionth time, and Cade was still a mind-numbing contradiction to him. Then . . . then he saw it!

Mother of God! Cade had shot Danby *deliberately*!

Before he could even begin to guess what that meant, there was a loud knock at his door, and a harsh voice announced, "DeVito, this is Roth. Open up."

DeVito stopped the video, opened the door, and a grim-faced Roth entered the room.

"You're done," he said. "As of now, you're no longer part of Orpheus' protection detail. You're to proceed to Washington, where you will be separated from the service."

"Gee, Arnie," DeVito asked, "was it something I said?"

"Be out of this room by oh six hundred hours, DeVito. I don't want to see you anywhere near this campaign again."

"I know what it is," DeVito replied. "You're upset. You miss your playmate, Danby. The two of you were close, weren't you?"

Rage flared in Roth's eyes, but before he could say anything someone else entered the room. DeVito turned to see Orpheus walk in with his Secret Service escort.

"Am I interrupting something, gentlemen?" the candidate asked.

"Mr. Roth has just told me my services are no longer required, Senator," DeVito informed Del. "And he's urged me not to sleep in tomorrow."

"The director's decision," Roth explained.

"I see. Perhaps it's time I had a talk with the director."

"That's your prerogative, Senator."

"Just as it would be my prerogative to forsake Secret Service protection entirely."

On that point, both Roth and DeVito started to object, but Rawley held up his hand.

"I haven't reached that decision—yet. But I will allow no question as to who is in control of this campaign. Each and every detail of it. Mr. Roth, you tell the director he is to call me at seven A.M. tomorrow. We are going to have a discussion concerning all personnel matters. If he isn't on the phone to me at that time, and in a damned agreeable mood, I will discharge all of you gentlemen—and how will that look to the public?"

Rawley turned to DeVito. "Special Agent DeVito, if I can't persuade the director to see things my way, you will be the head of my campaign's new private security team."

Roth was too busy grinding his teeth to object. He gave DeVito a murderous glance and left. Rawley asked the other agents with him for a moment alone with DeVito. They stepped into the hall and closed the door behind them.

"Senator, please listen to me. Roth's an asshole, but it'd be a mistake—"

"Special Agent, I haven't committed myself to any action except letting everyone know who's the boss around here. Now, if I can't even keep control of my own campaign, what kind of president would I be?"

DeVito relaxed and smiled appreciatively. "Yes, sir."

"The reason I wanted to see you is there's someone I want you to check out for me."

"Who?"

"A man by the name of Garvin Townes."

"Senator, I can tell you who he is."

"You know him?"

"Not personally. But I know that three months ago he was appointed to head Treasury's new Departmental Internal Management and Oversight unit. Townes is Arnold Roth's boss."

Rawley hadn't known that because filling the newly created job hadn't required the approval of the Senate. But there was no question who had put Townes into place.

"Townes is a presidential appointee."

"Could be the secretary of the treasury put Townes where he is," DeVito responded.

"Yes, possibly." That would give the incumbent the shield of deniability.

But Del Rawley knew who was ultimately responsible.

J. D. was in his suite with Jenny Crenshaw—not taking advantage of the night of grand passion she'd promised him as a token of gratitude for his heroism. He was staring out a window at Mission Bay. It seemed to Jenny, sitting on a sofa behind him, that he'd been brooding over something all day.

She said, "I really don't understand you. Your son is cleared of a murder charge. You save the life of the man who will be the next president. I offer to show you a *very* good time . . . and you act like your best friend just died."

J. D. turned to look at Jenny. Her face was smudged with fatigue, but it was still one you could fall in love with at a glance. One you could love until your last breath. And all he could do was lie to her.

"I think I'm feeling what you did the other night, a sense of mortality. How I might have come very close to dying today."

He saw that she accepted, even sympathized with, the explanation. And why not? It was a plausible lie. He'd become very good at improvising lately: explosives, lies, whatever the situation required. He looked back out the window.

He couldn't fool himself, though. He'd fucked up badly.

Saving Del Rawley's life had been a serious mistake. Worse, he'd come to realize that he'd done it not for any noble reason but as a sop to his ego. He'd done it so Evan would be proud of him. So his son would think that he was more than just a killer, someone who did people in without leaving a trace and then sneaked away.

Of course, that hadn't kept him from shooting Danby, had it?

Evan would have been far better off if he'd simply played the coward and let Prentice Colter shoot Del Rawley. Because the discovery of the second M-100 had convinced him that the second-assassin threat was no mere ploy. That madman Townes actually was running a contest: first assassin to kill Del Rawley won, loser suffered the consequences. Only in his case, Townes had set things up so Evan would suffer the consequences.

J. D. was sure that his son's reprieve in the matter of Ivar McCray's death was only temporary. Townes would have some other card to play. Say, a witness waiting for his cue to come forward and say he had seen Evan filch the incriminating shoes from the Salvation Army store. He should have thought to warn Evan's lawyer of such a ploy.

J. D. saw only one short-term solution to his problem. He had to eliminate his competition. He had to kill Donnel. Then there'd be no way the second assassin could finish first.

And if J. D. couldn't find Townes quickly and eliminate him . . . he'd have to kill Del Rawley, too.

Jenny came up behind him. She put her hands on his shoulders, pressed her cheek against his back. It was of small comfort to him that he'd decided not to fabricate nude pictures of her with the senator. She started murmuring words of encouragement to him, how brave and strong and wonderful he'd been. She was praising him, but she was also feeling sorry for him, and he couldn't have that. He couldn't let her get too close to knowing what was really in his heart. To knowing who he really was.

He turned and put his hands on her hips. He smiled briefly and kissed her.

"I'll be fine," he said. "Give me a day or two and I'll be ready to take you up on your generous offer."

Jenny repaid his kiss with one of her own and left J. D. alone with his thoughts. He tried to call Evan at his hospital room but the line was busy. He'd no sooner put the phone down than it rang. He regarded the instrument warily, let it ring again, and then picked up the receiver.

"Hello."

"Mr. Cade, I'm sorry if I'm disturbing you."

"Not at all, Senator. What can I do for you?"

"Mr. Cade, have you ever met the president?"

The question was so unexpected J. D. didn't know what to make of it.

"No. Never met him. Never even seen him in person."

"How about anyone else in Washington? The secretary of the treasury, perhaps?"

A sudden jolt of nervous energy rushed through J. D. Had Del Rawley discovered the connection between him and Townes? He continued in what he hoped was a normal voice.

"No, Senator. I don't know if Ms. Crenshaw told you, but I was *averse* to politics before I became aware of your campaign."

"She did mention that to me, yes. Well, I apologize for the late call . . . but as long as I have you, I'd like to ask if you could join me for breakfast. Say, eight o'clock?"

"My pleasure, Senator. I'll see you then."

J. D. hung up, trying to sort out the situation. If Rawley had learned of his relationship to Townes, that had to be the beginning of the end for him. He'd never succeed in killing the man with anything short of a kamikaze blitz.

But if Rawley had found him out, why invite him to breakfast?

Unless it was a ruse to lull his suspicions.

Unless it was a trap.

Jenny lay in bed, still awake, still bothered by J. D. Cade's somber mood, when her phone rang. "Hello."

"Your humble servant calls."

Don Ward's voice was more spectral than ever.

"Don! I'm so glad to hear from you."

"A pleasure I won't be able to provide for very much longer, I'm afraid. The end is so near I can almost foretell the hour."

"Oh, Jesus, Don. I want so much to see you a—"

"No, no, Jenny. Far better that you don't. I'd only horrify you. I'd rather you remembered me as I once was."

Jenny started to cry.

"Please, my dear, don't do that," Hunter Ward said. "A broken heart is more than I could endure in my present state . . . and we both have more work to do."

Jenny held back her tears and, understanding the implicit warning she'd just heard, she asked, "You have more news, Don?"

"Senator Rawley is going to be smeared again tomorrow . . . in time for the morning news shows."

Jenny's sorrow hardened to anger. "What kind of smear?"

"The president is going to say that the FBI has been unable to find the assassin who's out to kill Senator Rawley because there isn't one. He's—"

"What!"

"Please, my dear. Allow me to finish."

"I'm sorry, Don," she said, chastened.

"The president is going to say that the Justice Department has received an anonymous tip, which they're investigating with every resource at their command, that Rawley partisans staged both the attempt on the senator's life in Chicago and the attempt on Special Agent DeVito's life in Los Angeles to create sympathy for the senator's candidacy."

"That's—" Jenny bit her tongue and forced herself to continue listening.

"That's what they're going to claim. Both shots were deliberate misses."

"What about that super sniper rifle, the one that was found in Marina Del Rey?"

"It turns out that isn't the genuine article but a copy. A poorly made knockoff. Just what you'd expect from a hoax."

"What about Prentice Colter in San Francisco, goddamnit?" Jenny calmed herself before she went off on a rant. "I'm sorry, Don. I'm not swearing at you. But this is so infuriating." She took a deep breath. "What are they going to say about Colter? That we put a mentally ill busboy up to making an attempt on Del's life? Or was he supposed to miss his target, too?"

"No, they'll admit that one was real. But the president, if asked, will say it was the work of a random lunatic. And was possibly inspired by the staged events."

Despite her resolve, Jenny muttered a torrent of curses under herbreath.

"They're desperate, Jenny," Don told her. "They can read the poll numbers. They know if they don't do something fast, they're finished."

"So now they throw mud at us, attribute it to an anonymous source, and put Del on the defensive. Then they wait until after the election to say 'Sorry, looks like that tip was unfounded.' And by that time they're preparing for their inauguration."

"As I said, my dear," Hunter Ward repeated, "we have miles to go before we sleep."

The Secret Service agents standing at his side didn't like it, but Del Rawley sat on the balcony of his suite, stared out at the great black void that was the Pacific, and explored thoughts as dark as the night.

Foremost among them: Was the president trying to have him killed?

The president had appointed, directly or indirectly, Garvin Townes to his position in the Treasury Department. Townes' man, Roth, was heading his protection detail. Townes' former army subordinate, J. D. Cade, had become part of his campaign. Cade liked to fire rifles.

It was too neat, though, to think that Cade was the man

who had tried to kill him in Chicago. Because if he had been . . . why would he have saved his life in San Francisco?

What kind of a man would be capable of such a contradiction?

Still, it had to be more than coincidence that Cade shared a common history with Townes. Now, the question was what to do with J. D. Cade. Distance him or let him stay close?

With a man who liked to fire rifles over long distances, maybe close was better.

It would be a lot harder for him to slip a weapon past the Secret Service at close range, that was for sure. But then how far could he trust the Secret Service?

Not far enough to tell them he had the handgun DeVito had smuggled to him.

And if Cade turned out to be an assassin, could he, Del Rawley, kill the man who'd saved his life? Yes, he could. Because if Cade was on some kind of kill-him-save-him-kill-him cycle, he was crazier than Prentice Colter. He'd have regrets, but he'd kill Cade to save his own life.

The whole thing would be a lot easier, Del Rawley thought, if DeVito could come up with something more on Garvin Townes' background and how he came to have his current job.

The candidate's thoughts were interrupted when another agent stepped onto the balcony. "Senator? Ms. Crenshaw's here. She says it's urgent."

Evan Cade stared at Blair McCray incredulously and said, "Dead?"

He had been about to watch the digital video disc that Jeri Perkins had brought him when Blair stepped into his hospital room. He'd come to tell Evan that Deena Nokes had shot the man they'd all sought: the killer of Ivar and the Laneys.

Evan felt a surprising sense of disappointment. It stung him that he'd lost his chance for vengeance. He sat back against the bed feeling he'd failed Pru once more.

Then he and Blair watched the DVD on his laptop computer.

Pru's tearstained face appeared on the screen and it broke Evan's heart to see her again. The pain was made worse when he heard her confess that she'd learned her father had been involved in a scheme to make it look like Evan had been responsible for Ivar McCray's death. Only her father had sworn to her that the plan hadn't been for Ivar to die; he was only supposed to be framed for extortion. That was what the man who had paid Barton Laney all that money said he wanted: to send Ivar to jail for a long time for defrauding him in a business deal. And Evan wasn't supposed to be blamed for any killing; he was supposed to be the hero who tipped off the police to Ivar's extortion attempt. Then everything went wrong when Ivar died.

The man had explained to her father that when somebody died accidentally during the commission of a felony it was just like you planned to kill him. It was murder and her father would be executed for the death of a worthless biker unless he let the blame be laid off on Evan.

The man had even told her she could be locked up for being an accessory after the fact.

Pru apologized to Evan for not coming forward to clear him, but she couldn't let her father face the death penalty. Not when he'd done what he did only to benefit her. She promised that if Evan went to trial for Ivar McCray's killing, she would come forward. Her father would have had enough time to run somewhere far away by then.

Pru repeated how sorry she was . . . and that she still loved Evan.

Tears ran down Evan Cade's face.

"That statement exonerates you," Blair told him in a soft voice.

Evan looked at him and asked, "Weren't you sorry that it wasn't you who nailed the sonofabitch?"

"I got to see him shot through the head. That was enough for me."

The morgue was in the basement of the hospital, four floors below where Evan Cade talked with Blair McCray. There was only one attendant on duty and he had his nose buried in a Dean Koontz novel right up until the time the Toad creased his skull with the barrel of his pistol.

The Toad put the attendant on an empty gurney and covered him with a sheet. He left him among the four other bodies awaiting the medical examiner's attention. A classic example of hiding something in plain sight.

Farrel was under the second sheet that the Toad lifted. He looked at Farrel's fingertips: no ink stains. So he hadn't been fingerprinted the old-fashioned way. A quick search of the morgue revealed no biomorphic scanner, so he hadn't been printed the modern way, either. Which saved the Toad a lot of trouble. If someone wanted to try to track down Farrel under the name of Jack Armstrong, good luck to him.

The Toad dropped the sheet back into place and wheeled Farrel out the door the meat wagons used when they ferried bodies to and from the hospital. Per his custom, the Toad had rented a full-sized car with a huge trunk. He made Farrel fit easily enough.

Motoring away, the Toad thought it was as neat a job of morgue robbing as he'd ever done. Of course, small-town hospitals with their nonexistent security were no great challenge. Still, details like not allowing the local cops to get any clue as to whose body they had briefly held were part of the drill when you ran a first-rate covert operation.

And the Toad had sold himself to the Gardener as indisputably first-rate.

He'd bury Farrel's body in one of the endless stretches of national forest that lay so conveniently close at hand. Then he'd plan how to take care of the rest of his chores. He kept envisioning that trailer in the woods as the silver basket into which he'd put all his eggs.

"There is one thing about Prudence Laney's statement that bothers me a great deal," Blair told Evan, "something that's just not true."

"What?" Evan asked.

Blair began to pace the room.

"She said the reason that sonofabitch went after Ivar in the first place was that Ivar cheated him in a business deal somehow." Blair shook his head. "No way. If Ivar disagreed how a pie got sliced, he'd certainly fight you about it. But it'd be bare knuckles. He wasn't given to guile and sneakiness. Didn't have the capacity morally or mentally. So if it wasn't that . . ." Blair stopped and looked directly at Evan. "It's almost as if Ivar was chosen to die to start up the old feud again."

"And the blame would be pinned on me." Evan carried Blair's idea one step farther. "Maybe there's someone else out there. Maybe somebody who planned this whole thing. Maybe a second thug ready to do more dirty work."

While they considered that possibility, the room's telephone rang. Evan answered, listened, and said, "Just a minute."

He extended the phone to Blair. "Your in-law, the chief. You were seen entering the hospital. He was notified and figured you'd be here."

Blair took the phone and said, "Hello." A moment later he added, "I'll be right down."

He gave the phone back to Evan, who hung it up.

"What'd he want?" Evan asked.

"No question we've got somebody else involved," Blair told him. "Somebody just broke into the morgue downstairs and stole the body of the man Deena Nokes killed."

Dixie Wynne rolled into the driveway of his home in Gainesville, Florida, with his lights out. He tapped the button on his garage door opener and watched the door roll up. Then he eased his GMC 4 x 4 inside and lowered the door behind him.

He slipped into his house without turning on any of the lights. His plan was to stay in his house a day or two without letting anybody know he was back. He'd do a little peeking out from behind his blinds and drapes. If everything seemed okay, he'd emerge like he'd just returned from the hunting trip he'd told his neighbor Tag Olney he'd been on. If anything at all seemed wrong to him, he'd slip away in the middle of the night and accept that he'd have to make a new life for himself somewhere else.

Dixie lay down in the comfort of his own bed. After having slept on the ground far too long for a man who wouldn't see fifty again, he was asleep within minutes. He never knew that as soon as his garage door had gone up, a circuit had been closed and a signal had been sent to his former colleagues on the Gainesville PD SWAT team.

The neighbors would be evacuated first and then they'd come for Dixie.

Before going to sleep, J. D. checked for a message from Pickpocket and found one:

Might be on to something big re Townes. Will advise if it pans out.

    Haven't found Donnel Timmons' new line of work yet, but made another interesting discovery. He has a Michigan permit to carry a concealed weapon.

THIRTEEN
Wednesday, September 22, 2004

It seemed to J. D. that he'd been asleep for only minutes when the phone rang. He blinked twice to clear his vision and saw that it was in fact 2 A.M. His heart went cold when he thought that somehow the call would bring him bad news about Evan.

His voice was little more than a grunt. "Hello."

"J. D., it's Jenny. I'm sorry to wake you, but we have a crisis here."

"Where?" he asked.

"I'm calling from Del's suite. He asked if you could sit in with the rest of us."

"Now?"

A new strain of anxiety swam through his mind. It was the middle of the night. No innocent bystanders around. They were springing the trap on him.

"As soon as you can make it. Can we expect you shortly?"

What could he say? "Give me ten minutes."

A pair of Secret Service agents was waiting for him when he opened his door. Not to arrest him, but to escort him to the meeting. So he'd just been feeling paranoid. This time.

Del Rawley convened the predawn meeting around a

conference table in his suite. With the candidate were Jenny and the rest of the brain trust. Also present was Donnel Timmons. J. D. was the last to arrive. Donnel gave him a small nod when he entered the room.

Everyone listened to what Jenny had learned from Don Ward.

J. D. kept his face impassive when he heard the M-100 that had been found was a copy. His weapon had been a copy, too. A perfectly lethal copy. If the second weapon had belonged to Donnel, J. D. was sure it could do the job, too. The claim that it was a shoddy knockoff had to be spin to support the president's claim of a hoax.

But the others had different concerns.

"This is despicable," Alita said. "Del almost dies and they say it was all a scam to gain sympathy."

Baxter was uncharacteristically restrained, which meant he was thinking as hard as he could. "Despicable, but pretty damn smart. How do we disprove their assertion? Ask the assassin to step forward and say a few words on our behalf?"

J. D. maintained his mask of neutrality.

"We can expect big, *big* drops in our numbers if we don't find an effective way to fight this," Jim Greenberg informed them. "And if this lie gains popular credence, we're finished."

Del looked at Jenny. She was the campaign manager. She was the one who had to figure out a way to fight back. But at the moment she seemed as stuck for an answer as any of them.

"I'll think of something," she assured everyone.

"Better be fast," Baxter Brown replied.

J. D. was surprised that he had an idea and a reason to offer it. If, for whatever reason, he failed to keep both Evan and himself alive, if he didn't, in fact, kill Del Rawley, who did he want to see as president? It was crazy . . . but what wasn't these days?

He gently cleared his throat and all eyes shifted to him. "I'm new to all this. So I don't know if this is a good idea or not."

"What's that, Mr. Cade?" Del asked, very interested that the man who liked to fire rifles had a suggestion. Then a thought occurred to the candidate: If Cade really was the man who had taken the shot at him in Chicago, and he was now working so closely with the campaign, who would ever believe that the attempt on his life hadn't been a fake?

"You believe the incumbent is using this tactic strictly for political advantage?" J. D. asked.

"Yes."

"And he, in fact, knows that the assassination attempts were real?"

"Yes."

"Well, then, why don't you invite him to campaign with you?"

Everyone was stunned by the notion, but Jenny smiled brightly.

"Sure, I see it. Call his bluff. Ask him to share the same stage with Del, where *he* might wind up in somebody's gun sight . . . Oh, I'm sorry, Del, I shouldn't have put it that way."

The candidate smiled thinly. "That's pretty much what it amounts to." He turned to J. D. "Make the man put up or shut up, that's the idea, Mr. Cade?"

J. D. nodded. "Turn it around on him, Senator. If he says you're a fraud, he should have no reason to be afraid of making appearances with you. If he refuses, he's either a liar or a coward." J. D. asked Jim Greenberg, "What'd that do to the numbers?"

Del smiled. "I think you have an aptitude for this business, Mr. Cade."

"Beginner's luck, Senator."

While the candidate and his brain trust started to work

out the details of their response to the incumbent's ploy, J. D. went back to his suite and gave the matter further thought. What was it Rawley's political adviser had said? Could they ask the assassin to step forward and admit he'd been working in deadly earnest? No, of course they couldn't.

Even so, Colonel Townes couldn't take the chance of letting J. D. ever reveal the truth. So if there was a new strategy in place to eliminate Del Rawley politically rather than mortally, and the current propaganda had it that there was no assassin and never had been, it then became a necessity to get rid of anyone who could prove that assertion wrong. Him.

Donnel, too.

Of course, that assumed that Townes was working directly for the president.

The problem with that was, from what J. D. knew of Townes, the colonel never worked directly with or for anyone. His mind was too twisted to proceed along straight lines. It was entirely likely that the president's political people had come up with this strategy independently of what Townes was doing.

His attempt to kill Del Rawley and the two attempts to drive Rawley from the race politically seemed to be the products of two separate sets of thinking. Two different planners. So there could be crosscurrents at play here. J. D.'s guess was that Townes still wanted to see Del Rawley dead. If not, why would he have placed *two* assassins so close to the man?

Having lost his M-100, Donnel would have to get the job done up close.

And if anything, Donnel's access to Rawley was even better than J. D.'s.

———

Garvin Townes walked along Mission Beach in the predawn darkness. He heard the soft lapping of water on sand. The sound murmured in his ear like a lover's invitation: Join me. The notion of suicide had occurred to him before. It was especially apt now when, one way or another, the consequence of failure at the game he was playing would be the loss of his life.

Death had been his lifelong companion. Granted, he'd been its agent, but being so intimate with the mortality of others, he had lost all fear of his own. It was not dying that was to be feared, Townes knew, it was dying *badly*.

Dying young was bad, Townes conceded. So was dying at the hands of an enemy. Dying one day at a time in a prison cell was very bad. Perhaps worst of all, in Townes' view, was dying and leaving important work undone.

Of the latter two, which were the only possibilities he could see applying to him, he was sure that he could take his life to avoid imprisonment. And if someone took away from him the last opportunity he had to do something significant with the remainder of his life, then suicide seemed like a choice he could . . . No, you couldn't say live with, could you? But should he be denied what would be his crowning achievement, killing himself was something he could see doing without regret.

As long as he removed J. D. Cade and maybe a few others first.

Del Rawley showed up at the CBS affiliate in San Diego at 4:25 a.m. One of the anchors of the local morning news show was an old friend who used to work in Madison, Wisconsin, where Rawley lived. He trusted her. She and her coanchor were stunned to have the leading presidential candidate drop in out of the blue five minutes before airtime, five minutes before the president was to make what was billed as a crucial announcement concerning the election.

The anchors had thought they would be part of the mob fighting for Rawley's reaction to whatever it was the president had to say. Del Rawley was quickly patted down with makeup as the show's producer called New York to let the network know about their unexpected guest.

Jenny and the Secret Service detail looked on as the anchors started to question Del.

Did he know what the president was going to say?

Could Senator Rawley give them a preview of what he was going to say?

Had he heard the rumor that the president might drop out of the race?

The last question made Del smile. "No, I didn't hear that one."

The president went on the air at 7:30 Eastern time from the White House press room.

He made the disclosure that the Justice Department had received an anonymous tip that the shots fired at Senator Rawley in Chicago and at one of the Secret Service agents protecting him in Los Angeles were hoaxes designed to elicit sympathy for the candidacy of Senator Rawley. The weapon, previously believed to be an M-100 sniper rifle, had been shown to come from neither the armories of the navy SEALs nor any of the factories of McLellan Munitions, Inc. The FBI was already hard at work investigating the allegation of fraud, the president said. He continued, saying that he was making this news public only because he considered the situation a crisis for American democracy. The possibility that a deceit of historic proportion might influence the outcome of a presidential election had persuaded him that the American people must be told.

A reporter asked the president if there was the slightest

bit of corroborating evidence for such an outrageous allegation against Senator Rawley. The president replied that he was not accusing Senator Rawley of having any complicity in or knowledge of such a plot, if it existed. The president said political partisans often took measures of which candidates were unaware.

But what evidence was there that Rawley supporters might be behind such a scandalous deception? The president said that there was no evidence against specific individuals, but what made the allegation impossible to ignore or to keep quiet was that it squared completely with the fact that the FBI had been unable to find any trace of a real assassin.

Could that be because the assassin, while not yet successful, had been better at his job than the FBI had been at theirs? The president bristled at the suggestion and told the reporter that was an interpretation of events *he* would never make.

"Mr. President, how would you feel about having *your* campaign investigated at this point in the race?"

"In Senator Rawley's place," the president said, "I would welcome such an investigation."

In San Diego, Jenny gave the finger to the president's image on a TV monitor.

As soon as the president was off the air, Del went on. CBS magnanimously made their feed available to all the other networks—at Del's suggestion. Del's old friend from Wisconsin asked simply, "Senator Rawley, what is your response to what the president has said this morning?"

"My response is simply this: Mr. President, I invite you to join me for the rest of the campaign. Let us make joint appearances all across our great country. Let there be no public venue where one of us is seen without the other. If I truly have nothing to fear, then you have nothing to fear by appearing with me. In fact, sir, I don't see how you could possibly fail to accept my invitation. Because if you do, you will automatically undercut the credibility of the allegation you say the Justice Department has received. The allegation you deemed so important that it compelled you to speak to the nation. And by campaigning together, Mr. President, you'll have the opportunity to investigate my campaign firsthand. Perhaps you'll be able to ferret out the culprit behind such an act of ignominy . . . should such a culprit exist outside the imagination of *your* partisans."

The other anchor asked Del if there was any precedent for major presidential candidates campaigning together.

"Actually, there is. John Kennedy and Barry Goldwater planned to do it in 1964. The idea was that they would travel together from town to town. At one stop, Kennedy would speak first and Goldwater would rebut. At the next town, each man would take the opposite role. I would be very happy to offer the same arrangement to the president."

"But that plan was obviously never put into effect—"

"Because President Kennedy was assassinated," Del completed the thought. "But neither the president nor I should have to worry about that if the man who shot at me is just a prankster."

Jenny smiled grimly. She had come up with the story about Kennedy and Goldwater. Now, if the president refused to accept Del's invitation—his challenge—it would show not only that he was afraid but also that he didn't measure up to a major hero from each party.

"On the other hand," Del continued, "perhaps the president remembers Anton Cermak."

"I'm sorry, Senator," the anchor replied. "You'll have to help me with that one."

"Anton Cermak was the mayor of Chicago. In 1933 he attended a political rally in Miami and had the honor to sit in an open car next to my namesake, Franklin Delano Roosevelt. A man jumped out of the crowd that was watching the president motor by and fired a shot at Roosevelt. He missed the president but the shot struck Mayor Cermak . . . who died of his wound."

"You think the president should worry about something similar happening to him if he campaigns with you?"

"No, not if he believes the allegation of a hoax he felt it was his duty to share with the country." Del looked directly into the camera. "On the other hand, let's see how he responds to my invitation. The phone lines are open, Mr. President."

DeVito jumped when the phone rang in the coffin-sized office he was using at the Federal Building in San Diego. He'd been hunched over a computer for hours in unfamiliar surroundings, and he wasn't expecting a call. He reached for the receiver with suspicion, as if it might explode in his hand.

It didn't, and the caller, an agent with Orpheus' protection detail, had good news. The candidate had spoken with the director and DeVito still had a job. But everyone was leaving for Costa Mesa in an hour. So haul ass back to the hotel.

DeVito hung up and slipped the printouts of the work he'd done over the past several hours into a binder. The life and times of Garvin Townes. Public records of his early life and education were easy to come by. The man had been born and raised in Lawrence, Kansas, and came from a locally prominent family. Townes had gone off to Yale, and after graduating he took a job with an international construction firm, Amcon, Inc. Townes' starting position had been that of a troubleshooter. Two years later his job description had been changed to termination consultant.

Given the man's connection to J. D. Cade—the long-distance shooter—*termination* might take on a very sinister meaning.

But, to all outward appearances, Townes was an upstanding citizen. Had joined the National Guard in Virginia, where he had his official residence. Got called up and sent to Vietnam—as a captain. Okay, maybe he got a big leg up because he was an Ivy League grad. But within a year he was a major and the next year a full colonel. DeVito had heard of rapid battlefield promotions, but Townes was supposed to have been in a warehouse in Saigon keeping the guys who parceled out socks and jocks from robbing the store blind. Something wasn't kosher about his army career.

Especially when DeVito saw he'd stayed over there for *five years*. Gung-ho combat lifers hadn't stayed that long. And a guy with a Yale sheepskin had found a career in Pilferage and Inventory Control? PANIC, they'd called it. Yeah, must've been a real scream, DeVito thought sourly. A million laughs to stay in that goddamn country so long.

Then Townes had left the army in '72 and . . . disappeared. There was no record of him even being alive until he showed up where? In the Treasury Department. Head of Departmental Internal Management and Oversight. DEIMOS. Which DeVito had just looked up in a reference database because it sounded sort of familiar. The monitor in front of his weary eyes told him Deimos was one of the two moons of Mars.

Maybe that was where Townes had been hiding all those years, DeVito thought.

A link on the screen offered to call up further references for the word. DeVito wasn't sure it was worth the effort. He'd been told to hustle back to the campaign. The circus was about to leave town. He got up from the desk and headed toward the door, but he stopped, thinking he'd better not leave the computer on; somebody might come along and see what he'd been doing. The thing to do was go back to the starting menu and shut the machine down.

But when he got back to the desk his hand reached out for the mouse, almost of its own accord, and clicked on the link for further references. Up came a screen that informed him that in Greek mythology, Deimos was the son of Mars, the god of war.

Below that, in small type he had to blink to see, was one last reference.

Deimos was Greek for "panic."

J. D. had gone back to bed to catch up on his sleep and managed to get another three hours. After a stingingly cold shower, he felt relatively rested and alert. Room service brought breakfast, and he was done eating and dressed by 6:30.

He accessed Pickpocket's private chat room, hoping that the little thief might have . . .

> *Bingo! You wanted to know about Townes? You think having his autobiography might help? It's called "In the Defense of Liberty." Instructions to Townes' lawyer say it's to be published fifty years after his death. The damn thing was protected by safeguards that took Red and me all night to figure out. Great fun! Hope this helps you fuck the people who had me shot.*

J. D. quickly downloaded the attached file and started to read with his heart pounding.

The first thing he noticed was that the manuscript had an index. He quickly scanned it . . . and found his name. Continuing on, he found a reference for Alvy McCray, and for the PANIC unit.

J. D. had no doubt that Pickpocket had read at least the material that pertained to him. Most likely Red had, too. Little by little his secrets were slipping away from him. But in this case, he felt sure they wouldn't go any farther. After all, Pickpocket wouldn't have met his new girlfriend or even be alive to continue plying his trade if not for J. D.

Besides, when you'd learned somebody you knew had killed people, you probably didn't want to get on his bad side.

But J. D.'s feelings for the little thief and his friend were overwhelmingly positive just then.

They'd given him the key to get out of Townes' trap without having to kill anyone.

He was still reading when the phone rang and Jenny asked him to return to Del Rawley's suite—immediately.

J. D. said he'd be right there, but he took the time to assign a password to Townes' memoirs. Then he shut down the computer and locked it in his suite's safe. Another pair of Secret Service agents escorted him to Del Rawley's suite.

"They're waiting for you, Mr. Cade," said one of the agents at the door.

J. D. entered the room where the Rawley brain trust had gathered around a large-screen TV. Jenny spotted him and told him to hurry over. J. D. picked up his step and stood behind the sofa on which Del Rawley sat.

The candidate looked up over his shoulder at J. D. and said, "We're about to see how your strategy played at the White House, Mr. Cade."

The TV showed the press room at the executive mansion. The lectern was unmanned. Then the president's press secretary strode into the room and stepped behind it.

He began without preamble. "The president has instructed me to inform you that he accepts Senator Rawley's invitation to campaign with him. The president's campaign manager, Mr. Ronald Turlock, will be calling the senator's campaign manager, Ms. Jennifer Crenshaw, as soon as I've completed my remarks."

The Rawley suite erupted in cheers. Del looked up at J. D. and grinned. Special Agent DeVito slipped into the suite, noticed only by his colleagues.

"The president, furthermore, will make the gracious first gesture of altering his schedule to meet Senator Rawley in Los Angeles tomorrow. There he hopes to sit down with the senator and successfully negotiate an itinerary that will meet the needs of both candidates. I have no further information at this time and I will be taking no questions."

Which, of course, didn't keep the newsies from screaming a blizzard of questions at the press secretary anyway. The din died when Del Rawley clicked off the set—just in time to hear the phone ring.

"I believe that's for me," Jenny said. "I'll take it in the next room."

The candidate stood and extended his hand to J. D. "Thank you, Mr. Cade. You've done me another service."

Unaware of all that had transpired in the hours he'd spent in the federal building, DeVito watched Cade shake hands with the candidate. Once again he'd come back to find that the man he was increasingly sure was an assassin had turned out to be a hero.

He just couldn't under—

DeVito saw Roth enter the room. Roth's features were impassive, all except for his eyes. His eyes—looking squarely at J. D. Cade—blazed with hatred. No, even that was not adequate to describe what Roth was feeling. It was something more. It was . . . *betrayal.*

In a moment of revelation, DeVito was suddenly sure he knew what was happening.

Cade, the guy from PANIC, was supposed to be working

for Roth, the guy from DEIMOS. But he'd turned on Roth. Fuck, he'd *shot* Roth's partner, Danby. Maybe he was even going to go after Roth himself.

DeVito made sure his own face was a mask as Roth approached. At first he thought Roth was coming to say something to him, but the prick didn't give him so much as a glance, just walked up to Orpheus and asked if he expected to depart according to schedule.

DeVito thought Roth was clearly a man with a lot on his mind . . . like maybe *he'd* have to kill Orpheus if Cade wasn't going to do the job.

The only other person in the room who noticed Roth's mute rage was Donnel Timmons.

Blair McCray's pickup truck pulled up in front of Belle Cade's house on Lark Lane. He'd brought Evan home from the hospital. After talking with Chief Billy Edwards in the morgue last night, the two lawmen had gone up to Evan's room. There the chief had watched and then taken possession of the digital video disc that Pru Laney had made for Evan.

Evan had already copied the confession to his hard disk.

The chief begrudgingly admitted that it seemed to exculpate Evan in the matter of Ivar McCray's death. And with the Laneys and the man who killed them all dead, that left him only with finding Deena Nokes and whoever it was that had stolen the body from the morgue.

Billy Edwards had told them, "You two have clean noses right now as far as I'm concerned. Keep 'em that way. Don't go poking around in my business."

Blair intended to ignore that admonition quite soon; Evan, somewhat later.

"You over that dizzy spell?" Blair asked.

"It's passing," Evan said.

Evan had thought he'd recovered, and for lying down in a hospital room, he had. But when he'd started walking from the hospital exit to Blair's pickup the disequilibrium returned. Still, he insisted on going home. If rest was what he needed, he'd be more comfortable at his grandmother's house.

"You want me to—" Blair saw Belle Cade step out her front door. "I guess your grandmother can help you inside."

Evan watched Belle approach and then turned back to Blair.

"She's not carrying her shotgun, anyway," he said with a smile.

"Yeah, things must be looking up."

"You going to talk with Deena?"

"Yeah. See if we can't find that body snatcher. Though I can't imagine how."

"Good. Maybe by the time you come up with a plan, I'll be back on my feet."

Blair McCray steered his pickup truck into the clearing where Deena Nokes' trailer sat. He pulled up close to the front stoop. He put his eyes on the tumbledown log cabin but saw no sign of Gorbachev, and when he looked back at Deena's trailer she was standing in the doorway with her gun in her hand.

She beckoned him to come inside. He entered, closed the door behind him, and looked around.

"Where's your friend?" he asked, referring to LuAnne, the other biker mama.

"After what happened at Giant City, she started flakin' out. So I put her on a Greyhound to Ypsilanti. Where's your buddy?"

Blair told her he was at home, recuperating from his

head injury. Then he informed her that the body of the man she'd shot had been stolen from the morgue.

"Stolen before the police had a chance to ID him," Blair added. "My friend and I think whoever is behind all the killings had it done—and maybe the guy who did the body snatching is still around. Another strong-arm type who can lead us to whoever planned the whole thing."

Deena frowned at the idea . . . and then her mind went back to the night before at the restaurant. There had been that one creepy-looking guy near the door who hadn't been the least bit afraid while everyone else had been busy soiling their drawers.

"There was this one frog-faced sonofabitch last night. Real ugly."

"You think he could be involved?" Blair asked.

"Something was wrong with him. Acted like seeing someone shot dead was no big deal to him. But if he was partners with that bastard who killed Ivar, why didn't he try 'n' grab me?"

"You had a gun in your hand," Blair pointed out.

Deena shook her head. "Mighta been a squirt gun, for all he cared."

"Well, if he wasn't afraid, he might not have wanted to do anything to call attention to himself. It would have made stealing the body later a lot more risky."

"Yeah," Deena said. She could buy that.

"You remember this guy's face well enough to sketch it?" Blair asked.

She grabbed a pad of paper and a pen, sat down, and went to work laying down harsh strokes of ink. In a matter of moments a cruel, blunt face took shape.

"That's the man?" Blair asked.

"That's him," she said.

Blair studied the face. "You're right, he is ugly. Ought to make him easier to find."

"You know what I'm thinking?" Deena asked. "If the bastard I killed had a partner, maybe I got the wrong guy. Maybe it was Froggy that killed Ivar."

"I had that same thought myself," Blair told her.

Roth waited at the candidate's limo and communicated with his subordinates to make sure that all the details for the security of the motorcade's trip to Costa Mesa were in place. Everyone reported that preparations were complete.

Roth was a little surprised that he could keep functioning, attending to all the mundane details of his cover, when all he wanted to do was kill J. D. Cade.

Just a few minutes ago he'd been standing right next to the bastard in Rawley's suite. So close he could have done the job with a knife. Better yet, with his bare hands.

Of course, Cade had been close enough to do in Rawley the same way. Standing there behind the man, all Cade had to do was grab the candidate's head and give it one good neck-breaking twist. What the hell could anybody have done to stop him?

Roth had tried *willing* Cade to do it.

Go ahead, motherfucker, kill him now. Right here in front of everyone. Then I get to kill you and don't have to wait any longer.

Only Cade hadn't. Instead the sonofabitch had saved the day. Again. Rawley had said so himself. The only person Cade had killed was Bill Danby. The bastard had lined up Bill like he was making a trick shot in some cabaret act. Shot Roth's best friend right through the throat and severed his spine.

Roth had never disobeyed one of Garvin Townes' commands, but he really didn't think he'd be able to wait much longer. He was going to kill J. D. Cade soon—whether the prick had gotten Rawley or not.

A voice reached Roth through his earpiece: Orpheus was coming.

Much to the surprise of Jenny and the other members of his brain trust, Del Rawley decided that he was going to ride to Costa Mesa with only Special Agent DeVito for company in the back of his limo. As soon as they hit the freeway moving north, DeVito handed Rawley the information he'd been able to obtain on Garvin Townes. The candidate read the file quickly and DeVito handed him a legal pad on which he'd written his analysis—and a warning.

Don't talk. The Secret Service sometimes listens in without you guys knowing.

Del frowned upon receiving that piece of news.

It's not like we're blackmailers, the note continued in anticipation of the candidate's reaction. *We're just obsessed with knowing everything we can to protect our principals . . . although what we hear is good for an occasional laugh.*

Now Del smiled and nodded.

My view is that Townes has to be a spook, the note continued. *The CIA has always been big on Ivy Leaguers, and they probably grabbed him right out of Yale. The construction job and the army posting (PANIC) were fronts. After Townes left Vietnam, he just disappeared. Who knows what he was doing? But he had to be active in some covert capacity or he never would have been picked for his new DEIMOS unit—deimos is the Greek word for "panic."*

Del looked up sharply, and DeVito nodded. DeVito's next paragraph had been crossed out and Del had to flip the page to pick up the narrative.

I crossed out the last paragraph because I saw something this morning that maybe explains a few things to me. Cade (from the PANIC unit) has to be working for Roth (of the

DEIMOS unit). *There's no way in hell I'd buy the presence of both men in your campaign as a coincidence. But this morning Roth was looking such daggers at Cade I thought he might shoot him. Then I realized that by saving your life and helping your campaign, Cade has betrayed Roth (and Townes), and that's what made Roth so mad.*

So—maybe—Cade could have been the guy who took the shot at you in Chicago, but after that, something made him change his mind.

That's the way I see it. What do you think, Senator?

DeVito handed a pen to Del. The candidate looked at DeVito a moment, thought, and then started to write.

Your assumption is possible. But does anything in your research on Cade suggest that he was anything but a business-man after leaving the army? Were there any contacts between him and Townes or any other intelligence community personnel? Most important, what—under your assumption—would motivate a 180-degree change of heart?

Here's another way to look at things. Maybe assassin A was used in Chicago. After he failed, he was dismissed. Was disposed of? Then Mr. Cade was brought in (coerced?) to be assassin B. But for whatever reason he isn't going along with the plan. Isn't that possible?

I know you've made the connection between the PANIC and DEIMOS units and I think that's valid. But there have to be other men from that old army unit around. I know one personally: Donnel Timmons. Did you know he and Mr. Cade served together?

Rawley handed the pad back and DeVito read. He looked at Orpheus and it was clear the candidate had given him more to think about.

No, I didn't know about Mr. Timmons serving under Townes, DeVito wrote. *And no, I couldn't find anything sus-picious about Cade—if you can overlook his marksmanship with a rifle, which I can't. Now that I know—all right, as-*

sume — that Townes' unit in Vietnam was a front, I wonder if Cade's shooting skills were learned in the army and what he did with them. I don't know what could make a man go from trying to kill you one day to saving your life another. So maybe you do have it right that Cade is a successor assassin — or that's what Townes wants him to be. Hell, it would even explain why Roth was so mad at him. Maybe it wasn't betrayal I saw but just plain insubordination.

But at this late date, Senator, I have to tell you that my gut says Cade was the guy with the rifle in Chicago, even if I can't explain what turned him around. One more thought: Who could make a copy of an M-100 rifle without anybody knowing? The CIA.

Del read DeVito's conclusion with an impassive face. He took up the pen again. *Thank you for all your help, Special Agent DeVito. Keep an eye out for me, will you?*

DeVito wrote back, *Yes, sir. Anybody wants you, he'll have to go through me first. But I hope you're still carrying your gun.*

Del looked at the agent and responded. *At all times.*

J. D. had been assigned to ride in a limo with Donnel. The two men lounged in opposite corners of the backseat, unspoken tension filling the space between them. Then Donnel smiled casually at J. D.

"You care for a drink?" he asked.

"No, thanks, but you go right ahead."

"Believe I will."

Donnel helped himself to a glass from the limo's minibar, added ice, scotch, and a splash of soda. He raised his drink to J. D., who nodded in return. Donnel took a sip, then looked out the window.

J. D. watched him for a moment and then said, "I heard something interesting today."

Donnel regarded J. D. impassively. "What's that?"

"An old friend of ours wrote a book."

"Someone we know wrote a book? Who?"

"Think of the last person in the world you'd ever suspect would tell his life story."

J. D. could see that for a second Donnel thought he was referring to himself—but when Donnel came up with the correct answer his eyes went wide.

The opaque privacy screen was up but Donnel still wouldn't say the name aloud. He silently mouthed, "Townes?"

J. D. nodded. "What I heard, he names names, too."

Donnel looked down and rolled the glass between his hands.

"A friend of mine happened to find the only copy of the book," J. D. said. "I'm supposed to pick it up from him tonight after we get back to L.A."

Donnel looked at J. D. "The *only* copy?"

J. D. nodded. He didn't know for sure that was the truth. It was possible Pickpocket had made a copy for himself. But Donnel didn't have to know that.

"You gonna do the right thing with it?" Donnel asked.

"What do you think?"

Donnel thought he'd take a hit of his scotch and soda. Then he said in a soft voice, "I heard a story on the radio this morning about another old friend of ours. You hear it?"

J. D. looked surprised and shook his head.

Donnel continued, "You remember Dixie Wynne? Good ol' Southern boy like you. Even *looked* something like you, the way I recall."

Beauregard "Dixie" Wynne. J. D. remembered him, all right. The PANIC unit's most eager beaver. Hadn't been anybody that sonofabitch didn't like to shoot. Dixie hadn't been a bad-looking guy, so J. D. let the remark about a resemblance slide.

"So why was Dixie on the radio?"

"He shot himself a couple of cops, then did himself in."

Donnel summarized Dixie's story: shooting a robbery suspect who'd surrendered, disappearing, being indicted in absentia, and coming home to a trap.

"Dixie barricaded himself in his house," Donnel told J. D., "and set up his shooting stand on the second floor. The Gainesville cops knew who they were dealing with, so they came in force and took every precaution in the book. But Dixie still managed to kill two of them with head shots. Both the cops he killed were described as former friends. At that point, the SWAT team mounted an assault on Dixie's house with an armored vehicle. When they found him, he'd blown his own head off."

Donnel concluded, "Goes to show none of us knows how much time he's got left."

J. D.'s thought had been to lure Donnel into a trap that night. Thinking J. D. was going to pick up Townes' memoirs, Donnel would follow him to make sure he did the right thing with them. J. D. had also thought maybe he *didn't* have to kill Donnel. Only put him out of action.

But Donnel seemed to be hinting just now that he was playing for keeps.

Evan Cade was alone in his grandmother's house. He'd assured Belle that he'd be okay while she went grocery shopping. But he still had a dull headache that aspirin didn't seem to touch, and anytime he moved too fast or even turned his head too quickly, he got dizzy again.

He tried to distract himself by reading and watching television, but he couldn't concentrate on either activity. He wanted to be out helping Blair. He wanted to put his hands on whoever was responsible for Pru's death.

Feeling useless and frustrated, he went upstairs to his

bedroom to nap, hoping that more rest would get him back to normal. He didn't see the gray sedan stop out front.

The Toad gazed at the neat frame house. From where he sat, he didn't see anyone moving about inside. The other houses on the block were similarly quiet and the sidewalks were empty. He got out of the car, thinking the time was right to take a peek at the back of the property. It would be premature to move on the boy without final approval from the Gardener, but he wanted to get a feel for the place. For when he came back later.

FOURTEEN

Del Rawley took the stage at the South Coast Symphony Hall. The audience gave him a standing ovation. It went on and on until Del urged everyone to take their seats.

"You do me too much honor," Del said, his voice thick with emotion. He cleared his throat. "Before I get into the substance of my remarks, I'd like to introduce to you the man who made it possible for me to be here today—the man who made it possible for me to be *anywhere* today. Ladies and gentlemen, Mr. J. D. Cade."

J. D. stepped a few paces onto the stage as the audience rose to its feet again and buried him under an avalanche of applause. Jenny had persuaded him that he'd have to face the media sooner or later and it was better to do it on his own terms. He waved and smiled, intending to stay for only a moment before exiting, but Del Rawley extended a hand to him, compelling J. D. to join the candidate at center stage. Once he was there, Del triumphantly raised J. D.'s hand.

J. D. looked into the wings and saw Jenny. She was clapping, too. If you only knew, J. D. thought. If all of you only knew. Then he noticed DeVito, and it was instantly clear to him that maybe one of them already did know.

Del lowered J. D.'s hand and in a moment the audience was seated again.

"Mr. Cade," Del told him, "this is your opportunity to speak to the world."

The candidate stepped back to give J. D. the lectern to himself. He looked out at the crowd and it seemed vast to him. He saw the red light of a television camera on him and knew he'd be seen by more people than he could meet in ten lifetimes. He felt naked and revealed.

He began by saying, "I'm far more scared today than I was yesterday."

The audience laughed appreciatively.

"I can't say I'm a hero, and I won't say it," J. D. continued. "I'm the furthest thing possible from a hero. I acted without thinking. . . . I . . ." At a loss for words, he could only shrug. Then he turned to Del. "I found myself in a situation not of my own making and I really had no choice about what happened next. I had to react the way I did."

J. D. looked back at the audience and smiled ruefully. "I wish I could say I was more noble . . . but I'm really not a very good liar."

J. D. stepped back from the lectern and Rawley put his arm around J. D.'s shoulders as another round of applause filled the room. Del whispered to J. D., "Brief and self-effacing. Very nice, Mr. Cade. If not a liar, you certainly have the makings of a fine politician."

"Coming from you, Senator, I'll take that as a compliment."

"Please do."

Del raised J. D.'s hand one more time and then let him depart to further applause.

J. D. took with him an important new piece of information.

When Del Rawley had put his arm around him, J. D. had felt something hard.

He was sure the candidate had a gun in his pocket.

"You can't be serious," Jenny Crenshaw said into her PCR ninety minutes later as the motorcade headed for Anaheim. This time she rode with Del Rawley, who looked on with interest as Jenny talked to her opposite number, Ronald Turlock, the incumbent's campaign manager.

"I'm entirely serious," Turlock replied. "The president has agreed to the senator's invitation, but he feels that implicit in that invitation the senator is questioning either his honesty or his man—" Turlock remembered to whom he was speaking. "Or his courage."

"So you expect Senator Rawley to make his first appearance with the incumbent at an *outdoor* venue. The Secret Service would never allow it."

Turlock laughed. "Come, come, Ms. Crenshaw. They may *hate* it, but they have no choice except to go along. What else can they do, resign? Wouldn't be good at all for their image. No, if the senator doesn't wish to appear, then there may be a problem with his . . . courage. And we may have to rethink this whole matter of campaigning jointly."

"Hold on," Jenny snapped, and pushed the hold button.

"What is it?" Del asked.

"The president has booked the Hollywood Bowl—for tomorrow night!"

Del considered the situation, a grim smile on his lips.

"They don't think I'll do it."

"You shouldn't. It's a cold-blooded attempt to put your life in jeopardy."

"Or to make *me* look like the coward. Somebody on the president's side has just pushed their whole pile of chips to the center of the table, and they're hoping I won't call their bet."

"You shouldn't," Jenny repeated. "You should denounce this as the cynical political move it is. People will understand."

Del shook his head. "No, they won't. Remember what our motto is these days: This campaign will not be stopped. Well, that's just what refusing the president's choice of venues would do, stop us dead. The campaign would be finished."

"Even if it came to that . . . better the campaign should die than you."

Being confronted that starkly gave Del pause, but only for a moment. He'd committed himself to a course of action. The only thing he could do now was pray he'd come out of it alive.

"Tell the man we'll be there," he said quietly.

"You can't—"

"Tell him, Jenny."

"Del, for Christ's sake!"

The candidate took the PCR from his campaign manager and tapped the talk key.

"Mr. Turlock?"

"Yes?"

"This is Senator Rawley. We accept. The Hollywood Bowl it is. And Mr. Turlock?"

"Yes, Senator?"

"Please let the president know that since this was all my idea, I'll extend to him the courtesy of speaking first. He can say his piece, take however long he likes, and I'll wait patiently to reply."

Del Rawley clicked off before Turlock could respond.

"There," he told Jenny. "If we're gonna do this thing outside, that little prick can sweat being in the spotlight first. I'll wait in the shadows."

"Better yet, sit right behind him."

"Why?"

"That way if someone wants to shoot you, the bullet has to go through him."

Del gave his campaign manager a look and then laughed long and loud.

"What?" Jenny asked. "It wasn't *that* funny."

The candidate rubbed a tear of mirth from his eye. "I think you've got it backward. The more politicians you lined up to kill with one shot, the more people you'd have shooting at them."

Shooting at *us*, he corrected himself privately. Then Del's thoughts of mortality were brushed aside by an important political concern.

"About the tickets for tomorrow night at the Bowl—"

"Don't let the incumbent pack the house."

"Exactly."

"That was one of the first lessons in politics I ever learned, Del. Get at least half the tickets and make sure they're where your people can be seen and heard. But for tomorrow night I think I'm going to demand something different."

"What?"

"I think I'm going to have *all* the seats filled with Secret Service agents, and I'm going to ask the city to bulldoze all the hills within a five-mile radius of the venue."

Del smiled. He put a hand on his campaign manager's shoulder.

"I'm going to be all right, Jenny. Tomorrow and the day after that. We're going to win this election. I'm going to be president. I'll do some good things for our country, and then I'm going to retire and watch my grandchildren and their children grow up. When my time comes, they're going to find me sitting under a shade tree next to a stream with a rod and reel in my hand and a fish on the end of my line."

"Yeah . . . okay. Meanwhile, *I'll* die of a heart attack tomorrow night."

"Now, that'd make me sad," Del said, shaking his head gravely. "That'd be about the only thing that could keep me from winning this election."

Jenny laughed. "I'd slug you if you didn't have so damn many bodyguards around."

"You don't have to; I beat myself up every day."

Del gave Jenny a wink and then called his wife to let her know that he'd be speaking outdoors again tomorrow night, exposing himself to the world and all its madmen.

After the speech in Anaheim, Jenny rode with J. D. this time as the motorcade made its way back to Los Angeles. He said, "Explain something to me."

"What?"

"Why is it good that Senator Rawley will be campaigning with the president? If the president had refused the challenge, okay, then he's a coward or a liar. But by accepting hasn't he, in the public's eyes, called Senator Rawley's bluff? I didn't think of that when I suggested the idea."

Jenny took J. D.'s hand, privately glad that he didn't understand politics as well as he'd seemed to at first. It wouldn't do to have gifted amateurs ruining things for the pros.

"Your idea was win-win," she told him. "If the president ducked Del's challenge, he would, as you said, undercut himself. But by accepting he was forced to do what every politician hates most: jump through a hoop set up by his opponent. So that's one point for Del right there, and when Del gets the president onstage with him he's going to demolish the man. That's what we were so happy about when we heard the news."

"So everything's looking good?" J. D. asked.

Jenny frowned.

"What?" J. D. wanted to know.

"The president's side just made us jump through a hoop." She told J. D. that the first joint appearance would be outdoors and asked, "Have you ever been to the Hollywood Bowl?"

"Sure. Back when I had an intact family, we'd come to town two or three times a year to hear a concert there. We'd stay over in a hotel, do some shopping, make a weekend out of it."

"Would the Bowl be a risky place, do you think, for Del to speak?"

"Could be," J. D. said, thinking about it. "There are lots of trees around the Bowl, and there are hills around it, too. Could be a place where . . . you know, someone could take a shot. If not at the stage, then at one of the approaches to the Bowl."

"I want to check it out. Will you help me?"

J. D. frowned. "Jenny, if both candidates are going to speak there, you can bet the Secret Service will be swarming all over the place."

"They were swarming everywhere in Chicago, too, but Del almost got killed. And frankly, I don't trust that sonofabitch who's the head of the protection detail now. He looks . . . I don't know. Maybe not crazy, but not completely right."

"I don't care for the man myself," J. D. agreed, thinking of Roth. "But if you want to go scouting—when, tonight?" She nodded. "We're going to need some kind of official escort."

"Who?"

J. D. smiled thinly. "How about that guy DeVito, who thinks so much of me?"

"*Him?*"

"Yeah. He might be up for it."

The Rawley campaign settled in for the night at the Century Plaza Hotel in Los Angeles. J. D., despite having a new home in town, took a room at Jenny's suggestion. She said she'd like him to be close in case she needed to . . . talk to him.

Del informed Jenny that his wife might be flying out to join him, despite his wish that she remain at home and out of harm's way.

And DeVito was recruited to accompany Jenny and J. D. on their scouting trip to the Hollywood Bowl. The special agent was surprised that it was Cade's idea that he accompany them, but then he thought that Cade using him for a cover was possibly the sneakiest thing the bastard could do.

DeVito did agree not to mention their little expedition to Roth.

Using a government car, DeVito drove Jenny and J. D. up to Mulholland Drive, the road at the crest of the Hollywood Hills. He saw a turnout between Cahuenga and Outpost and pulled over. No sooner had the three of them exited the car than an LAPD unit pulled in behind them. Two cops got out of the black-and-white. One approached them, while the other stayed at the patrol car with his gun drawn.

DeVito announced who he was and showed his ID to the cop. Then he introduced Jenny and J. D.

The cop, a sergeant whose name tag read DE LA HOYA, informed DeVito, "At the request of your agency, we're keeping a tight watch on all the sites overlooking the Bowl. But we were told not to expect any of you people until tomorrow morning."

"Ms. Crenshaw wanted to take a look for herself this evening," DeVito explained. "Make sure security is up to snuff."

"After Chicago, I worry," Jenny elaborated.

"Don't blame you, ma'am. And this other gentleman with you is here because . . . ?"

"I asked him to be. He's the one who thought we should bring Mr. DeVito along."

"That was a real good idea, sir. Saved us all a lot of trouble." The cop turned to DeVito. "Mighta saved us even more if you'd called ahead to let us know you were coming."

"That's my fault, Sergeant," Jenny intervened. "I wanted to see what would happen if we appeared unannounced."

The cop looked like he had to bite his tongue. Then he said, "Well, I guess now you know. You folks going to be doing any more snoo—looking around?"

"If you don't mind. Just a little."

The cop nodded, not happy. "I'll have to inform our people up here. Wouldn't want anyone to get nervous and make a mistake."

"No, we wouldn't," J. D. agreed.

The cops got back in their car and De La Hoya spent a minute on his radio. He was looking at DeVito and nodding. Then they drove off, not bothering to wave goodbye.

DeVito said, "The sarge just checked me out. Made sure I'm for real. Roth'll know soon if he doesn't already."

"Hard to keep a secret these days," J. D. told him.

Now DeVito was the one who had to bite his tongue.

Jenny watched the two of them for a second, then looked down at the stage of the Hollywood Bowl. The two men joined her at the overlook, one on either side of her.

"Could Del be shot from here?" she asked.

J. D. shook his head.

"Why not?" she asked.

"Yeah, Mr. Cade," DeVito added. "What would you know about such things?"

"I know that we were braced by those cops two seconds after we stepped out of our car. What do you think they would have done if one of us had a weapon in his hand?" J. D. turned to Jenny. He inclined his head toward the hill-side that fell off sharply below them. It was covered with thick vegetation. "Down there. Seems to me if you could find a spot where the elevation hasn't fallen off too far to ruin your sight line, a spot where there's enough brush to cover you but still allow you a clear view, that'd be where you'd find a shooter. Might be a few other spots on a hill-side off this road where a man with a gun might set up."

"You sound very knowledgeable, Mr. Cade," DeVito said, a clear taunt in his voice.

J. D. noticed that Jenny was looking at him, clearly inter-ested in his response.

"Just know what I read in the papers," he said with a shrug. "That and common sense. A man with a gun has to find a place to hide until he can make his shot. Somewhere down there is where it would have to be. Of course, you Se-cret Service people and the LAPD will be working these hills with dogs to make sure nobody's hiding in that brush, won't you?"

DeVito didn't say a word.

But Jenny persisted. "Well, won't you?"

"I'm sorry, Ms. Crenshaw, I can't give away that kind of information."

"Then let me put it this way," Jenny countered. "You'd damn well better."

Just like that, DeVito was the one on the defensive.

For the next hour they made stops in the hills. One was at a home perched directly above the back of the stage. They tried to gain access but nobody responded when they rang the bell at the gate. While waiting outside the house, J. D. asked DeVito if the security detail had considered that an assassin might use something more powerful than a rifle, say, a light antitank weapon. Fire right through the back of the building and take out *everybody* on the stage. At another stop, J. D. noticed a TV station helicopter buzzing overhead, and he asked if one of those things had ever been hijacked. A two-man team with automatic weapons could steal a news copter and make a strafing run if the air defenses weren't tight. With every scenario J. D. concocted, DeVito had to reassure Jenny—without going into detail—that the Secret Service had thought of everything.

"Everything but that man in Chicago."

The very mention of which rubbed DeVito's wound raw. He had to lock his jaw to keep from saying anything. But the crazy thing was that DeVito's gut told him Cade really wanted the security to be airtight now.

Back at the hotel, Jenny thanked J. D. for his help, gave him a kiss on the cheek, not caring that DeVito was there to see it, and said she would see him tomorrow. She still had a lot of work to do tonight. The two men watched her go.

When she was out of earshot, J. D. turned to DeVito. "There was one thing I didn't want to mention in front of Ms. Crenshaw."

"Yeah, what's that?" DeVito wanted to know.

"All the security in the world won't help if the shooter comes from inside."

DeVito stared hard at J. D. "You mean inside the campaign?"

"No," J. D. said, meeting DeVito's eyes squarely. "I mean inside the protection detail."

The Gardener considered his options. At this point in the game, he conceded that he had but two choices: to follow the aggressive path, as he'd been urged, or toss in his cards. If he went aggressive, he'd be stepping outside the guidelines of a carefully conceived plan. Any number of unpredictable—and inevitably bloody—consequences might follow. Things might turn out quite differently from the way he wanted. But one thing he was sure of: Any carnage that might ensue would not be traced back to him.

On the other hand, if he gave up the game, he would be abandoning his vision of the future, of how politics in the United States would inevitably come to be conducted. *He* might leave this strategy behind, but within a generation some bright, ruthless young man—or woman, to be fair— would pursue it. Then how would he live with himself? He might as well be . . . Well, no, he'd never want to share that coward's fate.

He couldn't really withdraw, anyway. He'd already set too many forces in motion. Their momentum was independent of his wishes now. Since he could do nothing to recall them, his only real choice was to give them another shove forward.

If things didn't turn out the way he'd planned, he'd at least be able to learn a few things from his mistakes—for next time. The Gardener tapped out a number on his phone.

When his call was answered, he said, "Harold, take Evan Cade."

"There's no way I can change your mind?" Del Rawley asked, speaking on the phone.

"Baby," Devree Rawley answered, "you've been trying for the last hour, and I'm just about packed now, and for the last time, the answer is no. I'm coming. When you step on that stage in the Hollywood Bowl, I'm going to be right there in the front row."

"The children, then."

"Del, our children are grown. They're strong, wonderful adults. They're as adamant with me as I am with you. They will be there, too."

"The grandchildren, then."

"I'm working on that one," Devree conceded. "They're still youngsters. I'd love for them to see their grandfather onstage and—"

"Devree, I will not allow it. You tell Eleanor, Colin, and Bobby that if they bring any of their babies with them, I'm withdrawing from the race."

"You won't."

"I will!"

"All right, I'll tell them. But don't be surprised if—"

"Honey, if I see those babies in what might be harm's way, I will be forced to keep my eyes on them at all times; I will have no focus on the debate; and in the words of Mr. Reagan, I might even forget to duck—if something should happen."

"You really think . . ." Devree Rawley couldn't bring herself to finish the sentence.

"I don't know."

"Then I'm certainly going to be there with you, and I know the children will feel the same way. Maybe we can work things out so that the grandchildren can see you backstage and then be taken back to the hotel."

"That would greatly ease my mind."

"I'll speak to the children."

"I'm sure they'll see the light. I love you, Devree."

"I love you, too . . . Mr. President."

"Not yet, baby."

"Won't be long, though," Devree Harper Rawley assured her husband.

J. D. sat at a table in the hotel bar for the better part of an hour. He nursed two glasses of sparkling mineral water with twists of lime. He engaged in a pastime usually reserved for the more celebrated denizens of L.A.: being seen.

Specifically, he wanted to be spotted by Donnel Timmons.

Any number of campaign regulars passed by. The brain trust came in and took a table of their own. Then Alita Colon stopped by to say she had a million requests from the media to interview him. She was putting them off, but if he changed his mind about talking to the press, he should let her know. A pair of special agents strode directly up to him, giving him an uneasy moment, but all they wanted was to shake his hand and tell him he'd done a balls-out job saving Orpheus yesterday. The last visitor to his table was Vandy Ellison. She came in with a silver-haired gent who looked like he could write the campaign a big check or two, but when she saw J. D. she excused herself and sashayed right over. She sat down next to him and kissed his cheek—while running her hand up the inside of his thigh. She said she could only stay for a moment but promised that someday soon she would show him some real gratitude for his heroism.

Finally Donnel entered the bar.

He noticed J. D. immediately but didn't come to his table, just nodded and took a seat at the bar. J. D. spent a moment finishing his drink, then went to the men's room. When he came out, he made a call from a pay phone. To get the correct time. The artifice of pretending to make contact with the "friend" who would deliver Townes' memoirs proved unnecessary. When J. D. looked up, he saw that Donnel had already left the bar.

Donnel couldn't possibly be uninterested in getting his hands on Townes' book. But maybe he had smelled the trap.

Or he could be in a car outside somewhere, waiting for J. D. to make his move.

Either way, J. D. had to play things out. He stepped outside.

A valet brought J. D.'s Lexus to the hotel entrance and handed him the keys in exchange for a tip. J. D. got in and turned south on Avenue of the Stars. He made a left at Pico. Scant seconds later, another car made the turn after him, just beating the red light. But then the driver was content to drop back, doing less than the speed limit. In L.A., driving that slowly meant you were either a tourist, a drunk trying to be clever, or someone who didn't want to be spotted following someone else.

There was still enough traffic that the interval between J. D. and his pursuer was soon filled by two other cars. So he couldn't tell for sure that it was Donnel behind him. But he'd given no one else a reason to follow him tonight.

He checked his watch; the phone call had confirmed it was accurate. He had to time his drive just right. It was 9:49 P.M. when he turned left on La Cienega. The tail car was still behind him, again racing to make the light and then falling back.

He used the PCR to call the number of a movie theater and a recorded message confirmed the information on which he was relying. Twelve minutes later he stopped for a red light at the intersection of La Cienega and Third Street. Just ahead on his left was the massive, eight-story, dun-colored Beverly Center, a mall that sandwiched four levels of enclosed parking between its ground-floor restaurants, hair stylists, and Hard Rock Cafe and the top three floors of glitzy retail chains, food court, and cineplex.

The retail shops all closed at 10:00, but the last feature at the cineplex began at 10:15. So, as J. D. remembered from a previous visit, the automated barriers to the parking levels kept raising their arms until 10:05. When J. D. drove up to the winding ramp to the parking structure and stopped at the barrier, the clock on the ticket machine stood at 10:04. Just enough time for him to get through and Donnel to follow.

He took the ticket, the barrier lifted, and he goosed the Lexus up the ramp.

He turned right off the ramp and into the third-floor parking level. It was a huge doughnut-shaped space that wrapped around the auto ramp. On the east side of the parking area a pedestrian exit led to canopied escalators that ran along the exterior of the building and went up to the retail shops and down to street level. Lighting was up to code, but nobody would ever be blinded by the glare. Only a few widely spaced cars remained parked on that level, just as J. D. had hoped.

He didn't want any company. Any witnesses.

He pulled the Lexus around the enclosure of the auto ramp. Here he was shielded from the pedestrian exit, where somebody going past on an escalator might see him, and he was as remote as possible from the street below and the shopping complex above.

He parked the Lexus, got out, and positioned himself behind a support pillar ten feet away.

His plan was simply to shoot Donnel. For which purpose he carried the pen gun he'd originally bought to shoot Del Rawley. He hoped to hit Donnel in some critical but not vital part of his body. This being Hollywood, his gun hand would be good. But if it got down to kill or be killed . . .

J. D. heard the squeak of the tires on the concrete as a car hurried around the ramp enclosure. Headlight beams splashed past J. D. He was hidden but the Lexus was in plain sight.

There was another squeal of rubber as the car braked abruptly. Donnel was trying to figure out where he was, J. D. thought. How best to get at him. The car's headlights were extinguished, leaving only the undifferentiated parking structure illumination.

After that, J. D. heard gears being shifted and the whine

of a car being driven in reverse. More tire shrieking reached him as the car backed around the ramp enclosure. Finally he heard a pair of soft metallic clicks: a car door quietly being opened and closed.

Donnel meant to come after him on foot now, J. D. thought, and undoubtedly he'd brought more firepower than a .22 caliber pen gun.

He considered his options for several moments and then carefully poked his head out from behind the pillar to see . . . that the pursuer's car hadn't been abandoned after all. It had crept back around the curve, with its lights off, and slowly enough not to make the slightest squeal. Donnel Timmons wasn't sitting behind the wheel, either.

Arnold Roth was—and when he saw J. D. he smiled.

J. D. knew immediately that his only chance was to get to the escalators, and he bolted. The roar of the car's engine and the scream of accelerating tires told him that the chase was on. If that wasn't enough, a gunshot echoed crazily in the cavernous space. The round struck something hard enough to deflect it; J. D. felt the ricochet whiz past his head, trailing a banshee wail.

He dodged behind one of the few remaining parked cars, then made a beeline for the pedestrian exit. His path was shorter and far more direct than the one Roth had to take, but as J. D. glanced to his right, he saw that the car's speed would easily overcome his temporary advantage.

Still, he feinted as if he would make an all-out effort to get to the escalators, and then he sharply cut back and ran for the opening of the ramp by which he'd entered the parking area. He darted through it, turned right, stopped quickly, and pressed himself against the wall. He pulled the cap off the pen gun. He heard mechanical growls and the shriek of tortured rubber as Roth sought to catch him. He fired his shot as soon as Roth came careening through the opening.

But the sonofabitch made the turn far faster than J. D. had expected. His shot took out the rear passenger-side window of the car but didn't come close to hitting its target. Worse, Roth managed to get off a shot of his own. While it didn't hit J. D., a sliver of the concrete that the round blew out of the wall next to him nicked his neck.

He quickly ducked back into the level-three parking area. His first hope was to get to his car and put the chase on a more equal basis. But Roth came barreling off the ramp in reverse. J. D. dashed once again toward the pedestrian exit. Roth came roaring after him, still driving backward. He didn't try to shoot J. D. now. He meant simply to run him over.

J. D. looked desperately for a parked car or support pillar to duck behind, but the nearest shelter was impossibly far away. With sweat running into his eyes and the reek of his own mortality in his nose, J. D. tried to fake left and right, but the one glance he dared take over his shoulder showed him that Roth had not been fooled.

The bastard was bearing down on him, smiling as ferociously as if he would eat J. D. alive.

The hellish image abruptly disappeared as the rear window of Roth's car was blown out. It was only afterward that J. D. realized he'd heard a gunshot, the report of a weapon far larger than his paltry .22. He caught a glimpse of a familiar figure standing in the pedestrian exit, holding a gun, firing once more at Roth, who'd braked sharply, had put his car into drive, and was racing away for all he was worth.

J. D. didn't count himself delivered yet. He ran behind a pillar. He grabbed for the one spare cartridge he'd brought with him and reloaded the pen gun. By the time he did that, he could hear the sound of Roth's car receding into the distance.

That left only the man who'd shot at Roth.

Donnel Timmons *had* followed him. Him and Roth. The man J. D. had intended to shoot, if not kill, that night had saved his life.

But when J. D. carefully looked around the pillar for him, Donnel was gone, too.

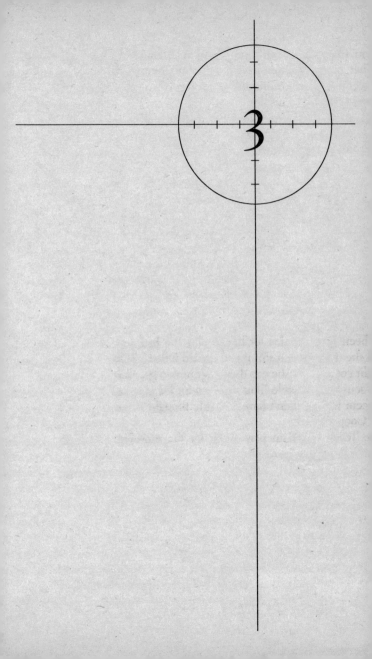

FIFTEEN
Thursday, September 23, 2004

By midnight the Toad knew that there were just two people inside the house. He knew how he was going to break in. He'd rehearsed in his mind how he'd stash Evan Cade in the trunk of his car. The only question left to be answered was, did he need to kill the old lady?

The answer to that was entirely pragmatic. He'd just have to wait and see how things went. He didn't feel particularly bad about dusting old folks. The way he looked at it, they had all their good times behind them, anyway.

The Toad backed his car into the driveway. He switched off the dome light so it wouldn't illuminate him as he opened the door. He got out and closed the door quietly. He walked at a normal pace with a normal posture—as if he belonged there—around to the back of the house.

The home's elevation cut off most of the light from the street lamp out front. He didn't bother trying the kitchen door or any of the ground-floor windows. Even in small towns people were pretty good about locking them these days. But on the second floor a double-hung window stood with its lower sash raised to let fresh air circulate through the house.

Laboring swiftly and silently, he lifted a wrought-iron patio table and placed it next to the house. On top of the table, he carefully stacked all four of the accompanying chairs. He made sure they were firmly joined together and then agilely clambered atop the highest one. From that point, the Toad had to jump less than two feet to grab the sill of the open window. He managed the leap with ease, his feet producing only a slight thump against the side of the house.

He pulled himself through the window and saw by the glow of a night-light burning in a bathroom to his right that he was in a hallway with three other rooms off it. The door of the first room on the left was open. As his eyes adjusted to the low light, the Toad could make out a sewing machine, an ironing board, a love seat, and a TV. He passed by.

That left him two rooms to check. Each had its door closed. So before he opened either of them he went to each one and sniffed. Which made it easy.

The room on the right had no particular smell, but the one on the left smelled like his own mother's room. So unless Evan Cade was into wearing Shalimar and the old lady used only a deodorant soap, he knew which room he wanted. He opened the door on the right and closed it soundlessly behind him. For a moment he stayed right where he was, letting his eyes adjust to the deeper darkness there. The outline of the bed became discernible.

He listened to the breathing pattern of the person in the bed. It was somewhat labored but regular. It was also too deep and strong to belong to an old woman. Now the Toad made out the form of a body: large, clothed, male, and lying on its back. He stole across the room to it.

As he hovered above the person he could now identify as Evan Cade, the young man's breathing changed and his eyes popped open. The Toad's right hand shot out and his thumb and index finger closed on Evan's carotid arteries, intending to shut off the blood supply to his brain and render him unconscious. Much to the Toad's dismay, however, he felt Evan Cade's hand close agonizingly around his penis and testicles.

Both men squeezed.

The Toad had the more difficult time of it. He had to keep Evan quiet while at the same time refrain from screaming bloody murder himself. He was also under orders to take Evan alive, but as he felt his balls being crushed to jelly, he had no choice but to squeeze with all his might, regardless of outcome. Evan Cade's hand fell away from his crotch.

Waves of nauseating pain continued to pulse so strongly through the Toad that he collapsed on top of Evan. It was several minutes before he was able to push himself upright. When he checked Evan, he found that his victim was unconscious but still alive. The Toad took the opportunity to hobble to a closet, pull clothing from a laundry hamper, and use it to bind and gag Evan. After giving himself a few more minutes to recover further, he rolled his victim in a blanket from Evan's bed and put him on the floor. Then he pulled the coverlet up and neatly made the bed. Using a penlight he'd brought with him, the Toad found Evan's wallet and keychain on the nightstand next to the bed. He put them in his pocket.

He managed to sling his captive over a shoulder and carry him down the stairs, hugely grateful that they didn't squeak and alert the old lady. He was certain that she could have finished him off at the moment.

The Toad eased Evan into the trunk of his car and closed him in. Then he went around to the back of the house again and with equal silence but much greater difficulty moved the patio furniture back to its original positions. That done, he returned to his car and drove off—but he went only three blocks before he pulled over and parked at the end of a residential street that faced a large commercial boulevard.

He got out of the rental car and walked as briskly as he could back to the Cade house. He used the keys he'd taken from the nightstand to reenter the house and drive the Honda Prelude out of the garage. It was easy to assume that car belonged to a college kid rather than the Oldsmobile that was parked next to it. He left the Honda in the parking lot of a Kroger grocery store across from the side street where he'd parked his rental car. Signs posted prominently around the parking lot said any cars left there between 12 A.M. and 6 A.M. would be towed. Which was just what the Toad wanted. He didn't leave the keys in the Honda or the windows down—too obvious—but he left the doors unlocked and walked back to the rental car.

He had to wait only forty-five minutes before he saw a tow truck arrive, put Evan Cade's car on the hook, and drive it off to an impound yard somewhere.

It was only then, when he was fairly certain that his voice wouldn't emerge in a soprano squeak, that he called the Gardener. "I have Evan Cade, sir."

J. D. had to take the time to go to the Refuge, shower, and change his clothes before returning to the Century Plaza. Otherwise, anyone who had his eyes open would have seen him for what he was, a man who'd just escaped death. As it was, there were few people in the lobby when he arrived, and nobody paid him any attention as he crossed to the elevator.

When he opened the door to his room he saw the piece of paper on the floor. Someone had slipped it under the door. He squatted to examine it.

I have your son.

That simple. Four laser-printed words. No need to spell

out any threat. No need for the author to identify himself. Nevertheless, the message hit J. D. like a sledgehammer to the heart.

Evan had been kidnapped by Townes.

He had to get away from there before he lost control. Before he lashed out at the wrong person.

He stood, grabbed the garment bag he'd yet to unpack, and, without ever touching the piece of paper, pulled the door shut behind him. He took the elevator down to the lobby, retrieved his car, and drove within the speed limit back to the Refuge.

He sat at the table by the pool and waited. Thirty minutes later he had e-mail on the PCR. A telephone number. He memorized it and made the call. It was picked up on the first ring, and J. D. listened to a voice that he had last heard when he was twenty years old. Of all the people he *should* have killed . . .

"I have your son, Cade."

By now J. D. had readied his response. "And I have you by the short hairs, Colonel."

Which was hardly the reply Gàrvin Townes had been expecting. So he buttressed his point. "Would you like to hear him scream, Cade? I can arrange for you to listen."

"Would you like to have your memoirs published fifty years early, Colonel? You can explain how assassinating a presidential candidate and murdering a young man are acts done in the defense of liberty. You were so busy planning your offensive against me, Colonel, you forgot to post a rear guard."

There was a profound silence on the line. "See what I mean, Colonel? By the short hairs. Think about going to trial. You'd be the star witness against yourself."

"Then I'll have company, won't I, Cade?" Townes replied. "Because you're in my book, too. You and Alvy Mc-Cray."

"You think I'm going to give a shit about myself if my son dies? Here's what you have to remember, Colonel: If Evan goes, we all go."

There was another lengthy pause. J. D. could almost hear the gears turning in Townes' head as he sought some advantage for himself. And this time when Townes' voice returned, it was so agreeable it scared J. D.

"You're right, of course, Cade. If you can't have what's most important to you, nothing else matters. I had just the same thought quite recently. Thinking that if somehow I couldn't make you do what I want, I would end my own life."

"What?" J. D. asked incredulously.

Townes laughed. "Surprises you, doesn't it?"

"I only wish you'd taken the jump a long time ago."

"No, no, Cade. You won't get to me that easily. It's really a wonderful feeling that has come over me. A sense of peace, odd as that might seem. I can't imagine how you obtained my memoirs, but there will be no time to publish them other than posthumously. There will be no trial for me.

"It's really quite simple," Townes continued. "Senator Rawley dies in the next twenty-four hours or your son and I die. I think . . . I think I'll leave instructions that you be allowed to live. It would be so much harder for you that way. You'd either have to live with the pain of knowing you allowed your son to die, or accept the shame of committing suicide . . . *just like Daddy did.*"

J. D.'s mouth filled with the taste of bile. He had no doubt that Townes was completely sincere. It almost sounded to him as if Townes would like him to defy his wishes. Then Townes could meet his death without regret because he'd know how much pain he would inflict on J. D.

J. D. had been so sure of himself since receiving Townes' memoirs. He'd seen those rantings as the key to freedom for both him and Evan. The key to life for Del Rawley. He had even gone so far as to suggest improvements in Rawley's security. But now . . .

"And if the senator dies?" J. D. asked, his own voice barely a whisper.

"Then I get what I want and you get what you want."

"And if you try any comebacks against me or my son, your memoirs get published."

"And if you publish my memoirs, you and your son get killed." Townes laughed softly. "It's just like the good old days, Cade. Mutual assured destruction. What could be finer?"

J. D. regarded the question as rhetorical.

"So what's it to be, Cade?"

"We'll soon find out, Colonel."

Arnold Roth's return to the Century Plaza had been even more problematic than J. D. Cade's. He'd had to blast past the stunned parking attendant at the shopping mall and then quickly ditch his shot-up car. He'd been unhurt by the three rounds that had been shot at him, but he'd been brushing bits of broken glass off his clothes for blocks after he'd abandoned the car. He'd have to report it stolen in the morning. Another goddamn humiliation.

Not wanting to take a cab, Roth had to walk back to the hotel. As if that hadn't been enough, Townes had called him on his PCR as he hiked and told him to slip a piece of paper under fucking Cade's door. At least the news he had to deliver cheered him. They had the bastard's son. Cade would squirm now.

But back in his room, taking another call from Townes,

Roth couldn't believe what he was hearing. He asked Townes to repeat himself.

"*Don't* kill Cade," Townes said curtly. "Not unless I explicitly reverse this order."

Cade's ambiguous response to their standoff had left Townes unsure how to proceed. He added a further instruction for Roth. "In fact, if Cade appears to be in mortal danger from any third party, you are to intervene on his behalf."

Roth had never done drugs in his life; he even shunned alcohol. So all he could think was that his brain had to be shorting out from the stress he'd just been through. Because even hearing his orders a second time, he couldn't make sense of them.

Townes went on. "I just spoke with Cade. Caller ID showed a number other than that of the Century Plaza. So I want you to check his room at the hotel. Make sure he took the note you left for him. If he didn't, destroy it. Roth . . . are you there?"

"Yes, sir."

"You heard everything I've told you?"

"Yes, sir." Heard it all. *Understood* none of it.

"Good." Townes disconnected.

Leaving Roth to look at the phone receiver in his hand. "Fuck you, sir."

Goddamn Townes. What the hell did he think he was doing, writing off Danby's death?

Might as well have told him his own life wasn't worth a damn.

Protect Cade? Roth thought he should have told Townes how he'd just tried to *kill* him.

Maybe he ought to kill Townes, too. Be like Cade, kill one of your own. But that thought was so alien to Roth's nature and training it almost made him sick to his stomach.

Fuck it, he told himself. He'd had enough for one day.

He was going to bed. Which he did. He was almost asleep when he remembered the note Townes had told him to retrieve from J. D. Cade's room.

Fuck that, too.

DeVito sat in his room, sipping a ginger ale. He'd have liked to add a knock of scotch to his glass, but he needed a clear head. He had to sort things out, and fast. Goddamn Cade had turned him inside out, to the point where he couldn't even trust himself.

He was truly convinced by now that Cade had been the guy in Chicago who had taken the shot at Orpheus. The idea that Cade could have been a successor assassin, as Orpheus had proposed, complicated things too much. It was a much cleaner line of reasoning to assume that Cade had made the first attempt, failed, and was back to try again.

The fact that Cade was a marksman with a rifle, and that his army unit had undoubtedly been a cover for something somebody hadn't wanted to do publicly—gee, maybe Cade killed people—only underlined his conviction. But he hadn't known any of that the first time he'd seen Cade; he'd only known the guy should have had a manicure to complete his look.

There had been something just a touch off about him from the start.

Maybe there was a *smell* that accompanied treachery. God knew, with his beak he should be able to sniff out anything: treachery, deceit, an unpaid college loan. But thinking of Cade's warning to watch out for someone inside the protection detail, sniffing it for all it was worth, he couldn't find anything wrong with it. Cade thought one of their own was going to kill Orpheus.

And there was no question whom Cade had in mind.

Arnold fucking Roth. If you looked at the videotape of the San Francisco assassination attempt with any kind of critical eye, you knew that Cade was trying to get Roth—right after he'd gotten his buddy Danby. And you took one look at Roth and you knew that he was practically dying to kill Cade.

So how did it all make sense? Why would Cade first try to kill Rawley, then save him, then make sure his security was perfect, and then warn DeVito that there was a threat from Roth?

It *didn't* make any sense.

So go back to the man's history, DeVito told himself. Cade was involved in some kind of spook-shop operation in the army. Then he got out and left all that shit behind. He started a normal—hell, a successful—life. Why in God's name would he leave a sweet, safe setup like that? Common sense said he would stay right where he was and keep on keepin' on.

If DeVito had been in Cade's shoes, you'd have had to . . .

Force him to do anything different.

The lightbulb went on. Somebody was *blackmailing* Cade . . . and who'd know enough to have the dirt on him but his old commanding officer, Garvin Townes? Sure, he had to know about something Cade had done in Viet—No, wait, there was the thing with Cade's kid in Illinois, a murder charge. That had to be—Jesus! Did Townes have *two* things on Cade: one on him, one on his son? That could be enough to make a man do almost anything.

So, then, the only thing that could change Cade's mind was . . . he'd gotten out from under. Yeah! Somehow Cade had outwitted Townes. Got his kid's murder charge dropped and slipped out of the corner he was in, too. He wasn't going to kill Rawley anymore, and so . . . and so he took out Danby and warned DeVito about Roth because they were the backup team.

Sonofabitch! He'd figured it out.

Some of the details might not be exactly right but the broad outline sure worked. Cade was a bad guy who'd become a good guy. DeVito's gut instinct about Cade had been right, and now his brain had connected all the dots. Or most of them, anyway.

He wondered for a moment why he hadn't thought earlier about the possibility of Cade's being blackmailed. Then he realized it was less than twenty-four hours ago that he'd made the connection between Cade and Townes. And only a few days before that he'd learned about Cade's kid being arrested. Up till then—on paper—Cade had looked squeaky clean. So why should he have thought of blackmail?

Okay, he hadn't slipped up, but now what the hell did he do? Because he still couldn't *prove* jack shit. Who did he talk to about this? DeVito couldn't just go over Roth's head and tell the director of the Secret Service; he was still a pariah. If he started spouting, everyone would look at him like he was crazy. Worse, they'd think he was just trying to fuck over the guy who'd gotten his old job.

DeVito laughed quietly to himself. The guy he'd like to talk with right now was Cade. Take him aside, confide in him he'd figured the whole thing out, say no hard feelings, see if the two of them could work something out. Yeah, sure. Cade would probably shoot him.

Or arrange to have a meteorite hit him.

DeVito went to his minibar and grabbed one of those airline-sized bottles of scotch. He'd sip his drink. See if he couldn't think of something brilliant to do.

————

Jenny Crenshaw was back in the Hollywood Hills. It was night, but the kind of night they had in the movies, where you can still see everything clearly even though it should be pitch black. What Jenny saw was J. D. Cade, and not just one of him. He was everywhere.

Behind every rock, tree, and bush, there was J. D. And every time she saw him he was holding another kind of weapon: a handgun, a rifle, a rocket launcher, a crossbow.

All the weapons were pointed at the stage of the Hollywood Bowl. The only illumination on the stage was a tightly focused spotlight. From the audience in the amphitheater below, Jenny heard applause begin and people start to cheer. She knew Del was walking onto the stage, moving toward the spotlight. As he did, the crosshairs of a telescopic sight appeared on the circle of the spotlight. But Jenny knew that you would have to be above the stage to see it. The people below had no idea of what was about to happen. Their roar of approval grew louder as Del neared the spot where he would die.

Riven with panic, Jenny looked around to find J. D. and beg him not to do it. A moment ago she had seen him everywhere, but now she couldn't see him at all. Still, she knew he hadn't left; the threat was more imminent than ever.

She felt something descending upon her. She looked up, and there was J. D. hovering in the air, kept aloft by black wings. Horns she'd never before noticed protruded from his head. He had cloven hooves instead of feet. He looked at her and there was fire in his eyes. All along he'd been the devil in disguise.

Turning his attention to the stage, the winged demon raised a sniper's rifle just as Del's leading foot broke into the cylinder of light. Jenny tried to yell for help, but her voice was gone. She looked around frantically for someone to stop the monster. Where was the Secret Service? Where were the cops? Why wouldn't somebody do something to prevent this tragedy?

Then she saw DeVito standing on the pavement of Mulholland Drive, but he was shaking his head. He held up his hands and Jenny saw they were heavily tied. Jenny looked back at the stage. Del's leg had entered the light, and an arm and shoulder were following. He was in the light now, oblivious to the fact that he was approaching his death.

The demon spared Jenny one last glance and then turned his fiery eye to the rifle's telescopic sight. Del Rawley stood directly in the crosshairs. The crowd cheered wildly.

Desperate for some way to save Del, Jenny looked around and saw a mask lying on the ground. It was the face of J. D. Cade, the one the demon had wanted the world to see, the guise it no longer needed. She grabbed it. It crumpled and compressed in her hands, forming a ball with a thousand razor-sharp points that tore her flesh. She hurled it with all her strength. It hit the demon and he shattered like glass, but she was too late. The creature had gotten off a shot.

She tried to turn and see if Del was . . . but something terribly strong seized her.

Jenny woke up to find a Secret Service agent shaking her shoulder. "Ms. Crenshaw," the man said, "wake up. You were having one hell of a dream."

Jenny looked around, just starting to get her bearings. A second agent stood in the background. The one with his hand still on her shoulder regarded her with concern.

"You okay now? You were screaming so loudly we thought someone was being killed. And when we heard the crash we had to come in." He nodded at a wall mirror that had been shattered. "Looks like you did that with a water glass. Must've been one hairy nightmare."

"It was," Jenny replied weakly.

"Should I call for the hotel doctor?" the agent asked.

Jenny shook her head. "I'll be all right."

"Okay. Be careful of the broken glass, then, until we can get someone to clean it up."

Jenny nodded again, and the Secret Service agents left.

The dream was still so vivid in her mind it made her shiver. How could she have imagined J. D. that way? He'd been the one who was so helpful last night. He'd been the one who got DeVito to think of all the possible ways that . . . How *had* he been able to think of so many ways Del could be attacked on that stage?

J. D. had told DeVito it was just common sense, but it was almost as if he was revealing an *expertise* in the matter. Maybe without even being aware of it. Then with her consciousness brightening and the horrible dream receding, she remembered that there was no question that J. D. had been trying to protect Del, not hurt him. J. D. had *saved* Del's life.

The nightmare had turned everything inside out. Were all of DeVito's suspicions poisoning her subconscious? Mindful of the broken glass, Jenny tiptoed to the bathroom. It was not yet five o'clock but she had a million things to do today, and number one on her list was to see J. D. Cade.

If only to make sure he hadn't grown any horns.

Blair McCray and Deena Nokes had spent all of the previous afternoon in a futile search for the frog-faced man Deena had seen at the restaurant. Then they'd stayed up until the wee hours sharing their respective memories of Ivar. It was the most meaningful memorial service that had been held in honor of the departed biker.

Just about sunset last night, their reminiscences had been interrupted by a deep grunt at the trailer door. Gorbachev had arrived and announced it was time for his dessert. Deena insisted upon having the animal forage in the woods for his own meals, but she provided sweets for him at least once a day.

She went to her tiny fridge and pulled out a half-gallon tub of ice cream. Deena took the ice cream out to the bear, pulled the lid off, and set the container down at the foot of the stairs to the trailer. Blair watched from the doorway. Deena looked over her shoulder and smiled at him.

"Don't worry about Gorby. He knows you're a friend of mine now."

Blair inclined his head. "Does he really live in that old cabin over there?"

"He pretty much bunks there through the winter. Gets out of the rain there, too. When the weather's nice, he moves around a lot."

"Does he really heed you?"

"About fifty-fifty," Deena told him. "Same as any other male, I guess. Let's see how he's feeling today. Gorby." The bear looked up at Deena, his muzzle pink with strawberry ice cream. Deena whispered, her voice filled with feigned menace, "The Cossacks are coming."

Immediately the bear's head whipped around. His eyes scanned the woods and he went into a defensive posture and growled. Deena looked at Blair and arched her eyebrows questioningly. The lawman nodded, impressed.

"Moscow is saved!" Deena told Gorbachev.

The bear relaxed and turned back to Deena with an expectant look.

"I don't know what half this shit means," she told Blair, "but that's the way the old Russian who raised Gorby trained him." Then she added, "In the cabinet next to the fridge there's some candy. Fetch Gorby a peanut butter cup, would you? He loves them damn things."

Blair got the candy and at Deena's urging unwrapped it and tossed it at Gorbachev. The bear plucked it out of the air with his mouth. Blair would have sworn with his hand on a Bible that Gorbachev grinned as he masticated the treat. Then he lumbered off, content with the boost in his blood sugar, heading for the trees.

"You just made a friend for life," Deena told Blair. She picked up the ice cream container and the two of them went back inside.

They talked for hours, always keeping an ear out for the sound of someone approaching the trailer. In the morning they'd go out looking for Froggy again.

That sense of purpose was what wakened both of them almost at the same time after only three hours of sleep. Deena pushed herself up on an elbow on the unopened sleeper sofa where she'd spent the night, and Blair sat up in his sleeping bag on the floor. Each of them regarded the other somewhat sheepishly in the first light of day, remembering how much of their pasts they'd revealed to someone who was all but a stranger.

Blair gestured to Deena that she should use the bathroom first, and she was just about to close the door when, looking out the window, Blair murmured, "Jesus Christ!"

"What is it?" Deena asked, alarmed.

She hurried over to the window. What she saw made her draw a sharp breath. Someone had been outside the trailer last night. Had been very close by, and with all their chattering, they hadn't heard him. Hadn't known at all that someone had come and tied Evan Cade to a tree.

Ben Cade was moving about the kitchen of his home in the town of Anna as the day began. He was the one who made breakfast in his family. He had just cracked four eggs into a bowl to scramble and butter was melting in the frying pan when the phone rang. He said hello and heard J. D.'s voice on the line.

"Ben, I need a favor," J. D. told him.

"Anything at all, J. D. Just name it."

"I've been told Evan's been kidnapped."

"Dear God Almighty! You coming home again?"

"As soon as I can. But I need you to see if you can find him."

"J. D., we've got to go to the police with something like this." Ben was worried when his cousin didn't respond immediately, and even more disturbed when he eventually did.

"Ben, if Evan has been kidnapped, the people who have him will kill him if they see any cops. I need you not only to find Evan, I need you to do whatever it takes to free him."

This time the silence that ensued belonged to Ben. He knew that the time had come for him to repay J. D. for freeing him of the need to kill Alvy McCray. In all the years that had passed since Alvy's death, Ben had thought he would gladly kill for his cousin J. D., and now it looked like he was facing just that possibility.

Ben Cade told his cousin, "I'll do whatever I have to, J. D."

"Thank you. I don't know if my mother knows what's happened yet, but I have to think if Evan's really gone, she'll find out sooner rather than later. Could Marie stay with her?"

"You bet. What do these people want, J. D.? Money?"

"I only wish. All I can say, Ben, is if we don't get Evan back, something terrible is going to happen."

The Toad saw two faces appear in the window of the trailer, first the man's and then the woman's. They stared fixedly at Evan Cade tied to his tree. Trying to decide if he was still alive, no doubt. If their vision was adequate, they'd soon see his chest rising and falling. Yes, they'd noticed. They were talking, and now they were looking for who had trussed up their friend.

The Toad made his entrance, stepping from the shadow of the trees to the sunlight of the clearing. But he was ready to duck back quickly if they opened fire on him immediately—which they should have done but didn't.

"As you see, I have your friend," the Toad called out. "He's alive and well, but he won't be for long if you don't come out."

The two faces disappeared from the window, which was the second best they could do: get out of sight and keep quiet. Taking the next carefully calibrated step, the Toad fired a round into the ground. Two seconds later the woman's face appeared at the trailer's window. She fired through it. Three distinct rounds. A revolver, not a semi-auto. But she was too late. The Toad had stepped back behind a tree and none of the shots threatened him. But one kicked up a clod of dirt a foot from Evan Cade.

"You almost killed your friend," the Toad announced.

"No skin off my ass, Froggy," the woman replied.

The Toad's features tightened. *Froggy.* He knew what he looked like but he'd always hated that particular name. Toad he could live with. Indeed, he wore it comfortably. Toad had a certain weight to it, an earthy dignity. But Froggy? She'd pay for that.

"So I should just shoot him, then?" The Toad stepped out from cover and pressed his pistol to Evan Cade's temple. He watched the trailer carefully for any sign of a gun pointed his way. The woman was no marksman, but there was no point taking chances.

Still hoping to do things the easy way, the Toad called out, "Have you ever seen that famous film clip from the Vietnam War? The one where the South Vietnamese general calmly walks up to the captured VC suspect, puts his gun to the man's head, and blows his brains out? It's my favorite. Such decisiveness. Such . . . *dispatch*. Well, here goes."

The door to the trailer opened. The man stepped out first. The woman followed, clearly the more reluctant of the two, and she had a revolver in her hand. But it wasn't pointed at the Toad.

"Drop your firearm," the Toad told Deena, his gun still at Evan's head.

Instead she flung it into the trees. "Fuck you, Froggy. The one thing you ain't gonna do is kill me with my own gun."

The Toad stepped back from Evan. He pointed his weapon at Blair and Deena and told them, "That's quite all right. There are so many other things I can do."

Then, at the Toad's direction, Blair and Deena untied Evan and carried him into the trailer. Once inside, with his prisoners all settled nicely on Deena's sofa at the rear of the trailer and his gun trained on them, the Toad called the Gardener on his PCR.

"Yes, sir. This is Harold."

"*Harold*," Deena snorted. "I'd prefer Froggy myself."

The Toad's eyes narrowed. This one would indeed get special attention.

"No, sir. No problems. I've just taken the woman who killed Farrel, and Blair McCray. My prisoner count is now up to three."

Jenny Crenshaw went to J. D. Cade's room at the Century Plaza. She had decided not to phone ahead. She wanted to make it a cold call. Get a first impression of him in whatever state he appeared at his door. But after knocking hard, harder, and door-rattling hardest, she concluded that he wasn't inside.

She listened for the sound of a shower running, a TV

blaring, or some other competing noise that would mask her assault on the door. But she heard nothing.

She told herself that J. D. might simply have stepped out for an early breakfast. He might have gone for a workout or a swim. He might even have made a trip to his house to pick up, say, a change of clothes.

But, coming on the heels of her nightmare, not finding J. D. Cade where she'd expected him to be disturbed Jenny more than she wanted to admit.

She thought to bang on the door one more time, if only to vent her distress, but she restrained herself and started back to her room. Maybe he'd be there, calling on her.

But if he wasn't . . . if he wasn't back soon . . . if there wasn't some completely mundane reason for him being in some very ordinary place . . .

Maybe he should stay away.

At least until Del's appearance at the Hollywood Bowl was over.

J. D. was at the Refuge, sitting at the desk in the den, Pickpocket's laptop computer in front of him. He was, he had to admit, putting his affairs in order. Planning what he knew might be the last day of his life.

He made two digital copies of Townes' memoirs. He'd mail them out that morning: one to his lawyer and one to Ben. He included instructions as to what should be done with the copies in the event of his death.

With the mailings ready to go, the next thing he needed to do was to find a reporter. Jenny had told him how the campaign used the media. J. D. was going to see if he could do it, too.

He called the *Los Angeles Times* and asked for Tom Hayashi. Hayashi was the investigative reporter who'd broken the story of the discovery of the M-100 at Marina Del

Rey. His specialty was politics, with an emphasis on exposing corruption. He used to cover the legislature in Sacra-
mento, but his nose for scandal was so good that the paper
had moved him to national politics.

J. D.'s name was sufficiently hot to get the reporter to
pick up his phone, but he told J. D. that heroes were really
not his area of interest. If J. D. felt like talking, Hayashi
could hook him up with another scribe at the paper.

J. D. needed a reporter, but not one with a blasé attitude.

He said, "Thanks anyway. I'll find someone who's interested—because what I really want is to trade my story for a
favor."

"A favor, huh?" Hayashi did his best to play it cool, but
J. D. could hear the newfound interest in the reporter's
voice. "So maybe there's more to your story than everyone
thinks?"

"No . . . well, I can't promise you anything. But listen, I
like your stuff, been reading it for years. So I'll *give* you
something, but this has to be one of those anonymous
deals, okay?"

"Yeah, sure. Anonymous." Now J. D. could hear skepti-
cism. "What've you got?"

"The president has only one ball," J. D. revealed in a
deadpan tone. He'd promised Jenny never to reveal that secret, but that was the least of his betrayals.

There was a moment of silence and then Hayashi guffawed. "You're shitting me, but that's pretty funny. Hey, are
you really J. D. Cade?"

"I'm really J. D. Cade, and I'm not shitting you. If you
don't believe me, check it out. Now I've got to find someone who's interested in doing me a favor. See you around."

"Hey, wait! If you *didn't* make up that one-ball story, you
must have some pretty interesting connections. Maybe we
should get together. Just to get acquainted, you know."

"That worth a favor from you?" J. D. asked.

"Depends on the favor."

"I want to find out if someone I used to know is in town with the president's entourage for the Hollywood Bowl debate tonight."

"But you don't want this someone to know?"

"Yeah."

"And there's no story there, huh?"

"Wouldn't want to make a promise I couldn't keep."

There was a pause, then Hayashi asked, "What's this someone's name?"

"As you said, let's meet somewhere and I'll tell you."

"You're pretty cagey, Mr. Cade. I like that. Okay, we'll meet."

The reporter gave J. D. a location.

"I'll meet you there at noon," Hayashi said. "That'll give me time to see if I can track down the president's urologist."

Another task started: finding Colonel Townes. With the president coming to L.A., J. D.'s money said that Townes wouldn't be far behind. If he hadn't arrived already.

Putting the pieces together, J. D. had realized that the reason Townes so badly wanted to see Del Rawley die was that he wanted to guarantee the incumbent's reelection. Which meant, plain and simple, Townes was going to be a player in the next administration—if his man won.

Del Rawley had said that J. D. wasn't sucking up for a job in Washington, but Townes clearly was. Undoubtedly a bigger job than he'd ever had before. And if the colonel wanted something badly enough, he wouldn't care who he had to kill to get it.

The new wrinkle was Townes saying he'd kill himself if he didn't get his way. J. D. had to admit that the twisted bastard had sounded sincere about committing suicide . . . but J. D. wanted Hayashi to find Townes for him to make sure there would be no backsliding on the colonel's part.

If J. D., Evan, and Del Rawley were not destined to out-live this day, then J. D. wanted to be sure that Townes' life expectancy was similarly limited.

The place where J. D.'s thinking hit a sticking point was at Donnel Timmons. How could he even think about shooting Donnel now, after his old comrade in arms had saved his life? In the hours since he'd almost died at the Beverly Center, J. D. had asked himself many times *why* Donnel had saved him from Roth.

Was it because they'd once been friends?

Or was it only because Donnel knew from him that Roth worked for Townes, and Donnel had feared Roth would intercept Townes' stolen memoirs and return them to him?

When Donnel wanted to take them away from J. D.

In either case, finding the will to even wound Donnel now . . . he just didn't see how he could do it. He'd have to do something else. Maybe decoy Donnel out of the picture. But the more he thought about how Donnel had saved him, the less he could accept that Donnel would actually go through with an assassination of Rawley. After all, Donnel had been closer to Rawley—more likely to fall under the spell of his considerable charm—for far longer than J. D.

He hoped to hell he wasn't just romanticizing an old friend. A friend he knew for a certainty had killed at least eight people. One more than him.

Unable to take that line of thought any further for the moment, J. D. decided he'd better check in with Jenny. She might be wondering where he was by now. He tried to reach her at the hotel but she wasn't there. He tried campaign headquarters and his call was taken, but not by Jenny.

Instead Vandy Ellison cheerfully greeted him. "Hi, J. D. How'd you like to go out with me tonight?"

"I beg your pardon."

"Well, Jenny just spoke to me. She was on her way out so she asked me to say that she tried to call on you at the hotel this morning but you weren't in your room."

"What's this about going out, Vandy? Del's at the Bowl with the president tonight."

"Yes, exactly. Jenny thought you and I should watch the debate at the Westside Studio lot—in a screening room with a bunch of Hollywood types. We'll be Del's surrogates and answer any questions the people there might have."

"The A-list isn't going to be at the Bowl?" J. D. wanted to know.

"Jenny's idea. There'll be a few exceptions, like Marva, of course, but Jenny decided to give Del's seats to everyday people who want the chance to see him. She thinks this will contrast nicely with the incumbent filling his seats with the pols and poobahs from his camp."

J. D. looked past the politics to the crucial point. "*I'm* not going to be at the Bowl?"

"I know," Vandy commiserated. "I'm not, either. But with all the celebrities Jenny's turned down, she thought she'd better do something to placate them. And *you* are still a very hot commodity. People will turn out for the chance to talk with the man who saved Del's life. As for me, I'll console myself that I'll finally get to spend some time with you.

"So, what do you say?" Vandy asked. "Can I drop by your house in a little while and we'll work out all the details?"

J. D. felt as if he was about to be sucked into a whirlpool. Without the access to Del Rawley that he'd come to take for granted, there was no chance he'd . . . He wondered if he'd gone too far last night. Had he overplayed his hand by suggesting possible threats against the candidate at the Hollywood Bowl? Had he made Jenny uneasy? Was she deliberately easing him out?

"J. D.? Are you there?" Vandy asked.

"Yes, I'm here."

"So, can I come over?"

He couldn't turn her down. Right now Vandy was his only unforced link to the campaign. But he was going to stall.

"Sure, Vandy. But listen, I have to catch up on some personal business I just can't put off. Why don't you stop by, say, an hour before we have to leave for the studio? That way we should have enough time to go over . . . well, whatever you think needs going over."

J. D. was sure Vandy had heard the innuendo in his voice, because there was a lilt in hers when she said, "I'll see you at six, then."

Just then J. D. had a moment of inspiration. "Maybe there's one thing you can think about before you come over."

"I'll be thinking of all sorts of things, but tell me what you have in mind."

"Well, Jenny might be overestimating my box office appeal, and it wouldn't do to play to less than a full house. Maybe you could hint that besides you and me, there might well be a special surprise guest. That should pack 'em in."

Vandy understood immediately. "You mean Del? That's brilliant! Have him drop by after he's done at the Bowl. That way he can be a man of the people, and he won't put any of Tinseltown's perfectly sculpted noses out of joint, either."

"I was just thinking of a tease to guarantee a good turnout, but if you think . . ."

"I do. And as long as you're so humble, maybe I'll take credit for the idea."

"By all means."

"I'll get right on it," Vandy said.

See that you do, J. D. thought. See that you do.

DeVito poked his head into Jenny's office—Vandy's assertion to J. D. notwithstanding, she hadn't left campaign headquarters. She had just been about to make a phone call, but put the receiver down as the special agent took a seat in one of her guest chairs. "What?"

"Where's your boyfriend?" DeVito wanted to know. "I've been looking all over for him but I can't find him. So I figured he had to be with you or you'd know where he is."

"You're referring to Mr. Cade?"

"You got another boyfriend?"

Jenny knew there was no use trying to fool the Secret Service about who was sleeping with whom in a presidential campaign. "No, I don't."

"So where is he?"

"I don't know."

"Don't know or won't say?"

"He just called in, but I had Vandy Ellison talk to him."

DeVito knit his brow. A lover's spat? he wondered. Normally he wouldn't give a damn, but nothing was normal anymore, so he spoke up. "Trouble in paradise, Ms. Crenshaw?"

"No," Jenny said frostily.

"Things just ran their course, then."

"Special Agent DeVito, this is really none of your business. If you want to find Mr. Cade, see if Vandy Ellison can help you. Now, I really have a lot to do."

But DeVito persisted. "You'll see Cade tonight, though, right? At the Bowl?"

"Mr. Cade will *not* be at the Hollywood Bowl tonight. He's been asked to appear at the Westside Studio to speak to an audience of entertainment people."

Cade *wouldn't* be at the Hollywood Bowl? DeVito was amazed. What the hell was going on here? What could have made Jenny Crenshaw change her mind about Cade? Something merely personal . . . or something he should know?

DeVito knew he couldn't strong-arm Jenny to find out—but there was nothing that said he couldn't drop a bomb on her.

"Are we done, Special Agent DeVito?" Jenny's tone clearly implied that they were.

"Sure. Just one thing. If you happen to see Mr. Cade, tell him from me: That guy he warned me about, my considered opinion is that guy's coming after him."

"Coming after?"

"Yeah. I think that guy wants to kill your friend, Mr. Cade."

There—DeVito saw it. The alarm in her eyes. She still had it for Cade, even if there was some new kink in their relationship he didn't know about. Just as Jenny was about to question him, DeVito got up, threw her a mock salute, and left.

Let Miss Bossy run after him if she wanted the details.

Let her come clean first, tell him how come Cade had been sent down to the minors.

Still shaken by what she'd heard from DeVito, Jenny returned to the phone call she'd been about to make. She tapped out the numbers to reach Don Ward. As before, she wondered if her old friend and mentor would be alive to receive the call. She heard the phone ring once on the far side of the country and then a set of relays clicked in her ear. She knew that meant her call was being forwarded to another number. A moment later the phone was picked up.

"Don?" Jenny asked.

"I was hoping it would be you, my dear," Hunter Ward told her.

His voice sounded so ghostly that she wondered half seriously if the phone company had call forwarding to the Great Beyond.

"Are you busy preparing for your man's big night?" he asked.

"Yes," Jenny replied. Then she added, feeling great guilt, "That's why I called. I wanted to ask if there would be any last-second dirty tricks—or threats—that I should worry about."

There was a moment's silence. Then Hunter Ward told her in the barest whisper, "There will be no more tricks, no more threats. I've found him, Jenny dear. I've caught up with the man who wants your candidate dead."

Jenny was stunned—and then elated.

"That's wonderful, Don! Tell me who he is and I'll have the Secret Service take him into custody immediately."

"No, no. This is something I must do myself."

"Don, how can you say that?" she asked, panic filling her voice. "You're . . . dying."

"All to my advantage."

"Don, *please*. Let's do this right. Let me help you."

"I've always loved you, Jenny."

Those last words were spoken so softly she wasn't sure she hadn't imagined them, but she knew for certain that her phone connection with Don Ward had been broken.

After he'd made his call to the Gardener, the next thing the Toad did was to allow Blair, Deena, and, when he came around, Evan to use the toilet—leaving the door to the tiny water closet open, of course. Deena uttered not a word of protest but turned her back in the Toad's direction and, after dropping her jeans, broke wind in his direction.

The Toad refused to take umbrage. Having done what he thought was necessary to make sure his captives would be reasonably comfortable, and therefore more likely to be docile, he had them reseat themselves on the sofa with Evan, Deena, and Blair positioned left to right. Then the Toad tossed a coil of clothesline and a pair of scissors that he'd found to Deena.

"Cut six four-foot lengths of line," he instructed her. "If you try anything stupid, I'll shoot all three of you."

With a scowl on her face, Deena did as she was told. The Toad told her to put the scissors and the remaining rope on the floor and kick them over to him. He then had Blair use one length of clothesline to bind Deena's ankles together. After that, he had Deena tie Evan's and Blair's hands behind their backs—making sure the bindings were tight—and then tie their ankles together. Finally, he had Deena lie facedown on the floor. With his knee on her spine and a promise to break her back if anybody tried anything, he put his gun down and bound Deena's hands behind her back, too. With that accomplished, the Toad hefted 170-pound Deena as if she was a toddler and deposited her between the two men.

The four of them had occupied the trailer for only thirty minutes, but already the air was rank with body odor, the space compressed by the certainty that death would soon be joining them. The Toad helped himself to a soft drink from Deena's fridge and surveyed his prisoners once more.

"What's your name?" he asked Deena.

"Fuck you, Froggy."

"Her name's Deena Nokes," Blair said.

"Don't be telling him nothin' about me," Deena ordered Blair.

She gave him an angry bump with her shoulder for emphasis. Then she looked back at the Toad. His can of soda sat on the breakfast bar, and he had his gun comfortably cradled in both hands on his lap. Seeing this, Deena smiled.

"Bet you like to play with yourself a lot, don't you, Froggy? That, or your women have to blindfold themselves so they can cop your joint without looking at you."

The Toad compressed his lips.

"Bet you can snatch a housefly right outta the air with your tongue, can't you, Froggy?"

A tic appeared at the corner of the Toad's left eye.

Blair watched their captor carefully, taking great pains to remain still. He didn't even want to let the guy see his muscles bunch up—something that could be entirely obvious in someone with his development.

Before they'd surrendered, he and Deena agreed to play a variation of good cop–bad cop. Along with throwing away Deena's Smith & Wesson, it was part of their plan. They wanted this plug-ugly SOB to think they were unarmed, and he hadn't bothered to search the trailer. But, in fact, Blair's Browning semiauto was under the seat cushion on which he sat.

It had been Deena's idea for her to play the bad cop. She'd said she didn't give a shit if the bastard killed her as long as Blair got him. So she was doing her best to get their captor to focus on her while Blair watched for his chance, trying to seem like he didn't have a hostile thought in his head. Mr. Cooperative.

But the Toad refused to play along for the moment. "Why'd you kill Farrel?" he asked.

"Who?" Deena wanted to know.

"The man in the bar. I saw you shoot him."

"He was with you?" Deena asked.

"You steal his body from the morgue?" Blair put in.

"Yes to each of you."

"Well, hell, if I'd'a known he was with you, that'd be enough right there," Deena replied.

"But you didn't know."

"Yeah, you're right about that. If I'd known, I'd'a shot you, too."

"Answer the question."

"I shot him because he killed my Ivar. I shot him because I saw him kill an innocent girl and her daddy."

Interesting, the Toad thought. He'd noticed a flash of anger in Evan Cade's eyes for the first time. He thought perhaps it was time to introduce a new line of tension to the dialogue, have his captives focus their hostilities on each other and not him.

"That young woman . . . let me see if I can recall her name." Having been in on the Gardener's planning from the start, the Toad had no difficulty in doing this. "Prudence Laney, I believe. A friend of our young Mr. Cade here."

Blair and Deena glanced at Evan, who looked angry and not overly concerned that he was tied up and the Toad was holding a gun on him. Blair gave Evan a small shake of his head in warning. He and Deena hadn't risked their lives to save Evan only to have him go kamikaze on them now. The Toad noticed Blair's concern and was amused.

"Blair McCray," he said, and the Kentucky lawman turned to face him. "That would make your father . . . Alvy McCray."

"That's right."

The Toad smiled, looking more reptilian than ever. "Did you know, Mr. McCray, that Evan Cade's father killed your father?"

Then Harold the Toad told them all just how J. D. Cade had done it.

"I want to meet the man who saved my father's life," Eleanor Rawley Walker said.

Del's family had arrived and was with him and Jenny in the candidate's suite.

"Yes, where is Mr. Cade?" Del asked. "I haven't seen him all morning."

"I'm sure we'll see him before the debate tonight, won't we?" Devree asked.

Jenny shook her head. "Well, no, actually. Mr. Cade is going to be speaking tonight as a surrogate for the senator. He'll be at a gathering of important movie people."

That came as news to Del and he said so.

"It was something I thought of just this morning," Jenny explained. "I'm trying to keep a *lot* of people happy. I thought if Mr. Cade and Vandy Ellison were over at the Westside Studio—"

"I don't want to mess up anybody's plans," Eleanor said quietly. "I'd just like to meet the man. Give him a hug and tell him I'll always be grateful. Introduce my son to the man who saved his grandfather. It really doesn't have to take more than five minutes."

The other Rawleys all agreed, including the one who mattered most.

Jenny suggested, "Let me go talk to Vandy Ellison. Maybe she'll know if Mr. Cade is free to visit with you this afternoon."

"Thank you," Eleanor Rawley said.

After Jenny left, Devree took her husband aside. "You know, with you standing on an outdoor stage, even with all your Secret Service people around, I wouldn't mind having that man, Mr. Cade, right there in the front row with us. He saved you once. Who can say it wouldn't be a good idea to have him nearby again?"

Del was not about to tell Devree that he'd learned from Special Agent DeVito that J. D. Cade was a marksman with a rifle. He wasn't going to get into any of the unsettling facts about the head of his protection detail, about Garvin Townes, or about his suspicion that the president himself might be in on a plot to assassinate him. Nor did he intend to share with his wife the fact that, except for the moment, he carried a gun these days.

So he responded with a politician's answer.

"Let me talk to some people, Devree. Then I'll let you know."

In a bar filled with fair hair, freckles, and faces as Irish as shamrocks, J. D. took the Asian-American gent coming out of the men's room to be Tom Hayashi. The reporter had told J. D. to meet him at Molly Malone's, a bar on Fairfax just off Sixth. He'd said J. D. should have a pint if he was a few minutes late. When J. D. had arrived and hadn't seen his man, he'd ordered a ginger ale. The bartender had looked affronted but served him nonetheless. Then he'd told J. D. his money was no good in the bar, but neither was the bleedin' swill in his glass.

Hayashi motioned J. D. over to a corner table.

"Favorite watering hole of yours?" J. D. asked, sitting down.

"Love my Guinness," the reporter replied as a waitress placed a pint of stout in front of him and departed. Hayashi raised his glass, "Health—and the devil take our enemies."

J. D. raised his glass. "I'll drink to that."

The two men put their glasses down and looked at each other frankly.

"You're the man who saved Senator Rawley, all right," the reporter said.

J. D. nodded and responded, "Try as I might, Mr. Hayashi, I don't see the Irish in you."

The reporter laughed. "My stepfather's name is

Desmond Walsh. He's a wonderful old guy who stepped in and saved the day for my mother, my sister, and me when my dad died. He gave me three loves: the use of language, the folly of men's ambitions, and stout."

"Sounds like a fine man."

"Made me who I am today," Hayashi said. Then he got down to business. "Who do you want me to find for you, Mr. Cade?"

"Can we keep my identity private in this matter?"

Hayashi chewed his lower lip for a moment and looked at J. D. "I think it might be interesting to know you, Mr. Cade. So yeah, this one's on me."

"The man I want to find is Garvin Townes." J. D. spelled out the name.

"You think he's traveling with the president?"

"He may be."

"Is it okay to ask what Mr. Townes does?"

J. D. thought about that and an idea occurred to him. "Right now he's got a spot with the Treasury Department. Heads a unit called Departmental Internal Management and Oversight."

"D-I-M-O?" Hayashi asked.

"D-E-I-M-O-S. Are you going to the debate at the Bowl tonight?"

"Sure."

"You know if they're going to take questions from the media?"

"A formal Q-and-A hasn't been decided yet. But that doesn't mean someone with a strong set of lungs can't shout out anything that comes to mind. What might come to mind, Mr. Cade?"

"Ask the president what job he has in mind for Garvin Townes if he's reelected."

"That's where the story is? The job this guy's getting?"

"Story might be in how the president reacts to your question."

The reporter looked at J. D., rubbed his chin, and then smiled again.

"I like you, Mr. Cade. I get the feeling you're hanging your ass out here, but I don't know just how. It's going to be fun finding out, though."

"I'm glad I could brighten your day. You might enjoy thinking about this, too. If you can't find Townes' name on any official roster of the president's entourage, run a count of the rooms the president's party has booked. See if there's one more than they should need. Look for something like that or any similar discrepancy."

"This Townes guy likes to stay in the shadows."

"It's pretty much his life . . . when he isn't writing his memoirs."

The reporter's eyes opened wide. He knew what he'd just heard. J. D. Cade either had in his possession or had read the bio of some spook who might be getting a big job from the president if he got reelected. But Hayashi also knew better than to expect J. D. to come across with something like that right away. He had to prove himself first.

"Did you know you were followed here, Mr. Cade?"

J. D. shook his head but kept his face impassive.

"A friend of mine told me while I was in the men's room."

"You had me watched as I arrived?"

The reporter shrugged. "I've made a number of people mad at me over the years. My Irish friends are well versed in the subject of getting even; they like me to take certain precautions before meeting someone who calls out of the blue. They look out for me."

Another reason for meeting at this particular bar, J. D. thought. "What's this person following me look like?"

"Black, middle-aged, nicely dressed . . . able to take care of himself, if need be."

Donnel. "Thank you for letting me know, Mr. Hayashi."

"Sure. Where can I reach you when I find out about Townes?"

J. D. gave the reporter his PCR number, and just then the device's pager element beeped. He looked at the number. "Have to make a call," he said.

"If you want to use a public phone, there's one back there by the john. I'll call you as soon as I know something." He gave J. D. his business card. "Or you can call me if you need to."

The two men stood and shook hands.

"By the way," Hayashi said, "you were right about the president having only one ball."

"You found someone to confirm it?" J. D. asked, more than a little surprised.

"Talked to the White House physician."

"He wouldn't have said anything."

"He barked out a very defensive 'No comment.' If the story wasn't true, he'd have just laughed and politely reminded me that people's medical records are nobody's business but their own. So you're right, Mr. Cade. Sometimes it's how people react that tells you the story."

J. D. called the number that had paged him and Jenny Crenshaw answered.

"It's me," he said deadpan. "Spokesman to the stars."

"Hold on a minute, will you?" J. D. heard her put the phone down and then in the background a door closed. "I'm back."

"You paged me."

"I've been trying to reach you."

"It's okay. Vandy Ellison talked to me. I'll do the Westside Studio appearance . . . but then I think I'm calling it quits. Politics isn't what I'd hoped it would be."

After a moment of silence, Jenny asked, "Are you mad at me?"

"More puzzled than angry, but women have left me guessing before."

"It wasn't my intention to . . . I was just . . ."

"It's okay. You don't have to explain. One day you're everybody's friend, the next you're on the outside looking in. It happens."

Stung, a new note of formality entered Jenny's voice. "Del's family has arrived in town and his daughter, Eleanor, would like to see you this afternoon. She wants to express her thanks to you for saving her father's life. The other members of the family feel the same way. Can I tell them you'll make it at, say, one o'clock?"

That development took J. D. completely by surprise. Meeting a grateful Rawley family was the *last* thing he wanted to do. But if access to the candidate via Jenny had been cut off, and he knew that was what had just happened, another entree might provide a golden opportunity.

"They're at the hotel?"

"Yes."

"Tell them I'll be there. Is there anything else?"

"Yes," Jenny replied. "Special Agent DeVito stopped in to see me this morning."

"What did he want?" J. D. asked.

In a dispassionate tone, Jenny answered, "He said the guy you warned him about probably wants to kill you."

J. D. had to shake his head in admiration of DeVito's instincts. The man was something else. DeVito wouldn't be surprised to hear what had happened at the Beverly Center. Not that J. D. would ever tell him.

"I'll make a note of that. Thank him for the warning, will you?"

When J. D. stepped out of the bar a moment later, he looked all around, making no effort to be subtle, but he couldn't spot Donnel anywhere. He wondered if Donnel sensed that the end was near, too.

He wondered if he was making Donnel nervous.

"So your dad did it?" Blair asked Evan quietly.

"Yeah," Evan admitted. "My father killed your father."

"Hey, this is all real interestin'," Deena Nokes said in a bored voice, "but true confessions make me thirsty. And it's hot as a ten-dollar Rolex in here. How about a drink, swamp breath?"

The Toad had been enjoying the dialogue between Cade and McCray. There had been no denial on Cade's part, no recrimination on McCray's, no anger from either. Just a melancholy and entirely civil acceptance of what he'd divulged to them. In fact, he was the one who'd been surprised that young Cade had already discovered so much about his father. The only reason the Toad could see that the revelation had not caused any hard feelings was that intuitively the two men had understood that it meant nothing in the context of their impending deaths. They were resigned to their fates, and you couldn't ask for a better attitude among condemned men than resignation.

But then the woman had to open her big—

"Hey, Froggy, goddamnit! I'm sweating like a pig here! You got the three of us joined together like we were born this way. Get me something to drink, reptile dick."

The Toad stared hard at the glaringly defiant woman.

The only reason he hadn't shot her already was that he hadn't wanted her corpse raising a stink in the trailer. But he'd promised himself that she'd suffer and he saw no reason why her pain shouldn't start immediately. He looked through the cabinets behind the breakfast bar and found a bottle of Lysol. He held it up to show Deena. "Think this might quench your thirst?"

"That stuff's poison," Blair warned.

"Exactly," the Toad answered with a grin as he removed the bottle's cap.

He gestured to each man with his gun not to interfere as he advanced on Deena. She had her mouth clamped shut and her chin pressed to her breastbone. The Toad evaluated the two men. McCray might make a move. Cade was watching but his face was impassive. His body sat slack. The youngest of the three captives, he seemed to have lost his spirit the fastest.

The Toad held his gun in his right hand, convenient to the side of the sofa on which McCray sat, and the Lysol bottle in his left. If he had to shoot McCray, he would—and at that point he'd have to abandon creativity and shoot the woman as well. Then he and his remaining captive would simply have to endure the mess and the stench until it was time for Evan Cade to die and him to leave.

Normally all that was required to open a mouth was to squeeze a nose shut, but the Toad's hands were full. He thought the solution to his problem was to give the woman a sharp blow on the top of her skull with his gun, not hard enough to knock her out, but sufficiently hard to force her mouth open in a scream. Then he'd jam the bottle in and clean up the woman's vocabulary.

Before he followed through on that plan, though, the Toad thought it wise to give Blair McCray one last warning with the business end of his gun. As the Toad looked at Blair, Evan came to life with the suppleness of youth and the speed of a snake. He slid his back down onto the seat cushion of the sofa and, angling to his left, whipped his feet up in a sharp jackknife motion.

The Toad saw movement out of the corner of his eye and turned just as Evan's kick arrived. The open bottle of

Lysol went flying from the Toad's hand and a sheet of the harsh liquid cleaner splashed directly into his protuberant eyes.

The Toad bellowed with pain, and Evan pulled his feet back and launched himself at his pain-wracked captor.

SIXTEEN

Jenny met J. D. at the door to Del Rawley's suite.

"Thank you for coming," she told him coolly. Then she turned and led the way to where the candidate and his family were rising from their seats with expectant looks on their faces.

Donnel was also present. Mrs. Rawley had been sitting next to him. He didn't bother to get up. But a glance told J. D. that Donnel was watching him closely.

"Mr. Cade," Del said, stepping forward to shake J. D.'s hand. "Good to see you again. I hope we haven't interrupted any of your plans for the day, but my family wanted to meet you." He guided J. D. over to the others. "May I introduce my wife, Devree Harper Rawley. Devree, this is Mr. Jefferson Davis Cade."

"Pleased to meet you, Mrs. Rawley," J. D. said, taking her hand.

"The pleasure is ours, Mr. Cade." Devree made no attempt to disguise the fact that she was studying J. D.'s face, taking his measure. She placed her free hand over J. D.'s, clasping it now in both of hers. "Has something hurt you recently, Mr. Cade?"

The question clearly caught J. D. off guard, but before

an answer became necessary, Eleanor stepped forward and her mother gave way. J. D. extended his hand to her but, true to her word, she stepped past it and hugged him.

"Thank you, Mr. Cade. Thank you so much for saving my father's life."

J. D. looked past the young woman embracing him to the candidate.

"My daughter, Eleanor," he said.

She stepped back with a sheepish grin. "That's right, I didn't even tell you my name. I'm sorry. I'm Eleanor Rawley Walker." She turned to a young man standing behind her, who handed a small boy to her. "And this is Benjamin Franklin Walker, age fifteen months. He still has his grandpa because of you."

To everyone's surprise, the boy reached out and grabbed J. D.'s nose.

"Ben!" his mother chastised gently, and pulled him back.

Not discouraged in the least, the toddler made another lunge and everyone laughed.

"Would you like to hold him, Mr. Cade?" Eleanor asked. "He seems taken with you."

"I . . . yes, I'd like that very much." Out of the corner of his eye, J. D. saw Donnel lean forward. Almost as if he was getting ready to make a move on J. D.

Eleanor carefully shifted her son to J. D.'s arms. He held the child with a natural ease; the boy was both comfortable and secure.

"You do that very well, Mr. Cade," Eleanor said. "You must have children of your own."

"A son." J. D. nodded. "He's grown now, but I guess some things you never forget." He looked at the boy and gently took his nose between thumb and forefinger. The child swatted J. D.'s fingers away and laughed.

"My son did exactly the same thing," J. D. said with a

haunted smile. He handed the toddler back to his mother. "You've got a good one there."

Eleanor smiled in agreement. "Who knows? Maybe it won't be long before your son makes you Grandpa Cade. Then you can put your old skills back to use."

J. D.'s smile faded.

Del sensed the conversation had strayed to sensitive ground. He stepped in and continued the introductions of his other children, their spouses, and his grandchildren. After everyone had had a few minutes to chat, he politely called a halt to the activities.

"Now, I think we've all taken enough of Mr. Cade's time. We'll have to let him get on about his business." He shook J. D.'s hand. "Thank you for coming. Let me see you out."

J. D. waved farewell to the Rawley family. He nodded to Donnel, who was once again seated next to Devree Rawley. Del ushered him toward the door but stopped short. The two men were equidistant from the Rawleys behind them and the agents guarding the door. It was a zone of relative privacy.

Del said quietly, "Jenny tells me you're leaving the campaign."

"Yes. It's . . . it's best for me to get back to my regular life."

Del Rawley laughed softly. "Well, there's precious little that's regular about politics, and nothing at all about campaigning. But I'll be sorry to see you go. I've enjoyed the occasions when we've had a chance to talk. You're not like anyone else I've met on the campaign trail."

"That's probably just as well."

"I want you to know, though, I'll see you one last time."

"How's that?"

"Vandy Ellison talked to me. Pointed out there will be some good and very generous people at the movie studio tonight and I'd be foolish to neglect them. So I intend to drop in on your gathering after we're done at the Bowl. Keep the crowd warmed up for me, won't you?"

"Do my best," J. D. replied in a neutral tone.

"I'm sure you will, Mr. Cade."

The candidate shook J. D.'s hand once more.

Over Del's shoulder, J. D. saw the little boy, arms out, still reaching for his nose.

Roth heard the scuttlebutt not fifteen minutes later from Landers, his new second in command.

"Cade's leaving."

"Leaving what?" Roth asked, careful not to sound too interested.

"The campaign. Tonight's his last night."

"Who told you that?"

"Thomas was on the door of Orpheus' suite. Guy's got great ears. He overheard Orpheus and Cade talking."

"Why's he leaving?"

"Well, that part's speculative. Some people think it's because Cade and Jenny Crenshaw had a falling-out. They were—"

"Yeah, I know they were."

"That's one theory. Another is Cade really dislikes the way the spotlight got turned on him after he saved Orpheus' life. Contrary to that, another school of thought has it that he's leaving to sell his story to the movies."

Despite himself, Roth snorted.

"Don't buy that idea, huh?"

"Not for a minute."

"Well, anyway, the part about him leaving seems solid."

Having dispensed with that subject, Roth and his lieutenant went over the day's business, ticking off one detail after another of not only having to keep Orpheus alive and well, but now also handling the additional burden of protecting the man's newly arrived family.

After that, Roth was alone with his thoughts.

Cade was leaving. He wouldn't be at the Bowl. He'd be across town at a movie studio. How the hell would he be able to kill Rawley from there? Answer: He wouldn't. So what was he doing, then? Writing off his son, giving him up for lost? Roth couldn't buy that, not after his run-ins with the bastard. Cade had something up his sleeve.

Unless Cade had decided there was absolutely no way he could hit Rawley short of a suicide attack. So if he thought he'd lost any chance to save his son, it made sense he'd give notice to the campaign . . . so he could devote himself to hunting down his enemies.

Like Roth himself. Whom he'd almost managed to drop a mountain on in his spare time. So now Cade was going to be out there with nothing else to do but draw a bead on *him?* While he was stuck heading Rawley's protection detail? Fuck that.

No, what Cade had done by announcing his departure was guarantee that Roth would get him—by hook or fucking crook—tonight.

After J. D. had left, Del excused himself from his family, Jenny, and Donnel, saying he had to work on his opening statement for the debate. He stepped into the suite's office. DeVito was there waiting for him.

"Could you hear anything?" the candidate asked.

DeVito shook his head. "Just that everything sounded friendly."

"Oh, it was. Just what you'd expect. Except for one thing."

"What?"

"When my wife shook hands with Mr. Cade she felt something, intuitively."

Making sure he watched his tone, DeVito asked, "Mrs. Rawley's psychic?"

The candidate gave the special agent a chastising look. "She's empathetic. She was a nurse. She's a mother and a grandmother. She knows when something's wrong with people. You should be able to understand that; I hear you often rely on your instincts."

DeVito nodded. "You've got a point. So what did Mrs. Rawley feel?"

"Devree asked Mr. Cade if someone had hurt him recently. So I'd have to think that she was feeling pain."

A flip response occurred to DeVito, but he stifled it. Maybe Mrs. Rawley's instincts were more acute than his own. He figured that Cade had pretty much gotten out of the box he was in and now he wanted the senator to live. But if Cade was feeling pain, who the hell knew what was going on in his head or what he might do?

"Cade thinks you're going to show up at the movie studio where he'll be speaking tonight, right, Senator?"

"That's what I told him."

"But you haven't confirmed that with anybody else?"

"No."

"So if Cade thinks you're going to come to him at the studio, he has no reason to try to get through all the security at the Hollywood Bowl. He'll wait for you right where he is. Then if you don't show up, he's shit out of luck, pardon my language."

"That assumes he is an assassin, which I still haven't concluded. But if he is, what's to say he won't simply leave the campaign, disappear, and try another long-range shot?"

DeVito shook his head. "I don't think so. He's managed to get too close to you to pull back now. And he's seen how tight security is at the Bowl, and he can bet it will be just as tight at any other outdoor appearance you might make. The fact that he's leaving the campaign after tonight tells me that if anything is going to happen, it will be before the day is out."

"So what you're recommending to me is . . . ?"

"Stiff him. Skip the appearance at the studio. If I'm wrong about Mr. Cade, you can always apologize later. But if I'm right, you'll have scammed him out of his last shot at you."

"What about Mr. Cade's warning to you about Roth?"

"I'm going to cover him. He steps one foot out of line, he's gone. I'll take the heat."

Del Rawley looked at DeVito, mulling his choices. "I'm going to withhold my decision for the moment about going to the Westside Studio."

DeVito bit his tongue but was clearly unhappy.

"There's something I want you to find out for me," Del told DeVito.

"What?"

"See if my wife was right. See if someone has hurt Mr. Cade recently."

Evan's escape attempt had failed. He and Blair and Deena were back on the sofa.

The Toad had his gun on them. He rubbed one eye and then the other, trying to clear his vision, but the world was a blur to him, and his eyes burned as if they'd been scoured with ground glass. But his prisoners were still tied up and under control once more. For the moment, that was all that mattered.

Evan hadn't been able to tackle the Toad after he'd kicked the Lysol into his eyes, because just as he'd gotten his feet back under him to dive at the Toad, Deena had tried to get up from the sofa and sent him sprawling in a completely unintended direction. That had given the Toad time to backpedal. Not that Blair hadn't tried to go after him, but he'd tripped over the sprawled Evan. Then the Toad had let off a round in the trailer, which had left everyone perfectly still while their ears rang like crazy.

He'd waved his gun back and forth over his captives and told them to get back on the sofa or he'd kill them all right then. It was plain to Evan, Blair, and Deena that their captor couldn't focus his eyes, but the way he kept waving that gun, all he'd have to do was open up and in that confined space he'd inevitably hit all of them. They'd done what they were told and struggled back into position on the sofa.

For a moment it had looked as though the Toad meant to wreak his vengeance on Deena. He tried to sight his weapon on her. Then Blair had leaned his torso in front of Deena, and Evan had leaned his body in front of Blair.

Now the air in the trailer was filled with the reek of the detergent and cordite, the stench of the captives' desperation, and the brimstone hatred pouring off the red-eyed Toad. Everyone was sweating from their various exertions, and the heat they had produced seemed trapped like an animal in the metal enclosure. There was a sense that soon they'd all asphyxiate.

The Toad started forward, holding his gun in front of him. The captives stiffened involuntarily, fearing he was moving in for a better shot. But when the Toad reached the end of the breakfast bar, he moved to his right and found Deena's little fridge. He opened it with his free hand, reached in, and came out with a bottle.

He held it up for the others to see. "Tell me what's in this bottle. If you lie, I'll shoot all of you."

"It's water," Evan said flatly. "Bottled water."

"Carbonated?"

"No."

The Toad found his way back to his stool at the breakfast bar. He twisted off the bottle's cap, and to be safe, he sniffed the contents. Looking back in the general direction of his captives, he said, "If you try to move again, I'll shoot you. I'll empty the clip. I'll get all of you."

Then, being very careful, he tilted the bottle of water and poured a stream into his left eye . . . and immediately screamed in agony. Nobody moved, nobody said a word as *suds* came out of the Toad's eye.

But Deena smiled fiercely.

And Evan and Blair began to strain against their bonds. Not grunting and going for broke. Just doing steady reps. Stressing the clothesline, pulling against the knots, relaxing and doing it all over again. Hoping to get free before the gargoyle with the foaming eye could see again.

Belle, Ben, and Marie Cade searched every single place in town where they might possibly find Evan. They'd looked all over the sprawling SIU campus. They'd been to the town library, the Salvation Army store, the law offices of Richard Shuster. They'd been to restaurants, bars, and parks that Evan had frequented. All without result.

Now Ben and Marie's minivan sat in a remote corner of a shopping mall parking lot off Route 51. Ben and Marie were trying to assure Belle that Evan would be all right while they waited for Ben's neighbor, Sawyer Price, to arrive. With each disappointment they'd faced in their search, the old lady had become more grim.

The afternoon shadows were growing long when Sawyer Price arrived. He came in a pickup truck with a camper shell on it. From inside the shell came the barking of excited dogs. The one place the three Cades had yet to look was the Shawnee National Forest: 270,000 acres of woodland with 1,250 miles of paved, gravel, dirt, and grass roadway running through it. If you kidnapped someone in southern Illinois, you couldn't ask for a better place to hide.

Ben climbed out of the minivan, and Marie slid in behind the wheel.

"We'll go out to Giant City first," Ben told the women. "We'll look around the lodge and the facilities. Then we'll go into the woods. Belle, if Evan's out there, we're going to find him."

The old lady looked at Ben but didn't say a word.

She was keenly aware that Ben hadn't—couldn't have— promised to find Evan alive.

After leaving the Rawleys, J. D. returned to the Refuge. He took Pickpocket's laptop out to the table by the pool. The task to which he addressed himself was pulling up every story he could find on the demise of his old comrade Dixie Wynne. He quickly read all the news articles. He weighed the information he learned against what he hoped to do with it. He probed for any deficiency. Much to his surprise, he couldn't find any. It all fit. At first glance.

He put the computer to sleep and turned a second analysis of Dixie's story over to his subconscious, trusting it to be less inclined to see what he wanted it to see.

He looked at the patterns of sunlight dancing on the water of the pool and his mind drifted back to his meeting with the Rawleys. He could still feel that little boy's fingers on his nose. What was his name again? Ben . . . Benjamin Franklin Walker.

Thing was, when he'd told Eleanor Rawley Walker that Evan used to clutch his nose the same way, he'd been telling the truth. J. D. remembered holding his infant son in his arms. Evan had looked right at him with his big green eyes shining brightly and gone straight for his nose every time. He'd held on tight, too. When J. D. had tried to gently grasp Evan's tiny nose, his son had smacked his hand away and laughed as if he'd devised a strategy the old man could never figure out for himself.

J. D. had never tried to plan Evan's life. Duplicating himself was the last thing he'd wanted. He'd hoped only for the joy of beholding his son as he discovered himself. So he'd encouraged Evan's inclinations, never pushed his own. Helped him to see why doing the right thing was the right thing to do. He never issued commandments from on high. He'd tried to set a good example of what a man should be, but left room for Evan to see that there were other worthwhile ways, too.

The only point on which J. D. had been completely rigid was that he had always and unapologetically done whatever he thought necessary to keep his son from coming to any irreparable harm. But now that bastard Townes had kidnapped Evan and was holding his son's life hostage. The taste of failure was bitter in J. D.'s mouth.

He couldn't let Townes succeed. Couldn't let the sweet little boy he'd held in his arms be sacrificed to a madman's ambitions. Himself, yes. He could accept his own death if that was what it came to. He'd killed people. He had blood on his hands. So let him die.

But not Evan. *Never* Evan.

J. D. forced his mind back to Dixie Wynne. Most of the stories he'd read had rehashed the same details: Wynne's shooting of the robbery suspect at the convenience store, his killing the two police officers at the siege of his house, and his suicide. But within the text of other stories J. D. found the information he sought.

No one had been able to account for Dixie Wynne's whereabouts during the weeks he'd been away from home. His neighbor, a man named Tag Olney, said Dixie had gone hunting, but nobody knew where. The angry SWAT cop and former PANIC sniper had dropped out of sight. If he had gone out to the wilds and hunted, as he'd told his neighbor, he'd lived off the land. That and paid cash for any necessities. If Dixie had used credit cards to pay for motel rooms, meals, or filling his gas tank, his trail would already have been known. He'd have been tracked down. The only clue as to where he might have gone to hunt was the vague description he'd given his neighbor: He was going hunting where nobody would complain about what he killed.

Who was to say that hadn't been Chicago? It might be suggested that Dixie had received a call from his old army commander, a man who appreciated a good sniper and wasn't nearly as squeamish about who got killed as the Gainesville PD. The idea was pure disinformation but, as J. D. saw it, squared neatly with the facts—and the idea of using another sniper from the PANIC unit as a stepladder out of the hole Colonel Townes had dug for him held great appeal for J. D.

The other significant piece of information he'd gleaned from his reading was the race of the convenience store robber Dixie Wynne had killed: black.

To those who'd known him, Dixie had been the salt of the earth, an equal-opportunity killer. But maybe he'd been just a mite ticked off that he'd gotten in trouble for shooting a black man. One of the news stories had even suggested that the police department might have swept Dixie's poor judgment under the rug if the criminal he'd shot had been white. Such considerations might have inspired a bit of racial animosity in Dixie Wynne.

Finally, maybe it hadn't been just the possibility of having to face the rap for shooting a convenience store bandit that had made Dixie go postal when he saw all those cops surrounding his house. Maybe it had been because he'd thought they'd come to arrest him for trying to kill presidential candidate Senator Franklin Delano Rawley.

That was more disinformation, of course, but it would be impossible for anyone to rebut. Just as it would be beyond proving that Dixie hadn't called his old army buddy J. D. Cade from a public phone somewhere and told him what he'd done up there in Chicago. Which had led J. D. to join the Rawley campaign to see that Dixie didn't succeed if he made another attempt.

J. D. dug out the business card Tom Hayashi had given him and called the reporter at his *Los Angeles Times* office. He wasn't in, so J. D. tried his PCR and Hayashi answered. He had good news for J. D.

"Got your man. The rest of the president's entourage is at the Beverly Hills Hotel, but he's at the Peninsula. You know where that is?"

"On Little Santa Monica Boulevard, right?"

"You got it." Hayashi gave Townes' suite number to J. D. and told him it was being paid for out of the same account as the rooms at the Beverly Hills Hotel.

"I won't ask you how you found that out."

"Good, because I wouldn't tell you."

"How many people from your paper besides you are going to the Bowl tonight?"

"That's a funny question," the reporter replied.

"Enough so maybe you could slip one extra name on the list and I could use it?"

"That's a damn funny question."

"Could be worth a *very* good story if you help me."

J. D. could almost hear Hayashi shift gears as he took that into account.

"How good?" he asked finally.

"Tell you who took the shot at Del Rawley in Chicago."

"Jesus! How could you—"

"I'm the guy who knew the president has one ball, remember?"

There was a deep silence on Hayashi's end of the conversation.

"You're the man with the great nose for news, right?" J. D. asked. "Listen to me and decide if I'm telling you the truth: I know who took the shot at Senator Rawley in Chicago."

"Sonofabitch," Hayashi whispered after several seconds. "You do know."

"That good enough to get me a press pass to the Bowl?"

"Two things . . ."

"What?" J. D. inquired, having anticipated the first question any good reporter would ask.

"Was it you?"

"No." Ready for the question, he answered firmly without either rushing it or waiting too long. He didn't let Hayashi's long following silence draw him into saying anything else, either. He could only wait to see if Hayashi's judgment was truly infallible. He was beginning to sweat when he finally heard the reporter speak.

"Okay. So you know who did it and it wasn't you. The other thing I have to ask is whether you know if there will be another attempt on Senator Rawley's life tonight. I couldn't keep something like that to myself."

"Neither could I. The reason I want to be at the Bowl tonight is I'm trying to *save* someone's life. I hope you can believe that, too."

"Shit, shit, shit."

"What?" J. D. asked. "You don't believe me?"

"No, the problem is I do believe you. And I want this story so bad it makes my teeth ache. But listen, Mr. Cade, there's no two ways about it: I sneak you in, I get fired. I might have a great story, but it'll be my last."

"Maybe not," J. D. hinted.

"Don't fuck me around, Mr. Cade. If you've got something more, tell me. Maybe I'll start my own Internet rag."

"I've sent some material to a friend," J. D. told the reporter. "Help me, and I'll arrange to have him send it to you . . . if anything should happen to me."

"Jesus," Hayashi whispered. "You think *you're* going to get killed?"

"You were the one who said I was hanging my ass out, remember?"

"Yeah . . . and if I don't help you and you get killed, I'll never find out what you know. If I let that happen . . . Hell, either way I'm finished."

"But my way you get one very big story and maybe a second; the other way you don't."

The reporter finally gave in. J. D. said he should have the press pass messengered to the Refuge. J. D. promised he would never reveal how he got it if Hayashi never revealed the source for his story.

"I called you cagey, Mr. Cade, but that doesn't cover the half of it."

J. D. hoped he was as clever as the reporter thought— showing up at the Bowl when everyone expected him to be at the studio—because if he was going to save Evan, he'd have to take a lot of people by surprise tonight.

The valet at the Century Plaza brought Jenny Crenshaw's car up for her. She was reaching in her purse for a tip when Dante DeVito came up from behind and took her elbow. Jenny was so startled she jumped, but by the time she saw who had his hand on her, she was already angry.

"What do you think you're doing?" she demanded, and pulled her arm free.

"We need to have a little talk."

"I don't have the time. I don't have a free minute all day."

"Me either. But Senator Rawley gave me a special job to do, and it involves talking to you—so we're *going* to talk."

Jenny saw that she was not going to get rid of the special agent.

"You drive," she said. "If you want to talk, you can drive."

DeVito nodded. He got behind the wheel and Jenny slipped into the passenger seat. He asked, "Where are we going?"

"CBS. Television City. It's on Beverly Boulevard and—"

"I know where it is." DeVito steered the car out of the hotel driveway and into traffic.

"So talk," Jenny said.

DeVito did, keeping his eyes on the road. "You were there when Cade met the Rawleys. Did you hear Mrs. Rawley ask Cade if someone had hurt him recently?"

"Yes."

"The senator wants me to find out *who* might've hurt him." DeVito glanced at Jenny. "I figure one person could be you."

Jenny turned bright red. DeVito faced forward again but kept talking.

"The two of you had a thing going. Everyone in the protection detail knows it. Now you and Cade are on the outs. Normally that's nobody's business but yours. And if you tell me to fuck off, that's your business, too. But it's also what I'll have to tell the senator."

After a long pause, Jenny asked, "Why is this so important?"

"You know I've always had my doubts about Cade. I've shared them with the senator."

DeVito had expected some sort of complaint from the woman at his side but when he heard none he looked over at her again. "The senator doesn't necessarily agree with

me that Cade is the guy who shot at him in Chicago. But
he does agree it's important to understand the man's frame
of mind. So if you tell me he's just upset over a lover's quarrel—and we don't need the details, believe me—then that
will ease everybody's mind."

"It wasn't a quarrel," Jenny said.

DeVito stopped for a red light at Beverly and Crescent
Heights and stared at her. "Then what was it?"

"A dream. I had a dream that spooked me." She told the
agent of her nightmare that J. D. was a demon killer who
assassinated Del Rawley at the Hollywood Bowl. "And I
think the whole damn thing was your fault, sowing seeds of
suspicion in everyone's minds. J. D. Cade hasn't done a
damn thing to make me think he's an assassin. He *saved*
Del's life. But I have one silly nightmare and I let it scare
me so badly that I alienate the man personally and push
him right out of the campaign."

The light turned green and DeVito stepped on the gas.
"You tell Cade about this dream?"

"No. I'm embarrassed that I've told you."

"Don't be. I believe dreams can tell you a lot."

"Sure, especially when they play right into your precon-
ceived notions."

DeVito considered debating that point but let it go. "So
as far as Cade knows, you just lost interest."

"No, he's too smart for that. I'm pretty sure he knows I
doubt him now . . . and how can I tell him it's all because
of some damn nightmare I had? I'd sound like an idiot."

DeVito disagreed, but he was not there to give advice to
the lovelorn.

"Donnel Timmons is the only other person in the campaign Cade is close to personally?"

"Yes, as far as I know. Vandy Ellison would like to be
close to him, but I don't think he's obliged her. Not yet,
anyway."

DeVito pulled into the parking lot at Television City. "Have you heard of anyone else who's important to Cade?"

Jenny Crenshaw looked at him and said, "His son."

DeVito parked the car and left Jenny to call for a ride back to the hotel.

As she watched him go, Jenny felt torn that she hadn't informed DeVito that Don Ward had told her he'd found the man who wanted Del dead. She still wasn't sure Don had really done it.

But a part of her was afraid that he had—that he'd found out it was J. D. Cade.

J. D. was driving east on San Vicente Boulevard when he called his cousin Ben. While traffic whizzed past him in L.A., Ben answered the call on his PCR in the stillness of the vast Shawnee National Forest. The news from Ben was not good. He'd failed to find Evan in town or at the Giant City visitors' complex and was now searching the woods for him with the help of his neighbor and his dogs. Ben told J. D. he would call just as soon as he had anything to tell him.

"Good or bad," J. D. instructed Ben. "Either way, let me know immediately."

"I understand," Ben replied.

J. D. left his car in the underground parking lot at the Century City Mall—watching carefully that Arnold Roth was nowhere nearby. He walked northeast on Little Santa Monica Boulevard. It was a half mile from the mall to the Peninsula Beverly Hills Hotel. J. D. had the sidewalk to himself the whole way. He was grateful there were stretches of L.A. where it was virtually impossible to follow someone on foot and not be noticed.

The Peninsula, however, was right around the corner from the Wilshire Boulevard retail corridor of Beverly

Hills, where people shopped on foot and even arrived at the hotel without the presence of a car.

J. D.'s appearance passed muster with the doorman and he received a smile as he entered the building. Finding a house phone, he asked the operator to connect him with Mr. Garvin Townes' suite. Townes' phone rang four times and then the hotel's voice mail center kicked in. J. D. hung up. Townes was either out, in the shower, or busy with his coven. Any such distraction would serve J. D.'s purpose.

He found his way to Townes' suite, feigning the assurance of a frequent and valued guest of the establishment. There was no one in sight as he approached his enemy's door, but when J. D. stopped opposite it, the reason seemed to be that he'd noticed his shoelace had come undone. He stooped to tie it and in doing so momentarily lost his balance and had to put his hand on the floor to steady himself.

With his hand thus extended he performed the simple legerdemain of sliding a small slip of paper under Townes' door. Then he tied his shoe, continued down the corridor, took the stairs back to the lobby, and made his way back to the mall.

The message J. D. had delivered to Townes's suite read: *Tonight in Hollywood . . . but only if you're there.*

DeVito found Donnel Timmons in his hotel room. He got the impression the man had been about to go out and was none too glad for the delay. Too bad about him.

"What can you tell me about your old army unit?" Agent DeVito asked.

Donnel regarded DeVito impassively. Accepting at least a momentary delay in his schedule, he settled himself comfortably in an easy chair. He gestured to DeVito to have a seat.

"What do you want to know?" Donnel asked evenly.

DeVito remained standing. "Tell me what your unit did."

"1st Logistical Command was the army's Wal-Mart. Pilferage and Inventory Control was store security. Simple as that."

DeVito looked at the prosperous middle-aged black man. He knew that Donnel Timmons had been a big supporter of Del Rawley from the start. Now he also knew that Timmons had been a part of the same army spook-shop operation in which Cade had served. Belatedly DeVito had the uneasy feeling he should have given this man a much closer look. He had to admit the racial thing had blinded him. What black person wouldn't want to see the first black president?

But as a professional, he chastised himself. He should have asked: What could be better camouflage in this situation than having a black skin?

"Mr. Timmons, what would you say if I told you that you were full of shit?"

"I'd say I musta forgot to eat my prunes." Donnel's smile mocked the special agent.

DeVito wasn't amused. He said, "You and Cade were part of a covert operation in Vietnam, Mr. Timmons. Your army service had as much to do with inventory control as my job has to do with writing parking tickets."

"Might be your *next* job. Real soon."

"Are you working with Cade, Mr. Timmons? Are you part of whatever he has planned?"

"Yeah, I am. See, what we both plan is to get Del Rawley elected president." Donnel looked around as if to make sure no one would overhear what he had to say next. "Then we're gonna make connections at the Pentagon and corner the market on army-navy surplus."

Donnel laughed at his joke, made sure DeVito saw he was laughing at him.

This time DeVito turned red.

"You're a very funny man, Mr. Timmons. You going to be the court jester in the Rawley administration?"

Donnel got to his feet and for a second DeVito thought he was going to take a swing at him. That'd be all he'd need, getting into a fight with a prominent *black* supporter of the candidate. He'd be gone so fast—

But Donnel walked calmly past the special agent and opened the door for DeVito, letting him know their discussion was over.

"If I do go to work at the White House," he told DeVito, "maybe I'll see to it you're the one who walks the family dog. Picks up after the messes he makes."

Garvin Townes returned to the Peninsula from a meeting with the president. He was outwardly happy but, in truth, he was a highly conflicted man. His position as national security adviser in the next administration, heretofore dangled as a carrot, had just been confirmed. What should have been his greatest moment of triumph was marred by his gnawing doubts about what that bastard Cade would do. Or refuse to do, even at the cost of his son's life.

In hindsight, Townes knew he should have had Cade killed years ago.

Townes pushed open the door to his suite and stopped dead when he saw the slip of paper on the floor. He observed it from the doorway. Not hotel stationery. Plain white bond of an ordinary quality. He could see fragments of type, but the message as a whole was concealed by the fold in the paper.

The old covert warrior looked into the suite. He could sense no one lurking nearby who would fall on him should he stoop to retrieve the message. With a frown, he quickly looked behind him, but there was no one about to attack him from that direction, either.

Stepping into his suite, closing the door behind him, and picking up the slip of paper, Townes read the message. But at first the words themselves were lost to a far more important bulletin: Cade had found him!

Townes' eyes darted around the suite once more, all but certain a sadistically smiling Cade would step out from concealment with a gun in his hand, bent on vengeance. Townes had a weapon of his own in his bedroom and he slinked toward it, ready to make a dash if need be. But when he had the reassurance of holding his Glock in his hand, he realized that Cade was not present. No, Cade had only slipped the note under the door.

The note! *Tonight in Hollywood . . . but only if you're there.*

A trap. What else could it be?

The answer came readily to Townes. It was a *challenge.*

Cade wanted to bring all the players into one forum, test them, and see who won. Townes had to smile. That was as it should be. How could he, as national security adviser, be expected to best adversaries from all around the world if he couldn't outwit his own former subordinate? Yes, this would be his crucible, and he would emerge victorious.

By early that evening the Toad had lost all sight in his right eye. In his left eye, where he'd splashed the water—an exercise in agony he'd been unable to repeat in his other eye—there was now only a small circle of focus through which he could see clearly; it was like looking through a corrective lens with the circumference of a soda straw.

In order to watch his captives, he had to move his head to point his partially sighted eye at what he wanted to see. But each time he moved his point of focus off one of the prisoners, the other two seemed to move. Not to lurch forward at him, but to rock gently back and forth. Each time he tried to catch them at it, the one he focused on was stationary again.

Blair asked Evan, "How come you admitted your father killed mine?"

Evan sighed. "Well, in a practical sense, it doesn't matter. Mr. Ribbit over there is just waiting to get the word to kill us."

"That right, Froggy?" Blair asked.

The Toad rotated his head. His appearance was truly ghastly. His right eye looked like melted wax. The left eye was less deformed but the pupil was reduced to the size of a pinhead. The Toad's only response to Blair's question was a cruel smile.

"The other reason is," Evan continued, "if he's going to kill us, why not make peace before we die? How long have our families been killing each other and where has it gotten us? Right here is where it's gotten you and me."

"What do you mean?"

"I mean, I didn't kill your cousin Ivar, but frog dick and his friends made it look that way. They put me in a lot of trouble with the law and raised the possibility of starting the feud all over again. But why? I haven't pissed off anyone that badly."

"But maybe your father has?"

"Apparently. So if I'm framed for Ivar's murder and Dad is revealed to have killed your father, what happens then?"

"Blood starts flowing in two states."

"Pretty strong hand to use for blackmail," Evan said.

"Not as strong as the one that sonofabitch over there is holdin' now," Deena said. "Why didn't they just grab you in the first place and leave the rest of us the hell out of it?"

Evan shook his head. "That wouldn't have left my dad enough room for hope. The way they were framing me, I bet they had someone or something ready to pop up and either hang me or clear me. I was in jeopardy, but my fate wasn't sealed. So my dad had reason to think that if he went along with whatever they wanted, maybe things would work out. But the situation must have gotten desperate. Dad is probably outsmarting them somehow. That's why they kidnapped me—and they obviously didn't give a shit how many other people got hurt or killed."

Deena ground her teeth in anger and told the Toad, "You aren't worth the sweat off my Ivar's ass, you amphibian cocksucker."

Evan said, "Don't feel too bad, Deena. Whatever they have in mind, it's not going to work. They've had me long enough by now to notify my father, so I'll tell you just what he's doing. He's hunting them. He knows they're never going to let me go. So it might take a little while, but Froggy over there, and all his friends, they're just as dead as we are."

Blair asked Evan, "What is it these shits want your father to do for them?"

"I don't know."

A deep, rumbling laugh emerged from the Toad.

"Would you like to know?" he asked. "I might as well tell you. I bet your old man does just what he's told; I bet he hopes he can save his sonny boy right up to the last second." For effect, the Toad leaned his gruesome face forward and said in a stage whisper, "Your father . . . is going to kill . . . Senator Franklin Delano Rawley."

Evan, Blair, and Deena all looked at each other in disbelief.

"You're crazy!" Evan asserted. "My dad *saved* Senator Rawley's life!"

"He also took that shot at him in Chicago that *just* missed," the Toad said with a gargoyle's grin. He threw his head back and laughed again. Then he leaned forward once more and said, "And you know what? This time, I bet he gets it right."

By 6:00 Belle Cade had decided that she'd had enough of Ben's wife, Marie, hovering around her. Marie meant well, but every few minutes she was at Belle's side, touching her elbow and asking if she could bring her a cup of tea, something to eat, anything at all. That, or she would just place her hand on Belle's shoulder and look at her with an expression that was meant to keep Belle's courage up. Marie was driving Belle to distraction at a time when she felt she had to do some serious thinking.

"Marie," Belle Cade said in a very firm voice, "I appreciate that you're trying to comfort me, but the best thing you could do right now is find something to read and be as quiet and still as humanly possible."

Marie looked as if she was going to utter words of protest or explanation, but she thought better of it. She simply nodded, took the family Bible off a bookshelf, and sat down to read. A moment later her lips moved in silent synchrony with the passage she was reading. The twenty-third Psalm, it seemed to Belle.

"Thank you, Marie," she said softly.

Left with no one to bother her, Belle said a brief prayer of her own for the deliverance of her grandson. She knew that without question her heart would break if Evan died. It would be the final blow in a life that had seen all the men she'd loved leave her.

Landon, her husband. She'd tried so hard to make him love her, make him love their son. But the sadness that ate away at him—over the wartime death in England of the girl he'd truly loved—was something that in the end nobody could overcome, and he took his own life.

It seemed barely a heartbeat later that J. D. had had to

flee after causing the death of Alvy McCray. Yes, she had visited J. D. many times in California, but for much of the last thirty years he had been absent from her life.

When Evan had arrived to attend the university and live in her house, that had been one of the most joyous days of her life. She had been able to see personal legacies from both her son and her husband in Evan, and for the past three years she had felt as if she was being repaid for all the time she'd missed with Landon and J. D. Repaid with interest, because Evan was his own wonderful, unique man.

She just couldn't lose him, too.

Leaving Marie in the living room, she went to the kitchen, closed the door behind her, and picked up the phone. She was going to do something she never would have imagined possible: ask for help from the spouse of a McCray.

"My name is Belle Cade," she told the man who answered her call. "I need to speak with Chief Edwards immediately. It's a matter of life and death."

SEVENTEEN

When J. D. returned to the Refuge, he noticed a manila envelope leaning against his front door. He drove into the garage, walked through the house, and retrieved it. The envelope was from Tom Hayashi at the Times. He opened it in his living room.

He found a press badge with his picture and name on it. An accompanying note explained that Hayashi's editor was happy to have J. D. write a story for the paper about what had gone on behind the scenes at the Rawley campaign on the day leading up to the debate at the Hollywood Bowl. Watching the debate from the press section at the Bowl would, of course, be a necessary part of J. D.'s report.

Hayashi had proven more than a little cagey himself. He'd given himself cover for getting J. D. into the Bowl. So he wouldn't lose his job after all. And if J. D. went berserk, why, poor Tom Hayashi had been duped. A blow to his ego and possibly his career, but not the kamikaze ending J. D. had scripted for him.

He took the press badge with him into his bedroom. He selected the clothes he would wear that night and put them out. He placed the pen gun and a small notepad into the outside pocket on the right side of the coat. The actual Mont Blanc pen he put into an inside pocket.

He looked at the digital clock on the nightstand next to the bed: 4:45. An hour and fifteen minutes until Vandy Ellison was due to arrive. He was bone tired, not having slept at all since finding the note that Evan had been kidnapped and talking with Townes, but he knew if he was to lie down for a nap, he wouldn't get up for hours.

He went into the bathroom to splash cold water on his face. He was drying himself off when he noticed something on the counter next to the sink: the remaining chloral hydrate capsule. What was it the flight attendant had told him when she'd given the capsules to him? Don't mix them with alcohol.

J. D. hadn't touched alcohol in over twenty years, not counting the sip of champagne he'd had with Jenny, but when he'd leased the Refuge he'd noticed that the liquor cabinet was fully stocked. He went to it now and half filled a tumbler with scotch.

He took the drink and the capsule out to the table next to the pool. He brought the PCR, too. Just in case his cousin Ben called to tell him the worst about Evan. If that happened, he wondered, could he really kill himself? Would that be a better choice than seeking vengeance?

For just a moment he felt a flash of sympathy for his father.

He looked out across the pool and the garden. Palm fronds rustled in a soft breeze. An idyllic place, a place to be at peace, but he couldn't lose himself in the beauty that was all around him, not even for a moment.

Evan was at the center of his mind, and all his other thoughts hurtled around his son in eccentric orbits. He wished he could look at Evan just one more time. But all the photo albums with pictures of the two of them together were at his Santa Barbara home. Still . . . he did have a shot of Evan in his wallet. He pulled the billfold out and flipped it open—remembering too late the details of the picture.

There was his son in a candid pose with his girlfriend, Pru Laney. Evan had sent it to him last year so J. D. could see and admire the girl he was dating. Now he wondered if Evan wouldn't soon be as lost to him as Pru Laney was to . . . no, her parents were already dead.

J. D. closed his wallet and dropped it on the table.

He did his best to remember the good times he'd had with Evan. But the memories became elusive and when he latched on to one it fought him, refusing to yield its life-sustaining joy. Soon his attempt at nostalgia became an exercise in masochism.

He put his wallet back in his pocket, picked up the drink, the capsule, and the PCR, and walked into the house. He sat down at the small desk in the bedroom, scribbled a terse note, and stuck it into the pocket of the coat he'd wear that night. He put it next to the genuine Mont Blanc pen.

He left the PCR in the bedroom and took the drink and the capsule into the bathroom. He put the tumbler of scotch on the counter and emptied the chloral hydrate into it. He tossed the empty capsule into the wastebasket and stirred the drink with his finger. No reason not to be prepared, if that was the way he decided to go.

He stripped and gave himself a fresh shave. Then he took a cold shower to clear the remaining cobwebs from his mind. When he stepped out of the shower stall Donnel was there pointing a gun at him.

He told J. D., "Believe you were away on R and R, that time your father died, when we got the briefing on surreptitious entries."

First assassin to get the job done wins. The thought came unbidden to J. D.'s mind.

"You mind if I put my robe on?" J. D. asked. "Or you want to shoot me the way I am?"

"You can put your robe on. We've got some things to talk about."

Out of the corner of his eye Donnel noticed the tumbler of scotch.

"I understood you weren't a drinking man anymore." Donnel picked up the glass, sniffed, and smiled in approval. "Scotch. Good stuff, too."

"I thought I'd make an exception just this once," J. D. said deadpan. He slipped into his robe as Donnel took a precautionary step backward.

"Looked around while you were cleaning off. Hope you don't mind. Had to see if we were all alone."

"We are."

Donnel nodded and smiled. "Saw your press credentials. You planning to show up at the Bowl when everyone's expecting you to be over at the studio?"

J. D. didn't say anything. He didn't have to.

"You sure are something, J. D.," Donnel said with real admiration.

"Appears you are, too." J. D. tied the belt of his robe.

"One thing I didn't notice was Colonel Townes' memoirs. Or did you make that up, hoping I'd have a heart attack?"

J. D. shook his head. "It's on digital disc. In a safe in the den."

"Why don't you show me?" Donnel took another step back to give J. D. room and waved with his gun hand for J. D. to take the lead.

On the way they came to the liquor cabinet. J. D. stopped and asked, "You mind if I get a drink, since you have mine?"

"You be real careful all you reach for is a bottle," Donnel

told him. "Do it like that, you can drink anything you want."

Keeping all his movements slow and obvious, J. D. picked out a bottle of soda water. He opened it and didn't bother with a glass.

"Don't want the scotch anymore?"

"The moment's passed," J. D. said.

"Don't know what you're missing," Donnel replied with a smile. He took a careful sip from the tumbler.

J. D. watched to see if Donnel noticed anything amiss with the taste of his drink.

But his smile widened. "Like I said, good stuff."

J. D. led the way into the den. He dialed the combination to the safe and then Donnel waved him to the other side of the room. Donnel opened the door.

"No gun . . . just a disc."

Pickpocket's laptop was on the desk, booted up but asleep. Donnel woke it up and loaded the disc. He sat down behind the desk and pointed to a chair with his gun.

"Take a load off and tell me the password to get into the disc," he told J. D.

J. D. did as he was told and took a swig from his bottle of water.

Donnel, responding instinctively, took a second sip of scotch.

Then he put the glass down and deftly fingered the keyboard with his left hand.

The file came up and once again Donnel murmured a heartfelt, "*Sonofabitch.*"

J. D. said, "There's an index. You can look up specific page references for your name." Then he took another pull at his bottle of water.

Donnel checked to make sure that his name had in fact been included in Townes' tome. When he saw that it had, he picked up the glass and took a hefty jolt of the doctored scotch.

"Don't know why one of us didn't kill the fucking colonel a *long* time ago."

Donnel's left eyelid drooped abruptly, half covering his eye. He rubbed it vigorously.

"I've been thinking about doing just that," J. D. replied. He took another drink of water.

"Probably never find the cocksucker even if you did decide to kill him."

J. D. told Donnel where Townes was staying. Donnel found it interesting that J. D. knew. He took another sip of the scotch.

"Townes is the one put your boy in trouble . . . ain't he?" Donnel wasn't slurring his words, but they were coming harder.

J. D. finished off his water. He didn't answer Donnel's question.

"That's why you gotta . . . kill Del Rawley. Motherfucker Townes pullin' your . . . strings. Let's see what all he's got on you." Donnel finished the scotch, then went to type out J. D.'s name on the keyboard. But his fingers weren't nearly as adroit as they had been. He had to look at the keyboard now.

The moment the other man took his eyes off him, J. D. hurled the empty water bottle at Donnel. It caught him hard on the forehead. By itself, the blow wouldn't have been enough to knock him out or even keep him from getting a shot off. But added to the stupor in which he already labored, it stunned Donnel.

J. D. wrested the gun from Donnel's hand without a shot being fired, and after a minute of clumsily trying to grapple with J. D., Donnel collapsed in his arms.

Vandy arrived at 5:30, half an hour early. Just about when J. D. had expected her. He was fresh from a second shower. He'd needed it after lugging Donnel off to the bedroom normally used by a housekeeper.

Vandy appeared wearing a T-shirt, running shorts, and sneakers; she had a garment bag slung over her shoulder.

Looking at J. D. in his robe, she scrunched up her face. "Oh, I'm *too* early. I'm sorry. I thought I'd get here just a *little* early, we could make our plans, and then I could change so my clothes wouldn't look all rumpled and lived-in." She brushed J. D.'s still-damp hair with her free hand. "I thought you might even let me take a shower."

"Come on in, Vandy," J. D. said graciously. "What's mine is yours."

There was never any question where they were headed, and a minute later they were in J. D.'s bed. But J. D. had a fleeting moment of uncertainty whether he'd be able to perform. By using Vandy, he was making a whore of himself, and that was something he'd never done before.

Then a cynical voice in his head reassured him. What's a little whoring, it asked, compared to all the other things you've done?

Almost an hour later, a well-satisfied Vandy propped her head on one hand and said, "I think we'd better get going. We can shower together and discuss our plans for the evening. What do you say?"

J. D. pulled her down on top of him and kissed her. "Something's come up."

"What!" she shrieked, pushing away from him.

"Don't worry. I'm not abandoning you."

She collapsed atop him with relief.

Then he told her he'd been asked by the *Los Angeles Times* to do a story on the campaign. It would be terrific publicity for Del, J. D. said, but he'd have to miss the first part of the evening at the studio. That shouldn't be a problem because everyone there would be watching the debate on television. He promised he'd be there to talk to everyone by the time the debate was over.

"You'll cover for me, won't you, Vandy?" J. D. asked.

She drew her head back and said, "You just better be there, buster."

"There?" J. D. asked, reaching out with his hand. "Or there?"

"There," Vandy directed. Then she gasped. A true professional to the end, she added in a tremulous voice, "And at the studio, too."

Once they were showered and dressed, J. D. helped Vandy into the Lexus as it sat in the garage. Then he asked her to excuse him for just a second; he'd forgotten something and would be *right* back.

He was. Right after he'd left the front door of the Refuge standing open.

The first time DeVito called the Carbondale PD and asked for the chief of police, he was told to try back tomorrow and was disconnected. The special agent could only look at the phone receiver in disbelief for a moment. He had to leave with Orpheus for the Hollywood Bowl in ten minutes and this was what he got from some Podunk cop shop? He slammed the keyhook for another dial tone and savagely stabbed the redial button.

"Police department," answered the same voice that had cut him off.

"Listen to me," DeVito ordered in a menacing voice. "My name is Special Agent Dante DeVito. I'm with the United States Secret Service. I want to talk to the chief of police and I want to talk to him now. If you don't see that I do, I'll find out who you are and I'll make the rest of your life a *living hell*. Do you understand me?"

DeVito heard a sharply indrawn breath and then nothing. He thought he'd been cut off again. He could not fucking be —

"I don't care who you are, you sonofabitch," came an outraged voice in DeVito's ear, letting him know he'd only been put on hold, "you threaten any of my people like that again, I'll kick your ass till you shit through your teeth."

DeVito replied, "Sounds like we're both up against it, Chief, but I had to talk with you."

"Make it fast, goddamnit. I have no time whatsoever."

DeVito heard the urgency in the man's voice and wondered what could possibly have a little town like Carbondale in such an uproar. Then DeVito felt an iron fist grab his guts and twist for all it was worth. Whatever the chief's problems were, he'd bet —

"Hey!" the chief yelled. "You gotta talk to me but all of a sudden you fall asleep?"

"I'm calling about Evan Cade," DeVito said softly. The silence from Illinois was so profound he knew his instinct had been right. "Something happened to him, didn't it?"

A moment later the chief responded, "His grandmother just called to tell me he's been kidnapped."

"*Kidnapped?*"

"Yeah. How the hell did you know something was wrong?"

"I . . . It was just . . . Someone out here got the feeling the boy's father had been hurt recently."

"Well, if he hasn't, he will be. I don't think this one's gonna have a happy ending."

Then the chief was gone, leaving the federal agent with the phone in his hand once more. DeVito put it down. Was it just a coincidence J. D. Cade's kid got grabbed the same day Del Rawley was scheduled to speak outside again? DeVito asked himself. Not a chance in hell.

The way DeVito saw it now was that Cade had taken the

shot in Chicago because his old army commander, Garvin Townes, had had both him and his kid blackmailed. Then Cade had somehow worked his way out of that jam, and that was when he saved Del Rawley's life. But Townes struck back, kidnapping Cade's kid and undoubtedly telling him the kid would die if Cade didn't kill Orpheus.

So now Cade had been forced back into being an assassin. For the first time DeVito almost felt sympathy for the man.

He looked at his watch. Time to go. He had to stop Cade, but that wasn't all. He also had Roth to worry about. Cade had as much as told him Roth was the backup killer, and Roth would be at the Bowl. Cade would be at—

DeVito grabbed the phone again and called the number he'd been given for the Westside Studio, where Cade was *supposed* to be. He identified himself to the person who picked up the phone and was quickly passed along to Vandy Ellison.

"Is Cade there?" he demanded.

Vandy knew DeVito's voice; it was one she'd come to loathe.

"Yes, he's here."

"Let me talk to him."

"Can't."

"*Put him on.*"

"Sorry. He's just going—"

"*Going where?*"

"To the men's room. I have to tinkle, too. Bye."

Yet again DeVito was left with a dead phone in his hand. But now he had to run. He'd be at the Bowl with Orpheus watching Roth. Cade would be at the movie studio waiting for Orpheus, who would never come.

DeVito wasn't going to let J. D. Cade get within shooting distance of Orpheus ever again.

Jenny was crossing the lobby of the Century Plaza when she saw DeVito almost yank Del away from his family. Luckily, nobody took a picture of this incredibly rude and unprofessional act. She decided then and there that after tonight DeVito was gone. She didn't think she'd have to put the matter on a him-or-me basis to Del, but if that was what it took—

"Pardon me, Ms. Crenshaw?"

Jenny turned to see the hotel manager, who had a look of deep concern on his face. What now? she thought. Had the damn check for the hotel bill bounced?

"Yes?" Jenny asked politely.

"We were informed that Mr. Cade would no longer be needing his room."

"Yes, that's correct."

"So housekeeping was sent to the room to prepare it for our next guest . . . and the maid found this." He handed Jenny a slip of paper. "As you can see, it's not *overtly* threatening, so I didn't know if I should give it to the Secret Service or you."

On the slip of paper were four words: *I have your son.* J. D.'s son!

Jenny wouldn't have believed that anything could have shocked her more at that moment, but then the hotel manager took a package from a bellman standing next to him.

"This just came for you. I thought you might like to see it before you left for the evening."

The package was a long, narrow cardboard box, the type used by florists to deliver their blooms. Indeed, that was just what it was. Jenny opened it to find a bouquet of . . . *lilies*.

The accompanying card read: *Fresh from my garden.*

After dropping Vandy off at the studio, J. D. made one stop on his way to the Hollywood Bowl. He made a call to 911 from a public phone.

"Listen," he told the emergency operator, holding a handkerchief over the phone, "I'm making a delivery at this house in Santa Monica Canyon. I get there, the door's open. I poke my head in, shout hello . . . To cut to the chase, I find this black guy passed out on a bed, barely breathin'. Who knows if he's gonna make it? You better send somebody fast."

J. D. gave the address of the Refuge. He declined to give his name.

It had already been some time since Donnel had passed out, and he hadn't checked to see if Donnel was still alive before he and Vandy left, but he felt he owed his old comrade some chance.

The Toad finally caught Evan Cade rocking back and forth.

He pointed his gun at him and ordered, "Stop that."

"Stop what?" Evan asked, sitting still.

"You were rocking. Trying to loosen your bonds."

"I wasn't."

The Toad cocked his weapon.

"Fuck you and your handgun, too, Froggy," Evan said wearily.

The interior of the trailer was now lighted by a single sixty-watt bulb. It was the only source of illumination the Toad had been able to find easily. He was leery about moving around, and with his prisoners bound hand and foot he couldn't order them to turn on a light. In the dim glow, with his ruined vision, it was possible that he had imagined Evan Cade moving, but he didn't think so.

Evan sneered at him. "You won't shoot me, Kermit, or you would have already. I'm the guy who crushed your nuts in my hand. I'm the guy who blinded you. But I'm still here."

A murderous look crossed the Toad's ravaged face but he didn't pull the trigger.

"See what I mean?" Evan continued. "Whoever you work for has you very well trained. You *won't* kill us until you get the word. By the way, when's the last time you replaced the battery in your PCR?"

The Toad swung his pistol toward Deena.

"No!" Evan screamed. He threw himself sideways, falling across Deena's lap. He frantically pushed with his bound, numb legs until he was sitting atop Deena's leg on one side and Blair's leg on the other. Evan leaned in whichever direction the Toad pointed his weapon.

In the end, the Toad lowered the gun and shrugged.

"You were only partly right," he told Evan. "I *probably* won't kill you without receiving orders first. But the way this situation works, I wait to receive word only until midnight. That's the deadline. And *dead* is the operative part of that word."

The Toad laughed with such menace that all three of his captives shared the same chill.

Using Evan Cade's body as a shield, Blair McCray started stressing his restraints again—and this time he exerted a lot more effort.

Jenny was supposed to ride in a limo with the rest of the brain trust to the Bowl, but she left them wondering if she'd lost her senses when she told them to go on without her; she'd catch up as soon as she could.

Baxter Brown had wanted to know what was so important she wouldn't be coming with them. For just a moment Jenny was tempted to tell him. She thought she might need some help, but then she remembered that Baxter, for all his size and bluster, came from an upper-middle-class family that had sent him to prep school and Princeton, where he'd been a member of the glee club, not the football team. Jenny finally told him that there was simply one more task she *had* to handle before she went to the Bowl, but they were to assure Del that she would be there.

After the others had gone, she used a phone in the hotel lobby to call the florist that had delivered the flowers—lilies, the symbol of death—and see if she could persuade the merchant to give her the address of the customer who'd sent them. If her powers of persuasion failed, then she'd have to involve the LAPD to get the address. She already knew the customer's identity.

To her surprise, instructions had been left to provide her with the address if she called. She was given the number of a house on Mulholland Drive. The location sent a chill racing up Jenny's spine.

"Do you know if that's near the Hollywood Bowl?" Jenny asked.

"Yes, ma'am. It's quite near the Bowl. You should be able to hear whatever is going on down below."

Hear the gunfire and screams, Jenny thought. That would make the Gardener happy.

Jenny drove northeast through the city, speeding, running lights that had just turned red, and otherwise blending in perfectly with the more aggressive drivers on the road. She knew she was going to need help when she got to the house on Mulholland; she was pleased that the hills would be filled with special agents from the Secret Service as well as cops from the LAPD. She'd recruit whatever help came to hand. Then she'd force the goddamn Gardener to reveal just how he planned to kill Del—hoping she wouldn't be too late.

She had to fight back tears of anger as her car raced into the mouth of Laurel Canyon, snaking along that winding road as it climbed to the top of the Hollywood Hills.

"Oh, Don, goddamn you," she complained bitterly. "You found out who wanted to kill Del, all right. You knew all along."

Roth was at the Hollywood Bowl. He stood in the wings, stage left. People were starting to enter the amphitheater. Each and every one of them, humble or exalted, had to pass through a metal detector, put their coins and keys in a little plastic container, and hand it to security, just like at the airport. Only the Secret Service was paying much closer attention than the minimum-wage types who merely had to make sure an airplane didn't get hijacked or bombed.

The only exceptions to the security screening were the people in the immediate entourages of the two candidates. Nobody was going to frisk the First Lady or Mrs. Rawley. The seats for those VIPs were right up front in the area referred to as the Pool Circle. But Roth knew that Cade wasn't supposed to be traveling with Rawley's inner circle anymore, and even if he somehow had pulled a switch on that account and got a prestige seat, what was he going to do? Stand up and make like some latter-day John Wilkes Booth? He'd be smoked before he got his knees unbent.

The seating area began to fill in as Roth watched. He'd considered looking for Cade as he first entered the amphitheater, but the point of this exercise wasn't to stop the prick from getting in, it was to kill him after he got Rawley. Even if Roth saw which gate Cade entered through, he still wouldn't know which seat he took unless he followed him closely enough to see him sit down. And he knew Cade would spot him if he tried that.

Roth ground his teeth. Fucking Townes had given him an impossible assignment. He kept scanning the crowd, hoping against hope he could pick Cade out of the growing sea of faces. It would have been much easier for him to go to Cade's house in the canyon after the debate and grease him there, the way he'd planned before Townes had changed his mind again.

A hand tapped Roth gently on the shoulder.

Landers, his second in command, said "Orpheus is here. He's in dressing room B backstage."

Roth nodded. He'd gone ahead to scope out the Bowl; Landers had worked the motorcade.

"No hitches?" Roth asked.

"No. Only DeVito asked where you were."

That cocksucker. Roth had forgotten about him. "You told him?"

"Sure. What was I going to say? You stepped out for coffee?"

Roth was not in the mood for gibes at his expense and it showed.

"I'll get back to Orpheus now," Landers said.

"Wait," Roth ordered. "You got a list of where all the VIPs will be sitting?"

"Yeah." Landers handed it over. "Got this if you want it, too." He passed another sheaf of papers to Roth. "It's a list of all the accredited media people who will be here."

Roth was about to thrust it back. What the hell did he care about reporters? Cade would never be sitting with . . . There was his goddamn name! At the bottom of the first page. Cade, J. D.—with the *Los Angeles Times*. How the sonofabitch had managed that he'd never know, but fuck him if he cared.

"Where's the press sitting?" Roth asked.

"That section right there." Directly in front of the wing of the stage where he stood.

"Are Orpheus and Primus—the president—going to be taking questions? Will those press jack-offs be jumping up and down, screaming and trying to get their attention?"

"Yeah. Both sides gave in on that an hour ago. Can I go now?"

"Yeah," Roth said absently, "go ahead."

He shook his head in grudging admiration. You had to hand it to that sonofabitch Cade. He'd found a way to include himself in the one group that was allowed to act like assholes in front of the Secret Service. If Cade could find some way to sneak a weapon in, and Roth had no doubt he would, then he should be able to get off a shot at Rawley. And if Rawley didn't duck like last time, he'd bet Cade nailed him, too.

As for himself, now that he knew where Cade would be, even if he opened up with his Uzi on full auto, he wouldn't hit any innocent people. He'd just take out a raft of political reporters.

Be a goddamn public service.

Garvin Townes arrived with the presidential motorcade, fourth car in the pecking order for now. Still, Townes was included in the group that joined the president in dressing room A. He discreetly exited as those present were posed for an official campaign picture. Townes noticed as he eased the door shut behind him that even in the midst of family, friends, and hangers-on, the president couldn't quite disguise the fear in his eyes at the prospect of confronting Del Rawley before the whole world.

Take courage, Townes silently urged him. It could well be over before it begins.

Never one to forget his own advantage, Townes had come to the debate armed. And why shouldn't he? Wasn't he the head of a special unit of the Treasury Department? He was making his way to his seat when he recognized the face of Devree Rawley. The challenger's wife held pride of place among a multigenerational group of black people sitting front and center. The Rawley family had come out of hiding. He noticed one empty seat next to a young woman holding a small child on her lap. On impulse, he decided to take it. The special agents on guard around the Rawleys nodded respectfully at Townes as he displayed his identification.

Still looking at her child, the young woman sensed a presence arriving on her left.

"It's about time you got here, Mr. Donnel Tim—" She turned to see Townes. "Oh, I thought you were . . . I'm sorry, but this seat is reserved for a member of my father's campaign."

"I know," Townes said, showing Eleanor Rawley Walker his ID, "but it shouldn't have been. You see, I'm something of a superior to these gentlemen behind you, and what with all of the unfortunate events surrounding your father's campaign, I asked to be seated with the Rawley family on this occasion."

Now Devree and the others were looking at Townes.

"When your friend shows up he can use the seat I was mistakenly assigned. It's right over there." Townes nodded. "Quite a nice seat. I hope you don't mind, but I'll feel so much better if you'll allow me to sit with you."

Devree Rawley nodded. Then she and the other members of the family went back to their conversations. But Eleanor confided to the silver-haired official, "My father didn't even want us to be here. His children, I mean. Then he didn't want his grandchildren to be here. He even threatened to pull out of the race if we all showed up."

"Really?" The irony made it almost impossible for Townes to keep a straight face.

"Yes, but we spent all day persuading him that we had to stick together as a family."

"And evidently you did."

"Only at the very last minute," Eleanor said, turning back to her toddler, who was beginning to fuss. "And even then it was because my father said the danger was elsewhere."

This time Townes couldn't keep a wicked grin off his face, but the young mother beside him and the special agents behind him didn't see it.

J. D. arrived at the press entrance. Tom Hayashi was there waiting for him somewhat anxiously. "I thought you weren't going to make it," the reporter told J. D.

"Had to make an unexpected stop," J. D. said.

The two men approached the security station. Hayashi went first, dumping a recorder, PCR, pens, notebook, billfold, keys, and change into the pass-through container for inspection. He walked through the metal detector without a problem. A Secret Service agent on the other side checked him off.

J. D. took out his wallet, keys, notepad, PCR, and a Mont Blanc pen and put them in the container for inspection. He was about to step through the metal detector when he stopped short. "Oh, wait a minute. I forgot I have a spare pen."

The special agent inspecting his PCR looked up.

J. D. dug it out of his coat pocket but fumbled it to the ground. Then, making matters worse, he accidentally kicked it under the table next to the metal detector. Apologizing for his clumsiness, he stepped through the metal detector without setting it off.

The agent on the other side of the barrier had picked up the dropped pen. He looked at it closely. "Darn nice pen. Too bad it got scratched." He took off the cap and gently drew a small circle on the back of his hand. "Still works, though."

He looked at J. D. and his press badge. They'd never met

but the man said, "You're the guy who saved Senator Rawley's life, aren't you?"

"Yeah."

"I saw the video. That was nice work." Then the agent inclined his head at Hayashi and grinned. "So what're you doing going over to the enemy?"

"It's only for one night," J. D. assured him. He retrieved his pen and the belongings from the container the special agent extended to him; only the PCR had been given more than a glance. J. D. tucked the PCR, the notepad, and the uninspected pen gun back into his coat; the wallet and keys went into his pants pockets.

"Hope I run into you again sometime," the special agent said. "Like to buy you a beer."

Hayashi cleared his throat.

"That'd be great," J. D. replied. "But right now I've got to get going."

As the two men entered the Bowl, the reporter whispered, "All right, payoff time. Who took the shot at Senator Rawley in Chicago?"

J. D. told him, "His name was Beauregard 'Dixie' Wynne. He was an old army friend and . . ."

Del looked around at the members of his campaign staff and the protection detail crowding his dressing room. "Where's Jenny?" he asked Baxter.

"She said she had some last-minute job she just *had* to do," the political adviser answered, rolling his eyes. "She said to tell you she won't miss the show."

Del frowned. Under normal circumstances he might possibly be understanding about such a development, but with everything that had gone on . . . Still, he knew that this was no time to cause a commotion.

He shooed everybody—even his Secret Service agents—

out of dressing room B. He said he needed to be alone with his thoughts for a minute. When he was by himself, the candidate closed his eyes and bowed his head.

"Give me strength," he whispered solemnly. "And please keep my family safe." About to raise his head, Del had one more thought of supplication: "If J. D. Cade's son is in trouble, Lord, please see him through it."

The news he'd received from Agent DeVito about the kidnapping had shaken Del Rawley to his core. Learning that Cade's son had been taken persuaded him that the man who had saved his life in San Francisco might well have been coerced into trying to take it in Chicago . . . and would be forced to try again.

Del asked himself if he would do such a thing if he was in J. D. Cade's position, if the life of one of his children or grandchildren was held hostage to his actions. What if Devree's life was on the line? He hated to admit it, but he couldn't imagine *anything* he wouldn't do to save one of their lives. Even sacrificing his own.

He was sure J. D. Cade would do no less.

Del Rawley most certainly did not want to die, tonight or anytime soon. But because he could imagine the excruciating pressure J. D. must be under, he found it impossible to hate him, to bear him any ill will.

Now, the sonsofbitches working behind the scenes to force J. D.'s hand—they were another matter. He was good and mad at them. He'd forget every lesson he ever learned about justice and fair trials if he could find them. Put the motherfuckers right up against a wall and shoot them.

The question foremost in his mind was whether his opponent, the president, was in on this whole evil design. The politician in him said no. The president would want the strongest measure of deniability possible should a horror show like this ever be exposed, and that would mean that he actually didn't know.

But in the end he was the one responsible. He was the one who had put into place the people who conceived and executed this monstrous scheme. He was the one who had articulated and spread the win-at-all-costs mentality that had turned hardball politics into covert warfare.

Del Rawley was not feeling too kindly disposed toward his opponent right now. He meant to take the man apart— verbally. But because of the atmosphere of terror that had been fostered—and Jenny Crenshaw's sudden and disturbing absence—he meant to take one other precaution with him onto the stage.

He went to his personal attaché case. He dialed the combination that only he knew, and opened it. There it was: the handgun that Agent DeVito had given him. Since Devree's arrival, he'd been forced not to carry it so that she wouldn't find out just how dangerous things had gotten.

But now . . . now it went right back into his pocket.

And if by some strange twist of fate he found the president besting him in the debate, maybe he'd just take it out and shoot the sonofabitch.

No sooner had that thought crossed his mind than there was a knock at his door.

Alita Colon peeked in and said, "Del, it's time."

Jenny reached the address on Mulholland Drive that the florist had provided her. It was the same home directly behind the Bowl that she, J. D., and DeVito had been unable to gain access to last night. Then the entrance to the grounds had been closed; then no one had responded when they'd rung the bell. Now the gates were open.

She pulled just onto the driveway and stopped. She realized what she should have done was call for help en route. With that option no longer available, she took out her PCR, called 911, identified herself, told the operator that the man who was behind the assassination attempt on Senator Rawley could be found at the Mulholland address, and for God's sake hurry. The debate at the Bowl was about to begin.

The operator told Jenny to keep her connection open and stay right where she was.

Jenny responded that she would leave her car parked at the entrance of the property . . . but she was going into the house.

DeVito was as taut as a piano wire. Special Agent Landers, Roth's number two but not some bullshit DEIMOS prick, had told him where Roth was. DeVito stood in the wings, stage right, across the stage from Roth. Stage right was nearer to where Orpheus would be when he and Primus went onstage. Roth, both symbolically and literally, was on the president's side. But DeVito could see that the special agents on Primus' protection detail stood apart a step or two from Roth and their sidelong glances at him said, What the fuck's this guy doing here?

DeVito noticed that Roth was looking out at the audience. The sky was dark now but the seating area was still illuminated as the late arrivals were taking their seats. DeVito tried to determine whom Roth was trying to find.

It seemed to him as if he was observing . . . the Rawley family? Then DeVito noticed a guy seated in the aisle seat of the Rawleys' box who looked like a GQ version of Lavrenti Beria. With a jolt, DeVito realized he recognized the man; he'd seen a picture yesterday when he'd been doing research for Orpheus at the Federal Building in San Diego. That sonofabitch was Garvin Townes. Why the hell would he be sitting with the Rawleys?

DeVito's alarm grew when he saw Roth and Townes exchange a nod. What did *that* mean? Roth was going to take his shot at the senator? No, Roth was inclining his head toward the seats in front of the left side of the stage. Townes turned his gaze to look that way. DeVito's eyes followed and ... The house lights went down as the white-haired journalist who would serve as the moderator for the evening stepped onstage to polite applause.

The man's words sounded throughout the Bowl but De-Vito didn't hear any of them. What had Roth been nodding at? DeVito asked himself, straining to see through the darkness. What had Townes turned to see?

DeVito was vaguely aware of movement behind him and then he was snapped out of his reverie by thunderous applause. He looked out at the stage to see the moderator shaking Orpheus' hand; the candidate waving to the crowd.

Which was when it hit DeVito: Cade was out there!

That had to be what Roth was telling Townes. Cade was in the audience ... somewhere in that section on the left. That little bitch Vandy Ellison had lied to him about Cade being at the movie studio. He was going to kill her. But first he had to—

Another rousing ovation made DeVito focus on the moment. Now Primus had taken the stage and he and Orpheus were shaking hands. How the hell could DeVito pull Orpheus off the stage now without making him look like an absolute fool? He couldn't.

What he had to do was find Cade ... and kill him if the sonofabitch made one wrong move.

But he couldn't forget about Roth, either. Roth was the backup man. DeVito turned and saw Landers, Roth's honest lieutenant, right there where he should be. He grabbed Landers' arm and pulled him aside, urgently whispering in his ear.

"Jesus!" Landers said, going pale. "You're sure?"

"Absolutely. If you see Roth go for his weapon, *shoot* him."

"But . . ."

"Listen," DeVito commanded, "there's no time to argue. Just watch him. You'll know what he's doing won't be right. Trust your own eyes if you don't trust me. Just don't let that sonofabitch get off a shot."

Then DeVito took a flashlight off the stunned special agent and as the debate began, he descended from the stage and into the crowd to hunt J. D. Cade.

As Jenny approached the house, a stark chain of white cubes joined in an almost whimsical fashion, she saw that the front door stood open. That was when her thoughts clicked together in a far more logical pattern than the architecture she beheld. First the lilies at the hotel, then the gates at the entrance to the property being swung wide, now the door to the house standing open? Someone had all but spread a trail of bread crumbs to lead her right where he wanted her to go.

The realization of who that someone was made her stomach turn over. It also made her painfully aware that you really did have to be careful about what you wished for, even when all you wanted was to see an old friend one last time.

Jenny stepped across the threshold of the house.

"Don?" she called out. "Where are you, Don?"

"We're back here, my dear," came the sepulchral voice. "The room off to your left."

She followed directions and entered a softly lit, harshly modern room. Abstract paintings hung on shadowed walls, their images morphing into Rorschach monsters. The rear wall was made of sliding glass panels that had been opened to the night. The view of the city was panoramic. Waves of sound coming from the Bowl just down the hill seemed shockingly loud.

Especially when a huge cheer erupted, followed by a somewhat lesser ovation.

Hunter Ward, hairless from chemotherapy, scarred from where his skull had been opened, and pale as winter moonlight, was seated near the entrance to the room. He had both of his hands wrapped around a gun, but the barrel of the weapon danced through the air in small jerks and twists as if controlled by a nervous puppeteer.

He told Jenny, "Your man just got the bigger ovation; the greeting for Tom's candidate was a mite less enthusiastic."

Jenny looked at the man seated opposite Don, the man at whom the gun was pointed. He was Hunter Ward's former partner, one of Jenny's two former bosses.

"Aren't you going to say hello, Jenny?" asked Thomas "Killer" Laughlin.

A. k. a. the Gardener.

"This is true?" Hayashi demanded of J. D. in a quiet but urgent voice. "All of it?"

"Just make sure you get the chance to ask the questions. See what the president says."

"Hey, shut up, why don't you?" said another newsie. "Some of us are trying to pay attention to what they're saying on the stage, you know."

Hayashi gave the finger to his colleague from the fourth estate, but he pulled J. D. closer and lowered his voice. "I ask these questions, it's just as likely as not I get stonewalled. Or, worse, I'm accused of trying to smear the president for Rawley's benefit. Either way, everybody's going to want to know my source for the information."

"You don't give away sources, do you?"

"Hell, no. Never."

"And how effectively can the president stonewall if he wets his pants in front of the whole world?"

Despite his anxiety, the reporter grinned. "You think he might?"

"I guarantee, you ask those questions, you'll get some big reaction."

"And if I don't? Ask the questions, I mean."

"Then you've got one less stone than the president."

Hayashi jerked back as if he'd been slapped. His face was a mask as he turned from J. D. without saying another word, but now J. D. was as sure as he could be that the reporter would ask the questions. That or Hayashi would have to find a new line of work, one where he wouldn't have to worry about self-doubt.

J. D. glanced at the stage. Del Rawley had just said something that drew laughter from a majority of the crowd, but J. D. hadn't heard a word of it and was in anything but a humorous mood. He could wait no longer. He had to go find a quiet spot where he could call his cousin Ben and find out if there was any news about Evan.

He was just about to step into the aisle when someone shone a flashlight in his face.

EIGHTEEN

The Toad sensed that something was going on with his three prisoners. He tried to see what it was, but his field of clear vision was far too narrow to take in all three of them sitting there in a jumble. Evan Cade was effectively shielding the other two from him. He didn't know what any of them could possibly do with their hands tied behind them, but he nevertheless felt increasingly uneasy that they were up to something.

The problem was, he didn't know what he could do about it. If he ordered Evan Cade to go back to his place, he was likely to get nothing more than an insolent refusal. Cade would protest that the Toad would shoot his friends. Which was precisely what he would do. Those two were of no further use to him. Come to that, maybe Evan Cade was of no further use to him, either. Given his circumstances, it was time for him to exercise a little independent judgment.

The Toad raised his gun and lined it up as best he could on the center of Evan Cade's chest . . . just as a loud grunt sounded outside the trailer. The Toad turned his head to listen. The grunt was followed by a snort and then a low growl.

Gorbachev was outside and unhappy that his daily dessert was late in being served.

"What was that?" the Toad demanded, trying to comprehend what he'd just heard.

By way of response, Deena yelled, "Gorby, the Cossacks are coming!"

The Toad was in the process of swinging his gun back toward Deena when there came a growl so thunderous that the Toad thought some predator was about to fall on him. That didn't happen, but a blow was delivered to the Airstream that rocked the trailer on its foundation. Another deafening roar followed, as did a second rattling blow, and then the face of the bear, all bristling black fur, glittering amber eyes, and massive fangs, appeared at the trailer's window. Gorbachev looked directly at the Toad, roared yet again, and slammed the trailer once more.

The Toad fired a round, but the shot only grazed Gorbachev.

Deena shouted, "Moscow is saved!" Gorbachev promptly dropped out of sight.

That didn't keep the Toad from firing five more rounds directly through the trailer's aluminum skin, but there were no howls of pain to indicate the animal had been hit.

While the Toad was firing at Gorbachev, Blair McCray finally managed to pull free of the ropes that had bound his hands. His wrists bled from being rubbed against the rope and his hands were swollen, but he brought them forward and, flexing his fingers as best he could, grabbed Evan around the waist.

"Get ready," he told Evan, speaking directly into his ear. "Jump when you feel me lift."

The Toad went to the window to look for the animal. He saw lights moving among the trees. He heard dogs baying. It was definitely time to go. He turned to his captives, bringing his gun around.

"Now!" Blair shouted.

Evan pushed off the floor as hard as he could while Blair came up beneath him and flung Evan with all his might straight at the Toad.

The gap between Evan and his captor was only a matter of feet; he knew that as he was hurtling through the air. But it seemed as if he was floating. He took in every minute detail of the experience. He could feel his throat vibrate as he stretched his mouth wide to scream his rage. He could see Froggy's brow furrow as he desperately tried to make his one barely functional, grotesquely reddened eye focus on the body flying at him. He saw the muscles in the bastard's arm tighten as he struggled to bring the gun to bear.

Then the jarring collision as muscle slammed against muscle, the crack of bone banging against bone, the momentum of flight slowed but not stopped as the two of them toppled together toward the floor. The second stunning impact as they hit, bounced up, and settled back.

Finally the bang, the heat, and the searing pain of the gun going off.

The flashlight went out, and when the afterimage faded, J. D. saw DeVito staring at him. The special agent had his right hand inside his suit coat and J. D. had no doubt his finger was on the trigger of his Uzi. He was almost surprised DeVito hadn't shot him already, but then he understood the agent didn't want to take the chance of hitting anyone else. He'd shoot if he had to, but given a choice, he'd rather take J. D. alive.

DeVito motioned J. D. to take his seat and he did. The special agent settled into a squat across the aisle from him. The woman in the seat next to DeVito gave him a glance until he looked back at her. Then she stared fixedly at the stage.

J. D. likewise turned his attention to the debate. He tried to focus on what the candidates were saying. They spoke of matters of importance to the country and the world, but their words had no meaning for him. All he could think about was his son, being held somewhere unknown and far away. How soon would it be before Evan died? he asked himself. A tear fell from his eye.

DeVito was the only one who noticed.

Then the house lights came up and the moderator opened the floor to questions from the media. All around J. D., reporters leaped screaming to their feet. But with a bellow of "Mr. President!" Tom Hayashi outshouted the others and was recognized.

"The gentleman from the Los Angeles Times," the moderator said with a polite smile.

The president nodded at the reporter; he was ready to take his question.

"A two-part question, sir. Can you tell us, please, what position in your next administration you plan to offer to Mr. Garvin Townes . . ."

There was only a handful of people in the amphitheater who even recognized the name: Townes himself, J. D., DeVito, Roth, Del Rawley, and the president. They all tensed as soon as the name was spoken, and everyone saw that the president had stiffened perceptibly.

" . . . and are you aware, sir," Hayashi continued, "of the connection between Mr. Townes and a Beauregard 'Dixie' Wynne? Specifically, did you know that Mr. Wynne was the man who tried to assassinate Senator Rawley in Chicago?"

The Bowl went deathly silent as everyone watched the president tremble with rage—everyone except Eleanor Rawley Walker, who was busy trying to remember something.

The president shouted, "That's a damnable lie! Who's your source for this slander? I demand to know!"

Hayashi's eyes danced nervously in his head but he didn't look at J. D.

He didn't have to. J. D. stood up slowly, so as not to excite DeVito, and said, "I'm his source, Mr. President. I can tell you more about Garvin Townes than you'd ever care to know. But the real question is, what do *you* know, Mr. President?"

Then, as J. D. had promised, things began to happen.

Eleanor looked at the distinguished man sitting next to her and remembered the name she had seen on his identification. She screamed, "You! You're Townes!"

Townes, even more infuriated than the president, understood now that he'd been duped. Cade had just shown himself willing to sacrifice his own son's life to strike back at him. He never would have imagined Cade capable of it.

Benjamin Franklin Walker, previously asleep on his mother's lap, wakened and, sensing his mother's distress, immediately began to wail.

Townes saw the boy and instinctively grabbed him away from his mother. He had his gun against the toddler's skull before anyone could intercede. Eleanor Rawley Walker shrank away in horror, holding up her hands in supplication that her son's life be spared. The special agents standing only feet away held their ground but didn't move against Townes for fear of causing the little boy's death. Benjamin Franklin Walker strained to reach his mother, bawling fiercely, but she was beyond his reach.

"Cade, you perverse sonofabitch!" Townes yelled, standing up with the child in his arms. "Do you see what you've done now?"

Hunter Ward gestured to Jenny to take the seat next to him, and she did.

"You brought me here tonight, didn't you, Don? Tom never would have sent me those lilies."

"Not before he'd managed to kill Senator Rawley, certainly," came the ghostly reply.

Jenny turned to look at Killer Laughlin. She'd never been as close to him as to Don, but there had been a time when she'd considered him a friend. "Why, Tom? Why do you want to kill Del Rawley?"

"It's nothing personal," he said offhandedly. "It was Don's idea originally. Not that he had your precious Senator Rawley in mind, but one night Don and I were having drinks in my garden and he said that if you took what we did to its logical conclusion, you'd have to run a covert campaign and guarantee that your man won by literally assassinating his opponent."

Hunter Ward nodded. "It was my idea, but it was all a game, an intellectual exercise."

"He'd thought it out quite well, too," Killer Laughlin agreed. "He said you'd need some straitlaced loser to run the front campaign."

"Like Ronald Turlock," Jenny offered.

"Exactly. Then, in a real stroke of genius, Don figured out that the person you had to get to do your dirty work was some old CIA hand. Because if you found someone like that and things ever came unglued, any investigation would conclude it had all been some nefarious CIA plot. Think of what a *brilliant* gambit that is. The CIA has used any number of fronts for its dirty deeds, so wasn't it time they got used for somebody else's evil machinations? They're a perfect firewall. With all the blood on their hands, who would ever doubt that they weren't the ones behind the assassination of a presidential candidate? Should I go on, Don?"

Hunter Ward nodded.

"As it turned out, Don had a neighbor who he suspected

was ex-CIA, a fellow named Garvin Townes. We decided he should look into Mr. Townes' history, and you know how good Hunter Ward was when he started investigating somebody. He could give those spooks at the NSA lessons in how to snoop on people. In fact, I wanted him to give *me* lessons before he dies, but he refused. Anyway, he found out not only had Townes been CIA, but he even had dirt on a sniper he'd been saving for half of eternity, and he'd stayed in touch with a half dozen or so burnouts who used to work for him."

Jenny said intuitively, "The sniper was J. D. Cade."

"Yes. Take a look at that file on the table there."

Jenny picked up a manila folder from the coffee table that sat between her and Laughlin. She opened it to find three eight-by-ten black-and-white photos. The first showed a man who'd been grotesquely crushed when his pickup truck had turned over. The second showed a young J. D. Cade emerging from a forest with a rifle in his hands. The third showed J. D. removing a loop of rope from a dismembered deer's neck. Jenny closed the folder.

Tom Laughlin told her, "Your friend Mr. Cade killed that fellow in the truck by getting that deer to dart in front of him at just the right time. What he didn't realize was that his old commanding officer, Colonel Townes, was having him followed and photographed for reasons of his own. Best of all, when I visited the Rancho Durango Gun Club here in California to see if Mr. Cade might be useful, I discovered that he is still a crack shot."

"That was as far as I wanted to take it," Hunter Ward said in a whisper. "It was just a game to me . . . to see if . . . I never thought . . ."

"People thought I left Don because he got sick," Killer Laughlin said, shaking his head. "I'd never do that. I broke with Don because he went *soft*. He'd created this wonderful scheme and then didn't have the guts to use it. Then a person who will have to remain nameless came to me and asked what I could do to help the president's reelection effort. This astute person saw that Del Rawley would be a real threat to the president. I said I could guarantee the president a victory. For that guarantee, I was promised ten million dollars every year for the rest of my life. What with his brain tumor and his delicate sensibilities, that offer didn't hold the same appeal to Don."

"I'd *never* have done it," Hunter Ward answered, the gun in his hands trembling. Keeping his eyes on Laughlin, Don told Jenny, "Tom has found out my plan hasn't worked as well in real life as it did on paper. Garvin Townes has forced him to have Mr. Cade's son kidnapped. Townes has become an independent actor, not the pawn he was expected to be."

"Your plan also didn't call for you to try to force Rawley to leave the race by digging up an adolescent love affair or saying that the assassination attempt had been a hoax," Laughlin retorted.

"I was trying to save the man's life, you evil bastard. Save him from you."

"It was *your* plan, Don . . . and I still think it's going to work."

"It might at that," Hunter Ward said with sorrow. "And that's why you're here, Jenny. We'll listen for any great outcry from down the hill. If we hear it, if it sounds like Senator Rawley has been shot, I'll leave it to you whether I should shoot Tom."

Killer Laughlin shook his head. "Don, that cancer of yours must really have eaten away your *spine*," he said with contempt. "Trying to lay off the decision to kill me on poor Jenny."

At that moment, they all heard the sound of a siren approaching along Mulholland. The police Jenny had called were on their way. Hunter Ward swung his head to listen . . . and Killer Laughlin rose from his chair to leap for the gun that was pointing at him.

Jenny saw him coming, knew what he was going to try from the moment he bunched his muscles, knew that this was the man who was most responsible for the attempt on Del's life, and that if he ever got his hands on the gun, neither she nor Don would get out of that room alive.

She grabbed Hunter Ward's hand and with his finger still on the trigger—and Laughlin's eyes fixed on hers—she shot the Gardener right out of the air.

Before he crashed onto the table in front of them, Jenny heard the sounds of horror Don had forecast: machine-gun fire and the screams of thousands of horrified people.

Roth decided his moment had come. He knew that if Townes had been exposed, he would be, too, and neither a federal prison cell nor a lethal injection appealed to him. So he thought he might as well go out right now, but before he did . . .

Roth stepped out onto the stage brandishing his Uzi. At first, several terrified onlookers thought he was about to fire on Townes even at the risk of the child's being killed. But two men knew better: J. D. Cade and Dante DeVito.

The special agent reacted first. Even as Roth raised his weapon to shoot J. D., DeVito was diving at him and yelling at everyone in the press section, "Get down, get down!"

DeVito couldn't fire his own weapon at Roth without risking hitting the others on the stage. He saw Cade turn to look at him, amazed by what DeVito was doing. There was no time for words anymore, but the look that blazed from DeVito's eyes seemed to say: *Even for you.*

He sent J. D. sprawling, and as a result, he did what

every Secret Service agent was trained to do: He took the bullet. Many of them.

The effort of flinging Evan across the trailer knocked Blair McCray back onto the sofa. He'd barely landed against its cushions when he heard the Toad's gun go off. For one soul-shriveling moment, all the Kentucky lawman could do was look at the two bodies on the floor—and then he screamed with rage and despair as he saw the bloodied Toad crawl out from under Evan's limp form. Deena added her shout of fury to the din. It seemed as if their vocalized hate should have shredded the flesh from the Toad and left nothing more than a jumble of bones.

The Toad had lost his gun somewhere under Evan and seemed dazed by the collision, but he managed to stand and stagger toward the trailer's door.

Blair roared again and, using his hands for leverage, pushed himself to his feet. He intended to kill the Toad by any means available—with his *teeth* if need be. The Toad had no trouble understanding that he was no longer the master of the situation, and he lurched outside.

Deena yelled to Blair, "Untie us, damnit! We've got a gun under the seat cushion, remember?" Blair sat back down and pulled at the knot binding his ankles, and when that was done he set about freeing Deena.

The Toad saw that the lights in the woods that he'd seen from the trailer were considerably closer now. He got to his car, but in pulling the keys from his pocket he dropped them. There'd be no time, no way, to find them now.

The approaching dogs were howling madly now, baying, growling . . . and running. They had been set loose. The Toad whipped his head back and forth, wishing he could see clearly, wishing there was somewhere he could . . . He spotted the only possible place of shelter: the decrepit log cabin.

Moving as fast as he could, the dogs gaining ground, their howls raising the hair on his neck, the Toad scuttled toward the cabin, hoping the damn thing had a door he could slam on the dogs. Then he'd have to find some length of wood, some club, within the hovel that he could use to beat them off should they try to leap through the open window.

He reached the cabin mere seconds ahead of the frothing pack, and to his dizzying relief there was a door. He slammed it shut and it wedged fast in its warped frame. Even so, he leaned his weight against the door as it shuddered under the impact of the charging dogs.

He knew the animals might be stunned for the moment, but they'd soon sniff out the empty window frame. He had to find something with which to beat them back when they attempted to jump through the opening at him.

When the Toad turned to look for a weapon, he forgot all about the dogs. He was confronted with a far worse terror. But in the darkened cabin, with his hopeless eyes, he couldn't see it at all clearly. All he could do was remember what he'd seen before. The black fur, the merciless yellow eyes, and the great rending teeth.

Quaking with fear, the Toad bolted for the window, but he was seized in a grip that was implacably strong, and he was dragged back. Razor-sharp claws slashed into him. He dimly perceived the heads of the dogs peeking over the sill of the window. But even they turned away from what was about to happen and ran off whimpering. Then he felt a blast of foul breath on his face and tried to scream, but there was no longer time even for that.

Deena and Blair emerged from the trailer. Ben Cade and Sawyer Price stepped out of the woods, and Sawyer's dogs crowded against his legs for comfort. Three of the people present looked at each other, and tried to shut out the sounds of the carnage coming from within the cabin.

But Deena Nokes stepped forward with her eyes gleaming.

"Get him, Gorby," she whispered fiercely. "Get him for Ivar and me and everyone else."

Arnold Roth emptied his clip and was going for another when Landers, his second in command, the agent DeVito had warned about Roth, was finally able to get a clear shot. He took Roth out with one tight three-round burst. One bad guy down, but Roth had been the easy one.

Garvin Townes had literally dozens of gunsights lined up on him as he made his way to the stage of the Hollywood Bowl, and that was part of the problem. Who had the best angle? If more than one agent opened fire, it was all but certain Senator Rawley's grandchild would be killed. But the special agents were well trained and disciplined, and nobody shot.

Del Rawley and the president were still on the stage. The chief of the president's protection detail was the ranking special agent. He communicated with all the others that if Townes took his weapon off the boy and pointed it at Primus—or Orpheus—*he* would take the shot. Everyone else was to hold their fire until the little boy was out of harm's way.

But Townes knew that he was dead the second he pointed his gun anywhere else, and he kept it pressed against the squalling child's head. He looked at Del Rawley. There were tears in the candidate's eyes as he looked at his frantic grandson, but Del's jaw was clenched hard enough to shatter diamonds.

"Step forward, Senator. Right up here."

Del started to move, but several Secret Service agents interposed themselves.

"Get out of my way," Del ordered in a harsh voice.

The head of the president's detail nodded, and the agents stepped aside. Del moved forward until he was ten feet away from Townes, who told him he was close enough. In the front row, the Rawley family was weeping openly, except for Devree, who regarded Townes with a look that by rights should have killed him.

Townes darted a glance to the press section that Roth had leveled. Most of those on the ground were simply doing the smart thing and keeping their heads down, but more than a few were bleeding, some of them mortally. The only thing that interested Townes, though, was the one figure who dared to stand: Cade.

Townes called out to him in a chilling voice: "Are you willing to sacrifice this child, too? If not, join the senator and me right now."

As Blair McCray cradled Evan's head in his lap, he pressed his fingertips to Evan's neck and found a thready pulse. Ben had already punched 911 into his PCR and was telling the operator he needed an ambulance immediately for a gunshot victim.

Help was promised to be there within minutes. Deena said she would meet the emergency vehicle out on the highway and guide it back through the trees.

Ben listened to instructions from the 911 operator as to what they might do to help Evan—to keep him alive until the paramedics arrived.

Tom Hayashi was up on one knee doing his best to keep the reporter who'd told him to shut up from bleeding to death.

It looked to Tom like the man had been shot clean through his lower right leg. A broken bone jutted its jagged white edges through the man's slacks. Tom was trying to stem the flow of blood manually, literally squeezing the blood vessels shut. Then a photographer crawled over and tapped him on the shoulder.

"Try this," he suggested, offering him the strap from his camera.

Tom used it to bind the wounded man's leg just above the knee. The tourniquet seemed to stanch the flow of blood, but Tom was alarmed to see that the reporter, who'd been moaning continuously, had passed out. Tom looked around him. One woman—from a New York paper, he thought—was having her face covered with the jacket of a man who was sobbing piteously.

Looking away, Tom's face was drawn to the stage. Townes, with his gun still to the little boy's head, Rawley, and J. D. Cade were walking off the stage, leaving through the wings to the left. Special agents followed at a distance of several yards, and once they were all out of sight, the reporter half expected to hear the roar of gunfire.

Instead he heard the trill of a PCR on the ground next to him. Unable to resist, Hayashi picked it up and said hello.

A man identified himself as Ben Cade and demanded to talk to his cousin J. D.

"He can't come to the phone right now," the reporter replied. "He really can't."

Then Ben Cade told Tom Hayashi to give J. D. this message immediately. His son had been rescued. He was alive but very seriously hurt. He was on his way to the hospital.

"If J. D. doesn't get this message right away," Ben warned, "something bad might happen."

"I'm afraid it already has," Hayashi replied quietly.

Garvin Townes ordered Del Rawley to close the door to dressing room B and lock it.

Del did as he was told. Now he, his grandson, J. D. Cade, and Townes were shut inside and the rest of the world was locked out. Little Benjamin Franklin Walker had exhausted himself. He could do no more than hang limply in Townes' grasp and whimper now.

Townes said, "I really don't think they'll be foolish enough to rush the door or shoot through it unless they hear gunfire, but just to be safe, Senator, you go lean against it. And you stand next to him, Cade."

Del leaned against the door, as instructed. J. D. stood to his right.

"You hurt my grandson," Del said in a flat tone, "you'll never get out of here alive."

Townes only smiled.

"Oh, I know that, Senator. But what you should know is I have no intention of leaving this room alive. My time has come, and I'm ready to die. Just ask Cade there; I've already told him as much."

Del looked at J. D., who did not meet his eyes or respond in any way.

"You see, Cade was supposed to kill you. For me. Almost did in Chicago, but you had to bend over at just the wrong moment and cause all this trouble for everyone. Then tonight Cade was supposed to kill you again. But I misjudged him grievously. The bastard hates me even more than he loves his son. He thought he'd expose me in front of the world, have me captured, and what, Cade . . . save Junior in the bargain?"

J. D. had nothing to say to Townes, either.

"But I told you I'd never be taken alive, Cade. I told you I'd sooner kill myself, and that's just what I'll do. But here's the real kicker, Cade. You can *still* save your son. Just do what I've always wanted you to do. Kill the senator here. Do it not because it serves a purpose any longer, but just because it pleases me to finally bend you to my will. Do it and I'll make the call that sets Evan free. Don't do it and . . . well, the deadline for saving him expires shortly."

Del Rawley again looked at J. D., who still refused to meet his gaze.

Townes continued, "Of course, now I have one additional tidbit of motivation for you, Cade: Refuse me and the senator's grandson dies as well."

"Kill me," Del Rawley said to J. D.

Finally J. D. looked at him.

"Do it," Del pleaded. "Don't let my grandson die."

"The time has come, Cade," Townes decreed. "You didn't sneak into this place tonight without bringing a weapon. Show it to the senator, and then use it to kill him."

J. D. opened his sport coat and with thumb and index finger removed a Mont Blanc pen. He twisted the cap off. Townes' eyes glittered with amusement.

"A pen gun? Good for you, Cade. First you use a weapon designed to kill from almost two miles away, then you plan to use one that requires you to be almost close enough to squirt ink on your victim." Towne shook his head while laughing. Then his smile hardened to ice. "Well, I'm sure all those heavily armed gentlemen outside are furiously making plans to hatch some sort of rescue attempt, so let's get on with it. Place the gun to the senator's head and execute him."

"Do it!" Del commanded. "Please . . . for the love of God."

J. D. took a step away from Del Rawley and looked at him with the eyes of a lost soul. He flicked up the golden lever in the side of the pen . . . and then tilted his head back and put the pen under his own jaw.

"*Nooooo!*" Townes bellowed. Suicide was *his* way out, not Cade's. He couldn't let Cade escape him now. *He* had to kill him.

Townes at last took his gun away from the little boy's head and pointed it at Cade. The last thing he saw as he pulled the trigger was a jet of ink squirt Cade under his chin.

Then, while Townes' eyes were still widening in surprise and even as his bullet tore through J. D. Cade's chest, Del Rawley used the distraction and grabbed the gun from his pocket. Praying to God Almighty that he didn't hit Benjamin, he fired a round that struck the bridge of Townes' nose, killing him instantly.

Del lunged to catch his grandson in midair. Less than a second later, the dressing room door flew off its hinges under the weight of a Secret Service assault. Agents looked around frantically for someone in need of killing, but the only two conscious people they saw were Orpheus and his hysterical grandson.

"Take the child!" Del ordered, handing his grandson to the first available agent. He rushed over to where J. D. Cade sat slumped against a wall painted red with his blood. For a second J. D.'s eyes seemed to meet his, but then they lost focus.

Del Rawley, the old army medic, put his fingers to J. D. Cade's throat . . . but he couldn't find a pulse.

Inauguration day was bitterly cold, but that wasn't why President Franklin Delano Rawley kept his stirring speech brief and hurried back to the White House. No, this was his first chance to see J. D. Cade since that horrible day months before in Los Angeles. Cade and his son, Evan, whom Del would meet for the first time, were waiting for him in the Oval Office.

The First Lady was quite put out that she and the rest of the family would not be allowed to meet with J. D. Cade and his son, but the president was adamant. He told them that this was an official visit, not a personal one. He refused to explain what he meant, but was forced to promise he would invite J. D. Cade and anyone he cared to have accompany him to Camp David at his earliest possible convenience.

Striding through the West Wing, Del thought back to how J. D. had been clinically dead when he'd first reached his body. J. D. would have stayed that way if the Secret Service hadn't had the president's doctor right behind them when they broke into that dressing room, and if there hadn't been a helicopter standing by for the two-minute flight to Cedars-Sinai Hospital, and maybe even if Del hadn't forced his way into the operating room and prayed just as hard as he could for the man who'd saved not only his life but his grandson's as well.

No absolute proof had ever been found that Del's predecessor knew of Garvin Townes' scheme to kill him, though he had appointed him to a specially created post within the Treasury Department. Even so, the election had been decided when Del Rawley came out of dressing room B not only alive but with Benjamin in his arms. A man who had risked his life for his grandson, entered a locked room with an armed madman, and emerged a hero, he had carried all fifty states by the most overwhelming margins in U.S. history.

The assassination attempt on Del Rawley's life in Chicago was attributed to Beauregard "Dixie" Wynne. Information establishing Wynne's connection to Garvin Townes was first published by Tom Hayashi of the *Los Angeles Times*, who was still being fed horror stories about the life and times of the late Townes by an unknown source.

The official version of how Del had been able to escape with his life and save his grandson had given a large amount of the credit to the further heroism of Jefferson Davis Cade. He was said to have distracted Townes, allowing Del Rawley to wrest Townes' gun from him and turn it against him.

The fact that Townes and J. D. Cade were shot with different-caliber rounds was a secret that Del was content to keep. The Secret Service had persuaded him that letting people know he'd been armed during the course of a political debate would not reflect well on him or them.

Once Devree had been told the truth about Del having been armed, she felt compelled to inform her husband that she had placed a secret bodyguard with him from the beginning of the primary campaign: Donnel Timmons. He'd been left in place when the Secret Service came aboard after the nomination, and she never would have let herself be sent home after the attempt in Chicago if Donnel hadn't been on hand to call her with daily reports.

Stepping into the Oval Office, Del saw the Cades seated and waiting for him. He sat on the corner of his new desk and looked at them. Their eyes and hair were different colors but the resemblance between father and son was striking. Just looking at them together was enough to understand why J. D. loved his son so much.

The president reached out and extended his hand to Evan Cade. "Pleased to meet you," he said. "I'm Del Rawley."

"The pleasure's mine, Mr. President," Evan answered, shaking hands.

"Pardon us for not standing," J. D. said with a wry grin.

Both Cades were seated in wheelchairs. Evan had suffered, along with other damage, a spinal injury. Upon entering Evan, the bullet from the Toad's gun had passed through his liver, ricocheted off a lumbar vertebra, causing a spinal cord contusion, and struck the liver again, causing further severe damage to that organ.

J. D., once resuscitated, had seemed to be on his way to a remarkable recovery. Townes' shot had struck him outside the nipple line on the left side of his chest, missing the heart. After a tube had been inserted, en route to the hospital, to drain the blood and air from his chest, he'd seemed like a new man. He'd been expected to remain intubated and hospitalized for three to five days until a tear in his lung healed. But when he learned that his son's liver had been effectively destroyed, he insisted on donating a not insubstantial part of his own liver to transplant into his son. He'd been flown to Illinois after informing his medical team that there would be *grave* consequences if his wishes in this matter were not respected. Coming in the aftermath of a serious gunshot wound that had stopped his heart, he had been slow to recover from his liver donation.

The transplant had saved Evan's life; the contusion of his spinal cord had left him with the use of his upper body but, for the time being, not his legs.

"What are the prognoses for the two of you?" Del asked.

"I'm going to walk again, Mr. President. The doctors say maybe, I say absolutely."

"They tell me I'll be okay eventually," J. D. said. "Provided I don't get shot again."

"See that you don't," the president instructed him.

The three men chatted for a few more minutes and then the president asked Evan if he would excuse his father and him. Evan said sure. Del pressed a button on his desk and a Secret Service agent opened the door to admit Belle Cade. Introductions were made.

"Very nice to meet you, Mrs. Cade," Del said. "You must be very proud of your son and grandson."

"Yes, I am, Mr. President," Belle said, beaming.

After another minute or two of conversation, Evan and Belle took their leave.

When they were alone, Del told J. D., "I've talked with your mother, you know."

J. D. was more than a little surprised to hear that.

"I've talked with quite a few people about you. Even your old girlfriend."

"You spoke to *Mary Ellen McCarthy?*" J. D. frowned.

"Her name's Dr. Mary Ellen Brightman now, I believe. And I understand she has a daughter named Libby who had occasion to meet your son recently and was quite taken with him."

J. D. had nothing to say about that. He understood what

the president was telling him: that he'd had J. D. checked out down to his dental work.

But unless the man had actually had J. D.'s hospital room bugged—which J. D. doubted—there were still some things Del Rawley didn't know.

There were still things that J. D. didn't know.

During his time in the hospital, Donnel had come to see him.

"You sonofabitch," Donnel had told him, "you just sat there and let me drink a mickey."

J. D. replied, "The way I remember it, you were pointing a gun at me."

"I was worried you were going to kill Del."

"Didn't turn out that way."

Donnel had told him that after getting out of auto parts, to make productive use of all the skills he'd learned in the army, he'd become the silent partner in a private security firm that Devree Rawley had hired. She, of course, hadn't known about Donnel's PANIC background . . . and J. D. couldn't bring himself to ask whether Donnel had been worried that J. D. would try to kill Del because he'd wanted to protect his client or because Donnel had been, in fact, a second assassin.

J. D. didn't want to know—but maybe it said something that Donnel was as content as he was to let the blame for Chicago be pinned on the late Dixie Wynne.

Pickpocket also came by to see J. D., looking cockier than ever for having survived a shooting. The little thief brought with him interesting news. He had discovered that one name on the guest list of J. D.'s gun club had matched a resident of Arlington, Virginia, the location of the Post-Master Plus franchise from which the blackmail letters had been sent to him: Thomas Laughlin.

He'd found public-record pictures of Laughlin that had

been taken with his two former associates, Donald Ward and Jenny Crenshaw. J. D. never believed that Jenny played any active part in either the effort to blackmail him or kill Del Rawley, but the coincidence was very disquieting. It made him maintain a little distance when Jenny came to visit him.

She told him of her nightmare. She said she was sorry for acting like such a fool. While admitting nothing, J. D. told her she had nothing to be sorry about. It had seemed to him at that moment Jenny had a secret she wanted to share with him, but apparently she thought better of it.

What Jenny hadn't told J. D., thinking the time was not yet right, was that she'd kept the pictures of him at the scene of Alvy McCray's death from falling into police hands—and that she'd agreed with the now departed Don Ward to let Ward take the responsibility for killing Tom Laughlin. Jenny Crenshaw now had demons of her own to appease.

But her visit to J. D. in the hospital had been the start of a reconciliation. What remained uncertain was how they'd deal with the secrets they knew about, but kept from, each other.

J. D.'s gaze moved to a framed photo that had been set in a place of honor on the credenza behind the president's desk. Dante DeVito looked every inch of what a special agent of the Secret Service should be.

"He thought you tried to kill me that day in Chicago," Del told J. D. "By the end he was absolutely sure of it. Even had me persuaded for a while there."

J. D. could only sit mute under Del Rawley's scrutiny.

The president continued, "I've also spoken with your cousin Ben and a number of other Cades living in southern Illinois. I'm afraid I made them somewhat uncomfortable with my questions. Without responding directly, they hinted that you might be in legal jeopardy concerning the death of one Alvin C. McCray, who as far as I've been able to determine died in a highway accident."

Del Rawley stepped behind his desk and sat down. He took a piece of paper out of the top drawer. "This is the first time I've sat here as president, and this is my first official act."

He signed the document in front of him and slid it across the desk to J. D., who picked it up and read it silently. Then he looked up at the president.

Del said, "That is an absolute pardon for *any and all* crimes you may have committed in your life. No one will ever use Alvy McCray or anything else against you. And when I spoke with Blair McCray, he said that as far as he's concerned, the Cade-McCray feud is over."

J. D. nodded. Then he asked, "Any and all?"

"Yes," the president said. Del Rawley paused a moment and then asked, "Do you know my Secret Service code name?"

"Orpheus."

"Yes, Orpheus. The man with the wonderful voice, whose only mistake was looking back at just the wrong time. I'm not going to make that mistake. There are some things I'd rather not know. You think that will make me a weak president?"

J. D. remembered Del Rawley begging to be killed rather than let his grandson die.

"There is no weakness in you, Mr. President. None that I've ever seen."

Del Rawley remembered the note the Secret Service had shown him, the one they'd found in the pocket of J. D. Cade's sport coat when it had been stripped from his blood-ied body. *Garvin Townes has my son. Please save him if you can.* The words of a brave man and a loving father who had not expected to live long enough to see his son again.

"Nor in you, Mr. Cade. Now, please put that pardon

away, and if you don't mind, I'd prefer you keep it to yourself."

"Yes, sir." J. D. tucked the sheet of paper into his inside coat pocket.

Del pressed a button on his intercom and said, "Come on in, Jenny."

She stepped into the Oval Office. J. D. felt very strange seeing her again, especially while sitting in a wheelchair. But there was no denying he enjoyed seeing her smile at him just now, and she seemed to respond to his smile.

"I'm very busy today, J. D.," Del told him. "But as of now Ms. Crenshaw is at loose ends, casting about for something to do."

"Is that right?" J. D. asked.

Jenny said, "I never argue with the president."

Del Rawley laughed and then he said, "I'm going to want her back four years from now."

"We'll see," J. D. and Jenny said at the same time.

And they smiled at each other once more.

Among those journalists leaving Washington for reassignment after the inaugural festivities were over was a reporter who'd been among the media contingent at the Hollywood Bowl on that historic night. He was a scribe from the Perth Morning Standard, and unlike anybody else, he'd come away from that awful bloodbath with a memento. He'd been hunkering on the ground along with everybody else after the gunfire had started when a pen came skittering over to him. Just as if someone had kicked it to him. A bloody nice Mont Blanc, it was.

It had a wonderful heft to it. He'd thought it would make a grand pen to use in his work. Too bloody grand, really. He'd been carrying it around for months now and had never used it.

He decided what he'd do once he got home to Perth was encase it in Lucite and put it on his mantel. He'd tell his grandkids twenty years from now about the night the Yanks almost shot up their presidential candidates right under his very nose.

ABOUT THE AUTHOR

Look for Joseph Flynn's

THE CONCRETE INQUISITION

coming in Fall 2001

from Bantam Books

Sometimes a cop's job is pure murder. Other times, it's a lot more twisted.

"Doc" Kildare was a narc. One of Chicago's best. He put a Colombian cocaine king in jail and forty-five million drug dollars in the government till. That's the good news.

The bad news is that the drug boss has a contract out on Doc's life. His own police superintendent wants to see him hit before he can claim a share of the drug money. A serial killer prowls his neighborhood. A desperate mother is begging him to find her missing boy. His ex-wife is heating up a sexual relationship that once burned them both. And one more little thing: His left eye was blown away in his big drug bust. Now, he plunges into a maze of violence and treachery where he'll need eyes in the back of his head. . . .